MEDICINE GRIZZLY

By

Richard D. Seifried

Best wishes to Linda

Have an exciting life!

Richd D. Seif

april 18, 2011

ISBN: 0-7596-1366-4

Library of Congress Control Number: 2002101936

This book is printed on acid free paper.

Printed in the United States of America
Bloomington, IN

1st Books - rev. 5/20/02

Dedications:

This novel is dedicated to my wife, Norma Jean, who is my greatest inspiration.

PROLOGUE

Location: East slope of the Northern Rockies
Time: After European Contact

Something was in the willows, across the stream. She had seen a slight discoloration in the springtime greenery.

The late evening shadows didn't help. One had to be certain before an alarm could be raised. Only the rushing ripplings of the mountain stream intruded upon the evening quiet.

Sinopah stopped at the top of the bank. Faking innocence, the woman loosened the twist of grasses that held her long, raven hair in place. Freed, the black tresses slipped forward and partially covered her face. Now she could peer between the strands and the intruder wouldn't be able to discern that he was being watched.

Heart pounding with fear, the Blackfeet woman carefully picked her way down the river bank and dipped her water pouch into the cold depths of the Cut Bank River. Still feigning unawareness Sinopah dipped her cupped hand into the stream and drank fully before hoisting the heavy burden to her right shoulder.

There was the image again. A man's face appeared among the branches of the not-so-distant shore. Legs trembling, anticipating the swish and impact of an arrow, the woman slowly stepped up the path and reached the fragile sanctuary of the underbrush.

Eleven men, including Sinopah's husband, were reclining against their willow-backed resting supports. Their talk was casual, slow; not very important. The tipi's sides were up allowing a half foot of space between the ground and the rest of the shelter. A soft breeze showered a few sparks onto one of the warriors. Everyone chuckled as he swatted at the hot ashes. All looked up, surprised, when the woman hurried into their sanctuary. Sinopah still had the heavy water pouch upon her shoulder. Before they could scold her she blurted out the danger.

"Just now. Down at the water-gathering place. I saw a man peering at me from across the river. He is not one of our people."

She didn't have to say more. They all knew that very likely a war party was moving upon their camp. Quietly, having performed the same exercise many times in the past, they told the other men in the encampment of the invasion.

Within a few minutes they were peering into the near-total darkness toward where the man's face had been. The defenders were none too soon. As they watched, eleven men disrobed, wrapped their weapons in their clothing and as one, entered the icy water.

The enemy war party was halfway across when the Blackfeet sounded their war cries and fired their arrows in the direction of the startled invaders. Within seconds all of the raiders were dead except for the chief. Somehow, miraculously, the leader had managed to elude the deadly shafts and had found sanctuary in a thicket of willows.

While a few warriors watched the chief's hiding place the others waded out into the turbulent river and recovered the floating enemy clothing and what weapons they could locate. Knives flashed in the dull light as scalps were taken.

The hidden survivor saw the glistening steel and from his thicket sanctuary arose terrible roars and screams of fury. The Blackfeet warriors shuddered for surely he sounded like their awesome brother, the Grizzly Bear.

All night the surrounded enemy roared and growled. Crashings of underbrush and terrible sounds brought awe to the Blackfeet.

When the first light of dawn appeared the warriors rushed the enemy shelter. They were lucky. No one was even hurt. With only a war club for a weapon the chief was no match for his more than twenty adversaries.

His body was dragged ashore and turned over so that the lifeless eyes peered upward into the grayish dawn. The men gasped. Upon the dead warrior's throat lay a necklace of grizzly bear claws of a size they had never seen before. They were immense, curved instruments of destruction.

Surely, they thought, the dead chief was a powerful Grizzly Bear Medicine Man.

Their victory tasted bitter like death itself and they looked wide-eyed at one another. The camp chief spoke. "We move. Now!"

So they did. Within a white man's hour the Blackfeet camp was struck; the belongings hastily piled on the backs of the protesting horses. Men, women and children as well as dogs and young colts hurried down the narrow, forest-bordered valley to the safer sanctuary of the more open meadows a few miles below.

Warm June sunshine gave them comfort. Exhausted, feeling considerably safer away from the horrible Grizzly Medicine Man, they pitched their camp along the shores of the same stream. Sinopah righted her tipi poles, the three slender shafts placed to accept the remaining supports. She sighed from the exhaustion of the day's flight.

The woman looked toward her neighbor's upraised tipi just as the monster struck. The giant grizzly ripped out of the aspen and struck a woman with such a blow that her head was severed. Without stopping the bear raised up and grabbed the woman's man by the head and tossed him into the bushes. The tipi collapsed. People were running and screaming. Warriors rushed up to save the children of the dead couple. They were too late. Horses reared and fled. Men yelled and women screamed in fear. Old people (there were a few) hesitated and died. Before the carnage had ended more warriors lay dead. The survivors fled in panic from the horrible killer beast.

CHAPTER 1

March, 1984

The Great Beast stirred restlessly in his den.

Removing a powerful, clawed forepaw from his black nostrils it sniffed the cold, moisture-laden air. Ears twitched nervously, seeking to catch a sound that would explain the giant's apprehension.

Nothing. The drip, drip, dripping of snowmelt continued unabated. For three days unseasonably warm winds, out of the northwest, had resulted in periodic disintegration of the den. Thawing. Freezing. Day and night.

Yawning noisily he stretched and struggled to emerge from his semi-hibernated condition. Twice before he had left the security of the den, but March gales had hurled pelting sleet and huge, sloppy snowflakes into his massive face. The male grizzly had retreated to the warmth of the inner recesses of his tiny cave. This day would be different. Something had happened during the night. Animal memories conjured back strange calls, never heard before. Heavy breathing nearby. Once, the most dreaded smell of all had sought out his nostrils, the man creature.

Curiosity was just a fraction of the bear's motivation to leave the den. He was hungry. The last meal, a dead mountain sheep, had been consumed early last December. Rising, sniffing noisily, the grizzly half staggered to the den entrance and poked a hole in the thinning snow cover so that he could see out. A chunk of soggy snow stuck to his nose and he sneezed lightly.

There wasn't much for him to observe. Seemingly endless gray plumes of fog rose to merge with rain-laden clouds. Somewhere above his den, Apikuni Mountain stood majestically still, its long ridge buffeted by the storm.

Cold rain and the sharp wind helped reduce the dullness caused by the long sleep. Wheezing and snorting the bear relished the air's freshness, while at the same time he swung the great head from side to side so that he could observe the misty exhalations erupting from his nose and open mouth. ·

Again a faint odor. Caution. A vague segment of last night's beastly dream replayed itself in his memory. Those noises. Strange calls on a wintry slope.

During the month of March food is almost always scarce. He recalled his mother's survival lessons. Perhaps a search along the base of the steep slope would reward him with the fallen carcass of a mountain goat, or better yet, another sheep.

Seeking food would take effort. Further sleep was a tantalizing alternative. Rumblings within his intestines emanated with a flaccid-sounding, sulfurous stench. The bear decided he needed food.

Almost before he began searching, the grizzly found his meal. Strange. The creature that walks on two legs, was lying on it's back, spread-eagled in the snow. One of the man creatures. Unmoving.

The bear circled cautiously. Large melting footprints of another man-creature, a somewhat different scent, led off, down toward the fog-shrouded valley.

Memories, again of childhood. Beware of the man-creature with its foul odors and thundering sticks. Danger. Danger. Years of fear-laden experiences rushed back into the mind of the great beast.

The bear was hungry. Ravenous. Pausing only for a thoughtful moment, he began consuming the fallen man-creature. It was good. Powerful jaws armed with massive teeth began tearing away large chunks of groin and thighs. Methodically, with near machine-like precision, the bear ate his way into the stomach, consuming the intestines, and then up into the chest cavity. Being a beast, the grizzly never wondered at the freshness of the blood, which tasted so wonderfully salty. The human had not been long dead.

*

April 1984

April arrived. Only the long bones of the legs and arms remained. Even the skull had been crushed and consumed by the bear's mighty jaws. The body, what was left of it, gradually dropped and slid further and further down into the rock debris of the slide area. The remains were never found.

*

June, 1984

Hot, tired, burnt from the unrelenting wind, Douglas Jakowski drove down slope to the town of Browning, Montana. His destination, in Glacier National Park, was another fifty miles or so beyond the small Indian community. For all practical purposes Browning with a population of a little over one thousand inhabitants was the capitol of the once powerful Blackfeet Nation.

What met his eyes didn't thrill him by any means. Many of the buildings were woefully unkempt, run down. Some were empty. A few, a service station, motel, and restaurant obviously were flourishing. On a curve of the main street he observed a gift shop that actually seemed elegant, intrusive amid Browning's somber environment.

In his mind he acknowledged that he was observing through the eyes of a White Man and that Browning was the home of many good citizens. Never the less, irritated by the poverty he saw, plus his throbbing head, he grumbled to himself. Throbbing forehead was an understatement. He hurt. The hot, dusty wind had taken its toll. He was nearly sick to his stomach.

Native Americans and Whites walked slowly along the wide main street. Faded, work-worn clothes seemed to blend in with the swirls of brown dust and tumbling scraps of filthy paper, plastic and last year's desiccated weeds.

The dogs were there, as he knew they would be. Mutts. Large, lean mongrels also of faded hues of browns, grays and in-betweens. They staggered, exhausted, in the glaring sun or hid beneath vehicles, in shady doorways, along the darker sides of buildings. Some, the lucky ones from the ranches, rode in the backs of pickups, speeding in one direction or the other down the main street. One large, white, wolfish canine shared a truck's cab with it's master. Two rifles perched businesslike upon the gun rack in the rear window.

"What was it?" he mused. "If you see a pickup with two dogs in the back and two guns in the window, you know you're in Montana." He didn't laugh at the old joke. His head was killing him.

Having driven two-thirds of the way through town, he could see the west end of Browning a half dozen blocks ahead. He should have stopped for gas at the busy station on the east end. Just as he was about to turn around a convenience store of sorts came into view. Cutting across the street he pulled the Toyota up to the "Unleaded" gas pump. A sign read, "Pay First." He walked into the dark interior of the store. Three Indians were talking but when he entered they became silent, watching him, their faces expressionless. Not friendly.

"I'll take three dollars on pump two."

The clerk, a young man with a big belly, grunted agreement and took the three bills.

"Thanks," Douglas responded, with mild cynicism in his voice.

When he got back to the pump he found that the street side was broken so he backed up to go around the island to the inside pump.

Roaring with the surge of its powerful motor a large, black pickup truck zipped in ahead of him and stopped at the pump he had paid to use. Inside the cab sat a large, leering man. Perspiration ran down his face making his countenance even more offensive.

Douglas honked the horn lightly and waited. Nothing happened. The three men inside the station were looking out, mild amusement showing on their faces. He waited a few moments longer.

The intruder remained seated in his truck, the motor still running. Obviously he wasn't buying gasoline.

Slowly he opened the door and stood up. It was a trick he had used many times. The slow, seemingly endless increase in height resulted in a distorted idea of how tall he was. He was six foot four inches tall so the unbending of his legs and the slow steady rising of his frame took several seconds. The Indian's expression, seen in the trucks rear vision mirror, changed slightly. Douglas knew he was about to win.

Taking his time, looking the pickup over as if he was considering smashing it, he strolled up to the driver's door. Inside, the Indian remained motionless, the leering smile frozen, uncertain. He leaned down, careful to stay far enough away to avoid the powerful arms of the driver. He smiled.

"Hello." No response from within. The Indian's body was tense, awaiting the next move. He spoke again, pleasantly, softly, yet with a coldness that the driver could understand. "I paid three dollars to use that pump. Your truck is in my way."

No response. He continued, his voice nearly a whisper. "If you don't move your god-damned truck now, I'm going to drag your big, fat ass out of that cab and beat the shit out of you." The Indian moved slightly, still uncertain and tense.

"Now go! Look at me! I mean it! Move!"

For the first time the driver looked into Douglas's eyes. He gently eased out on the clutch and rolled the truck around the pumps and onto the main street.

Turning, Douglas gave the three inside observers an icy stare. They dissolved into the store's shadows. Bastards, he said to himself. One of these days I'm going to get myself mangled. He pumped his gas.

CHAPTER 2

Outside of Browning, heading westward, the highway led along a small river and then gained elevation. The land was lovely; grasslands, emerald green from the late springtime rains and warming sun. This was the western fringe, the final uplifting of the Great Plains, where mountains rose above the high, arid, short grass prairies. It was in this border region that the rolling hills of grass succumbed to the trees of the higher elevations. A few yards east of the pass, the forest finally conquered. Giant fir, hemlock, and the shorter aspen victoriously enveloped the mountain slopes in varied, somber shades of green. Gray trunks towered high along the sides of the road, hiding tumbling streams and threadlike waterfalls from the traveler's eye.

A little further along the highway Douglas exclaimed loudly and swung his car across the blacktop and parked upon the berm. Below him, hardly discernible between the trees, lay the crown jewel of Glacier National Park. Late afternoon haze slightly clouded the enchanting, lovely view. A magnificent lake, waters rippling, shooting sparks of reflected sunlight toward the pass, lay within the long, gently curving expanse of a glacier-carved valley.

Surrounding St. Mary Lake, mighty peaks stood guard, raising their sedimentary layers higher and higher until some of them became crowned with the soft gray-white hues of melting snows. Once, a long time ago, a great seabed had fractured and slipped upward upon itself, creating the mountain range that the young man observed. This overthrust, he realized, was to be his new home.

He arrived at the Hudson Bay Ranger Station an hour before closing time, five p.m. Vern Nielsson, the District Ranger, was busy so one of the secretary's assigned him a room in the sprawling dormitory. While he was unpacking, the clerk returned to inform him that he was to have dinner with the Nielsson's at 6:30.

A long, hot shower refreshed him. He dressed into a clean pair of jeans, a blue work shirt and comfortable shoes. Since the ranger's home was next to the dorm, there was no need for a jacket.

Carolyn, Nielsson's twenty-one year old daughter, answered the door. Douglas was pleasantly surprised to find himself looking into the smiling face of a pretty blonde.

Vern wasn't home yet. Mrs. Nielsson was preparing dinner. The two young people sat in the living room and conversed, somewhat awkwardly, for nearly half an hour. Every time his eyes would glance at her ankles or breasts, Carolyn would catch him. The talking languished and finally stopped. Embarrassment engulfed the couple. Soon, they were sitting in painful silence, a situation more likely to happen to teenagers than people in their twenties.

The District Ranger finally got home. Dinner was served. Douglas ate slowly, politely, ingesting bountiful portions of steak, potatoes, and gravy. Consuming the last fork full of peach cobbler, he looked up to find the three Nielsson's smiling at him.

"Evelyn's a fine cook, isn't she?" beamed her husband.

"Yes sir. She really is. Mrs. Nielsson, the dinner was excellent." Everyone laughed.

Douglas sensed that he had been accepted. Somehow, he had passed a test of sorts.

Evelyn, Mrs. Nielsson, suggested that "You boys" adjourn to the living room. The move was a short one because National Park housing was sometimes comfortable but almost always quite small.

The two men sat in silence. Douglas had an opportunity to observe his host. Nielsson was a big man, as tall as his guest. A massive, powerful chest, perched atop still-slim hips and narrow waist, indicated that the World War II mountain trooper was still in fine shape. He appeared to be resting, eyes closed, but Douglas found himself looking into penetrating, icy-blue eyes. Vern didn't speak but continued to gaze straight at him. He was becoming uneasy.

"So, Father has you under his infamous scrutiny," laughed Carolyn.

"I think that's what's going on," he grinned.

Both women arranged a tray containing a pot of coffee, cups, saucers, napkins, sugar bowl and creamer on the coffee table.

"That's a good idea," smiled Douglas. "Coffee on the coffee table." Only Vern didn't respond with a smile. Shortly, everyone had a filled cup before them or perched on their lap. The silence deepened. Obviously the women were to be in on the conversation.

Nielsson spoke. "Can I call you Doug?"

"Sure. Fine."

A slight smile cracked Vern's otherwise somber face.

"Doug, what is said in this room stays with the four of us. Oh, there's one more exception, but I'll get to him later. I've read your file. Not bad. For a young man, twenty-five years of age, you've had some tough jobs. Handling that jackass up in Wyoming, who fenced off the antelope from their winter range, was a masterpiece of patience and just plain guts. Then, there was the eagle slaughter in the Dakotas. Had to deal with the Sioux on that one. Most men your age aren't mature enough to handle problems like that. You'll find our Blackfeet easier to handle, most of them. Probably a situation with our Native Americans won't arise."

Vern paused. Large fingers arranged the magazines on an end table, placing them so the title of each was visible. "Officially you're here as Glacier's wolf man. The expert."

Douglas nodded in agreement.

"Well, you certainly have had the training. But, I want to tell you that we have a young woman here who knows more about wolves than anyone I have ever met. She is our..." he chuckled, "'Wolf Woman.' Not you."

Douglas stirred uncomfortably. He hadn't come to Glacier to be told he wasn't experienced enough for the assignment. Nielsson sensed the feeling. "Oh, you could do the job all right. What I'm saying is, we don't need you. Not as a wolf researcher, anyway.

"The Superintendent didn't hire you, Doug. Neither did the wildlife manager. I did. At least I urged that you be called in. I'm the one that stuck his neck out."

Pausing, the ranger slurped some coffee. The women remained unmoving. Intent. "No, Doug, your real contacts here are us. My wife, two daughters, Cindy isn't here right now, and myself. You come to us for help. No one else. Not ever! We are your support team. We can get you almost any kind of help you will need. You don't go to law enforcement. You don't go to wildlife management. The word is out. You are to be left alone. As far as the Park Service is concerned, you are on your own and everyone thinks that you are researching wolves."

Douglas remained silent. The answers to the questions in his mind were forthcoming.

"Our problem here, Doug, is bears. Not wolves. People kill bears and bears kill people. In 1980 we lost three visitors, two men and a woman. All to grizzlies. "Since then we have lost five more."

"Five more?" protested Douglas. "I thought—-"

Nielsson raised his hand for silence. "I know young man. You have heard of only one more. Well, and this is not to leave the room, four more people were killed last year. Four more, Douglas. Now what do you think of that?"

The young man's gaze turned to the women. They stared back, faces expressionless.

Vern spoke bluntly. "We think there is a murderer here in Glacier. That's your real task. Get this killer before more people die."

"Why me? I'm not a cop. Call in the U. S. Marshals. Get the F. B. I."

"No, no, no." The suggestions were waved off. "I've talked it over with those fellows and they claim that there isn't enough evidence to warrant an investigation."

"What evidence do you have? Maybe the bears did do it."

"Could be. But I know down here." He patted his chest, "I know in my heart that someone is doing these folks in. All four were loners, three of them drifters. Perhaps that isn't so much of a coincidence because bears are more likely to attack a lone hiker. I learned a long time ago not to accept coincidences. I don't believe in them as such, especially in this case. What would the odds be of four men being killed by the same bear and all of them just passing through, on their way to nowhere? I've never heard of a wild animal lurking along a national park boundary, waiting to attack lonely men." Vern cleared his throat. "What about women? Children? Good Lord, these visitors allow their kids to run all over the place without supervision. No woman or child has turned up missing.

"How is the problem kept quiet? You were going to ask me that, weren't you?"

Douglas nodded affirmatively.

"No relatives. No friends of the deceased except for the one victim. We've been working on keeping it quiet. All four cases happened in such a way that we were able to keep some of the information away from the media. For all they know, and we for that matter, the victims were probably killed somewhere, not necessarily in the park, by freak accidents. I know better. Doug, I've lived nearly my whole life in these mountains and something is going on that I can't fathom. We've found no bones. No kill spot. Not even a bloody sock."

Leaning forward in his chair Nielsson rasped, "Boy! They've all happened in my district! All of them. And we don't know how many more are out there. Bodies. Cadavers. You've got to help me. You are trailwise, tough, strong, a real outdoorsman. You are a rare breed these days. I need you to catch this weirdo. Keep the public pressure off the bears. Stop the killings. Will you do it?"

"Sure, but—"

"Good! I knew you would." The older man grinned. "Now we've got to get you out of the dorm. There's an old trailer along Lower St. Mary Lake; out on the reservation. You use it. I don't have much money but I'll cover your expenses." He was excited, almost laughing with relief. "Now, son, one more person is in on this. We've got a fine gentleman as our local deputy sheriff. His name is Henry Two Feathers. He is your contact for help on the reservation. I recommend that you work closely with him. Let him know where you will be. Feed him your knowledge. He is the one that convinced me that my imagination wasn't playing tricks on me."

Douglas interrupted. "This is all very flattering and sure I'm excited about it, but I just don't see myself as a detective."

"Sure you don't. Neither will anyone else, if you're careful. Just be yourself. Keep you eyes open. Study those animals. Move around. You'll stir something up."

"Yes sir. Just one more thing, Mr. Nielsson."

"Vern. Call me Vern."

"Yes. OK. But, Vern, I'm kinda' wild."

"Yes. I know, Doug."

"No. I don't think you do. Just today, in Browning, I—"

Vern interrupted again. "I know all about that, too."

"You do?"

"Henry told me. Nice work. Just don't embarrass the Park. OK?"

"Yes. Sure."

He once again became serious. "Henry will meet you outside of Black's Lodge in just about," he looked at his wristwatch, "a half hour from now. He's an older man, Doug, like me. Don't underestimate him. Henry is tough, wise and a real gentleman."

The three Nielsson's got up. Apparently the meeting was over. "And Doug?" There was a sparkle in Vern's eyes.

"What?"

"Stay away from my daughters."

He could have died. Right there. Everyone was laughing. He looked at Carolyn. Automatically his undisciplined eyes dropped to her shaking breasts. Oh, my god, he thought. I can't believe I did that.

Mrs. Nielsson said, "Doug, you'd better get out of here. You look flushed. Your face is red."

"Hot," corrected Vern. "See him to the door, will you Carolyn?"

"Sure, Daddy." She took the flustered guest by the hand and walked him the whole fifteen feet to the front entrance. It was her turn to tease. "Goodnight, Douglas."

"Night."

"Oh," as if an after-thought had occurred, "I've already got myself a boyfriend." She pushed him out the door. "Goodnight Wolf Man!"

Laughter followed him across the lawn. Douglas found himself grinning.

9

*

June was training time for all personnel, as it was every year. Douglas thought he should attend some of the sessions to prevent people from wondering why he was exempt. Besides, the meetings enabled him to meet most of the park staff, especially the east-siders. If foul play was responsible for the disappearances, then everyone was suspect; except for the newcomers. He remembered that from Agatha Christie novels.

Wildlife Management Officer Wade Leonard found out that Douglas was going to attend the East Side training sessions and immediately contracted a near fatal stomach pain which could only be soothed by an afternoon in his favorite saloon.

Bonnie Easton, Glacier Park's "Wolf Woman," was in the Kootenai Lakes area checking on some rumors of a wolf pack. That left the newcomer to give the wolf lecture.

The old timers, including Wade Leonard, who was by then in Kallispel, expected Douglas to fail to stimulate anyone. They were wrong. The seasonals and the few full-timers present experienced a fascinating forty-five minute lecture, with slides, on the North American Timber Wolf.

In the afternoon, right after the welcoming speech by the Superintendent, an incident occurred that gave Douglas his first suspect, a seasonal employee.

Helen Grigsby, the Assistant Personnel Officer, was speaking. "In conclusion, I might add that there were approximately eighty applicants for each summer opening. Every one of you scored at least 98 plus on your application or you wouldn't be here.

"Veterans, as the law mandates, got a five point preference and those with service-connected disabilities received ten points."

"That's not fair!" The statement was shouted in anger. Everyone turned to face the young man speaking from the tenth row of the auditorium.

"A person goes to college, studies hard, works years to get on with the Park Service and someone who was in the military, not nearly so well-qualified, can bump him! You call that fair!" It was a statement, not a question.

Helen Grigsby, as usual, remained calm. "What is your name?"

"I'm James. James Ballard. What does my name have to do with it?"

"Well Jim, Mr. Ballard, I do appreciate knowing who I am speaking with. Let me explain how this—"

"Yeah!" He was shaking with anger. "I've heard explanations and they're all the same. The truth is the veterans have a powerful lobby in Washington and anyone who didn't go to Vietnam is treated like scum!"

An older seasonal asked, "How about Korean veterans?"

"Them too! It doesn't matter what war they fought in. They are all alike. Expecting favors from Uncle Sam just because they were in uniform."

"What about me?" asked the unidentified man.

Most were embarrassed. Some sat in silence, heads lowered. A few nodded in agreement. The older seasonal looked at Jim with a blank stare.

Helen tried again. "Jim. Jim." She waited for him to stop shouting. "Mr. Ballard! Will you please get control of yourself and sit down!"

"I do have control. No, I won't sit down! I'm making a point. I've been screwed too many times."

"You are employed now," reminded the personnel officer.

"Don't try to soft-soap me. I have a Masters Degree in Outdoor Recreation. I have a right to a permanent position with the Park Service. These veterans make me sick. Always—"

"Bull shit!" The profanity cut through the tension that had built up. A few gasped. Douglas stood up.

"Excuse me, Mrs. Grigsby. I figured my favorite words were appropriate so that I could get everyone's attention." He smiled. "It worked."

People laughed. Jim Ballard seethed with anger. He was a big man, taller than Douglas, powerfully built.

"I suppose," leered Ballard, "you're one of those Vietnam heroes, eh Wolf Man?"

"No, Ballard. I'm not. I stayed safely in college just like you did. One could say it was a form of draft dodging, couldn't they?"

"Draft dodging! Are you calling me a draft dodger?"

"Look. Don't make a bigger ass of yourself than you already have. OK? Many agree with you and you may be right but I'm going to ask you one question. No. You needn't answer. Excuse me for being personal. There is a ten-point veteran in this room. I'd like for you, Jim, or anyone in here, to ask yourself if you'd like to trade places with him to get the ten points. Think about it."

Jim Ballard started to interrupt. "No. Now, wait a minute, Jim. I'm not finished.

"Now, place yourself in his shoes. In October of 1952 he was in Korea. This ten-point veteran was standing in a motor pool, smoking a cigarette and talking to his best friend. They were close, like brothers.

"Now, visualize that. Get the picture?

"Suddenly there is an explosion. A shell. The ten-point veteran's friend disintegrated into a red mist. Our ten-point veteran was also wounded, in the leg. But, worst of all, his buddy, his very best friend, was sprayed all over his face, arms, hands, and fatigues. Try as he did he couldn't get his buddy off of him.

"Now, Jim, with that picture in mind, do you still want him to loose the ten points? How about it?"

Ballard glared with hatred. "You son-of-a-bitch." The profanity came out low and personal.

"Mr. Ballard." It was Helen Grigsby again. "Please sit down. Don't jeopardize what will likely be a successful career in the Park Service."

Instead, Ballard stomped out.

Those near him heard Douglas mutter, "No guts."

*

The two men slurped coffee in the Ranger's living room. Nielsson was angry. Douglas knew he was in for a tongue-lashing.

"Look, Doug, I don't like profanity. Don't use it around me, my family, or my people. That's an order.

"You blew your cover."

"No I didn't."

Nielsson stood up. "Don't contradict me. You did. Jackson, that ten-point veteran you told everyone about, came to me. You can imagine what he said, can't you?

"Yeah. Well, I'll tell you, Doug. He asked me how you knew about his injury and the explosion and all of that. He was quite upset."

"What did you tell him?"

Nielsson sighed. "What could I say? I told him the truth. I confessed that I had violated his confidence and had talked to you about the incident. He wanted to know why and then I had to lie. I don't like that, Doug. You really put it to me."

"I'm really sorry, Mr. Nielsson."

"Vern."

"OK, Vern. Honestly, I'm sorry. I'll see Jackson and apologize to him, too. Everyone must realize he is the guy I was referring to." He felt terrible about embarrassing Jackson. "I'll see him."

"Right. Make it good."

"What about this Ballard? When you gave me the rundown on the temporary staff you talked so damned—"

The District Ranger frowned.

"Woops!" Douglas corrected himself. "...darned fast, I didn't get all the information."

"He is a seasonal. Yet, he lives in East Glacier the rest of the year. He didn't get a position his first year of applying so he moved into a small house. He's from Long Island."

"So he's been around since the bear maulings started?"

"Yes. He's a hard worker. People respect his know-how. Jim got a 100 rating on his application for this year."

"Then what is he complaining about?"

The ranger grinned. "Last year he wasn't hired. Remember? Veteran's preference bumped him off the hiring list."

"Oh. I see. What about his personality?"

Nielsson smiled again. "He is a sort of a pain in the you-know-what."

Douglas couldn't resist. "Ass?"

Vern laughed. "You had to say it didn't you? Son, you are going to be a bad influence on me.

"Speaking of that, we've got to cut your visits here to a minimum. Just as soon as Charlie and his boys get that trailer set up I want you to move in."

"What's the holdup? That should take just a few hours."

"Usually. The crapper leaks and we can't get parts here for two weeks or more. Besides, there isn't any water."

"Two weeks! Look Vern, I'll dig a pit. I'll haul water. Your boys can build me an outhouse to put over the hole. I've gotta' get out of that bunkhouse."

"Dormitory," corrected Vern.

"Right. Dorm. My roommate is driving me nuts. He's a California AV media guy and he's prying too much. I can't respond to his questions and he already knows that something is screwy."

Nielsson sympathized. "Just hang in there a little longer. By the way, how is he getting along?"

Douglas grinned. "I hate to admit it but this guy is terrific with the video camera. He makes excellent suggestions to the interpretive staff, too."

Vern sighed. "I was afraid you'd say that. I was against having an AV man following everyone around to 'help' them improve their presentations. Guess I'll have to eat a little crow."

13

"Maybe Jess and his camera will come in handy later on."

"Perhaps." Then Vern changed the subject. "How are you and our local sheriff getting along?"

"Henry?" Douglas was pleased that the subject came up. "Things couldn't be better. He is everything you said he was. A real sharpie."

Vern nodded in agreement.

Douglas explained, "We decided to split the territory just as you likely figured. He checks out the reservation and I watch for the killer within the park. That doesn't mean that we won't help one-another for we certainly will."

"Good. How do you think you two will get along?"

"No problem. He is a fine man. We relate to one-another on lots of subjects. Henry is Indian, though. I don't know how we'll get along if spirituality comes in to the picture."

"I don't know why the subject would come up unless you initiate it. Henry is a very modern man but he keeps personal beliefs to himself.

"Oh, I almost forgot." Vern frowned at his temporary loss of memory, "Martha, Henry's wife wants to meet you. Have you been to his ranch yet?"

"No."

"I thought not. It is time to meet our local sheriff's wife. They live out near Duck Lake, on the reservation. Here's a map I sketched for you. Drop in tomorrow evening around seven. Martha will have some fry bread and tacos to fatten you up a bit."

"Just what I need," he sighed patting a slight bulge of stomach fat. "Just what I need."

"That gut will be gone by the end of next week. Your training ends Friday and I expect you to be out on the trails from then on. This killer, if he exists, isn't going to come to you. You've got to go to him."

"That sounds easy but I'm still not certain I'm the right guy for this sh—"

"Yes you are." Vern stood up and slapped him on the back. "Now, I've got to do some paperwork. Get out of here, Wolf Man."

Both men smiled and shook hands.

*

Friday afternoon of the last day of training

There was no point in hiking any further. He could sit by the single-planked bridge until the new personnel returned from their overnight training session. He was waiting for one person in

14

particular. Her name was Julie. Just thinking of her caused his pulse rate to increase. He had admired her beauty for nearly two weeks. She worked as a sales person in the St. Mary Visitor Center and had been required to attend several of the training classes.

Chill winds, off the snowfields, competed with the radiant June sun. The young man shivered. No one was coming along the Red Eagle Trail, so he sat down on the leeward side of a grassy mound. Vaguely, he wondered who had piled the fine, rich loam alongside the trail. No matter. The grasses loved growing there and already the stems towered over two feet into the air. Undaunted by his movements, the cold winds sought secret paths among the thick grasses and whipped slender blades in rhythmic patterns, sometimes caressing the man's cheeks with still-soft, tender stems.

"Ahh." He sighed at the aromatic scents, which assailed his nostrils. Removing his cap, he thrilled to the wind's playful attacks upon his rusty colored strands. Impetuously he untied the leather thong and shook out the shoulder-length hair so that he could experience the full force of the chilly breezes.

Flowers again, delicate, small, mountain meadow varieties, some not familiar to him; he saw, peering up from the grasses, the tiny forget-me-not with its five blue petals and yellow center. An old friend. He leaned forward, his face coming closer to the minute blossoms. He smiled with the pleasure of the experience. The perfume of the grasses became stronger. He was sheltered almost completely from the chill. Using his daypack as a pillow he laid down to keep warm. Somewhere, nearby, a ground squirrel chucked in irritation that the human was lingering. He smiled again. He would rest a moment, enjoy the whole; the sky, the soft, warm earth, fragrant smells, beauty.

The man slept.

*

What was it?

He woke quickly, all senses alert. In the fraction of the second it took for him to waken he recognized the anxious scolding of the ground squirrel. The tone was different. No longer mildly complaining, the rodent was sounding its warning cry.

What was it?

The wind still blew. Grasses still swayed. Cottony clouds continued sailing across the blue heavens.

Something new was there. A tenseness, somehow, had intruded upon the mound. He was not alone. Something else was there, just a few feet away, hidden by the foliage. Whatever it was, it was large. Douglas felt it.

A man?

The simple thought sent danger signals racing through his frame. Whoever, whatever it was, was moving closer. No noise but he knew the intruder was inching nearer. In one movement he jerked from prone to upright position. When Douglas's head rose above the grass the thing leaped backwards, startled by the encounter with the wild-haired man-creature.

Ahead of him, still less than twenty feet distant, a deer stood trembling, eyes quivering, nostrils fluctuating; still not certain what she was seeing.

Both, in different ways, thrilled with the encounter; he knowing the joy of it, and the doe sensing danger, muscles tensed, waiting for the next move.

Douglas relaxed. His shoulders drooped slightly. Perhaps because of the slight shifting of posture or maybe because the wind was whipping the man's hair about his eyes, the deer turned. Stopped. Moved again. Stopped. Then, trotting with dignity, the creature hurried into the forest below.

The man's face lost its smile. He looked grim, almost frightened. The deer could have been a bear. A grizzly bear. A grizzly with cubs. If the latter had been true, very likely he would be dead. Unnerved, he arose, scanned the edges of the forest, and picked up his daypack.

When he first noticed the young woman she was standing, quite still, part way up the bank from the bridge. Her hair was half hidden by a blue cap. Denim blue jacket and jeans clothed her in a softness becoming to her beauty. Mud-smeared boots completed her attire. The top of a beige Kelty pack protruded above her head.

In that first instant of his seeing her she remained motionless, her expressionless face radiating glimpses of loveliness. Somewhat awkward, due to the unfamiliarity of carrying a heavy pack, she moved up the trail until she was within easy talking distance.

"Hi, Douglas." The voice was deep, complimentary to her race. Julie was a Native American, a member of the Blackfeet Nation. Unlike her White friends she could not call him "Wolf Man." That would have been disrespectful.

"Hello, Julie. How are you?"

She was puzzled. This man, by his very action, his body language, indicated that he had been waiting for her.

Not receiving an answer he asked, "Can I walk back to St. Mary with you?"

"Sure." That was all she said.

The trail to Red Eagle Lake was eight miles in length. For the last four miles the route dropped off the side of the moraines and became a rather swampy, forest-choked trail. The first four miles followed an abandoned road. Their walk was along the wide, dry roadway. Neither spoke. Both were by custom rather silent individuals. Except for random, shy glances, they did not look at one-another. They hurried on, painfully aware of the awkward silence, neither willing to initiate a conversation.

Another encounter broke the spell. The couple was walking along a somewhat narrower segment of the road where the forest-clad earth was higher on both sides. A loud crashing occurred, a small tree bent over, and out of the forest fell a very large black bear.

Plop! The large male lit on his rear end right in front of Julie. The two humans stopped. Obviously embarrassed at being caught in his awkwardness the bear looked appraisingly at the two startled people, lifted his head in false dignity, and began walking slowly along the road.

Both humans considered the situation very humorous. Julie giggled softly.

The problem was that the clumsy black bear was ambling along the road going in the same direction as the two hikers. He wasn't hurrying. Progress became agonizingly slow. The bear sniffed at every patch of strawberry blossoms and snacked from time-to-time on the succulent cow parsnips.

"Ahem! Ahem!" Douglas kept clearing his throat so that the bear would remember that the humans were nearby. A startled bear might possibly create a serious problem. "Ahem!"

Julie was still giggling softly. The bear turned his head impatiently and stared. Then he proceeded along the trail. Finally, partly because of the human sounds, possibly because the bear knew they wanted to pass and mostly due to a large cluster of parsnips just off the trail, the very large bruin strolled into the vegetation and began noisily feasting.

Still not wanting the bear to become startled Douglas whistled Jingle Bells, as loud as he could. The bear stared at them as they passed, parsnip stalks hanging from his half-closed lips.

17

Somehow Julie's hand had found its way into Douglas's. The awkward spell was over.

*

Seldom, at least in modern times, had a clumsy bear falling out of the woods resulted in so dramatic a change in the lives of two people. The slight, brown hand slipping into Douglas's large palm had not only provided Julie with the safety she so desired, but the simple act triggered the beginning of a rapidly developing romance.

Julie worked for the Glacier Natural History Association. Until Logan Pass opened for business she was stationed at the St. Mary Visitor's Center. There, she sold books and maps. Most of her time was spent dispensing information to the visitors. At first she found the job frightening, especially operating the cash register with it's many buttons. Then, because of the people she met, the sales job became a labor of fun and excitement.

The staff naturalists and association clerks were there because they liked people. From diversified backgrounds they melded into an efficient, caring group who made laughter out of long hours and tried, subconsciously, to meet the needs of every individual.

Douglas observed much of what transpired in the center. He used the employees as information gatherers. Always unassuming, he gleaned facts, opinions, and experiences from the staff. Such information helped him assess the happenings within the park. The almost immediate result was that he began to think that foul play, if there was any, was not contrived by the east side staff. They knew almost everything that went on and none of it reflected the violence that Vern Nielsson thought was happening. As far as Douglas could determine there were no suspects in the St. Mary area.

Sometimes he would sit sprawled in the uncomfortable plastic chairs in the lobby, and smile at the activities going on about him. Mostly he smiled at Julie. By July they were genuinely in love. She lived for the moment he would appear at the center. Unfortunately, for Douglas, his work kept him so engrossed that there were few spare moments for him to think of her.

The Thursday before the Fourth of July weekend marked the real beginning of their affair. Douglas appeared at the VC at 12:30 sharp. Melanae, another clerk who was Julie's best friend, was with him. Both were grinning broadly. "Come on, Julie. We're going on a picnic." Every employee in the center smiled with anticipation.

"But, I just have an hour for lunch and that's—"

"That is why I'm here," laughed Melanae. "I'll cover for you. Go on! Get out of here!"

Confused, blushing, Julie asked the Ranger in charge of the center, "Is that all right? Do you think it's OK if I go?"

The old man pulled at his Adams Apple and finally whined, "Well."

By that time the two were gone.

*

They became lovers that very afternoon.

*

Julie wheeled her pickup truck around the circular, graveled parking area below the 1913 Ranger Station, drove up to the split rail fence and parked.

Their eyes met, causing broad grins to appear. Douglas stepped out, pulled his bulging daypack from the truck's bed and carelessly slung it over his left shoulder. Julie locked the doors. Side-by-side they headed for the gate that marked the beginning of the wilderness. Tacked upon a gatepost was a brilliant, orange sign with a black image of an attacking bear. In bold letters, also black, the sign cautioned, "WARNING! Grizzly Bears have frequented this trail. Travel at your own risk."

Julie looked up at Douglas. "You have a gun, don't you?"

"No. We aren't going far. Don't worry."

Their route along the Red Eagle Lake Trail ran through a rocky flood plain. To their left, hills, mostly forest covered, alternated with tiny swampy depressions. Willows, mere shrubs, obscured their view of the lake to the west. The couple stopped at a tiny pond to gaze into the dark water coursing through the luxuriant grasses, sedges and countless other water-loving plants. The small stream was a special place with its own enchanting environment.

Upper St. Mary Lake, the most beautiful of the two called St. Mary, appeared from behind the willows. The blue waters sparkled with a myriad of silver waves; quivering mirrors. A lone duck paddled just offshore from a tiny spit of rock and sand. One time, not so long ago, the site had been a pier, a boat landing, which had serviced a log-structured St. Mary Lodge.

The landing was gone as were the lodge buildings. Where once they stood and where noisy automobiles had chugged, misfired, and roared, only fast growing stems of fireweed and little clumps of wild roses rustled and softly whispered in the warm mid-day breezes.

Their path led uphill, through a deep road-cut with high, still ugly, naked slopes on each side. They passed a thick forest of fir, and later, another.

Douglas stopped, took Julie's hand and smiled, "Up there!" He pointed to a grassy slope. "We'll go up there."

Booted feet made swishing sounds in the tender grasses; the hill was open, sunny, warm, almost hot. They went over a slight rise and found the second, the real summit, ahead of them. Below, the lake could be seen stretching into the sparkling, hazy distance, completely surrounded by snowcapped mountains with romantic names. Red Eagle, Mahtotopa, Little Chief, Dusty Star, along the south shore. Otokomi, Goat and Going-to-the-Sun mountains rising high above the north shore.

Dense forest obscured the view to the northeast. Eastward, the nearby summit of the hill hid a beaver valley from their eyes. But, to the south! The land wavered on and on, one moraine after another, marking the former lateral route of an extinct glacier. Those small hills were clothed with the brilliant greenness of new life.

Douglas peered over the summit of the hill, saw no movement in the valley below, and returned to the waiting Julie. Theirs was a very private place. No one could see them unless they walked right into the picnic spot.

The young man was spreading out an old army-surplus blanket when Julie spoke. "Douglas."

"Hum?"

"What were these old trenches for?"

"Well! You are observant, aren't you? I'm impressed."

"Well, what are they?"

"Some people think they are old toilet pits or refuse dumps."

"There aren't any old cans or bottles or anything laying around."

"Right again." He smiled, pleased with her observation. "I'll tell you what I think they are." Along the hilltop there were four, irregularly spaced holes, about the same size as a grave. They were old, sides caved in, partially filled with soil and fallen branches. He explained his theory.

"During the winter, elk move in very close to the ranger station."

"Yes," she interrupted, "I see them out on the flats near the VC."

"If it is a snowy autumn, they come in early. A bad spring and they stay around here pretty late. I'd guess that for one or more seasons a grizzly also came into the area. Perhaps several bears.

This hill is good grazing land. I'd guess the elk were here and the bear or bears killed a few and fattened up for the long winter ahead. Maybe those holes were made over a long time, say a span of five, ten or more years."

Julie asked, "What do the trenches have to do with it?"

"A kill was made. The bear couldn't eat a whole elk or deer so he dug an elk-sized pit and dropped the carcass into it. Then all he had to do was cover it with branches from these trees, brush, dry grass, dirt, easy for a big grizzly to do. Then he could stroll into the forest over there, to the north, fix up a day bed of fir boughs and sleep. If anything came by to steal his food the bear could run it off." Douglas added, "Or, add it to its larder."

"Oh." Her voice was low, uneasy.

"Come on Julie, it's almost July. There are few elk in this area now."

The young man held her by the arms. She could feel his warmth, more intense then that of the sun. Her body, without command, instinctively moved forward and blended into his. Her face nestled into the powerful, throbbing chest. Two round, wonderfully soft mounds, her breasts, radiated heat that burned through his cotton shirt. Retreating slightly, the man gently pulled his beautiful companion down to lie upon the blanket. They kissed. Slowly fingers moved across fabric as they undressed to perform their act of love.

*

She lay nude, staring up at a lazy fluff of cloud. Looking down toward her body, she observed her still-erect, dark nipples, quivering slightly as she breathed. The breasts seemed a little red. Whisker burn, she thought, almost laughing.

Her naked stomach, slightly rounded, was beyond her vision but an irregular rusty-red mass of hair marked the location of her lover's head. He was asleep, his face resting on her cushion of black, pubic hair.

She marveled at what had happened. Their passions had been great. Their desires had needed immediate fulfilling. Suddenly she had found her wild haired, freckle-skinned lover on top of her, powerful arms keeping him well above her soft, brown body.

During the act, they had steadily looked into each-others eyes, almost unblinking, two souls desiring so very much to be one. Each time the lover had thrust forward, shock waves of ecstasy had rushed out from her areas of sensuality until she almost cried for joy. Once

21

she felt fear, a woman's fear of un-fulfillment. His eyes did a funny thing. They rolled uncontrolled in their sockets and his gasps of extreme passion nearly became cries of anguish.

He was finished. He was finished and she was not.

Lying there, with her man sleeping on her special place, she blushed at what had happened next.

Slowly. Very, very slowly her spent lover had covered her with kisses; her face, neck, breasts, waist. She realized what was about to happen when soft lips and tongue reached her navel. She had tried, really tried, to resist. Out of control, her thighs had simply moved apart, as if having a mind of their own, allowing the wet, sensitive tongue to explore her secret places, caressing her tiny ridges, lips, and valleys.

Her orgasm had, she thought, nearly killed her. The woman smiled in remembrance, closed her eyes and slept.

*

The Great Bear stumbled across the deteriorating beaver dam. From time to time the massive head lowered and he noisily slurped the slightly acidic water of the dying pond.

Beaver no longer lived there. A decade before, the same grizzly had visited the dammed valley. That time he had waded out to the lodge. With great powerful sweeps of his paws and the ripping of powerful teeth upon the larger branches, the bear came close to penetrating the interior of the beaver den. A few weeks later a large black bear completed the den's destruction. The beaver family, realizing that their situation was precarious, had moved downstream, into a thicket of aspen. Since then the pond had become shallow; un-supporting of all but the most minute aquatic life including small fishes. The pond held a few small trout. There were no beaver. The bear, on a vegetarian diet, grunted and shuffled along the hillside. His memory was excellent. He remembered fifteen years before when his mother, sister and he had climbed the same hill to feast on a slightly decomposed elk that had been hidden in a shallow hole. The bear's mind deduced that perhaps another carcass lay there, waiting for him.

Westerly breezes carried the man-smell to the bear's sensitive nostrils. The strange two-legged creature was nearby. A more recent memory briefly came to focus. The beast salivated as it remembered the delicious flavor of the man-creature he had found just a few yards from his winter den.

Instead of fleeing, as he had usually done in the past, the giant stealthily made his way to the crest of the hill. For a moment or two he stood up, full height, looking downhill. When he saw the lovers he quickly dropped to the ground. The bear couldn't see them from a four-footed position but by crawling forward, slowly, silently, he once again gained the summit. Peering from between the grass blades the grizzly acted much like a big lovable dog lying on its stomach.

What was he observing? Confused, the grizzly raised his head slightly so that both of the humans could be observed. So unusual and new to the bear was the activity that he thought at first there was but one strangely formed human below him. The nakedness compounded his confusion.

His senses of hearing and smell told him that there were two man-creatures, a waft of perfume, a musky scent, two distinct voices. One voice was of grunts and deeper sounds of passion. That creature was pumping its rear end up and down, forward and backward. The other voice, high pitched, some moans, sighs, also heavy breathing, was emanating from the human lying on the ground.

Slowly the intelligent beast realized that the man-creatures were mating. He, himself, had just completed a five-day tryst with a blondish-brown female grizzly. The movements and sounds were somewhat familiar. Interesting. He hugged the earth and watched intently.

Human flesh, as tasty as it was to the Great Bear, was not the catalyst for his curiosity. His diet, since the beaver pond had produced no animal snacks, was still vegetable matter; bulbs, new grasses, leaves, and flowers were the present delicacies.

The bear couldn't see as well as he wished so he inched his massive torso forward until he could peer, unobstructed, at the humans. He was having fun.

Both humans became silent, still. They remained that way for a long time. The bear became bored. Forgetting himself he slapped at a passing bee. His movement resulted in a slight noise. The rusty-haired being raised up and peered up slope. At that moment the fickle wind shifted. Bear; the powerful, offensive odor swept downhill to seek out the nostrils of the already-alerted man and his still unsuspecting mate. Muscles tensed, the grizzly lay silent, wondering what the man-creatures would do next, now that they knew he was there.

*

CHAPTER 3

June 28, 1984

Around noon Douglas thought he heard a motor running just outside his trailer. The previous day had been quite strenuous, a fifteen mile, mostly upslope hike. Muscles aching, Wolf Man arose from his mattress bed and opened the door. There was Henry Two Feathers, sitting in the cab of his truck.

He waved, picked up a clean pair of jeans and began dressing. Before he could finish Henry poked his head inside the trailer, exhaling a gray cloud of cigarette smoke.

"Want to go for a ride? I want to show you something."

"Sure. Just give me a minute."

*

Douglas saw the coyote first. He yelled, "Hey! Look out!" The coyote crossed in front of the truck. It didn't run. Neither did it lope. The creature's gait was casual, unhurried. Gracefully it cleared the fence below the road, turned, sat down, and stared at the truck's occupants.

Douglas was fascinated. As quiet as he could with a truck, he opened the right door and slid onto the road. The coyote didn't move.

Somewhat stooped, hunched over in a submissive stance, he crossed the dirt road. The coyote, now but perhaps forty feet away, sat staring, tongue lolling out of the side of its mouth. Realizing that he'd probably get no nearer and thinking that the unusual behavior might be due to rabies or another illness, Douglas stopped.

The young man stared directly into the coyote's eyes. The color was different, more yellow, but the eyes reminded him of a red fox he had once encountered when he was a boy. Strange, those eyes before him now, filled with wisdom. "How could that be?" he wondered. Softly he spoke, "Hello, you old coyote you. What are you doing here? Why aren't you running away?"

The animal stared back, its eyes soft and moist in the early afternoon air. Rising off its haunches the wild dog turned, with head down, and walked away toward the distant Chief Mountain.

"You were talking to him," declared Henry. "You were having a conversation." The men were once more speeding along the Duck Lake road.

24

"Yeah," Douglas responded. "I really like the wild dogs. They are so intelligent." He was frowning, a puzzled look of mystification distorting his face. "You know, Henry, I could swear that as we looked at one-another that old coyote cried. I was sure I saw tears of sorrow. That just can't be."

Old memories again, rushing back to Henry of long, long ago legends, stories, campfire tales, the unwritten history of his people. Not knowing what to say the older man had responded, "Son, you must be part Indian to experience what you just did." He forced a smile.

"Naw! Indians don't have a monopoly on understanding the natural world. They just sometimes come a little closer to the truth."

A long somber silence prevailed. Only the trucks motor and metallic rattling could be heard. Behind them a thick column of grayish-brown dust obscured the route over which they had just passed. Wishing to break the mood Douglas spoke, "You know, Henry, you're right. I think I am part Indian."

"Yeah?" The sheriff saw a faint twitch of humor on Douglas's face. He waited for the obvious joke that was coming.

"Sure! My mother was part Blackhead and my daddy was half Flatfeet."

Moaning inwardly, Henry had forced a laugh. He had heard the stupid joke dozens of times before. Oh well, it had broken the silence. Why not laugh and make my young friend feel good, he had asked himself.

A half grin spread over Wolf Man's face. He thought he was pretty clever.

The old man added, "You'd better not tell that one around the boys at the Babb bars or you'll get a mauling you'll never forget."

Both men laughed heartily.

*

Their destination was way out at the extreme northeast corner of Route 464, a dirt road of considerable challenge for the occasional tourist. Where the road angled south, they drove north, then east again, over rough ranch truck trails, far out upon the vast expanses of the reservation. The trip took three quarters of an hour.

Although knowing one another but half a month the two men, ages twenty-five and sixty, had become good friends. They were, except for age, very much alike. Because of the coyote episode and the bad joke, Douglas came alive with conversation. Henry listened attentively. The young man, accepting his elder companion, poured out his thoughts, including his growing love for Julie.

Henry, without saying so, approved of Wolf Man's selection for a mate. In a mature, respectful manner he had admired the girl's firm, rounded butt. Her hips were perfect for birthing. A man had to consider things like that.

Douglas declared that Julie's greatest assets were her beautiful features and matching personality.

The older man had agreed and he remembered thinking of his Martha and how lovely she had been as a young woman. She had looked very much as Julie did in 1984. His reverie ceased when Douglas began telling him about the aborted picnic.

"First I heard a slapping noise, very faint. Then I detected two brownish, rounded ears sticking up over the uphill vegetation. I could feel it watching. That was the eerie part. Then the smell hit my nostrils. It was a bear sure enough."

He reported how they had casually packed up their belongings and slowly ambled down the hill, casting guarded looks backward to see if the bear was following. He neglected to tell Henry that they had worn only their boots; everything else had been wadded up and carried under their arms. The two lovers hadn't stopped walking until they reached the tiny meadow where the old lodge had once stood. Fortunately for them, bad luck for the fisherman, the only person around, was so busy fly-fishing that he didn't see them until they were completely dressed.

Henry swerved violently to avoid running over an already partly squashed skunk. Obviously the story was completed. Henry changed the subject. "Do you carry a gun?" His question startled Douglas.

"Why, no. The bear didn't make a hostile move. I don't think he was hunting for people food."

"I'm not thinking of your picnic bear. You don't have a half-assed idea of what you are looking for and what it can do to you. I don't think it can be called overreacting if you protect yourself a little bit. I'd label it, 'being smart.'"

"Yes. I suppose so. I hate to break a good habit."

"Good for you in the past, maybe, but not now."

"Yeah, I agree." Douglas sighed.

"By the way, what were you eating? Anything with a good smell that would tempt a grizzly? Chicken? Bologna? Ham and cheese? Potato salad?" He waited for an answer that didn't come. Looking at his rider he realized that Douglas's face was flushed a bright red. "Well I'll be damned!"

The conversation ended. Later Henry attempted to end the silence by saying, "I've got just the thing for you. On the way home let's stop at my place and get you fixed up with the proper weapon. Firearm," he clarified.

David Brown met the two men at a corner of the east pasture of the DB Ranch. Henry and David solemnly shook hands. Although the rancher gave Douglas an inquiring look, Henry did not make the introduction. Understanding the expression, the Wolf Man stood back a short distance from the two Indians so they could converse in privacy.

"She don't look good, this one," declared Brown. "Too many funny things about it. I don't like this none."

"Let's take a look," replied Henry. "Maybe we can figure out what happened."

The cow, a Hereford, was lying in the open. Only a few very small plants of sagebrush plus a sparse growth of grasses covered the area.

Henry and Douglas climbed over the barbed wire fence. The rancher obviously wasn't going any nearer. "Here are Brown's tracks," mused Douglas. Henry grunted. The rancher's boot prints led straight out to the corpse and the same shaped prints returned.

"Shit!" Henry swore strongly, yet quietly. Douglas knew why. There were no other tracks in the arid soil, not even the deceased steer's.

"Got a camera?"

Douglas nodded.

"OK. I'm going to look away for a few minutes and I want you to shoot this scene from all four directions."

"Right." Douglas pulled a Nikon from his daypack and began taking photos.

"OK, I'm done."

"Good. I didn't see you take them. OK? If the authorities find out they'll confiscate your film and camera. The whole kit and caboodle."

"Sure."

Henry walked up to the carcass. "Look here. The upper right lip's been cut away. See the funny looking grooved incisions? If you look close you'll notice that the tongue's gone, too."

"What's this all about?"

Henry ignored the question. "I'll turn away and you shoot it." Douglas's camera clicked twice.

"Now, look at the anus."

"It's gone!"

27

"Damn right it's gone. So is the udder. Look here. A whole section of the stomach area is missing." He shook a cigarette out of the pack. "OK. Mr. Wolf Man, tell me what's wrong."

"Cow's dead."

"Of course it's dead. What else?"

"Well, there are no tracks except for Brown's and ours." A frown appeared on Douglas's forehead. "Let's turn it over."

"Why? I might get a hernia."

"There's no kill spot that we can see. No blood."

"You're right," agreed Henry, "and there won't be any underneath either. No god damned blood at all. Before we turn it over, look at the cut area where the lips used to be."

"It's dark along the edges, like the tissue was burned. Say, Henry, let me cut a cross-section of tissue out and I'll send it to Joe Gibbons at Montana State. He's a friend of mine."

"I have to say 'no'," answered the sheriff. "I'm going to look the other way and block Brown's view of this so don't take too long doing whatever you will do. I'll have to answer a lot of damned questions and I don't want to see any picture taking or know for sure that any tissue was taken either."

Rolling the heavy cow over had been a real chore. Nothing unusual was found on the other side of the carcass.

"See anything else funny with this critter?" challenged Henry.

"Not funny. No. Nothing."

"Then, look at the face."

"The eyes are bulging, but that's not peculiar," observed Douglas.

"Aw! Come on Wolf Man." Henry had never called the young man that until they had arrived at the site. "Think!"

Cold realization struck him. He looked about. "No Magpies! No Ravens!"

"You've got it, son. Normally the birds are pecking the eyes out almost before the animals are dead. Every time, I'd say." Henry paused and cleared his throat. Unwillingly, he looked up into the clear blue sky.

"What is this? What's going on?"

Casting a look backwards to make sure the rancher couldn't hear Henry whispered, "Cattle mutilation."

"Really?" He almost laughed. A grin spread across his face. "That's pretty wild stuff there, Henry." He'd heard of the rash of cattle mutilations that had plagued the West back in the 60's and 70's. For some reason the mystery had been hushed up or weakly explained away. Now, he was looking at the same phenomenon. He could only add, "Are you sure?"

"Yes. I remember very well. This is a real mutilation. Done by high technology. Look at the wounds again. You'll be surprised at the report you get back from your Bozeman friend." He added weakly, "If you took any tissue. And if it doesn't get lost somehow."

Douglas looked at the incisions. "Very neat. Efficient."

Henry became stern. He emptied a sandwich into his jacket pocket and handed the container him. "Now look, get that tissue sample into this baggy and stash it in your pack. Don't let Brown see you do it. I've gotta' call headquarters."

"Why? What will they do?"

Henry explained. "Our orders are very explicit. Bob, another deputy, apparently more trusted than I am, will come out here, load the carcass, cover it with a tarp and haul it to Bozeman. I'm not sure where in Bozeman. The rancher over yonder, Brown, will be given three hundred dollars and told either that predators or cults did it, depending on how much he observed."

The two men went back to the truck. "Henry, what if they find where I made the tissue cuts? What will they do?"

"What cuts?" Both grinned. "Maybe they won't," hoped Henry. "The carcass is starting to stink."

*

Henry didn't return his friend to his trailer until nearly 3 A. M. Douglas slept late; too late. Hurriedly he ate breakfast. The drive to the St. Mary Visitor Center seemed longer than usual. Impatient to get started on an important day hike, he chatted with Julie for just a moment. Fortunately she was busy, allowing him to make a quick exit.

Brisk winds were chopping St. Mary Lake into dark waves spewing dull, grayish froth across the surface. Aspen trees bent to the fury of the gale, their leaves quivering violently. The yellow Toyota bravely chugged out of the forest of deciduous trees. He was relieved to see Two Dog Flats bathed in brilliant sunlight. For some reason he felt a little bit unnerved, as though the weapon he now carried had created a new, intimidating environment. For a moment he considered taking the revolver out of the pack and stashing it behind the seat. Being in Glacier wasn't quite as much fun as he had thought it would be.

This particular backcountry hike had been chosen due to the short walking distance involved. As would be his habit, a sealed envelope was sticking in Vern Nielsson's mailbox at the station. Inside was Douglas's destination. Hopefully someone would always know where he was.

He parked the Corolla at the Rising Sun store's parking lot, just below the porch railing. It would be safe there. He wasn't yet accustomed to the near absence of theft and vandalism that Glacier enjoyed.

Rising Sun was a beautiful alluvial fan, the creation of thousands of years of sedimentary deposits tumbling down from the, sometimes turbulent, Rose Creek. The geological formation supported a mixture of coniferous and deciduous trees and a particularly enchanting meadowland. The area was partly desecrated by the ugliness of the parking lots, store, restaurant and particularly the motel units. Recognizing the necessity for the meager accommodations he put the tasteless intrusions out of his mind.

Just beyond the parking lot and below the motel area a large meadow flowed in slight billowy irregularities down to the lakeshore. One glance and he knew that he was looking at another western intrusion of the Great Plains, one last foothold of prairie grasses and wild creatures.

If he searched the meadow he would once again find his favorite flowers. Balsam root with its arrowhead-shaped leaves, waved in the breezes while the delicate prairie smoke hid reclusively from the same gusts. He thought that probably he would discover other familiar blossoms. He imagined an ill-tempered badger waddling bow-legged from burrow to burrow seeking out mouse, mole, and insect with unquenchable appetite.

Sighing, missing his beloved Great Plains, he turned away from the meadows and walked toward the trailhead to Lake Otokomi.

Rocky Mountain Maple trees grew profusely along the lower, beginning segment of the trail. Never becoming very large, even under the best of conditions, the maples were chopped off; stunted. During the winter season the local elk herd moved onto the delta and ravished everything above the snow. So did the mule deer.

Due to the cropping, and also because of the heavy snows, some of the trees were contorted into nearly horizontal mazes of branches clothed in large, veined leaves. He noticed that beneath the tangle of limbs there were sometimes dark, almost completely hidden "tree caves" large enough to hide a man, bear or any large animal.

Just beyond the grizzly bear warning sign he detected the unmistakable scent of bear. The smell was faint, stale. One of the animals had been using the tree shelters as a day bed. He scrawled a note on his pad to remind the bear management people of the site, all too close to the motel and campground.

He hurried on.

Soon the maples were left behind, replaced by a particularly dense, shadowy forest of moderate-sized conifers. The trail wound in long, graceful switchbacks, up and up, first east and then west and back east again, rising steeply at the bends and then leveling off somewhat for the long walk to the next turn.

Douglas, disgusted with himself, realized he was out of shape. He panted and perspired from the mild exertion. A single stream bisected the trail and at that point he stooped and splashed cold water on his face. "Must be the altitude," he lied to himself.

Eventually the trail led him to the edge of a very steep slope. There, beside the trail, stood a magnificent tree of peculiar bark design. He recognized it immediately as a Western Larch. The earth was clothed in a deep mat of golden needles. The larch was a unique conifer. Each autumn it shed all of its thin leaves. He rested beside the tree, touching the warm bark, listening to the high winds sighing through the upper limbs far above him. Pesky flies zipped in attempting crash landings on his unprotected arms, neck and face. One, lone, pale-blue butterfly bobbled from sunlight to shadow to sunlight and disappeared from view.

Douglas realized that his favorite animals, wolves, would love the Otokomi Valley. He leaned against the tree, almost hugging it, while his eyes took in the sun-drenched, V-shaped Otokomi canyon. A branch snapped!

Adrenaline surged within Wolf Man's body. All senses alert, the young man waited as he evaluated the noise. Why would a branch snap? The hard, dry sound was unlike a falling limb striking earth, rock or log. The noise had been abrupt, somewhat earthy in tone. There was only one logical answer. Something large was below him, probably on the trail.

He ran along the exposed slope, stepping purposely on a large ant nest. A few strides more and he faded back into the darkness, past small larches and into the seclusion of the gloomy Douglas firs. Crouching behind a fallen giant he waited, working to control his breathing; attempting to diminish its sound.

Panting was heard first, rapid, deep breathing, rasping. Moments later the coarse clumping of heavily booted feet upon the hard-

31

packed earth of the trail became audible. No bear or elk, that one. A human was hurrying up the trail.

He crouched lower.

The light gray of a sweatshirt flashed in the mottled sunlight of the trail. Broad shoulders on a tall body emerged. Then the man's hair appeared. Light brown. He didn't have to see the face to realize that the powerful body belonged to Jim Ballard. In a whisper Douglas announced, "It's that Anti-10 Point Veteran's Preference creep." Puzzled, he watched the newcomer.

Ballard was having far more difficulty catching his breath than Douglas. His labored gasps wheezed in and out of the trees, drowning out any small noises that might have been made by his observer. The man reached the larch and almost fell. Douglas realized that Ballard had been running. Disinterested, the man's eyes, hazed by perspiration, peered unseeing across the valley to the distant cliff.

Regaining his breath, Ballard took a few steps forward and saw the boot print in the anthill. Swarms of large reddish-brown insects were angrily scurrying about, seeking out the offender. From the ant nest the man could see a short portion of the trail ahead of him. It was empty. "Shit!" he exploded angrily and kicked viciously at the nest. He checked his watch and then glared menacingly at the empty trail ahead of him. Then he turned and staggered back down the trail.

Douglas realized that his adversary had carried no water. He had obviously rushed up the trail attempting to overtake him. He must have seen my Toyota, thought Douglas, or, maybe someone had seen me starting out on the trail and told him.

The man had carried no weapon. That was good to know. Wolf Man deduced that Ballard wasn't a very good woodsman either, or he would have known by the ant's growing activity that the nest had been stepped on just seconds before his arrival. If he had realized that then he could have deduced that Douglas hadn't had time to traverse the open area of the trail. Then, if the man had any brains at all, he would have reasoned that Douglas was probably watching him from the shadows of the forest.

Weird, he thought. I'd better keep a watch on him. He began to wonder if Jim Ballard wasn't somehow linked to the murders. The idea seemed illogical yet the man's behavior was irrational.

Brushing dried needles, and one small spider, from his jeans, Douglas moved back to the Otokomi Trail and proceeded on his journey.

Not far from where the larch tree episode took place, strong winds whipped down from the direction of Lake Otokomi. The still generally moist soil gave up only an occasional leaf or partially desiccated dust particle.

For some unexplainable reason he didn't like the area. Perhaps Jim Ballard's following him had made him uneasy. More likely the horror story of the bear mauling that had occurred on that very trail was sub-consciously creating anxiety. He never did find a good view. He couldn't catch a glimpse of majestic Goat Mountain or the somewhat lower summit of Otokomi. An occasional view of the opposite side of the valley wasn't particularly exciting.

Then, he encountered snow. A large drift covered the trail at a particularly steep section. He hadn't brought his crampons. It was too dangerous to attempt the crossing without ice ax and the steel-toothed equipment for his shoes. Angry with himself for not checking on trail conditions, he pulled out the topographic map. Wind, a steady, powerful force, tore at the map, whipped his hair about, threatening to push him off balance.

He decided to hike cross-country. The decision was basically sound. He would retreat downhill until the relatively gradual west slopes of Otokomi enabled him to hike up to a long ridge, which merged into East Flattop Mountain. Then he could follow the summit northeastward until he could drop down a rather gentle slope. From there it would be but a short distance to St. Mary Campground and the Visitors Center.

The route up Otokomi was a good one. The forest gradually thinned out and he found himself on a windswept spur of the mountain. Short, new-growth grasses hissed and reflected darts of rich emerald hues. The wind was ferocious. He took his hat off and stuffed it inside his jacket. The gale tore at his hair, tearing loose strand after strand until he unloosened the leather band, allowing the reddish mane to whip about his face. Once or twice he nearly fell. He remembered the radio in his pack and attempted to call the station. The batteries didn't work. Since he had changed his plans no one would know where to look for him if he became injured. Normally that wouldn't have bothered him. He had months of experience of living alone in the Wind River country of Wyoming, the Bitterroots, Salmon Mountains, and Yellowstone's neighboring wilderness areas.

The wind roared in his ears, confusing his senses. Above him, unseen, due to the curvature of the slope, a dead tree crashed to earth. The grasses and flowers were bent horizontally, surrendering to the rapid airwaves rushing up slope toward the near horizon. He tripped; rather, stubbed his boot on a jutting rock, fell forward, catching himself easily with both outstretched hands. He swore nervously. The wind increased its force. Another limb crashed loudly from behind him. He could distinguish small twigs flying away from dead or partially dead trees.

Turning, he abandoned his route of travel. Leaning carefully into the force he slowly, carefully retreated down the slope.

Once, at a rocky promontory, he stopped to get his bearings. The stone wall, providing shelter from the wind, felt warm, reassuring. An alarm of sorts went off in his brain. What caused it? Had he seen something? Heard a noise that wasn't wind-caused? What was wrong? Douglas pondered the mystery for a few moments, immobile against the cliff wall. His blurring eyes, moist from the wind tearing at the lids, observed and detected nothing. He took a deep breath of cold air through his nostrils. Nothing. Whatever had triggered Wolf Man's warning system was gone.

Or was it?

Somewhat ashamed of his apprehensions, he moved slowly down the mountain. If he were lucky he'd reach the VC in time to see Julie again.

*

The rock outcropping, against which he had rested, towered twelve feet above the surface on the downside of the slope. If he had walked a yard or so further south he would have encountered the formation where the top horizontally protruded from the mountainside. Fortunately for him he hadn't. Three sides of the outcropping were steep. The east edge of exposed limestone rose a mere two feet above the sparse soil. A few junipers and bear-berries, plus other hardy plants grew within the split surface. One crack, nearly a foot across, divided the entire outcropping. Erosion caused by thawing and freezing, had carved out a small depression. In that depression, the Great Bear slept, belly-up, absorbing the luxuriant warmth of the sun. He had been sleeping when Douglas leaned against the rock to rest.

Several changes of wind direction in the vicinity of the stone shelter carried man- scent to the bear's sensitive nostrils. He awoke slowly, yawned, sniffed and became fully awake. The man-creature was very near. Raising his massive head the bear saw the strange man with the flying hair disappearing down slope. The observation was short-lived, just a few seconds. It was long enough for the grizzly to recognize the same man-creature he had encountered on another hillside a few days before.

Puzzled, somewhat wary, the giant thought about the new encounter.

The June sunlight, sheltered from the wind, was almost hot. Lazily the bear licked up a few ants and a hapless beetle from the stone floor of his nest. Yawning, he shut his eyes. A low growl escaped his half-opened mouth. The bear slept.

*

Late June, 1984

"I think you had better get yourself another man."

Douglas's startling words had brought silence to the Nielsson household. The three family members stared incredulously at the Wolf Man.

"The facts are pure and simple," he explained. "I've lost my nerve. I imagine things, like being followed. Being watched. It happens to everyone, I guess, sooner or later. I'm in over my head. Too many weird, unconnected things going on around here. I thought Wyoming was strange! It doesn't hold a candle to this place."

Fascinated, the Nilsson's listened while the young man reported on his activities, including the mutilated cow. He concluded with the ill-fated hike up the Otokomi Trail.

Mrs. Nielsson, who was seated next to the youth, reached over and placed her hand upon the back of Douglas's massive fingers.

He was finished. He had nothing else to say. Vern sat in deep contemplation. He realized that he would loose his young investigator unless he made the right move.

Carolyn caught the nod from her mother and filled the half-empty coffee mugs from the large thermos that had been setting on the end table. If the mugs were full perhaps he would remain a bit longer.

There was no clock in the front room so the silence, except for their slight stirrings and breathing, was complete.

Vern sighed deeply, his powerful chest rising and falling. The leathery, furrowed face reflected the acute disappointment he was feeling.

Finally he spoke. "Your reasons are valid. Sound. You might be correct. Maybe I should abandon the whole theory. I might be wrong, you know. I don't blame you, a newcomer to the area, for being anxious. The mutilations are real. Been going on for quite a few years, since 1967. Isn't that right, girls?"

All three listeners nodded in agreement.

"You can ask anyone in Glacier County and they will tell you the mutilations are not imagined. People out there," he waved in the general direction of the plains, "are scared silly."

"Maybe whoever does the mutilations also got rid of our missing hikers."

"Could be," Vern agreed. "Common sense tells us that either the men got lost or a bear killed them. Perhaps some of each. That isn't so unbelievable. Two inexperienced men killed by bears. Two others lost by hiking off trail. Impossible to find." Turning his magnificent pale blue eyes on Douglas, his voice husky with suppressed emotion, Vern appealed to him in the only way that he knew. "What if I'm not wrong? What if there is a murderer here in the Hudson Bay District? In spite of the mumbo-jumbo that complicates things, there might possibly be a killer here, in my district.

"What am I going to do about it?"

No one responded. Shaking his head slowly Vern asked, "Do me a favor, Douglas? Try one more thing. Don't quit just yet."

The wolf researcher sat quietly, unresponsive.

"Have you ever heard of The-Hole-in-the-Wall? Glacier's; not the historical one?"

"No, I haven't."

"Go there. The place is magnificent! Go there alone and just think. Feel."

"Daddy," protested Carolyn, "The snow's too deep."

"Not for this man. He can make it."

Douglas opened his mouth to refuse but Vern's upraised palm stopped him. "Do it. Go there. The scenery is overwhelming. Go there. Think things out. Take your time. I'll plan a trip for you. Then, afterward, if you don't want to stay, you'll know you've given Glacier a fair shake.

"But, give her a chance, man. You don't know this place. It's special. Very special. Do this for yourself as well as for me."

Douglas heard himself saying that he would give it a try. He would go to The-Hole-in-the-Wall.

*

CHAPTER 4

Early July, 1984

Twelve thousand years ago, more or less, much of the vast mountainous area of what is now Glacier National Park was clothed in a merciless mantle of glacial ice. Each summer the ice sheets submitted to the unrelenting force of gravity and increased their downhill velocity, away from the naked rock walls that marked their beginnings.

Every winter, and winters were nine or ten months long, snow blew into the crevasses separating the upper glacial edge from the sheer mountain faces. In such a manner the rivers of ice perpetuated themselves until warming climate and decreased precipitation resulted in their extinction. The great valley glaciers exist no more, until the next ice age.

One of the truly wondrous results of the ancient rivers of ice is a series of long, magnificent lakes, nestled within the deepest recesses of the glaciated valleys. On the northwest side of the Continental Divide the lakes curl gently southwestward. A topographic map displays them as four giant claw-like digits of a massive paw. From north to south they are called Kintla, Bowman, the Quartz Lakes, and Logging Lake. Using a little imagination the map-reader can perceive Waterton Lake to be a dewclaw, the fifth digit, lying in a north-south direction.

For two years a young grizzly male had roamed the dense forests of the western slopes. The year he was born his sister became a snack for a male grizzly. His mother, distraught over her loss, pampered the remaining cub and kept him with her for two winters. During the month of June of the year that Douglas arrived in Glacier, the mother bear came into estrus. Her sexual desires outweighed her waning interest in rearing the young male. One day, because he didn't take hints easily, the female slapped the two-year old male so hard that he tumbled down a steep, rock-splattered slope causing the youngster to become dazed, disoriented, and sitting in the rushing torrent of springtime Quartz Creek.

Usually a young bear, having the love and care that the new orphan had experienced would be at a definite advantage. Two complete years of bear education prepares a grizzly for the traumatic existence of being the intellectually superior creature of the forest, next to man. That was not the case with the juvenile male floundering in Quartz Creek. To put it simply, he was stupid.

One night, following days of near starvation, the black colored grizzly drifted across Lone Pine Prairie and crossed the North Fork of the Flathead River at a particularly turbulent spot. Unnerved from the adventure, stomach aching with emptiness, the anxious grizzly decided to make a search around the out-buildings of a ranch belonging to a local character nick-named, "Poor Shot Willie."

Willie's chickens didn't care much for the shadowy figure snorting outside their shed. When the bear's claws ripped the first board off a side of the ramshackled building, mayhem in the coup resulted.

Rambo, the black and tan hound, who had been sleeping in the cabin with his master, crashed through Willie's kitchen screen door. Just as the delinquent bear forced his shoulders into the coup the dog sank his teeth into the protruding rump. Chickens yelling, the bear screaming in pain, and the dog growling fiercely all caused Willie to come out of a deep sleep. Instead of heading for the nearby woods the frightened bruin took a shortcut across the yard. "Poor Shot Willie," wasn't really that bad a shot. When the black shadow sped past the house Willie fired his 12-gauge shotgun. Two pieces of shot penetrated the fur and hide of the youngster and became imbedded next to the puncture wounds received from old Rambo. Rambo, barely missing the same shotgun blast, ran the bear to the river where he gave up the chase.

Still hungry, snorting from his wounds, the two-year-old-bear headed back into the relative safety of Glacier National Park. His temper was worsening. The grizzly was ready to put anything edible on his food list, including humans.

The encounter between Poor Shot Willie and the young bear happened the night before Douglas arrived at Bowman Lake.

*

A throbbing headache, which seemed to begin in his rear-end and course up through his body to the skull, caused Douglas to state, "This is the worst road I've been on this year." His voice trembled as the truck bounced over a washboard section of the dirt surface.

"Road!" thundered Elmo Turner. "This ain't no god-damned road! This is a gut-bustin', shock-breakin', son-of-a-bitch. That's what she is!" The Park Service pickup lurched to the right as Elmo avoided a giant chuckhole.

"Watch it, man! You just about ran off the road!"

"Don't you worry none, Dougie old boy. Any detour would be an improvement."

Douglas shook a weak nod in agreement.

The two men in the vehicle were moving slowly up the West Side Road, which serviced the western border of Glacier National Park. The vehicle wasn't in the park but was moving through a sparsely forested area called The Home Ranch Bottoms. Now and then a ranch building, usually made of logs, appeared briefly. They passed no one on the road. Elmo exclaimed, "There she be!"

Looking to the right, Douglas got his first view of Polebridge, Montana. He liked the settlement immediately. An American flag waved half-heartedly over the log-structured general store. Apparently the restaurant was closed. Except for a small house and a few other out-buildings that was the total makeup of Polebridge.

Elmo commanded, "Go inside the store. They've got a lot of neat junk in there. Look around a bit. I've got to see ol' Mike over there." He nodded toward the closed restaurant.

Douglas pulled his aching backside out of the truck and wandered across the road. It took some maneuvering before he found the right spot to take a picture of the whole settlement. He fitted it into one frame of his Nikon. Smiling with satisfaction he entered the store. A cheerful musical bell announced that he was opening the door. The inside was somewhat darker than he had expected on such a sunny day.

"Hello." A middle-aged woman spoke without raising her eyes from her paper work.

He wondered how she could have anything to do. "Interesting store," he remarked. His voice didn't seem to go anywhere. The inside was still, close, as if the contents had absorbed his words before they reached the woman. "Nice store you got here."

The woman looked up, stared at him, then returned to her invoices. Toward the back of the store, attached to the south wall, was a yellowish-stained box of an old telephone. "Oh, you've got a crank-up telephone." He smiled with pleasure. "I haven't seen one of those since I left the Bitterroots." He continued to smile at the antiquated phone. "Can I use it? I'd like to call Communications Center."

"Sure. Go ahead and crank it. But, it don't work."

"Oh." His voice revealed the disappointment.

"Sorry," apologized the woman. "The phone company's going to send a repairman out to fix it."

"Oh."

A puzzled look crossed the woman's face. Briefly she stared at the broken telephone. "You know, it's been nearly two years now and he hasn't shown up yet."

"Oh."

He purchased a Coke Classic for himself and a Cream Soda for Elmo. He opened the door to leave. The woman called out, "Good bye, Wolf Man." Everyone seemed to know him.

The remainder of the trip was smooth compared to what they had experienced. A lady ranger said, "Hi," when they passed through the entry gate called Polebridge Ranger Station. Elmo announced, "I'll stop here on the way back and get a free coffee." The driver winked and leered into the rear vision mirror.

Douglas almost voiced what he thought. Bull Shit! She wouldn't give you the time of day.

He became fascinated with the deep forest that enveloped the road. They had left the North Fork Road and it's potholes at Polebridge. Elmo, obeying a sign, turned on the headlights. The road to Bowman Lake was narrow. As if it was his original idea Elmo said, "Want anyone coming the other way to see us." Each time he spoke Douglas was deluged with whiskey fumes. Apparently Polebridge was one of the man's watering holes.

The single-lane road twisted constantly. They would gain a little elevation and then on the next turn they'd loose it. Gradually, without realizing it, they were rising above the ranger station. Douglas inhaled the cool, moist air and sighed. Maybe Vern is right. Maybe I do need this trip. He thought the sentences rather than speaking them.

"Just wait 'till you see the lake," Elmo remarked. He was right. The water was beautiful. The truck rolled into the campground area and stopped at the unloading area.

"OK, Doug. You're on your own from here. Bob, the local ranger is up at Quartz Lake." A devilish grin crossed his face. "Black bear troubles. No wolves around here."

Douglas ignored the remark.

"Just get your pack, head down to the lake, veer to the right and pretty soon you'll come to Bob's cabin. You'll find the canoe there. Have a good time and watch out for the Griz."

He realized that Elmo didn't like him much. It would have been proper for Elmo to show him the cabin. On an intuitive impulse he said, "Tell Jim Ballard that I said, 'Hi!' and that I hope he enjoyed his run up the Otokomi trail the other day."

Elmo's mouth gaped open, not comprehending his meaning. Douglas slung his Kelty backpack upon his broad shoulders and cinched up the waist strap.

"Say, Dougie." Elmo had an idea. "Where you comin' out?"

"The River Styx."

"Huh? There ain't no river called Sticks."

Douglas laughed. "Tell Jim-Boy the next time he follows me anywhere he'll have more fun than he can shake a stick at."

"Huh?"

"I'll whip his ass. Tell him that, will you? Thanks for the ride." Elmo Turner couldn't even qualify as a possible suspect. He was too stupid.

Bowman Lake nestled comfortably within a long glacial valley, which extended northwesterly into the distant mountains. All around the vast expanse of lake the forest covered hills paraded one after another toward the towering peaks that loomed over that enchanting cirque called The Hole-in-the-Wall. From a high mountainside Rainbow Glacier glistened in the afternoon sunlight. He walked out on the dock and stared. The uneasiness he had been living with seemed to fall from his shoulders. For the first time since he arrived at Glacier Park he felt at peace. He was no longer intimidated by the immensity of the wilderness, his assignment, or the people he dealt with. Although the killer or killers could be out there somewhere along the trail, he felt the odds were very high that the area would not give him the answers he sought.

Silent, unmoving, he stood, looking at nothing really, just feeling, sensing, absorbing. The land seemed to respond with warmth, gentleness, acceptance. The two, the man and the primal setting, blended into one. Complete. Tranquil. Belonging.

Unobtrusively, the sun slipped slightly to the west and he reluctantly moved from his place of meditation.

The ranger's cabin stood a few hundred yards along the southeast shore of Bowman Lake. Another log structure, its picturesque appearance seemed to blend into the forest as if it had grown there. There was a note on the door.

Hi Doug,

The supplies are hanging from the cable. Thank you for taking them to the upper campground. Be sure you string them up high at the CG. Leave the paddles in the brush a few yards north of the john. Have a nice trip. If you need help, call me!

Bob Lemon

41

The note was friendly. He felt better. Apparently all West Side personnel hadn't sided with Ballard in his dislike for Douglas.

*

He slipped the canoe out onto the shallow waters of Bowman Lake. The craft was an old, aluminum Grumman with a white-water keel down the center of the hull. His family had possessed just such a craft, years ago. He paddled slowly, getting the rhythm down so that muscles, back, arms, all moved in near effortless unison. Beneath him the water rippled gently along the side of the craft.

Since it was a calm afternoon, he struck boldly out into the center of the lake, into the deep, intensely blue waters. Once, a line of V-shaped ripples marked the flight of what must have been a very large trout, unusual for that time of day. The further out he ventured the more impressive the Cerulean Ridge, to his right, became. On his left Rainbow Peak towered high over its glacier. Directly to the north towered the ramparts of Numa Peak, splendid in it's massiveness. He didn't know the mountain's name, so placing the paddle across the gunnels, Wolf Man pulled out the topo map. He never did have an easy time memorizing names. Mountains were no exception.

Numa Peak changed as he sat gazing up at it. One moment it had been clear and distinct. Then the mountain succumbed to powerful blasts of wind. A long streamer of snow rose up from the slopes and spread eastward. A weak storm front had arrived, sweeping eastward from the Pacific. The great block of stone disappeared behind the flurry of snow, swept up from the mountain's flanks.

Anticipating high winds on the lake, he dug deeply with his paddle causing the Grumman to shoot forward, heading towards the distant shore. He smiled in satisfaction for he would make it to safety before the first icy gust struck.

There was no need to land. Numa Ridge and the forest that grew on it provided a buffer, a brake against the wind. Friction of air striking trees and rock slowed the velocity so that while out on the lake whitecaps rose and later were themselves blown flat by the force of the gale, he experienced only moderate winds just a few yards offshore. He donned his Army surplus poncho to protect his bare arms and neck from the cold. Carefully he altered his position, no longer paddling, using the poncho as a sail and the paddle as a rudder. He scooted along the shoreline in near effortless progress.

The brilliant sun still shone although the edges of storm clouds surged up Numa Ridge and would soon spill downslope to the lake.

He arrived at the campsite at the same time the first drops of rain splattered on the forest floor.

*

Cow parsnips were becoming coarse and of little nutritional value to the Great Bear. He was unable to digest the cellulose that became the dominant food in older plants. Early July did not provide the berries that August and September offered. He hungered for succulent, tender shoots of newly sprouted alpine grasses, the energy-filled roots of glacier lilies and especially the peppery quality of not-yet blooming spring beauties. Every time the bear's memory recalled the delicious flavors he salivated heavily, jaws dripping immense drools.

The dump, east of Highway 93 had been closed since 1980 yet his amazing ability to recall dictated him to return to the site at least once each summer. Perhaps he would find a mayonnaise jar for his long tongue to explore, or pork chop bones. Anything. People food was far better tasting than what the wilderness usually provided; except, of course, for the huckleberries. The Great One found nothing. The environment was changing. Life was somehow not as easy as in the good old days.

St. Mary Campground had been disappointing, too. So many of those unpredictable man-creatures! Dogs too; whining, yapping, growling creatures of odd shapes, sizes and smells. There were Rangers there, too. He didn't know them by that name but they were distinctly different from the others. He could distinguish them by their odors. Rangers smelled strongly of soap, lotions, and perfumes, depending upon their gender. They had a peculiar, subtle fragrance that emanated from their strange hats, the uniform itself, and the polished, immaculate boots. The bear knew all of this for he had met them, up close, although they hadn't known he was there. Campers smelled different. Their body odors were more powerful; wood smoke, white gas, insect repellent, and best of all, bacon. Backpackers were even worse smelling, the human stench sharp and penetrating. Unwashed bodies bathed in sunscreen. The bear hated meeting them on the trail or camped at one of his favorite feasting sites. Avoidance of all man-creatures was his preference.

Down the mountain, from where he stood, the bear observed the sunlight reflections and haze rising from the RV camp, just outside of the park boundary. If any place was a virtual hell for the bear it was the RV camp. Even two thousand feet above the site he could hear the confusing noises of revving motors, TVs, playing children, yelling parents, and Rock Music amplified far beyond reason.

The giant grizzly growled uneasily, deep within his massive chest. A blue haze hung over the valley. Dozens of needlessly large fires poured their smoke into the warm afternoon air. The bear didn't like the acrid smell. Memories of a wildfire flashed in his brain. He growled again, nervously. Turning his body away from the valley he ambled up, higher on the slopes of Flattop Mountain. A lesson learned from his mother would guide him to the fresh, new vegetation, springing from the snowmelt above Cracker Lake. The world would be quiet there. For a time.

*

Wolf Man was uneasy. Carefully he scrutinized the trail leading from Brown Pass. No one was moving along the narrow path that hung, as if by accident, half-way up the side of the precipice. Even though the trail was empty it took considerable mental adjustment to have a bowel movement in such an exposed location. The trees didn't really hide him that well, as he sat upon the primitive outdoor throne.

Habitually, he thought back over the events of his just-concluded trek.

Gradually the trail had steepened. By the time he broke out of the vegetation, along a wall on the north side of Bowman Creek, it didn't matter how difficult the going was. Leg muscles had firmed up, back and shoulder muscles strengthened. Once again he had experienced the sheer joy of possessing a powerful body, muscles rippling smoothly, overcoming the feelings of tiredness. He would ache though, before he slept that night. Wolf Man sighed as he relieved himself.

High up in the cloud-splotched blue a bird wheeled effortlessly on the early afternoon thermals. "Probably an eagle," he mused. The creature was a mere speck across the alpine valley. All that afternoon he sat or lay before his tent, absorbing the immensity of the place. Warm sunshine, cool breezes, and the cheerful noises of tumbling streams overwhelmed his senses with the awareness of what he was beholding. Douglas seemed to come alive, a spirit not unlike the distant wheeling raptor, totally aware of the flowers, grasses waving in the meadows, a falling fragment of limestone, even the varied insects that flew and scurried about him.

Suddenly he laughed and thought, damn you Vern Nielsson. You win! I couldn't leave Glacier after this. You hooked me you clever old cuss you.

Hole-in-the-Wall was as near to Heaven as one could get while still on Earth. The shadows raced across the bench upon which the campground was situated. The snowfields and possible glacier turned the color of salmon, then pale pink and finally, just before sunset, a deep bluish-purple that obscured the details of snow and rock alike.

Mosquitoes hummed, until it got too cold for them. Secure inside the tent, he lay peering out across the vastness of the great amphitheater. Ten P. M. came and went and still it was light. Eleven o'clock, a little darker and then, swiftly the black of night. A thin, knifelike sliver of a new moon crept among the peaks. High up beyond Boulder Peak an eerie glimmer of pale light silhouetted the mountain tops. "Alpenglow," whispered Douglas in recognition. Then he fell asleep.

*

CHAPTER 5

The hike down from Hole-in-the-Wall provided Douglas with a beauty rivaling anything he had previously experienced. Cascades of snowmelt plummeted over the upper trail, soaking his pack and upper torso. A rapid descent from Brown Pass led him into rather open country of gentle slopes blessed with two blue mountain jewels named Lake Francis and Lake Janet.

He popped in at the Goat Haunt Ranger Station, located at the south end of Waterton Lake. The reasons for the visit were more out of courtesy than for letting people know where he was camping. Park staff expected other members to be sociable, especially at such a lonely post. Too, he wanted to check over the people stationed there. None remotely suggested that he or she might be a suspect to the men's disappearance. Neither he nor Vern had expected the trip to solve the vexing problem of the missing men.

Iris Louie, the resident naturalist, greeted him with a big smile and a dainty cup of herbal tea. For a time he thought he might stay overnight at the station, but the intrusive shouting of young boys, coming from the direction of the shelter cabins told him to move on.

Douglas ambled back along the trail he had used just two hours previous, hoping he would catch a glimpse of a moose. A walk of a mile and a half along the trail, splattered with greenish bear droppings, brought him to the Kootenai Lake campground. There on a grass-covered spit of land he set up his camp.

The wind blew cool, causing dark ripples to race ceaselessly upon the surface of the pale water. Willows, which choked the river bottom and invaded the tiny lakeshores, shimmered in the penetrating July sunlight.

Iris Louie had informed Douglas that moose often fed in the ponds, just yards from campers. The thought of seeing the huge, ugly members of the deer family encouraged him to wander silently along the northern, brushy mudflats. His mind, for the second time since arriving at Glacier, reminisced about the magnificent long-legged wolves that he loved so well. They were the natural enemy of the moose. He had first studied them in an animal enclosure in Wisconsin. Much to his surprise, as well as to the amazement of the owners of the outdoor laboratory, he had discovered that he possessed the ability to telepathically communicate with the wild dogs. Occasionally he could understand what they were likely to do next. A year later, at Isle Royal National Park, he had again made mental contact with the beautiful wild wolves. They would approach his camp and sit, just outside of his "territory" and visit.

His wolves would love the area around Kootenai Lakes. Perhaps they were nearby. Alone, impulsively, he threw back his head and the chilling call of the timber wolf flowed from his throat and echoed back and forth along the valley floor.

Crash! Heavy steps and the snapping of branches moved ever closer to the trail. He realized that his weapon was inside the tent, which was a few hundred yards away. Another explosion of tree branches occurred; that time very close. A huge, blackish head stuck out of the thicket. Big, bulging eyes glared from the face of one of God's ugliest creatures.

Responding, as he always did to such a crises, he emitted the inevitable, "Oh shit!" Unimpressed by his profanity, the cow moose lurched toward Douglas, who was prudently running top speed for the only climbable, moose-proof tree in sight. He almost didn't reach the tree in time. His next observation revealed that the cow moose was a mother. Somewhere back in the willows there was a tiny, ugly replica of its guardian. He laughed. The moose glared in anger. To climb down would result in injury and perhaps even death.

He became tired of sitting on the rough branch. His hands were smeared with pitch from the tree trunk he had just scaled. Funny, he couldn't remember climbing up to his perch. Time passed. He tried explaining to the moose mother that he was not a wolf; that he had only been practicing. She was unimpressed. Then, as suddenly as she had appeared the cow moose padded back into the willows. He decided to wait awhile before descending. Another sound was heard. Turning, his eyes encountered the quizzical faces of two Boy Scouts.

"Hi," he volunteered. There was no response. "What are you kids doing out here alone? You'd better get back to your troop." Still no answer. "Go on! Get!" He was shouting, almost in anger. The boys, still open mouthed, turned and walked back up the trail.

He swung from his perch and dropped, with a sickening plop, into the water-saturated earth. He extracted his booted feet from the mucky soil. Another crash followed by fast, heavy, galloping sounds motivated him to re-climb the lone fir tree. That time the attack could have been labeled a "near miss." The charging moose surged past the tree, snorted and swung her awkward body about. Once again he found himself staring down into a pair of angry cow-moose eyeballs.

"But I'm not a wolf!"

47

The admission did not impress the irate mother. She stood, her fierce glare fixed on him for what seemed an eternity. Then, just as before, she stamped away, perhaps to check on her hidden calf.

"I bet it's illegitimate!" he yelled, then decided to wait a half an hour before trying to escape again. He waited too long.

"There! See? We told you!" The Boy Scouts were back and with them was a chubby man in a complete Scout uniform. Shorts revealed fat knees protruding above olive-drab stockings. Fancy stripes of scarlet decorated the outside of the knit footwear. Highly polished brown leather shoes, just a little bit muddy, protected plump feet from the wet earth. The leader's ample chest was nearly covered with medals and ribbons. Short sleeves were splotched with words, numbers and symbols, all of bright eye-catching colors. A "ranger hat" perched jauntily upon a head matted with thick, blonde hair.

"See!" said the one kid who Douglas was beginning to hate. "We told you there was a man sitting in a tree! You didn't believe us!"

Not knowing what to do, he stood up on the limb, holding on to the trunk. The Scout Master simply gawked in amazement.

"What's he doing up there Mr. Eberly?" the second boy inquired.

No answer.

"Hey! Man! What are you doing up there?"

Douglas felt his face heat up. He wasn't sure the blush was from embarrassment or anger.

"He's nuts, Mr. Eberly. Isn't he?"

"Shush! Don't say things like that," the chubby man responded. Obviously he had no control over the boys.

Douglas was angry and the man knew it. "Come on boys, let's go back to the ranger station."

"Naw! I don't want to," sneered Boy Scout number one, as he moved forward to stand directly under Douglas's tree limb.

"Yeah," agreed his companion, "We're going to stay and watch this guy in the tree." The scouts began making faces.

He lost control. He knew he shouldn't do it but he lost control. Douglas whipped out his penis and began urinating on the startled boys. They retreated to a safe distance, cursing and pulling at their wet garments. "Jeeze!" said one, "That asshole pissed on me!"

He jumped out of the tree again, but the second time he was roaring with anger. The boys and their leader disappeared amid cries of fear and childish curses.

Wolf Man finished his nature call.

His vocal display must have impressed the moose mother for her reappearance didn't take place, fortunately for the moose. He had armed himself with a large limb and a resolution to knock the overzealous parent senseless. He was not going to climb that tree again. Neither did he howl like a wolf.

*

The moose-scout incident was over but the night was a restless one. Moose slopped and floundered through the shallow pond, gorging themselves with water plants. Once, one of the great animals walked, or rather splashed, to within a couple yards of his tiny alpine tent.

No longer angry, the young man grinned in the darkness of his fragile shelter. The humor of the afternoon's encounter would make a good story in the Nielsson household. Well, he'd omit some of it.

*

The remainder of the backcountry trip wasn't anti-climactic. His senses, unused to such dramatic scenery, simply closed down to where he ignored the sounds, smells and especially the visual experiences that his journey exposed him to. Once, however, he came out of his semi-stupor. He had left the Kootenai Lakes and the moose behind. The trail he followed took him southward, slowly climbing through the broken forest and meadows of luxuriant newly awakened flowers.

The pack cut into his left shoulder, not much, but enough to cause minor discomfort. He stopped, took off the burden and was repacking his equipment when a doe appeared. The deer must have been standing there, just a score or so yards distant but for some reason had not been aware of the young man's approach. Her head lowered. A moment later it appeared again, large ears turning warily. During that time he had pulled out his binoculars. She moved, becoming more visible. He saw why he had not been detected. Between the doe's forelegs stood a tiny, spotted fawn. The mother had been licking her baby, cleaning the accumulated needles, bark and dried forest duff from its mottled coat.

The fawn was an ugly little creature. It's muzzle seemed flattened and oversized, yet, the helplessness of the tiny being won his heart. He pondered over the awesome maternal responsibility of the doe to rear such a delicate creature in such a hostile environment.

The mother lowered her head again affording him the opportunity to put the glasses aside and watch with eyes unhindered, the gentle, loving activity of the baby's bath.

Just as the doe periodically scanned the area for danger so did Douglas, searching the shadows, seeking out the rapid movements of a coyote or the larger, sensuous advances of a stalking lion. Neither was present.

The deer moved on, traversing a slope covered with moderate-sized, rounded, moss-encrusted stones. Her baby's ears twitched and pink tongue nervously licked at its tiny, yet oversized muzzle. Awkward, it's overly-long legs wide spread for balance, the fawn was able to stagger stiffly forward over the difficult terrain.

He smiled. From his memory a flood of impressions, rapid, instantaneous, fleeting, appeared before his eyes; of his mother, a deceased grandmother whom he had adored, his sister when she was an infant child, even the family cat licking the newborn kittens clean of excrement and mother's milk.

All of his memories had been of maternalism, all trapped within the convolutions of his mind, warmth, life, life renewal, the cycle of nature, of all that lived.

None of his thoughts were new or original. As a naturalist and simply because he was a man, he had pondered over the mysteries and emotions of life countless times before. Yet, each time they seemed to take on new meaning, more complete, as if his meager knowledge was developing toward a more complete reality of what life was. The day he saw the fawn was no exception. Julie.

The thought of her overwhelmed him. In a burst of consciousness he visualized her remarkable dark eyes, black tresses of hair lightly caressing her brown skin, of shoulders and strong, graceful neck. Breasts firm, yet invitingly soft, quivering from movement, each ending in a dark erect nipple surround by the slight aureoles of beauty, desire; her soft belly, rounding slightly downward to the exhilarating sensuousness of downy mound and smooth, wondrous inner thighs.

Like most men, he recognized the desire within his loins, the need to seek out his woman and cling to her, absorbing her warmth, tenderness; the mysterious wonder of her love.

He slung the pack to his shoulders, shifting about for comfort. Then he walked on. The deer, startled at first, recognized that in his movements no danger existed. The man-figure would not harm her child. Her baby had instinctively dropped its forelegs to a crouch, then hesitating, became motionless with hindquarters in the air, waiting anxiously to be told what it must do next. By then Douglas was out of sight.

*

If the month had been August, snow in the high country gone, he could have made the journey from his Kootenai Lakes camp to Logan Pass in one hard day's hike. He really didn't know what the snow conditions were, especially at the big drift near Ahern Pass. Rather than do something foolish the young man forced himself into a reasonable walk that neither strained his muscles nor covered many miles of trail. There was much to see. Progress up the northern flanks of the great mountain, which culminated beneath the majestic spires of Cathedral Peak, was not particularly difficult.

Once, halfway up the slope he encountered a flock of ewes and lambs of bighorn sheep. The shaggy beasts, shedding their winter fur, ignored him and continued cropping the flowers and succulent grasses. Late in the afternoon high cirrus clouds, feathery streaks of ice crystals, appeared in the azure heavens. He frowned. Such clouds could mean a storm. Whispering breezes, almost unperceptive, bent the sedges and flowers and at the same time teasingly wiggled the leaves of shrubs and willows. Conjuring up an old cliché, he said aloud, "The calm before the storm."

Uneasy, realizing his vulnerability in such high country, he got out his topographic map. Anxious eyes found little hope of finding adequate shelter along the trail. Most storms he could ride out but a very strong wind might give him problems. Better to be cautious. Somewhat reluctantly he decided on a down slope trail. In so-doing he lost nearly five hundred feet of elevation; five hundred feet that he would have to regain the next day.

Locating a sheltered, tiny meadow, he set up the tent and called his position in to communications center. Nielsson could find out where he was camped, if a storm stranded the lone hiker.

*

Douglas turned on his tiny flashlight. The wristwatch dial indicated 2:21 A.M.

He groaned, the sound barely audible in the turbulence of the storm assailing his tent.

Reluctant, not wishing to surrender his trapped body heat to the coldness of the shelter, the youth unzipped his sleeping bag just enough so that he could sit up. Struggling awkwardly in the darkness he threw his pack up over his legs so that it plopped into the corner of the tent facing the storm's main force. Perhaps the weight would anchor the lurching shelter so that his legs would stop jerking upward every time a wind gust struck.

One of the metal stakes, holding the tent's outer nylon sheet in place, tore loose and struck the shelter. Fortunately the metal object was on the leeward side. He visualized the annoyance. He hadn't been able to secure the stake satisfactorily due to a flat, rock shelf positioned just a mere two inches or so beneath the meadow's surface. The area had offered no stones or heavy branches for reinforcement.

He hoped the stake wouldn't cut or jab through the tent wall. Going outside would result in a soaking, chills and a miserable, possibly serious situation. He covered up his head. There was no point in remaining alert. The world was a black void of torrential rains and gale-force winds assailing everything including his little shelter. He didn't have to see to realize that the tent was tugging spasmodically, rising, straining against the metal pins, and falling once more into place.

Gradually the roaring subsided, not completely, but there was moderation. He uncovered his head and listened. Hard sounds. Heavy pellets. The rain, somewhat subsided in intensity, was freezing. The moisture stuck to the tent, half liquid, partly sleet, and froze upon contact. Outside an ice storm was coating the earth with an invisible, deadly layer of smooth, transparent slickness.

The wind died. He sensed rather than saw the tent sag beneath the frozen burden. By then he had decided to remain inside even if the shelter collapsed. There was nothing to gain by going outside. He curved his long frame around a sharp rock he had overlooked when he put up the tent. For the remainder of the night he slept fitfully.

*

Douglas wasn't the only creature to experience the force of the storm. The goats and sheep, veterans of the harsh environment, slept in sheltered rock overhangs or beneath ground-hugging juniper. Elk and deer had dropped down into the deep forests.

Far to the east, in the Cracker Lake cirque the Great Bear had retreated to a man-made shelter; a mine tunnel. He slept, belly bulging with recently consumed Glacier Lilly bulbs.

52

The park's wolf packs crowded together for warmth, huddled beneath thick canopies of alpine firs. The Alpha females snuggled their noses happily into their male's flanks.

Only the young, male grizzly, rear end burning from Poor Shot Willie's shotgun pellets, got caught in the storm. Stupidity again resulted in additional discomfort. The poor, dumb beast growled feebly, his body soaked, icicles forming on the belly hairs. For once luck was with the grizzly. He had wandered off an exposed meadow into the forest. Unable to see he stumbled into a thicket of fir, sending into flight an elk and her calf. The needles were dry and warm where the ungulates had been bedded down. Whimpering, vague thoughts of his warm, protective mother teasing him, the exhausted bear drifted off to sleep.

*

Dawn came with a light less than total; thick clouds hanging low, scraped the cliffs of the Continental Divide.

He awoke, forced himself to move and quickly dressed. He unzipped the ice-encrusted door, the metal teeth shredding their thick half-inch coating. Accidentally he struck the tent wall setting off a musical, tinkling of shattering ice, which broken free, slipped to the glazed earth's surface.

Gingerly he reached out and felt the ground. "Damn!" Trapped. To go outside would likely result in a fall. Crampons, on such thin ice, would prove awkward. Besides, the hard rocky surface beneath the transparent ice sheet would dull, perhaps even bend the steel teeth.

He settled back upon his bed, wondering how long he would have to remain. His map indicated a lower trail along Flattop Mountain and out to the loop on the Going-to-the-Sun Road. Then what? How could he get back up to Logan Pass and obtain a ride home? For all he knew the pass road was closed. No, he decided, better to stay up high. Stick to the original plan. The lower trail could be just as icy.

Rubbing his chilled hands together he got the circulation going enough to place his Svia stove outside the tent door, under the shelter of the canopy. Pouring a bit of white gas upon the stove's concave bottom he ignited the fluid. Thus heated, the gas inside expanded, increased in pressure, which allowed him to put another match to the slightly hissing vent of gas. Soon water was boiling and a hot cup of tea was ready for consumption. He heated a second container full of water.

Patters. Fog-like at first, miniature raindrops grew in size and intensity. Moaning in disappointment he expected the moisture to begin freezing again. The rain became steady, scurrying in sheets across the ice-encrusted surface of his tiny meadow; tiny rivulets running into depressions that became small pools that joined other miniature basins until the whole meadow's surface became a shallow, shimmering ice-bottomed pond.

Resignation to his situation set in. He stuffed himself with crackers, raisins, and nuts, chewing and swallowing the carbohydrates that would provide the energy to get him home safely. Water began collecting under the tent. Warily he eyed the liquid bubble squiggling back and forth at the rear of the nylon shelter. He figured that he was in for one hell of a day, or two, or three.

*

Something new was happening. The pools were diminishing in size. Rain still fell, the intensity the same, but the water was going somewhere else. He unzipped the door flap again and cautiously stuck his finger into the ice. Slush. The ice was thawing.

"Ha!" he yelled to the uncaring meadow. "The fucking ice is melting!"

Donning his rain gear Douglas stuffed his sleeping bag into its container and that down into the pack, remembering to place the revolver on top. Outside, he shook the tent half-heartedly and completed packing. The soggy shelter practically slithered into it's bag.

Feet slopping about in the melting ice and rainwater, he hurried across the meadow and back up the trail to his route home. Only once did he slip. Before he got halfway to the Highline Trail, he was perspiring. He could see very little in the feeble light. Through the downpour he could discern a few varied shades of gray. Most of the time the clouds hovered just a few yards above his head. Sometimes he was inside a low cloud, moving carefully, trying not to loose the pathway. Nearby were Chaney and Ipasha glaciers and later he passed close to Ahern Glacier. He couldn't have seen them on the clearest of days because a narrow stone ridge hid them from view.

Dawn had come early to the stormy July day allowing him, in spite of the icy delay, to begin his homeward journey shortly after the first real light arrived. By 9 A. M. he reached the famous Ahern Drift. The snowfield wasn't particularly steep but for safety's sake, acutely aware of his isolation, he strapped the steel crampons onto his boots.

Their jagged teeth plus the ice ax enabled the lone hiker to traverse the drift without incident.

The worst behind him, now relishing the challenge, he hurried on. The thought of Julie at Logan Pass had become more than a slight consideration. Reality was fog, rain, occasional snow, cold winds and the pure joy of moving forward in such an alien world.

He was almost to Swiftcurrent Mountain when he came upon a section of the trail that was disturbed. He stopped, studied the terrain before him, then moved slowly forward. There were horses' hoofprints. Mules, too. Why had they stopped so abruptly? Better to be cautious. He extracted the 44 Magnum from his pack.

Cowboy boots. Someone had been wearing high-heeled boots. More footprints told him that two men had stopped, the other wearing hiking or heavy work boots.

His eyes detected a faint glimmer reflecting from beneath a spirea bush. He stooped over and picked up a spent rifle cartridge. Someone had fired a shot. But why? A bear? He looked quickly about, peering into the fog. From the position of the boot prints in relation to the cartridge's location he decided that the rifle had been fired downhill. A few steps forward revealed a torn, rocky edge of the trail. Something large had slipped, then fallen over the side. He peered over, quickly ducked his head, and slipped the revolver from the black leather holster.

He raised his head again and peered down the steep mountainside. A mere hundred feet or less from him was the carcass of a dead mule. Likely the beast had fallen, became injured so severely that the men had shot it. Several heavy timbers were laying below the dead animal. Packers then. A pack train carrying bridge material had met with an accident.

He analyzed the cause swiftly for other factors demanded his attention. Below him, three grizzlies were tearing at the hapless mule's body. Two of the beasts, females, growled and snarled as they gorged themselves with the bloody flesh. A yearling stood behind its mother, darting in now and then to gulp down a scrap of meat overlooked by the two adults.

Most remarkable was the presence of a pair of wolverines, the largest members of the weasel family. The animals were powerful, built low to the ground, perhaps fifty pounds of taut muscle, the mythical reputation being that even grizzlies feared them. The bears were ignoring the wolverines. One of the latter, likely the male, kept inching forward, neck outstretched, body tense, black beady eyes concentrating on every move the grizzlies made. Both intruders were moving closer. Bloody flesh was just inches away. Hunger and a fearless courage drove them nearer to the feeding bruins.

The wolverines' best position to get some of the mule was also where the larger grizzly feasted, it's head partly submerged inside the mule's body cavity. The lead wolverine stretched out, ready to grab a chunk of meat. Swat!

Douglas almost missed the bear's movement with a blink of his eyes.

Without pausing in her eating the grizzly had struck the lead wolverine a killing blow, crushing it's neck. Sitting back, a piece of mule liver dangling from her jaws, the killer bear gazed, disinterested, at the nearly decapitated wolverine. The mate had fled to a copse of bushes, paused, looked back at her fallen companion and then wandered downhill in search of easier, less dangerous food sources.

Remaining motionless, he wasn't sure the action had taken place. The bear's movement had been so swift. If the wind shifted he could be the next victim. The weapon in his right hand seemed small, completely ineffective. His eyes almost missed the fourth bear. The juvenile was sitting, far downhill, propped awkwardly on its right buttock for some reason or another. The man wouldn't have seen the creature if it hadn't whimpered. Obviously the young grizzly wasn't going to get a share of the feast, either.

He took a good quarter of an hour, stooping low, inching his way along the trail. When he felt reasonably certain he couldn't be seen or heard, Wolf Man donned his pack, and with revolver still at the ready, jogged uphill for a good mile and a half.

*

"Where's Julie?" Wolf Man panted. The time was 5:30. The flag was down. The Logan Pass Visitor's Center was closing up.

"Gone," replied Esther. "She came up with the early shift and rode down with Lew and Bob."

"Damn!" he hissed. A couple of visitors looked at him, disapproval showing on their faces. He was too late.

*

CHAPTER 6

July, 1984

Tension!

Four people lounged uncomfortably on the Nielssons' stiff living room furniture. Vern, his wife Evelyn, Douglas and Henry Two Feathers made up the foursome. Each, in their own way, squirmed, uneasy, waiting for the conversation to begin. Each wondering how they had gotten into the agonizing silence of the moment.

The ranger cleared his throat, causing the other three to jump at the sound.

Odors characteristic of the Nielsson household permeated the room. Hot coffee. Home-made oatmeal cookies, slightly burnt. A clean house. Henry even noticed that his own clothing reeked of stale tobacco smoke. He was the only one that thought the odor smelled good.

Douglas had just completed his narrative concerning the bears and the wolverines. In the silence that followed he looked about, unsure of himself. The others didn't know what he had decided. Would the Wolf Man stay or would he abandon the investigation? They waited for his answer.

"Where's Carolyn?" He had blurted out the question, wanting the young lady's support.

"She's in Bozeman. Something about Fall Term at the university," volunteered the mother.

"Oh."

Henry coughed.

"I'm staying." The three listeners sighed in unison. All smiled at Douglas. "But, on one condition."

"What is it?" Nielsson asked.

"When we first talked you mentioned maybe five deaths. You've got to tell me about them. I need to know everything you can come up with. You've told me some of the mystery but let's go over everything again."

"Of course you do, son." Vern was smiling as he rearranged the magazines on the end table. "Of course you do."

Once again silence descended upon the group.

"Well," began Nielsson, "let's see. The first one was the Blood from Ft. Macleod. Wasn't it, Henry?"

"Yes. He lived near there. From what I was told."

Henry continued. "This Blood Indian was down here. Hung around St. Mary and Babb for a while and then ups and disappears. One of his drinking buddies told me the kid was going into the Cut Bank Valley; going to hike up to Morning Star Lake. That in itself is peculiar 'cause Indians don't...." Henry paused, "We aren't in the habit of back-packing anywhere. This guy had told his pal he was going on one of those old-fashioned vision quests. He needed to shake a drug habit."

"You mean his disappearance was drug related?" interrupted Douglas.

"Could be. Doubt it though. The man just up and disappeared. We contacted the Canadian officials but they didn't follow up."

"Why?" Douglas was puzzled. "I thought the Mounted Police were up on things."

Vern smiled. "Henry's talking racism, Douglas. Anglo-Saxon superiority rears its ugly head."

Realizing that Douglas was still confused Henry explained. "The Mounties don't give a damn for Native Americans. Some of them don't," he compromised. "The reality of all this is that the old saying, 'The only good Indian is a dead Indian,' still persists in the minds of many people on both sides of the border."

"You see," Vern took up the explanation, "You have been taught a myth about the Canadian police. The English like to believe that the Mounties are romantic heroes on horseback, the Bengal Lancers of North America. We Americans generally see them in scarlet tunics singing love songs to Jeannette MacDonald. 'Mounties always get their man.' That sort of thing."

"All bull shit," Henry mumbled.

Vern frowned at his friend. Henry ignored the silent reprimand.

"You see," Vern continued, "the Canadians, on this point, are more realistic. Most see their Mounties as screw-ups. Stumble-bums. Like we Americans visualize the CIA and the FBI. I'd guess the truth is somewhere between the American point of view and the Canadians'. Closer to the Canadian opinion, I'd guess."

Henry nodded in agreement.

"Who was this guy? What was his name?"

Douglas's question was answered by Henry. "Same first name as mine. His last name was Stone, or Black, or Trueblood, depending on who he was living with at any given time."

Vern interrupted. "The point is, the man vanished. No trace at all. A heavy rain fell after he went in toward the lake."

"Could a bear have gotten him?" offered Douglas. "Any in the area?"

"Oh, yes." Vern thought a moment. "There was one really big black bear around that area at the time. But, bears don't eat packs and shoes and all that stuff, especially not a Blackie. None do. This man just completely disappeared."

"That was a year ago last June," volunteered Evelyn.

"Right," agreed her husband. "Henry Stone would have had to go over the snow to get to the lake. We never found his prints."

"OK. Henry Stone." Douglas was taking notes on a small government-issue pad of paper. "Who else?"

Vern thought a moment. "I guess that was the Buick we found abandoned half way in to Two Medicine. Right Henry?"

The sheriff nodded in agreement. "Yeah, a really beat up old jalopy, that car."

"Don't know who he was," declared Vern. "License plates missing. One of the employees at Blacks thought he remembered pumping gas into the vehicle. The driver, if the attendant is correct, was a male, Caucasian, but that's all he remembers. The driver just vanished."

"Could be the vehicle was stolen and dumped. We checked that out too. No record," added Henry. He was hurting for a cigarette and his hands shook slightly.

"Two," announced Douglas.

"Yes. OK." Vern thought a moment. "The next two are similar. Both had backcountry permits. Used false names and addresses. Simply went in and never came out. We think. One of them was going over Dawson-Pitamakin, down at Two Med. The other hiker had signed up for Slide Lake."

"Up by Chief Mountain?" Douglas was surprised. "Why?"

"Good question. Fishing is good there and he wanted to catch some big ones. So he told April, the girl who gave him the permit."

"When was that?"

"Oh, let's see. When was that Henry?"

"First week of last September."

"Yes. That's right. Last September. Didn't even find his car. Just nothing."

"Did he have a car?"

"Well, he gave us a license plate number. Nebraska plates. The real problem is that the number belonged to the personal vehicle of the mayor of Valentine, Nebraska. The plates aren't missing. Neither's the mayor. Dead end."

"Could he have made a mistake on the number?"

"Sure. Could have," agreed Nielsson.

"Four. You said there were five."

"Well, yes, but, maybe six now. Last August a Brother; you know, a Catholic Brother. Like a Nun only a man."

"Yes. A Brother." Douglas understood.

"He was from Milwaukee. Hung around the park for a week or so and then simply vanished."

"What did he do for a week?"

"Day hikes mostly. Slept a lot. He had a room at the Rising Sun Motel. One day he was gone. All his things were gone too. Three weeks later authorities found his car in Seattle. Stripped. His religious order contacted us. That's how we found out he was missing."

Douglas sighed. "No wonder you guys think the problem is here. What a pattern. Lone hiker or traveler. Some hiding their true identity. Likely loners, or in the case of the religious Brother, away from an institution for probably an extended period of time."

"Two months," Henry confirmed.

"And this number six. When did he turn up missing?"

"Don't have much to go on," replied Nielsson. "Likely an itinerant. Henry's department thinks he might have dropped off a freight train last March." He paused. "Bad time to ride the freights. Too cold. He must have had a good reason."

"Running from someone or something, I'd guess," stated Henry.

"Right. Anyway, he was in Browning and then here, hanging around the bars. He was staying in a shack up on the hill above the highway. The man simply just disappeared. Left his bedroll behind."

"OK." Douglas reached for another cookie. "Can I see the papers on these guys?"

Vern smiled. "Of course. I've duplicated you a complete set."

"Now what?" asked Douglas.

The District Ranger sighed. "We wait. You hike."

*

"Something's going on up at Many Glacier. Get up there and give them a hand." Nielsson had hissed the words and Douglas knew that he was angry about something.

A little over half an hour later Wolf Man pulled his Toyota up to the ranger station at Swift Current. Inside he found the tiny office crowded with men. He knew all of them slightly. Albert Donnelson and Gene Hodgson belonged to the valley. They patrolled the backcountry and handled any problems that arose due to people, or animals that didn't perform the way humans thought they should. Ben Widley, the Swift Current ranger was talking in an unnecessarily loud, excited voice. Scott Murphy, a Bear Management seasonal ranger, completed the assembly. Douglas liked Scott. He had a good sense about bears.

Widley almost yelled, "About time you got here Wolf Man. We've been waiting for you."

Douglas knew that was a lie and smiled at the leader.

"Well, anyway," stalled Widley, trying to form his thoughts into words that would impress his men, "this is the problem." His two assistants fidgeted. Murphy smiled.

"About eleven this morning two young guys were coming down off Swift Current Pass. When they got to Red Rock Falls they encountered a bear. To hear them you would have thought it was the Cut Bank grizzly of Indian fame. But, I was able to calm them down and it seems we are looking for a sub-adult, black colored Griz. We had a problem up there yesterday and Albert here set a snare baited with the rotten carcass of a marmot. That was just above the falls, by the willows. If we're lucky it will have caught that son-of-a-bitch."

Douglas knew he would get a reprimand but he asked anyway. "What did the grizzly do?"

"If you'd have gotten here a little quicker you would have heard me tell these men. The damned bear growled. They dropped their packs and fled."

"So what's the problem?" Confused, Douglas looked at Scott. The Bear Man shrugged and smiled weakly. "A bear's walking along and meets a couple of guys and he growls because they are too close to him."

"Look, Wolf Man," Widley emphasized the title, "If you don't like it you don't have to go along. You wouldn't be here except that Nielsson insisted that I wait for you. There are too many damned bears in this Many Glacier area and I'm not going to put up with their crap in my territory."

Douglas smiled and said, "OK. Let's go."

Widley blushed with anger.

The four men put on their packs and hurried out the door. Douglas walked over to his Toyota, started the engine and drove to the end of the Swift Current parking lot where he waited for the rangers, who were, for some unexplainable reason, walking. As they passed Widley grimaced and ignored Douglas's smile. Wolf Man slipped on his own pack and fell in behind the little formation of men.

The trail took them through a not very attractive forest of small trees. The path was wide from overuse and carelessness, but it was smooth and a credit to the constant maintenance of the Swift Current trail crew.

When they reached the bridge that crossed Swift Current Creek they all, including Douglas, assembled their weapons. No one in the group underestimated the potential danger of encountering a young grizzly that was down on his luck.

Ben Widley, showing some good sense, like Douglas, loaded his .45 Magnum Smith and Wesson with solid point bullets. He shoved the weapon into a shoulder holster. Donnelson and Hodgson sported Winchester rifles. The Bear Management ranger alternately inserted rifled slugs and #4 buckshot into his powerful shotgun.

Douglas strapped on his gun belt and carefully inserted his weapon.

"What do you think you're doing?" growled Widley.

"I'm putting on my gun belt. I've found that's easier to get at than a shoulder holster."

"That is stupid. All of the fucking tourists can see it. You think you're a gunfighter?"

Douglas glared back. He didn't like a Park Ranger who swore in public. He knew they did but to him it was like a preacher cussing from the pulpit. "Well, there it stays."

"OK, Cowboy. Have it your way. This time."

Douglas couldn't help whispering loud enough for Widley to hear, "Jesus, Murphy, you'd better get that shotgun out of sight."

Fishercap Lake appeared on their left about the same time that they began hearing the roaring sounds. They all stopped. Each man felt cold prickly chills course up his neck for the cries of anguish and anger were terrifying.

"Something's in the snare," unnecessarily explained Murphy.

"Oh, my god," whispered Donnelson.

"Yeah," agreed Hodgson.

Not lacking courage the Swift Current ranger took the lead. The pace quickened. Gasping, for they all were out of breath from the emotion of it all, Murphy haltingly said to Douglas, "Don't let Widley get there before we do. He's liable to shoot it."

Redrock Lake came into view, below the trail. Douglas was grinning. His adrenaline was flowing and he knew that he was experiencing what a soldier feels in combat. Holy shit! I hope I don't crap my pants, he thought to himself.

The screaming rent the air with horror but the roars that followed engulfed the valley in a pall of anger that caused all creatures to flee. Even the raptors and ravens were gone. Squirrels, marmots and all the other small animals had sought shelter in the sanctuary of earth or hollow log.

One wild thing didn't flee. Above Red Rock Falls, hardly a safe distance from the trapped monster, the hapless, juvenile grizzly watched it's giant relative's gyrations in wonder. He had never seen anything so fascinating before. When the man-creatures appeared on the trail above the lake he simply hunkered down and waited for the next act of the drama to unfold.

The rangers all arrived together, automatically bunching up on the trail as they neared the beast. He was magnificent! None of the men had ever seen a grizzly that large and for a moment they looked, as if hypnotized.

The Great Bear also quieted. He saw the men as they scrambled up the rock to where he floundered in the deep pool of the stream, just above the falls. He knew they were the enemy. Yet, the giant's brain told it that nothing could be worse than what he had just experienced. Not resigned to fate, but rather, patiently waiting for an opportunity to strike, he sat still, emitting only deep, agonizing grunts of pain.

"Holy shit," swore Widley. "This is the wrong bear. The one we want is a black sub-adult."

"Like that one?" asked Douglas. The small grizzly had decided to vacate the valley and was running back up the Swift Current Valley.

"That's him!" yelled Widley. "He fits the description to a T. Let's go."

"Wait!" For the first time the Bear Management ranger spoke up. "You aren't going to leave this fellow here, are you?"

"You're damned right we are. He'll keep. Come on."

"No, wait." Murphy's voice made Widley stop. "We can't leave him here. You won't get the other one anyway. He'll outrun you."

"Listen, College Boy," sneered the ranger. "I'm telling you to let it be."

"I'm taking care of this big fellow. He's in pain."

"You're fired!"

"No he isn't." Douglas growled his words. "I'm staying too. If you know what's good for you, you'll get on up the trail and let us fix this old bear. If you give us shit then the animal rights people, Audubon, the whole damned bunch will be on your ass and your days as a hot shot ranger will be over."

Widley turned red and then blanched out white.

Douglas added, "Tell you what, Widley. None of us will talk about this. Just get on up the trail after your little buckaroo."

The ranger trembled violently, eyes looking at each of his companions. He found no support. "Come on men. Let the Boy Scouts stay if they wish." The three men disappeared up over the rocks.

"Oh god!" exclaimed Douglas. "I think I'm getting old or something." He felt drained of energy.

Murphy responded with a weak smile, "Thanks Wolf Man." He began opening his pack.

"What happens now, Murph?"

"We dart him. This stuff I've got is called 'Telazol.'"

"Yeah? Tell me about it. I want to get my mind off that dynamite sitting there in the pond."

Murphy methodically assembled the dart gun and made sure of the dosage as he calmly recited the information about the tranquilizer. "We used to use M99, still do, but this stuff is brand new so I ordered some on my own. I'm going to shoot him with an 8 mg/kg dose of this stuff which is prescribed for an adult bear." Taking careful aim the Bear Man fired the dart into the muscular part of the bear's rump.

"Ha! He didn't like that much, eh Doug?" The giant roared and showed his fangs, long strands of saliva dripping from his open mouth. "Watch this. He'll go into ataxia, loose his equilibrium and be unable to move, within minutes." Murphy checked his watch. "Damn! Four minutes. That's a record. He's a mighty tough one, I'd say." The bear was staggering, head rolling from side-to-side as he attempted to keep his balance. "Lateral recumbency will occur soon."

"Hey, Scott, easy on the jargon. I went to school, yes, but I have to really think about that one."

Murphy smiled and pointed. The bear had slipped and was lying flat on his side in the pond. "Lateral recumbency!"

"No shit. Look, Murph, he's puking."

"Oh oh, I don't like that. He could drown in his own vomit. He isn't supposed to do that. Hope his head doesn't go under the water."

They waited about ten minutes. The bear's nostrils slipped under the pond's surface.

"Come on Douglas. Give me a hand. We're supposed to wait twenty minutes but he'll be dead by then. Grab this hank of rope."

The two men floundered into the pond and slipped the rope underneath the giant animal's head. Eyes rolling uncontrollably, the bear attempted to muster enough concentration to grab at the quick-moving hands. He just couldn't. The drug was taking him deeper and deeper. Besides, when they pulled up on the rope the bear realized he could breathe again.

"We can't do this forever," groaned Douglas. "Man does he stink! If you cause me to get a hernia, Julie is going to get really pissed."

The rope slipped until only the end of the muzzle was out of the water. "Shit!" Douglas did all of the cussing.

"Look, Doug, you're stronger than I am. Work that big rock down off the bank and we'll slide it underneath the head. Somehow."

Douglas slipped and fell forward, soaking himself to the shoulders. The inevitable word came. "Shit!" Both men began chuckling at the situation they were in. That didn't help them any and both were sopping by the time the rock was under the giant's head.

The Bear Man sighed. "Now he can breathe."

"Won't he die of hypothermia?"

"Naw. We might, but he won't."

"That's nice to know," shivered Douglas.

"You don't realize how lucky we are," lectured Murphy. "We were tugging at him just ten minutes or so after I darted him. We aren't supposed to do that. Safety says twenty minutes."

"Now you tell me."

"Come on, Doug. He'd be dead by now and you know it."

"What now?"

Murphy recalled the training lectures. "Let's see. Safe working time forty-five to seventy-five minutes. Bear may be down for two hours. We have to watch for respiratory depression, but that isn't likely."

"Are you saying we'll, you'll, have to give him CPR?"

"No way. Thermoregulation is automatically maintained by the downed bear. See the white junk coming out of his mouth? That's saliva. It happens sometimes. Nothing to worry about. Telazol has a rapid induction time, quick recovery, wide margin of safety, and few adverse effects." He smiled at his memory.

"Yeah, Murphy. That's fine but what about the snare?"

"We lucked out, Doug old boy. Donnelson or Hodgson or whoever set the thing put it back far enough from the pond so that the snare is on dry land."

"It was Donnelson," clarified Douglas.

"Yeah. Whoever. I hate these things. Any innocent critter could get caught in one of them. A visitor could. That would make headlines. This guy Widley is one bum ranger."

"Tell me about it," agreed Douglas.

Murphy began explaining the snare.

"See here? That is the throw spring. The quarter-inch steel cable has two components connected with a swivel to avoid twisting. The gear is supposed to resist 1400 pounds of force.

"The first cable portion is the leg or foot loop which has a one-way locking brake. This brake," he was pointing to it, "allows that loop to be drawn up around the leg without it loosening. Unfortunately for our friend here he was so damned big that only his foot was caught. If we hadn't stayed, he'd have torn the pad right off the paw. He musta' got himself trapped just a little while ago." Murphy brushed the dirt from part of the snare. "This second cable portion is called the anchor cable, for obvious reasons."

Douglas saw that the cable was securely fastened to a large outcropping of limestone. Fragments of the rock had been sheered off due to the beast's struggling.

The lecture went on. "This is the throw spring which provides the means by which the foot loop is rapidly drawn around the leg; foot in this case. This is the spring's safety mechanism that I hope Donnelson used while he set the snare. The snare is a powerful and very dangerous piece of equipment. One man should never attempt to set one alone."

"Thanks for the lesson Murphy, but let's get this damned thing done with. To hell with the forty-five to seventy-five minutes safety factor. How about going for thirty?"

Murphy smiled weakly. With considerable effort the two men disengaged the injured paw from the steel cable. The bear was free. "Now I want to shoot him with this antibiotic so he won't get an infection and we'll just go back over there and watch to see that he recovers OK."

Douglas asked, "What about checking his teeth, his butt, and all that shit? Don't you take his temperature?"

"Piss on that stuff," grimaced the Bear Management ranger.

"My, my, you do know how to cuss."

Murphy grinned. "Let's go."

They took up their vigil up-trail so that Widley and his men wouldn't come stumbling down just as the monster woke up.

Murphy reported. "You know, Doug, he wasn't really asleep. That old man knew what was going on. He just couldn't do anything about it."

He was right. The Great Bear vaguely understood why the men were struggling to get his head above the water. It also realized that they did something to ease the terrible pain in his foot.

As the ability to move came back the head moved weakly back and forth. Then it slipped off the rock and he took in a mouthful of water. The two men watched anxiously. The danger was too great for them to try to save the grizzly. Another dart might overdose it. The bear was on his own.

He knew it. Strength surged upward to the neck muscles and the bear pulled his massive head back up on the rock. He was ill then. Bile and partly digested Glacier Lilly bulbs rushed out of the open mouth and floated quickly over the glassy edge of the pond, doubtless to become food for the hungry trout below.

Moments passed. Then minutes. Scott Murphy had been right. Forty-some minutes after he had gone down the bear tried standing. A quarter of an hour later he made it.

Although unsteady the Great Bear's mind began functioning normally. He swayed back and forth, peering at the two men who had rescued him. The thoughts were not of gratefulness, nor of recognizing friends. The malevolent nature of the beast caused it to feebly roar its protest, as if to say, "I'll get you one day." Awkwardly, but less so than moments before, the grizzly limped toward the steep slopes of Mt. Grinnell.

Douglas heard a sigh. Turning toward his companion he saw moisture running down the cheek facing him. Scott Murphy brushed the tears away. "I can't help it. I love those big monsters. Somehow they are important to modern man. A part of our past, our heritage."

"Yeah." The modest word was genuine. Douglas felt the same way. "Let's go home, Bear Man!" He slapped Murphy on the shoulder.

*

CHAPTER 7

1984

Since his hike in to Hole-In-The-Wall Douglas had explored nearly the entire Hudson Bay Ranger District of Glacier National Park. He'd backpacked through the Belly River country, seen the meadows choked with wildflowers, gazed at the not-so-distant peaks, and observed the living land so richly endowed with wild creatures.

On one of his days off, he had taken Julie up the steep trail to Ptarmigan Tunnel. They had sat on the stone wall, feet dangling into space, and gazed in wonder at the towering iron-rust red cliffs and the deep indigo blue of Elizabeth Lake far below; a miniature interruption in a sea of green foliage.

Twice he walked the Dawson-Pitamakin trail, crossing both passes, covering nineteen hard miles in one day. The second time the wind was so strong he had been forced to crawl over the summit of Dawson Pass, an experience he hoped never to repeat.

The realization had come to him on that trip, as he had gazed into the heavily forested grizzly country of the Nyack Valley. Perhaps the overwhelming scenery had shocked him into comprehension. Across the valley an alpine glacier perched tenuously on the edge of a distant cliff. The land was immense, too diversified, too rugged for a man to completely comprehend everything that he was seeing.

He knew that the killer, if there was one, would have to come to him. All the hiking in the world would not provide him with the answer to the mystery. Either a clue would be found or another violent act would give him the opportunity to catch the murderer. Douglas would have to patiently wait for his adversary's next move.

*

August 12, 1984

Around mid-morning Douglas drove his old Toyota to Logan Pass. Julie was working there, in the visitors' center and would get off work at 4:30. He had nearly six hours to kill so he unhurriedly walked up the rocky slopes to the summit of Mt. Oberlin. The view from the peak was, as were so many of Glacier's panoramas, overwhelming, enchanting, defying description. He sat up there for several hours, not really thinking of anything, not even of Julie. Right at three o'clock he started back and arrived at the center a little after four.

Julie met him at the water fountain, up behind the center. Her eyes were wide with anxiety. Obviously something was wrong.

"What's happened?"

Her voice trembled as she spoke. "I thought you'd never get here. There's a bunch of drunken' Indians down in the parking lot."

"I'm not law enforcement," he argued.

"Yes. I know. But, you're certified, aren't you?"

"Yeah," he reluctantly replied, not wanting to get mixed up in a problem that was not his.

"They're doing a war dance in the back of a pickup!"

"What?"

She didn't like his smile. "Don't laugh! It's not funny. They're drinkin' wine and beer and swearing at the tourists. Maybe they'll hurt someone."

Douglas looked around. "Where is that hot-shot ranger from Charlo?"

"He isn't going to do anything. He claims he's Flathead and they're Blackfeet. George says he doesn't want to get involved in an inter-tribal fight. Besides, there are six men and a girl."

He didn't move.

"George is waiting for you in the parking lot."

"How about road patrol?"

"Bonner is on his way up. Be here in fifteen minutes."

He sighed, "Well then—"

"But you can't wait. If you just go down there with George maybe he'll tell them to quiet down."

"George?" he grinned. "He'll likely not say anything."

By the time Douglas got to the parking lot George was walking beside him, talking rapidly. "There's six of 'em. They're drunk and I think they're buzzed up on something. Bonner will be here in five or ten minutes so we can wait a bit."

"Why? Seems to me you'd better quiet them down before they hurt somebody."

George swallowed hard and looked nervously toward the entrance to the parking lot. The patrol car hadn't arrived.

A blue pickup truck sat right in the middle of the crowded parking area. The vehicle had become the platform for the so-called war dance. Six young men, all slim and well built, were revolving around inside the truck bed in a counterclockwise motion. Either they were very intoxicated or they just didn't know what a war dance was supposed to be like. Douglas wasn't Native American but he felt ashamed for Julie and her fellow worker, Tina, who were.

One man, apparently the leader, raised a near-empty wine bottle to his lips and drank from it. George swallowed hard again and said, "Uh, you fellows had better keep the booze out of sight. That's against the law, you know."

Two of the drunks stopped and stared at the ranger. The leader continued dancing but his eyes were watching George. His voice became louder, more coarse, rising to a near scream. Douglas realized that that dancer was the one to watch; likely the one who had dreamed up the whole adventure. Turning his back on the dancers, yet watching from the corner of his eye, he slowly and methodically placed his pack on the hood of a visitor's parked car. He made a big thing of unzipping the main pocket, pulling the flap out, widening the opening, and then rooting through the contents. He found what he was looking for, a partially eaten chocolate bar. Acting as if it weighed a few pounds he placed the candy on top of the pack's contents. He turned and faced the Blackfeet. He'd eat the candy later.

The leader and one other drunk had been watching. What was in the pack? A gun? A knife? A club of some sort? Mace? Who was that tall ranger? George had called him Wolf Man. Was he part Indian? The dancers seemed a little less sure of themselves.

Douglas leaned back against the Buick, pulled his park service cap low, thus shading his eyes, folded his arms and with obvious self-assurance watched the proceedings. He wasn't going to take the men on. That wasn't his job. He intended to make sure that no innocent person got hurt. That was all.

George walked up to Douglas. "Uh, there's a man over there who claims his car has a vapor lock, so I'd better get back over and help him."

Douglas stared coldly at the ranger. George's eyes dropped and shifted nervously. He hurried away.

The fact that he found himself alone with a bad situation involving six drunks didn't bother Wolf Man too much. The Blackfeet seemed tired and with George, whom they obviously felt was a considerable irritation, out of the picture they stopped momentarily to catch their breath.

For the first time, Douglas noticed a young woman, also Indian, standing near the front of the truck. She seemed frightened and at the same time disgusted.

The dance began again, voices rising in falsetto, the typical sound of the Northern Plains tribes. Tourists were nervously moving away from the immediate area. Some, ready to go elsewhere, were afraid to approach their nearby cars.

Douglas didn't see the patrol car arrive. Chris Bonner, the law officer, appeared, standing halfway between Wolf Man and the drunks.

The arrival of the ranger changed the atmosphere dramatically. One could almost feel the electricity building up.

His physique was impressive. Bonner's uniform was immaculate, yet showing signs of wear. The Stetson was placed squarely upon the man's large head. His build was what caught the dancers' eyes. He was undoubtedly powerful. Short in stature, broad shoulders protruding above an equally massive chest, connected with muscular upper arms that bulged out from the short-sleeved shirt. He didn't seem to have a neck.

Checkmate, thought Douglas.

"Excuse me, sir." A tourist, around sixty, overweight, obviously not very bright, stepped in front of Douglas. Wolf Man moved to the side, for any change in the standoff could cause a fight.

"You are a ranger, aren't you?" queried the man.

"Yes sir. Look. I suggest that you move away from here because we have a bad situation which is likely to get worse and you might get hurt."

"Yes, Yes," the tourist was irritated. "I know. All I want you to do is tell me how to get to McDonald Lodge. You can do that, can't you?"

As politely as he could Douglas told the man to drive westward, down the Going-to-the-Sun Road and he would arrive at the lodge. Without thanking him the tourist walked away.

He'd missed it. "Damn!" whispered Douglas to himself. All six dancers had stopped and were facing Bonner. What had happened?

The leader whispered something to his companions. One of the men lifted a beer bottle from the floor of the truck.

Bonner spoke, his voice composed, authoritative. "Put the bottle away. Get it out of sight. You know your rights and one isn't drinking alcoholic beverages in this park."

The bottle disappeared but the man glared angrily.

Another dancer spoke. "This is our land. We can do what we want on our land."

"Yeah!" grunted another. "The White Man took this land from us and it is ours. We can do what we want, White Man."

71

"That's not the way it is," responded Bonner. "I'm part Indian, too, and this land doesn't belong to me any more than it does to you."

The leader's face contorted in anger. "You're no fucking Indian! You're a White cop. A National Park cop! You aren't from around here."

Chris Bonner broke in. "I'm from Louisiana. My grandmother was a full blooded Indian."

"Yeah? Horse shit! What fucking tribe?"

"She was a Kasihta."

"Kasihta?" laughed the leader. "That ain't no tribal name. That's the name for cowshit. Runny, green, slimy cowshit."

Now, thought Douglas, Bonner will take them on. Here we go.

The lone patrolman simply stared impassively at his adversaries. The minutes ticked slowly by. Five of them. Six. The Blackfeet were tiring of the staredown. Too many variables. Bonner had a revolver. They wondered what Douglas had in his pack, within easy reach. Was backup on the way? For the first time the Blackfeet began to think their little game was a mistake. If he didn't do something quick, the leader realized he would loose control of his men. "Hey, White Man," he called to Bonner. "What's that metal ring on your belt for?" He thought he had discovered a weak spot, a way to get the ranger to back off.

"This?" Bonner flipped the heavy ring with his left hand.

"Yeah, that! What's it for, White Man."

"That's where I carry my riot club."

"Ha!" laughed the leader. "Why don't you have one with you? Did you loose it?" His companions chuckled thinking that perhaps they were getting back the advantage their numbers had previously given them.

Bonner waited to respond, letting the silence do it's work. "No, I didn't forget it. My club is on the front seat of the cruiser, right next to the shotgun."

All six men broke out laughing.

The patrolman continued. "When I drove up and saw what the situation was I knew I didn't need it. So, I left it in the car."

What were they dealing with? This short, stubby man with the huge chest and arms? Did he really think he could whip them all? Each had concealed knives. Could they take him? Probably, but he could shoot two of them before they could get close enough to use the blades. Visions of prison had begun to appear in their alcohol-dulled senses. Better to wait. Things could get better with time.

Bonner hadn't moved since he arrived. His stocky legs seemed rooted to the blacktop. He moved. Casual, relaxed, the lawman walked over to the girl and spoke quietly. The conversation couldn't be heard by anyone else.

Turning, Bonner walked over to Douglas, the first indication that he knew the Wolf Man was there. "She's scared. Gave me the truck keys. She is cold sober. I'm going to have her drive these clowns down off the mountain."

George, who unobtrusively reappeared when the situation seemed to have quieted down, stood a few feet from Douglas, behind Bonner.

Two of the Indians looked sick. Another was sitting on the side of the truck bed, holding his head.

Chris returned to his former position. "Listen carefully." His voice was calm, authoritative. "You men are in real trouble. You could end up in jail for quite some time. Worse, I could turn you over to the tribal police. They'd love to beat the living byjesus out of you."

"But, I'm going to give you a break. I'm a peace-loving man and I like to think that people learn from their mistakes."

Bonner looked at the woman and she nodded resolutely.

"Lucy, here, is a fine lady. She's embarrassed about what you've done to hurt the image of her people. What you did in front of all of these visitors." He waved his left hand in an all-encompassing gesture, the right hand never leaving its position right above the holster.

"You men, sit down in the truck."

They hesitated.

"Do it! This is your only chance." Only the leader remained standing. Bonner ignored him, as if he didn't exist.

"OK. Now, Lucy here is going to drive the truck down to Blacks, just outside of the Park. I'll get on the radio and some of your people will meet you there and drive you home until you sober up. That's the story. The fun is over."

"Shit!" yelled the disfranchised leader. Everyone ignored him.

Lucy climbed into the truck. She seemed confused. The truck lurched forward and stalled. The men in the back grumbled. Two fell forward and collided with the back of the truck's cab. She killed the motor a second time.

Chris Bonner spoke to her a moment and returned to George and Douglas. "Hell! She can't drive a stick-shift."

"What'll we do? Let one of the guys drive?"

Bonner looked with disgust at George. "Of course not. You drive the truck down. I'll follow in the cruiser."

George paled. Sweat beaded on his forehead. He got an idea. "Hey, uh, Chris, why doesn't Douglas drive 'em down. I've got some flags and stakes and things to load up in the van. And some chains too. I'd better go do that." He started to leave.

"No. George, listen to me. You are going to drive the truck. I'm telling you."

"Why doesn't Wolf Man do it?"

"Because," answered Douglas, "It's not my job and for some reason or another I don't like you calling me, Wolf Man. This is your problem, so deal with it."

Bonner quietly ordered, "Get in the cab, George."

Turning to the six men he spoke, "Now, since Lucy can't drive stick shift, she's going to ride in the cab with George. I'll be right behind you in the cruiser. The shotgun will be on the riders seat. The first shell is loaded with rock salt," he lied. "So, you boys behave. No climbing into the cab. No standing up and no jumping out. He cleared his throat and spit for emphasis. "This is your only chance to get out of this mess. Screw up and your ass has had it."

Walking over to George he said, "Get in the cab, George. Now!" The frightened ranger scurried across the lot to the pickup and climbed inside, rolled up the window and locked the door.

Grinning, Douglas watched the two-vehicle caravan pull out of the Logan Pass parking lot. Thinking of George he said, "Chicken shit." A passing visitor, frightened by Douglas's comment, hurried to his RV, wondering what he had done to cause the ranger to be so angry.

*

August, 1984

A tragedy had begun on the day Douglas helped free the giant bear from the leg snare.

The grizzly had limped awkwardly uphill, cutting across the Swiftcurrent Valley just above Bullhead Lake, moving in the opposite direction from where the men had last observed him. The great beast's progress was slow, movement painful. His desire to escape, to once again be free of the man-creatures, drove the suffering animal onward until he climbed to slightly above the 6,400-foot level of the mountain. In a narrow defile he hid amid a mass of broken rock and debris, secure in the shelter of the avalanche chute. So he thought.

The bear's hideout was not completely secure. Another male, the young grizzly the rangers were seeking, was hunkered down behind a log, further up the ravine. He was crouched low, unmoving, the poor creature's heart palpitating rapidly. One of the pursuing rangers had fired a shot at him. Remembering Poor Shot Willie's shotgun attack, the youthful bear had sprinted until he had fallen in exhaustion.

Below, the giant licked its bruised foot and ankle. Sensing that he was in no danger the young bear gradually calmed down. Soon he was dozing in the hot summer sun.

*

During the next two weeks the youngster followed his huge fellow-grizzly. When the older bear would feast on succulent, tender shoots of newly sprouted grasses or sedges, the Follower would wait until the giant moved on and then he, too, would dine on the same type of plants. If the giant dug bulbs for a meal, the young bear did the same. The plan was a good one for the poor creature didn't have to think too much about staying alive. In a remote way, the great bear had replaced the young bear's runaway mother.

One day the older grizzly cut back on his own trail and smelled the scent of the Follower. Later that same day, by then rather uneasy, the bear turned again. That time he saw the Follower bounding away. No need to run in pursuit. The small grizzly could outrun the still-limping giant. Never the less, the older male became more and more irritable and wary. He sensed that somehow the presence of the Follower was compromising his security.

On two different days the giant lay in ambush, waiting for the Follower to come ambling along the trail. The first time he lay in wait a marmot had distracted the young bear. He chased the small mammal uphill, thus seeing the giant, down slope, secreted behind a boulder. Furious at being discovered, the elder bear roared in anger and charged uphill. His tormentor sped away, easily outdistancing him. Just before reaching the security of the forest, the young bear turned and stood to his full height. Unknown to the sub-adult, the stance was a sign of combat, of challenge. Instead, he had whimpered for acceptance.

Two days later, the giant tried again. The Great Bear had chosen a perfect spot for an ambush. The Follower would be within ten feet before he would be aware of the presence of the enemy. If a bear could gloat, the giant would have been gloating. His pest didn't have a chance. The day was warm, the wind just right, he was alive with anticipation. The aching foot had won him the right of the luxury of doing battle. Again fate played its hand. A flock of ewes and lambs, bighorn sheep, appeared moving downhill from the rocky palisades above. The new arrivals, although alert, smelled no scent of bear, saw no movement. Gradually they grazed within striking distance.

The giant leaped, roaring his power. The blood-chilling scream confused the flock, especially the inexperienced lambs. One hesitated and was felled by a powerful blow to the spine.

Hunger satisfied, very little left of the lamb, he moved on, temporarily forgetting about his Follower. Remnants of the lamb provided the youngster with a satisfying snack. He ate all that was left and then took up his following game once more.

The two male grizzlies hunted and fed along the slopes of the Wilbur Creek Valley for several more days. The giant became increasingly frustrated and ill tempered. His injured foot had healed and as it did the bear realized that soon he would be able to catch and eliminate the pest that followed him. One really good chase would run the smaller male right out of the area. By then, the thought of killing no longer entered the giant's mind.

The plan would have worked, except for an encounter with other grizzlies. The whole valley of Wilbur Creek and connecting slopes were alive with grizzlies. Several females prowled the mountainsides. Two of them had cubs.

One day the Great Bear, ill tempered as usual, came upon a female with three cubs. They were feeding on a bountiful hillside of huckleberries. The giant salivated at the thought of freshly killed grizzly cubs. They would be tasty morsels. Throwing caution to the wind he charged in on the feasting family. He had picked his victim, a little blonde female. Instead, he encountered the ferocious teeth and claws of the irate mother. Her teeth found one of his ears and ripped it down the middle. He howled in pain. Although the male could have fought and killed the smaller mother grizzly, he turned and fled. There were easier meals of berries and other edible vegetation nearby.

The Follower had witnessed the great bears aborted attack on the family. Unfortunately, the poor creature's mind analyzed the incident and, as usual, he misinterpreted what he had observed. He acquired the false assumption that by attacking the giant he could force the big fellow to retreat. The small bear felt safer and became bolder.

*

Up around Iceberg Lake snow was still melting in the more sheltered spots. Glacier lilies, the last of the season, were poking up out of the recently thawed, muddy earth. Everywhere else the lilies had bloomed and wilted, the essential nutrition used up in the flowering. The Great Bear knew this because he had visited the location each year for several summers. The roots would be bulging with stored energy.

Ann Davis sat somewhat apart from her hikers. Mosquitoes hummed about her face and hands. Thank goodness for long hair, she thought. Everyone else in the group was down at water's edge sunning themselves or munching on remnants of lunches. Ann, a Ranger Naturalist, was also grateful that the two children on the hike were well behaved, asked intelligent questions and were soft-spoken. One was a boy about ten and the other youngster was a twelve-year-old girl. Although both were somewhat shy they had become friends and were exploring the shoreline.

The limestone rock that Ann had selected for a seat contained a last-winter's fracture, the edges of the crack still sharp and close together. She shifted her weight. In doing so, part of her left buttock slipped into the slit and ceased to move with the rest of her body.

"Oh!" The ranger leaped to her feet to alleviate the pain. Her Stetson hat tumbled onto the ground. Blushing, she picked up the headpiece and attempted a casual walk to the lakeshore. A few people peered at her questioningly, wondering about her peculiar behavior.

The boy and girl were looking at a small floe of ice wallowing in the tiny, off shore waves.

Iceberg Lake was called that because a small ice field lay along the western edge of the pond, never completely melting. Except for three or perhaps four months of the year, the surface was frozen solid. During the warmer months chunks of ice would fragment off of the ice sheet and float about. In this, the second week of August, 1984, the tiny amphitheater, a glacial tarn, was three-fourths ice-free. The boy dipped his hands into the frigid water and extracted the tiny ice floe. The object was not quite a foot wide and probably four inches thick. "Look," the girl exclaimed in discovery, "The ice is made up of hundreds of tiny needles."

A few of the adult hikers walked up to get a better look. Ann explained that the peculiar, elongated honeycomb-like needle

77

formation was a characteristic of ice that developed during the thawing process. "Has anyone here read, <u>We Took to the Woods</u>, by, uh, I think the author's name was Louise Rich?"

None of the twenty-three adults had.

"That doesn't surprise me. The book was written in the late 40s or maybe a little later. You should read it. Fascinating. It's about a schoolteacher who marries a man who lives far up in the Maine north woods. Anyway." She had their attention. "The woman wrote about a day in late spring. She and another lady were sunbathing." Ann had to add, "In the buff."

The hikers chuckled, each imagining two naked women lying on a wooden dock. The men, in particular, liked the idea.

"Mrs. Rich wrote that the day was very hot. There was no wind. Not even a faint breeze. The ice became gray in color. It covered the entire lake surface. Suddenly the basking women heard a loud tinkling sound, kinda' like glass chimes. The women raised up and were astonished. The ice was gone. One moment solid ice and then only blue water. The ice was constructed of ice crystals, parallel needles stuck together, just as you see in David's hand. They had all collapsed instantaneously."

"Wow!" "Humm." "Huh!" The hikers were impressed.

The girl saw him first. "Look!"

"Oh, my god," whispered an older woman.

Ann looked across the lake. Although the south, west and northern slopes were extremely steep and barren a gigantic grizzly had appeared walking along the wall of the cirque, just above water level. No one had observed him until the girl had yelled. The Great Bear moved out upon the shrunken ice wall, gingerly picking his way to the top of the white accumulation. He rested when he was able to stand on bare rock.

Cautious, ignoring the humans on the far side of the little lake, he walked to the point where the ice accumulation was thickest. Looking about for a moment, out of habit, the bear seemed satisfied that he was safe. He leaped onto the steep icy surface and slid, his behind used as a toboggan, shooting down the slope, over the narrow flat ledge at the bottom, and into the lake. A huge spray of water rooster-tailed into the air.

Some of the people cheered.

Ann pulled her radio out of her pack and called the Swiftcurrent Ranger Station. The transmission was blocked by the sheer north face of Mt. Wilbur. There was no way for her to report the developing incident.

Rather clumsily the grizzly clambered out of the water, breaking off chunks of ice in the process. Concentric ripples moved rhythmically outward from the bear's splash point.

"Hey, look!" shouted the young girl's father. "He's going to do it again."

The bruin, moving up the ice sheet, stopped momentarily. He was watching a rock tumbling down slope, over the ice. He sat down. With all feet stuck straight up in the air the bear shot downhill. The rock struck the water first but the bear had almost caught it.

All of the hikers cheered that time, as the bear disappeared beneath the lake's surface.

Ann became anxious. Things were getting out of her control. "OK. Hate to break this up but it's time to go back."

No one paid any attention.

Not really irritated, rather uneasy due to the human activity on the not-so-far shore, the grizzly paddled gracefully to the open shoreline north of the ice floe. He could have just as easily crossed the lake to where the people were standing. There was no point in his doing so. The previously injured front paw seemed to ache in warning. The bear wanted to avoid the human creatures.

"Come on you people." Ann had become stern and official. "We're getting out of here before he cuts us off from our route home." The announcement got their attention. "Now look. Stay quiet. We'll keep close together for safety. Remember. No running!"

Appraising her group, Ann selected a man in his 40s who seemed calm. "Mr. Hamilton, you take up the rear. Don't let anyone lag behind. Once we get past the danger point I'll switch places with you. Lead the group to the falls before you stop to rest. OK?

"All right. Mr. Hamilton is in charge, too."

Hamilton smiled in agreement.

*

The Great Bear had found some glacier lilies, not yet blooming. The long, sharp claws became digging instruments, tearing the tundra apart. As they appeared, the roots were slowly masticated, the bear savoring every bit of flavor. He moved on to the next feeding area.

While the bear ate, the people hurried along the badly eroded trail; black ooze slopping up to cling to jeans, slacks and bare legs. Not a soul spoke. Rather, a peculiar sound followed the little group. Heavy breathing, partly exertion and partly fear, mixed with the sucking and slopping sounds of booted feet passing through the swampy pathway. Denim pant legs brushed against denim. Nylon swished as arms swung back and forth. The sounds were created by anxiety, even fear, which meant danger. The wilderness quieted. Small mammals, birds, even the insects seemed stilled in anticipation. What was about to happen? Danger. Danger.

By the time he reached the people path the last human had disappeared through the willows which bordered the trail. Pausing, he sniffed the foul human scent for information. Too many humans. Fear was present, a particularly unpleasant odor.

"Woof!" The Great Bear vocally expressed his disapproval. He stood up. The great massive body rose high, neck arched, forelegs held in front and to the side of the massive chest.

Although some experts say that bears have poor eyesight, the big male saw, in the distance, a human standing alone, above the trail, holding something black to her eyes. Ann had sent her group, under the care of Hamilton, hurrying back to Swiftcurrent. She had finally made contact with the Swiftcurrent Ranger Station. Her instructions were to watch the bear and to keep people out of his way. The Ptarmigan Tunnel - Iceberg Lake Trail was closed to hikers. Ann stood and watched for the remainder of the afternoon. Apparently her retreating group had convinced others to turn around. She was grateful that no eager-beaver photographer had shown up.

The giant was still feasting. Nearly a quarter of an acre of meadow lay in ruin. Plants, torn up, now lay covered with rich, black loam. A new, next year's crop of lilies had been planted by the, unknowing, bear. Torn and bruised vegetation slowly wilted in the cool mountain air. The sun dropped behind the high, narrow wall that marked the Continental Divide. Shadows were almost rushing toward the lone woman. She shivered in the late afternoon chill.

Someone was approaching, coming uphill toward her. Whoever it was, was considerate, for the newcomer every now and then scuffed his booted feet and cleared his throat. Ann was grateful. She didn't need a surprise.

"Hi, Wolf Man."

Grinning, Douglas nodded "Hello."

They both watched in silence.

"Hey! I know that one."

"You do?" responded Ann.

"Yeah. Notice the slight limp? We got him out of a leg-hold trap a few days ago."

She remembered hearing about the incident. "More like a week or two. Time flies."

"Yeah. Guess you're right."

The rangers watched in silence.

"Look." Douglas pointed downhill. "Over by that big tree."

Ann saw the young bear digging. "That stupid bear."

The young bear, the follower of the giant, had observed everything that had transpired. He'd watched the tobogganing, the people, and the Great Bear feasting. Hunger had finally overcome caution. The youngster was digging and eating his way on a collision course with the giant.

"Lord, Douglas. Watch this. He's in real trouble."

"Yeah."

The adult male first saw the Follower while still some distance away. Between the two lay the most bountiful lilly beds. Because food was there and also because of the comprehending mind of the giant, he dug and fed his way, in an unassuming manner, ever closer to the follower. Less than a hundred yards separated them before the youngster saw his adversary.

The bulbs were delicious. Apparently the Great Bear was also feeding contentedly. Foolishly, the smaller bear turned away and resumed digging. When he looked again the older bear was walking toward him. Remembering what the female had done to ward off the giant, the Follower growled menacingly. The giant continued to walk forward. Beginning to realize he might be in danger the youngster rose to full height and roared defiantly. The posture was that of combat. His threat didn't work. Time had run out.

He ran silently, a massive 800 pounds of killing machine, instincts in control, speeding at perhaps fifty miles per hour. He slammed into the small male. Thousands of years of hostile environment, countless enemies, had developed a genetic beast of destruction. Intuition told the giant that his adversary would bite so he made the young bear's face his target. Powerful ivory teeth crunched into the small bear's muzzle, ripping away the nose and upper mandible, puncturing the right eye.

Agonizing, shattering screams of anguish tore the wilderness silence, reverberating back-and-forth from palisade to cliff to mountain summit and back again into the depths of the valley. Ann and Douglas yelled in surprise and horror. At the junction where the Iceberg Lake Trail met the route from Ptarmigan Lake, a fisherman froze in terror and peed his pants. Throwing his catch of trout and expensive equipment aside he ran crazily down the trail to

Swiftcurrent. The Great Bear was on top of the dying youngster, using his teeth to slash and tear, ripping the throat out, feeling, tasting the hot blood pulsating from the torn arteries and the flowing veins. He was out of control. Days of pent-up anger and frustration were released in seconds. His tormentor, the Follower, was finally in his grasp.

Douglas and Ann watched, transfixed, nearly in shock, but realizing in a macabre way how lucky they were. Nightmares would certainly follow but they were privy to nature's ultimate savagery. The blood kill. Fury. Unbelievable animal power.

Astonished, Ann whispered, "He doesn't use his claws except to turn the body to the position he wants." The two rangers realized they were clinging to each other.

"Jesus!"

The killer had the body on it's back. With rapid, precise bites the genitals were snipped free of the corpse. Then the massive jaws ripped open the stomach and worked their way up to the ribs, tongue slurping body fluids, teeth pulling and tearing out intestines, stomach; all becoming a mess of shimmering, blood-splattered tissue.

Quite suddenly, nearly as instantaneous as it began, the tearing ceased.

Exhausted, adrenaline breaking down, the killer stood silent; blood matted his head, shoulders and forelegs. As if to emphasize the carnage that lay about, a portion of shiny tissue hung from the giant's neck, a necklace of sorts from the dead bear's entrails.

Grunting at each step, the Great Bear walked down slope, toward the snow-fed stream.

Silence.

"Let's get out of here." It was Wolf Man speaking.

*

CHAPTER 8

September, 1984

"Get out of here, Doug. Fast! Take off somewhere. Don't tell me where you're going and don't come back for three or four days." Nielsson's command had been urgent.

The drug bust of the previous afternoon, in the St. Mary Visitor's Center parking lot, had been a big one. Normally the park rangers would have handled the case but one of the people arrested was Raymond Phee, a famous, or infamous, political refugee from the Vietnam War. Phee had settled down in the Flathead Valley with his five wives, thanks to the CIA. The Agency had rewarded him for the cocaine trafficking he had directed into Communist-held areas of the Indo-China peninsula. He just couldn't behave and continually overstepped his liberties, getting involved in Colombian operations in the Northwest.

The National Park Service didn't play the political games like the Agency did. Someone had tipped off Hannibal Simms, the Hudson Bay District Law Enforcement Ranger, that Phee had a carload of stuff. When the Laotian refugee drove into the lot, rangers swarmed all over him. Other people, local citizens, were involved. The Blackfeet Tribal Council was screaming for prosecution of everyone involved, including the CIA who protected Phee.

Washington, not completely innocent in the complicated situation, was sending in special Federal Marshals to take over the case and try to settle things down. There would be inquiries. The already determined resolution of the problem, to let Phee go unpunished, would be screened by a senseless investigation of everyone in the area, including park employees. By the time the Justice Department and the Administration found out about the crime, Phee would be sailing on a cruise ship on the inland passage to Alaska.

Nielsson felt that Douglas, seeking evidence of the possible murders, was far too important to be exposed for no good reason. Besides, he was a rebel and if he refused to cooperate, they might dig deeper and blow the whole murder investigation. Among other things, the Hudson Bay District Ranger could loose his job.

Douglas didn't trust the White employees with a plan he concocted. But he did rely on the Blackfeet women who worked with Julie. They decided that Bonnie Trueblood would drive Julie's truck to her home and tell her parents that she had gone to the home of a friend's aunt in Browning for a few days rest. Such a story wouldn't be too unusual. Young Native Americans often decided to live with a relative for a few days, or even months.

The only problem was that Julie did not behave in the traditional Blackfeet manner. Her parents, especially her mother, would know something was going on.

"Well," sighed Julie, who had been listening to the plans for her love adventure being arranged without considering her, "I'll deal with Mother and Dad when I get back."

At first things had gone well. The lovers drove to Kalispell and spent an extremely passionate night in the best motel the town offered. Early the next morning the couple awakened, made love once again, and then breakfasted in the adjacent restaurant.

The splendid scenic drive along the west shore of Flathead Lake should have been one filled with happiness. Instead, Julie became pensive, seeming to withdraw and her mood evolved into being non-responsive to Douglas's comments.

They were going through Railroad Canyon when she finally declared that she was ashamed of their past-night's lovemaking. "It's not natural, that oral stuff. That's not what God wants us to do with our bodies."

Her comments resulted in a fight. Douglas declared that there was no moral basis for her position on lovemaking, as they had done it. He added that she was being unreasonable, old fashioned. "After all," he sharply added, "we did use the Missionary Position after the foreplay."

Confused about what he meant Julie fell silent.

Feelings hurt, disappointed, worrisome thoughts rushing into his mind, Douglas, too, ceased talking. The remainder of the trip to Missoula was silent and tense.

That night they made love once, briefly, unfulfilling for Julie. Finished, Douglas rolled over, away from the girl. He mumbled just loud enough for Julie to hear. "Missionary position." She still didn't know that the term referred to the usual position Christians were supposed to assume for sexual intercourse. Neither was able to comprehend what the other was thinking or even understand the deep feelings of confusion swirling in their minds.

The next day they went shopping. His mother was very wealthy and he had been provided with an unlimited credit card account. They went to the Mercantile, a popular department store, which carried excellent selections of clothing, especially for ladies.

He intended to buy Julie a whole new wardrobe for, as he explained, "when I take you home with me to Ohio."

Julie rebelled again. "Aren't I good enough for your family? What's wrong with my clothes anyway?" They fought while embarrassed clerks watched.

Miserable, barely speaking, the couple spent the afternoon and evening watching television, venturing out only to eat hamburgers and fries. When bedtime came, Douglas moved to the spare bed.

For a moment on the way back from Missoula, there was hope of reconciliation. A little. Julie placed her delicate brown hand on his giant paw and said, "I'm sorry, Douglas. Really." She smiled.

Hope returning, suddenly wanting to prolong the moment when they would part, he had wheeled the yellow Toyota in to the dusty parking lot of the Huckleberry Pie Restaurant. "Sweets for my sweetheart," he suggested.

"OK."

The interior of the restaurant was rather dark, everything wooden, little color to break the monotony. The dinginess and the close somewhat musty smell of the air reminded Douglas of many such Western, rural eating places during the winter. Outside winds would howl, piling the snow up to the rooftops, but inside, there would be warmth, quiet, and safety.

Thinking of past experiences he smiled. Julie looked at him quizzically.

The pie was good. Large wedges of crisp, flaky crust jammed with wild berries, recently picked, went down well with the help of iced tea. Eating slowly, thus prolonging the return to the car, they broke off small sections with their forks and chewed slowly. Both knew what they were doing and they laughed without explanation.

"Got me a Griz!"

The man was powerfully built, rather short, with massive neck and shoulders. His clothing reflected his trade, a logger. A heavy red and green cotton shirt hung loosely above soiled, badly worn blue jeans. Heavy work boots, badly scuffed and dusty, perched on the rungs of the sides of the barstool. He was drinking beer from a bottle.

"Yuh' did?" The waitress was curious. So were the two male locals who inhabited a table. Their lady companion sized up the speaker's physique with admiration and desire.

"Hell, yes I did." The man was enjoying his boasting. He had his audience's undivided attention. "I was walking up the old skid road about two miles this side of the dam. Thought I seen movement in some aspens, but I wasn't sure. Since I always carry my rifle, in case

I see varmints, like environmentalists - (his audience laughed) - I decided to investigate."

The bear killer grinned profusely. A little trickle of beer ran down his chin. "Sure enough. It was a Griz. Almost black she was, but a grizzly for sure."

"Wow!" the waitress was really excited. She reached out and placed her hand on the braggart's left arm.

"Never knew what hit her. A female. One shot. She went down slick as cat shit on a hot tin roof."

Everyone laughed. One of the men, becoming nervous over the confession of an illegal act, looked furtively about the room, his eyes settling momentarily on Julie and Douglas.

"Yep! One less god-damned grizzly to worry about. I drugged him into a ravine and threw brush all over him. He'll just rot away without anyone knowing it."

"Did you take the claws? The Indians ought to pay good for them." It was the waitress speaking.

"No way! I'm not havin' no son-of-a-bitchin' game warden or Fed fish and game man catchin' me with that stuff. No way!"

They all laughed again. One of the men ordered a round of beer to celebrate. Douglas looked at Julie. "Excuse me a minute. I'll be right back."

"No. Please. Don't make a fuss. I don't want any trouble."

He scowled. "Look, Julie." He spoke softly so only she could hear. "I'm a Fish and Game Officer, not National Park. I could arrest him right now. But, I want to find out who he is first."

"Please," she sighed. "Let's just go."

He glanced at her. "I'll be right back. Stay put." He was outside for a very short time. When he returned he walked to the far side of the restaurant, where the phone was.

The bear killer noticed the stranger first. The others turned and watched Douglas until he had ended his conversation on the telephone. Casually he walked toward the group at the bar, keeping a table between himself and the bear killer. "Is your pickup the red one or that black Ford?"

Actually there were five vehicles in the parking lot.

The man looked puzzled. Thinking someone might have hit his vehicle he replied, "The GM."

"Thanks," smiled Douglas. "I've got your license number and it's already turned in."

"What the hell for?" The bear killer rose up off of his stool, a mean look replacing the previous sneer.

"Just sit back down, mister. This won't take long. The sheriff will be here in a couple of minutes. He was over at the Dam Town Saloon, just across the street."

"Sheriff? What the hell is comin' off here?"

Douglas grinned. "Why you told all these nice folks that you shot a female grizzly. That's a federal offense. Likely there's a reward out for you. You are under arrest."

"Like shit I am!" The man stood up. Douglas thought he looked like a giant with his legs sawed off.

"Just sit back down, Sir. You don't want another federal charge against you, do you?"

"I'm going to take you, smart ass!" The threat was hissed between clenched teeth. Unable to control his fury the man stepped toward Douglas, throwing a chair that had been between them aside. "I'm going to beat the living shit out of you and then I'll drug your body out of here and dump you in a ditch."

"Drag," corrected Douglas.

"Huh?"

"Drag. Not drug. And you dragged the bear. You didn't drugged the carcass."

"You asshole!" The man lunged forward then suddenly stopped.

"Woah! Don't try it."

The attacker almost fell as he tried to halt his forward momentum.

"My Magnum looks pretty big, doesn't it Mister? If you are wondering if I will use it, you can bet your ass I will. Sit down! I'm a Fish and Game lawman."

A sheriff's deputy arrived. Very little discussion took place. The killer of the grizzly glared defiantly at Douglas while the other officer cuffed him. "I'll get you for this, Shitface."

Douglas didn't smile. He'd heard many such threats in his short career with Fish and Wildlife. He followed the cruiser to the deputy sheriff's little office, where he filed a federal charge against the killer. Julie, not speaking, rode to the jail and remained in the car while the man was booked.

Finally, an hour later, just as they started the long climb up the Going-to-the-Sun Road Douglas had to break the tension. "Now what's wrong?"

"You couldn't let it go, could you?"

"Julie, he broke a law. I'm a lawman."

"You could have ignored him. Maybe he was lying."

"You know better than that," he growled.

"Well I asked you not to get involved. You ruined our afternoon."

"Tough shit." He had whispered the words.

"What did you say?"

"I said, tough shit! There! Did you hear me that time?"

Not another word was said until they drove out the east entrance of Glacier Park, and into the town of St. Mary. "Pull over at Blacks." Julie pointed at the lodge. "I'll get a ride home from here."

"Oh for crap sake, Julie, I had to do that. Give me a break."

"I am. Let me out." She had opened the door while the car was still moving.

"For Christ's sake! Wait 'till I stop. You'll get hurt."

"Don't take the Lord's name in vain. Not around me. I'm not one of your cheap babes!"

He hit the brakes hard, throwing Julie into the doorframe. "Oh shit, Julie. I'm sorry. Did I hurt you?"

Crying, holding her bruised head with her hands, the girl flounced out of the vehicle and hurried, somewhat unsteadily toward the lodge.

Douglas sat there. The thought came to his mind that she was no longer his.

"Shit!" He banged the dashboard with his fist.

*

The day after the bear killer's arrest was completely taken up with the drive back to Hungry Horse and the legalities connected with the pending trail. For once, a judge strong on enforcement of environmental laws would hear Douglas's case. Usually the bench scolded the offenders and let them off with a suspended sentence. Wolf Man didn't think that would happen to the bear killer. The case was important for several reasons. Not only had the man killed a fertile female grizzly that had the potential of producing several offspring, but if the dead grizzly could be found that might mean the saving of another bear.

In spite of the precarious existence of it's grizzly population, the state of Montana permitted the hunting and killing of five each year. The safety check was that if a grizzly was killed by a train, truck or some other man-caused incident the number for the hunting season was reduced by one, for each man-related death.

Douglas joined the state game warden and the deputy sheriff in looking for the bear's carcass. Within two hours the dead grizzly was located right where the frightened prisoner said it was.

Night fell before he returned to St.Mary. Any chance of seeing Julie and appealing for reconciliation was lost.

The following morning was also disappointing. He was caught up in a maze of forms and irrelevant reports concerning the wolf study he was not doing. Finally, just before noon he managed to sneak away, eluding the visiting headquarters secretary, who was demanding the long overdue papers.

*

Douglas sat with feet perched solidly on the side of the tiny boat dock, waiting. A tiny black, hairy spider, perhaps a quarter of an inch across, was struggling up and down over the tangled mass of auburn hairs that covered the back of Wolf Man's left hand. He watched, unthinking, mind shut down, providing a brief respite from his anxiety. Instead of webbing itself to safety the spider caught a gust of wind and sailed out over the lake to its doom. He sighed, the restfulness ended. He'd arrived at Julie's home shortly after noon. For some reason she hadn't reported for work that morning. No one knew why. All he could do was wait until someone showed up at the house.

Lower St. Mary Lake sparkled in the autumn sunlight. All summer long storms had churned the long body of water into froth-streaked whitecaps. On this day, the 18th of September, except for the rare breezes like the one that carried the spider away, the surface was mirror-like, unbroken except where an occasional trout rose to suck in an insect. Three arrow-like trails were scooting along the middle of the lake indicating where ducks were paddling in search of food. Sighing deeply, because of his anxiety over Julie, the young man unhooked the leather thong that held his hair in place. He combed it out, bunched it together, and then replaced the strap. His efforts resulted in little improvement. Wear and tear from the long summer's adventures in the high country had ruined the long ponytail. Broken strands, individual bent hairs, all resulted in massive disorder, which did not compliment his appearance.

Oh well, he thought. He would be going home in a month or so. When he got back to Dayton he would get a decent haircut and give up the long hair. He thought about that. Time to give up the Hippie look. Be more serious looking. Business-like. The idea depressed him even more. Who wanted short hair? he mused, remembering how wonderful the long tresses had felt as they'd blown across his face, how warm they had been on those cold nights of back country camping.

"What you doing here?"

Douglas jumped, surprised that he had not seen or heard the Indian youth approaching.

"Hi! Nobody's at home." He nodded his head toward Julie's house.

Suspicious, the Blackfeet youth stared. "You waiting for Ben?"

"No. Julie. I'm waiting for Julie." He felt he owed his inquisitor an explanation.

"Well", grumbled the Indian, "You'd better go 'cause she ain't coming back."

"What?" Douglas scrambled to his feet.

"That's right." The newcomer looked a bit nervous. "None of 'em are. They don't live here no more."

He felt cold. The knot in his stomach became lead and despair coursed through his body. He didn't want to ask. "But, where...?"

"Ben took his family and moved out. My Father owns this place now. You'd better leave."

Wolf Man's eyes must have looked a bit wild. The Indian became uneasy and stepped back. "Look. I don't know you. You are trespassing. You'd better go now."

"Oh." He hesitated. "Where did they go?"

"Alaska."

"Alaska?" His word came in a whisper.

"Yeah. Ben, he sorta' had a problem with the government so he took off."

Douglas's face reflected his grief.

"Hey, man. I'm sorry. As I said, I don't know you. You'd better go now. OK?"

"Yes. OK." He started walking toward the Toyota. Turning, he called back to the still watching youth, "Thanks."

Numbness spread throughout his body. He'd lost her. Julie was gone forever. That lovely brown girl. Those perfect breasts. Eyes. Eyes soft with love, warm with tenderness, sparkling with life. Her father had taken her from him, a White man. He couldn't decide what to do. Gradually he began rationalizing the situation. If they had such differences so early in their relation perhaps her disappearing was for the good. No. He couldn't accept that. Too, he refused to recognize the fact that inwardly he was beginning to feel some sort of relief.

Click! A defense mechanism took over and he ceased to think at all. He started the car and drove north, along the lakeshore, toward the little settlement of Babb.

*

Douglas turned his little yellow car in to the bumpy parking lot of one of Babb's bars. A few years ago he had read somewhere, in National Geographic perhaps, that the old saloon was one of the toughest in the States. Very unlikely, but it made a good story and had brought some tourist business to the "barely making it" establishment.

He sat, staring out of the windshield at the parched, barren earth about him. The ancient logs did nothing to ease the view of desolation. He began to think again. Julie gone. He still couldn't accept the fact.

Worse yet, Douglas was unable to come to an understanding of his own feelings. Why wasn't he feeling more sorrow? He'd been in love before. Several times. Some of his affairs with women had ended congenially. Most had terminated in a fight. Verbal of course. And then there was Evelyn Cooper, back in Ohio. She loved him. They'd never had sex but they possessed a mutual respect for one-another. That made her something special. Yet, where was that feeling he should have had? Strange, he hadn't thought of Evelyn once since he had left home the previous spring.

Julie had been, still was, something special too, more so than Evelyn. Both of them had known that from the beginning. Neither had considered their cultural and ethnic differences to be a problem. Still, there had been difficulties.

Religion. Now there was what had caused much of their arguments. Both were Catholic. That was a plus. Religion forced a wedge between them only when the issue of morality became part of their conversation. Julie was more straight-laced, somewhat of a Fundamentalist. Douglas saw religion as a guide but more important, God was everything. God was Julie, his family, music, beauty, nature. Strange, he held the concept of God to be more like the Native Americans' beliefs. Julie believed more like the White Christians.

"No matter. She is gone, pure and simple." He became angry with his defeatist attitude. "Why in the hell don't I just go after her?"

He sat there for some time, not thinking anymore yet absolutely miserable. Slowly Douglas became aware of the heat building up. Funny. He always drove with the windows down on nice days. He had driven to Babb and was sitting in the car with all of the panes rolled up. He cracked the driver's window open a bit and then got out. No one was about. A scrawny brown and white hound peered at him with mild anxiety.

Richard D. Seifried

"Beat it," he mumbled.

The dog just stared.

He opened the door to the saloon and stepped inside. Coolness, darkness, mustiness, and, of course the smell of stale beer greeted him. The bar was empty. There wasn't any bartender either.

"Click! Wobble, wobble, wobble, thump!" The 5-ball barely fell into the side pocket of the pool table. Obviously the plump Indian woman shooting pool was the bartender. She didn't even look up.

He sat down at the bar, towards the far end from the front door. He waited.

The young woman finally cleared the table of balls. She wasn't very good. Then she started racking the balls for another game.

"Hey! Could you get me a Ditch please?"

The woman, irritated by her White customer's interruption, reluctantly walked behind the bar. "You want a what?"

"A Ditch."

"Huh!"

"Oh, just give me a double shot of Canadian Mist and some water."

"Don't have Canadian Mist."

"Pour something, will you? Not cheap crap, though."

"Well, OK." Slowly, with what she portrayed as extreme effort, the woman plunked a glass of questionable cleanness upon the bar and poured him a drink of cheap crap.

"Thanks." He tossed the liquor down chasing it with a sip of water. The taste was almost sickening.

The barmaid looked at him. "I suppose you want another one."

"Yeah."

"Look Mister, I'm trying to shoot me a coupla' games of pool. Do you mind if I pour you as many as you're going to drink so I don't have to keep running back here?"

He looked at her fat belly. The woman got the message. Her face scowled in anger.

"Set up four more. I'll pay you now so you won't have to over-exert yourself and ruin your day."

She turned to pick up the bottle. "Shit face." She spoke the words so he could hear them.

He chugged the second drink. She'd switched brands to an even worse tasting concoction. "Ugh!" He shook his head and grimaced. The woman, already back at the pool table, grinned slightly. She hated White guys, except the ones with long peckers. The woman

92

hesitated at the thought, looked at Douglas, and then shrugged her shoulders.

A half an hour passed before he tossed down the third drink. The burning in the stomach had ceased, replaced by a soothing numbness and a familiar warmth in his cheeks. The bar, except for the clicking of the pool balls, was quiet, comforting in its way. Nice not to think too much. Julie was fading a little bit.

Sunlight shattered the darkness as the door swung open. Two cowmen, Indians, walked in. They immediately spotted Douglas, connecting him with the yellow Toyota in the parking lot. The newcomers sat down near the door, unspeaking, watching the White Man, wondering what he was up to.

Again the door opened. Then twice more in a quarter of an hour. Exasperated the barmaid again said, "Shit!" put up her pool cue and resigned herself to being behind the bar making money.

There were five men plus Douglas. Some were talking quietly. Twice they laughed good-naturedly at some remark, not aimed at Douglas.

Except for the grossness of the barkeep Wolf Man was oblivious to his surroundings. As he watched the woman's fat butt and flopping breasts, barely constrained inside her T-shirt, he somehow allowed the image of Julie to filter back into his thoughts. He downed two of the drinks in rapid succession.

One of the Indian customers, just two seats down-bar from Douglas, slipped off his bar stool and moved to a table. This White Man is peculiar. Something bugging him. Better to avoid trouble.

Another man entered the dark room.

Douglas swallowed the last of his drinks, the fifth double. Ten shots of rotgut. Somewhat unsteady he looked about the room. "Hey, lady," he said not impolitely, "can I have a couple more?"

"I think maybe you got enough, mister."

He thought about that a while, then nodded in agreement.

Someone snickered.

"Where's the Rest Room?" Douglas felt the urge.

"Back there." She jabbed a thumb toward a not-so-distant door.

The place stunk. Stale piss. Wolf Man held his breath as much as he could, trying to hurry his urinating. Lowering his face he tried to breath through the fabric of his shirt collar, thus filtering out some of the stink.

He returned to his bar stool. Something had happened. The empty glasses were gone. Only the wet rings where the drinks had slopped over were left. He ignored the hint to leave. Lets see. Where was he in his thinking? Something about Julie. The emptiness was getting worse.

Loud laughter alerted his alcohol-dulled senses. Only two of the customers were talking. Something about him. Just ignore them. He'd just sit awhile longer. Let the whiskey wear off a bit.

"Hey! You in the blue shirt! Ain't you the one that runs with Henry Two Feathers?"

Douglas ignored the challenge.

"Seems like you don't pick very good friends."

No response.

"Henry, he's just an old Son-of-a-bitch!"

Douglas turned slightly to see who the speaker was.

"Yeah. He's one of them mother fuckin' sons-a-bitches that think they're hot shit. 'Cause they wear a star."

Douglas looked at the worried barmaid. "Give me a single shot." She did.

The pest was moving closer.

"Hey, Clarence. Take it easy. You don't want to mess with those quiet ones. He's a quiet one."

Douglas heard the agitator giggle. "Say, White man, you wanta' hear a good joke? What's the matter? Can't you hear me?"

Douglas swung on the bar stool so he could watch the man. His tormentor was Clarence, nicknamed Fang, last name unknown to Douglas; a big, skinny six-foot-four inch tall troublemaker that Henry had cautioned Douglas about. Wolf Man did not respond, wondering if Fang remembered the day he had given Douglas the finger, after Church.

"Well. So you lost your tongue." Fang laughed. "I bet I can make you talk." Pausing, recalling what he had been saying, the Indian smiled and continued. "Well, ol' ass hole Henry's friend, I'm going to tell you my joke whether you like it or not."

Douglas sat, staring, unblinking.

"Well, seems this dumb-ass Crow guy didn't like his Indian name. Excuse me. Native American name." Fang looked about to see if the others were laughing at his humor. No one was. Not discouraged, Fang continued. "So he goes to the son-of-a-bitchin' agent over on the Crow reservation and asks him to change it."

Douglas knew the joke. It was an old one.

"The Agent laughed and said that he didn't blame this guy for he'd change it too if it was his name. 'What do you want it changed to?'

"'Well', says the Crow, 'I want it changed to Robert'

"The agent said, 'Robert? You want it changed from George to Robert?'

"'That's right', says the Crow. 'I want my name changed from George to Robert Two-Dogs-Fucking.'"

Everyone in the saloon laughed except Douglas. He remained impassive.

"Hey, White Man. Don't you get it? He wanted to change his first name."

Finally Douglas smiled. Misinterpreting the smile Fang grinned, exposing a lone front tooth and lots of gums. "That isn't the way the story ends", explained Douglas.

"Shit you say! That's the way it ends. It's my joke. Sure enough."

"No that isn't correct."

"Well," Fang was a little puzzled, "you tell me how it ends then, White Ass."

Douglas looked at the barmaid and winked. "The way the story ends is that the Crow warrior wants his name changed to George Two-Dogs-Fucking."

"Naw!" growled Fang, "That ain't right."

"Sure it is. See, he wanted a better name."

"Why, that ain't better."

"Is too. You see his original name was even worse. His unmarried Daddy had named him Fang-Puke-Shit-Face, because he was so damned ugly."

"Why you!" Fang leaped forward colliding with Douglas's right fist. All six-feet-four inches slumped to the floor.

Douglas swallowed his last drink. "Thanks." He smiled at the barmaid and left her a dollar. Somewhat unsteadily he walked out of the quiet saloon.

*

Douglas couldn't sleep. Each time he lay down Julie's image came to him, her delicate, olive-brown features crashing into his aching head. By the time dusk fell softly on the land, he drained the last of the three beers his refrigerator held. The mixture of beer and previously consumed hard liquor made him mean. His policy was to never keep whiskey on the premises. Now he wished he had some.

Sitting outside didn't help either. The autumn evening chill penetrated Douglas's alcohol-dulled senses. He began to shiver.

He still had the presence of mind not to drive. Instead, considering hitch hiking too dangerous, he walked the few miles to town.

St. Mary was nearly deserted. The tourist season was rapidly winding down. Only a few vehicles moved along Highway 93 and through the large, nearly deserted parking lots.

He went to Blacks.

The St. Mary Lodge, called "Blacks" after the owners, was quiet, too. Staggering somewhat, he labored up the steps and entered the lodge. The gift shop was closed. A night clerk at the registration desk was working a crossword puzzle. The bar wasn't having a record night either. A middle-aged couple sat by one of the large west-facing windows. They were the only customers.

Behind the shiny, dark, wooden bar the bartender was washing a lone glass. He looked up as Douglas staggered in. Unobtrusively, the employee sauntered to the small open window that was used to pass drinks into the dining room. The drunk didn't hear the bartender asking a waitress to get the manager. Mentally confused, Wolf Man sat on the first stool he came to. He was ignored. He was still waiting when the manager arrived.

"Hi Douglas." The man placed a firm hand on Wolf Man's shoulder.

"Huh? Oh, hi."

"Do me a favor, friend?"

"Yeah. Sure." Douglas remembered something. "Say, how does one get waited on in here?"

"That's what I want to talk to you about. Come on outside, will you Doug?" He paused then added, "It's stuffy in here isn't it?"

"Naw! I want a Ditch."

"That's just it, Douglas. Let's go outside." He didn't touch Wolf Man any further than the initial contact. "Come on. Please?"

The manager's sincerity struck Douglas's clouded mind and he complied. Once outside the manager convinced him that he should just walk home.

The drunk, in fuzzy comprehension, agreed with Black's employee. He should go home and sleep it off. The manager went back inside and watched from the empty gift shop's store windows.

The St. Mary River growled and bumbled over the stream's boulder-choked bed, creating a somewhat soothing effect on the jilted lover. Two shadowy Mallard ducks, low and fast, shot past, straight as arrows from a strong bow. Their fleeting passage caused him to jump aside, though their passage was quite a few yards distant.

"Whoa!" he exclaimed to nothing. "Close one." Douglas looked about, puzzled. The river was right below him, racing under the bridge. "Woops!" He laughed and waved his arms at the night sky. "Wrong way. I was going the wrong way." Laughter, uncoordinated laughter, wobbled in and out of the river dominated night sounds.

Wolf Man's route led him through the Alberta Canada tourist center parking area. Pausing, he peered, hands cupped to each side of his head, face flattened against a giant windowpane, the slightly functioning mind recalling that the Alberta girls who worked there were quite attractive. Half-heartedly he thumped on the window and whispered loudly, "Hey! Anybody home? Come out, come out and I'll buy you a drink. A Ditch."

The empty, closed for the season, center didn't respond.

"Shit!" he cursed and struck the door loudly. Then, uncharacteristically concerned that he might have been heard swearing he exclaimed, "Woops!" chuckling to himself. "I've gotta' be more careful."

The Park Cafe was his next victim. Clomping up onto the aching wooden porch he yelled softly, "Hey! Got any blueberry pie?" As an afterthought, "Any coffee?" Since the proprietor of the Cafe was home in Iowa there was no response from the closed-for-the season restaurant. Blue Berry pie. The image reminded him of the grizzly bear killer who had helped him loose Julie. The memory of her didn't last.

His good intentions died. "Gotta' have a drink. Drink. Have a Ditch." Liquor wasn't really on his mind. The man was looking for trouble.

Within the obscure area sandwiched between the Travel Alberta office and the Park Cafe there were a few other businesses. One was a store with gas pumps in the front. A Blackfeet souvenir shop stood empty, dark, blending with the shadows, sinking into the total blackness of the moonless night.

A vertical rectangle of dim light miraculously appeared, instantly partially blotted out by a male figure. Hoodoo's, Douglas mused, remembering that the notorious saloon was there. He'd never been inside. He'd never been drunk since he came to Glacier either. He illogically thought that maybe going inside was just what he needed.

The shadowy man who had stepped outside walked heavily away from the front of the building and urinated, thus avoiding the stinking urinals inside. As he relieved himself, the Indian watched the faint figure of the intoxicated White Man, weaving unsteadily toward the door.

"Jesus! It's Wolf Man!"

Douglas reached the front door, a single, narrow, house-like doorway. He could smell the burnt stench of the frame. About a month before another drunk, angered at the door being locked, had burned it down. Whee! My kind of guy."

Douglas straight-armed the door. It flew open with a bang. Startled at the sudden report, the bartender and his three customers stared as the red-haired man nearly toppled over a chair, which halted his uncontrolled forward motion.

"Woops!" Sheepishly he grinned and walked to the bar.

"Barkeep! I need a double-Ditch."

"A what?"

"Double Ditch. You know. It rhymes with bitch." Wolf Man smiled at his cleverness. "A double whiskey." He looked, rather tried to look, into the fat man's eyes. He wondered if most bartenders were fat. "And don't give me no shit. OK?"

"OK." Angry, the man slowly poured out a double shot of his worst and shoved it at Douglas. "Five bucks."

"Huh? Five bucks? Republican inflation."

The bartender remained impassive.

"OK. I'll make you a deal, Barkeep."

"My name ain't Barkeep."

"OK." Douglas thought for a while. "Friend." He smiled. "Just give me the whole damned bottle and I'll give you thirty bucks. How's that?" He was smiling again. "Friend."

Friend grabbed the twenty and two five's and growled, "Deal."

The Hoodoo Saloon's three customers hadn't moved. All four of the men inside the bar stared at Douglas. One was the Native American who had blocked his gas pump the first day Wolf Man had arrived at Browning. He recalled the red hair and was still feeling the urge to revenge his humiliation.

By that time the man who had been urinating outside was racing his pickup to Babb. He hoped that Fang was still there. The skinny, one-toothed giant was. So were two of the Logan Pass drunks.

Douglas drank slowly, sipping the bitter liquid, feeling less and less. No thoughts came to his mind. Elbows supported him on the bar. Silence allowed him to sink deeper into a stupor.

Unable to contain himself any longer the gas pump Browning man spoke. "Horse's ass!"

Douglas hadn't caught the words at first. When he did realize what had been said only "horses" registered.

"Hey, barkeep! Woops. Friend. Sorry." He smiled for the last time. "Some ol' buddy told me that some son-of-a-bitch rode his horse in here last month. Is that right?"

"I did," answered the short, stocky man that Douglas thought he should know. "You've got two things wrong, Red. I rode Bucky in here last June. The other thing is that I ain't no Son-of-a-Bitch." The man got off his bar stool.

Douglas gulped the remaining whiskey from the bottle and got unsteadily to his feet. He was about to apologize when the door flew open with a bang. Fang and four companions walked in. "Well now," slurred Douglas, "I made a mistake. There's that Son-of-a-Bitch now." He pointed at Fang.

Only the bartender stayed put.

Douglas was facing eight angry men. As drunk as he was, he realized he was likely to die, or worse.

"Eight on one is Nigger's fun." He swung and missed, at the same time wondering why he had used a racial slur that he hated so. He picked up a chair and broke a leg off for a weapon. "Equalizer," he panted.

Fang struck him in the throat, sending Douglas reeling, hitting the wall, then just leaning there, half-fallen. Vomit shot out of his mouth splattering two assailants moving in for the kill. They stopped, which was a mistake. The chair leg became a missile of destruction. Both went down, temporarily. Blurry-eyed, wheezing, Wolf Man watched his tormentors. Identifying Fang he chanted brokenly, "Fang. Fang. Can't shit worth a dang."

The Indian's long arm shot out again, fist connecting with Douglas's left eye and cheek. He went down. Someone's booted foot connected with the injured man's side. White sheets of pain coursed through what should have been an alcohol-numbed body.

Another attacker pulled him to his feet. Fang again, bony fist connecting with the same eye. All eight were moving in. Douglas couldn't even raise his hands.

Somehow he was suddenly free again. Space between him and the angry attackers. A fuzzy giant appeared up close again. Fang, he thought. But what? Fang didn't have blonde hair.

Wolf Man swung, lost his balance and the last sensation he had was that of somehow sailing into the air and someone saying, "Dumb ass!"

CHAPTER 9

September, 1984

What was lying in the autumn grasses?

Raven, glistening black feathers of ebony reflecting weak, late September sunbeams like swift, golden darts of fire. Intense eye, darker than night, peering out of cocked head.

From the creature's open beak comes a low, hoarse croak. "Croak. Croak." It called again. Anxiously the powerful hooked bill tapped the center toenail of its right foot in nervous apprehension. He stepped forward in stilted fashion, moving closer to the yet undefined mass.

Whop. Whop. Whop. The rhythmic pattern of wing beats heralded the arrival of Raven's mate.

What is lying in the autumn grasses?

Together, courage strengthened, the two giant birds stepped ever closer. Nearer still. Senses straining for information, they recognized death. Nothing to fear of the mass.

Whop. Whop. Whop. Wing beats carry them to the unmoving corpse. The female, more dominant of spirit, though physically not so, jumps upon the exposed face and deftly slices the left eye open. Clear liquid flows quickly down the cheek. Both ravens push and shove to slurp up the delicacy. Then they peck, slash and swallow as much soft tissue as their massive beaks can reach.

Nothing else for them. Resigned to waiting, they flew to a nearby spruce. Upon the lightning shattered treetop they perched, emitting their harsh, yet somehow musical calls to attract the others. All they could do was wait. Perhaps, if they were lucky, a coyote, lion, or bear would come and rip open the body. If so, they will have an even greater feast. Patience was their greatest virtue.

*

Autumn, as if making up for summer's disappointing weather, was beautiful. Sun-drenched day after sun-drenched day marched through September toward October. The tenth month arrived, the weather held and the days moved forward to greet November. Just twice a trace of snow covered the high peaks, ever so lightly sprinkling the mighty towers of limestone.

The Great Bear was confused. As did the ravens far to the south he sensed a change. Sniffing the exhilarating breezes brought him no answers. He could see or smell nothing new.

Late October was time to begin seeking a den for the long sleep of winter. His coat glistened, silver tips, long hairs, shining strikingly in the daylight. The bear was heavy, with a winter's store of fat, collected from countless huckleberry patches, nutritious bulbs, plus an occasional hapless animal. Each time he walked he would grunt from the exertion. Thick layers of fat rippled underneath the fur not too unlike the waves of distant oceanic tides.

The warm season had been good to the Great Bear. Except for the injury caused by the mantrap, the months had passed happily, as a bear sees happiness. Digging up marmots, exploring the high country, sleeping in the deep shade of summer foliage, a little sex, and of course tobogganing down the snow slope into Iceberg Lake.

He should have headed for Apikuni Mountain where he had wintered the previous year. Instead, the Great Bear veered south. He would travel the low-forested slopes of Cracker Flats, Boulder Ridge and one night he would traverse the closed-for-the-season St. Mary Campground, then head up the Hudson Bay Creek drainage to Triple Divide Peak. Below the peak laid the tiny glacial-carved Medicine Grizzly Lake.

Along the tiny lake's shore line, in a slightly exposed grassy area, the still mostly untouched body of the former Medicine Grizzly continued to dissolve from it's own chemistry; the recycling process accelerating due to the sun's meager heat. The death of the bear, resulting from overweight and an aging heart, had resulted in a void within the ecological system of the area. The mighty bear spirit was gone. Somehow all creatures sensed his absence, the degree of comprehension depending on where a particular species stood in evolutionary development.

Too, a silence descended upon the tiny ice-formed valley. Not all at once, but within a few days the birds were gone. Only the ravens remained. The duck families left first, then the songbirds, that were migrating anyway and had stopped for a rest. Stellar Jays, not scolding for once, moved nervously down the Cut Bank Valley, where they would have gone anyway, when the snow and cold arrived. The few deer moved cautiously down to the warmer habitat. Even the young female lion hissed and snarled while she traveled on to other hunting grounds.

Most of the migrational activity happened when it did because the old bear had died. His spirit, soul perhaps, left behind an emptiness that could not be denied. In the old days, before European man, nature filled such emptiness with another great one. But now, with man's destructiveness, there was so little left. Would there be a replacement of the wild creature? What would it be? Another male grizzly? That had always been the case since the Blackfeet had killed the Grizzly Medicine Man and released his angry spirit; always a male grizzly.

Only the tiny rodents, the mice, voles and the few amphibians remained. Perhaps they too, in a fashion, also waited in apprehension.

What would come?

Miles to the north the Great Bear began his late autumn migration, not really knowing why. The Medicine Grizzly Spirit, now in his body, would once more inhabit the Cut Bank Valley. The creature that was coming was mighty indeed, as great as the monster that had slaughtered the frightened Blackfeet so many years ago.

*

Douglas stirred, a slight moan escaping his swollen lips.

Swiftly a soft figure glided across the tiny, darkened room and gently held his head. Nausea rushed up from his stomach. The parched lips emitted a feeble burst of vomit followed by strings of foul-smelling green bile.

Exhausted from the exertion the young man lay back and slept.

*

The next time Wolf Man awoke he felt better. A little bit. One of his eyes was swollen shut but he could see well with the remaining one.

Douglas recognized the shape of the room, the sink and refrigerator positioned to the left of the door. He was in the dormitory. The room, if the blind had been raised, would have been light and cheerful, very feminine. Lace curtains covered the only window. Pots of flowers, green plants, and germinating sprouts were everywhere the sun normally touched.

He was lying on the floor, on a mattress. White sheets, blankets, and a homemade comforter covered his aching body. He did ache.

Across the room, which was not so very far away, a young, fair woman slouched in a chair, deep in sleep. She was Ann Davis, the ranger with whom Douglas had watched the juvenile grizzly die. He held his breath for a moment, then exhaled softly. The woman wore a robe of white terry cloth. Sprawled as she was, the fabric had slipped aside exposing her lower legs and an ample portion of her left thigh.

Even with his many aches and pains, Douglas marveled at the beauty he beheld.

Ann Davis was respected by everyone on staff. She was perhaps the best Ranger Naturalist in the St. Mary Valley; not that being the best meant anything to her. Ann was most recognized and respected for her physical stamina. The young woman had scored higher than anyone on the Step Test, the notorious physical ordeal that one had to pass in order to qualify for fire fighting. On a hike Ann could keep up with any man, including Vern Nielsson.

Yet, there were her legs for Douglas to see. Not the oversized muscles he had imagined but graceful curves of feminine beauty. Wolf Man laid silent, eye drinking in the wonders of her magnificent limbs.

Again he slept.

*

"Hi, Wolf Man." Ann Davis's voice bubbled with humor. "Feeling better?" Douglas grimaced, tested his mouth with his tongue, and nearly became ill again.

"Here." She was bending over him. "Sit up and drink this juice. You'll feel better."

The lady ranger was right. The orange flavor helped. Douglas looked about questioningly. "Julie—"

She laughed again, that delightful rhythmic sound that he would grow to love. "Ann," she protested, "Not Julie."

"Ohh," he moaned. "I'm sorry. Guess I'm still sort of fuzzy." He tapped his head with a finger.

"That's OK, Douglas. I'll get used to the mistake. No harm done. As for what you are wondering, well, Jim Ballard rescued you and brought you here."

"Ballard?"

"Yes, Jim. I'd say you owe him a lot. Word was out that you were gunning for him because of last June."

"I wasn't 'gunning' for anybody. I thought he was looking for me."

"Jim likely saved your life. Want to hear about it?"

"Yeah. Sure." Douglas struggled to clear his head. "I'm not going anywhere soon, am I?"

More laughter.

"Do you remember going to Blacks last night?"

Douglas thought a moment. "Yeah. That was last night, huh?"

"Yep. Last night. The manager of the lodge called Nielsson and told him you were in a bad way."

"Oh, god! Now I am in trouble."

Ann ignored his remark. "Anyway, Jim and I were at Nielsson's house when the phone rang. Since Nielsson can't go barhopping after every misbehaving employee, he called Henry. The old man was out somewhere on a case but Martha said she'd get help.

Melanae, Tina and a couple more Blackfeet girls met Jim and me at Blacks just as a carload of guys pulled up in front of that dump up the road where you were having fun. The way those guys rushed in to the bar we knew you were going to have an even better time."

"Good time my..." Douglas caught himself.

"That's all right, Wolf Man," Ann giggled. "You can cuss around me. I wouldn't want to impede you using your best talent." She continued. "We all rushed down there and entered just as you were about to get brained. I didn't know what to do. Neither did Jim. But Melanie and her pals did. Those lovely young ladies pulled out the meanest looking knives you have ever seen. Switchblades, all of them. You could hear them in the deep silence of the saloon. Click. Click. Click. Boy, did they have the men's attention.

"Jim, taking advantage of the moment rushed in, dodged your stupid swing, lifted you up and carried you out like a sack of potatoes. He dumped you in the back of Melanie's truck. You were out." For a moment she was silent, reliving the scene. Admiration was in her voice. "He's really strong, Douglas. Quite a man."

"Yeah. I guess so. I owe him, don't I? Then what happened?"

"Pretty simple. All we had to do was beat it across the St. Mary River, on to National Park property and we were safe."

"Damn!" exclaimed Douglas with an enthusiasm not expressed since he woke up.

"Yeah. Hard to believe." She sighed. "You really screwed up, Wolf Man."

No response. They fell silent for a while.

He grimaced. "Do you hurt bad, Douglas?" Ann's voice had become soft, compassionate.

"Yeah. My ribs must be broken. Maybe two or three, I'd guess. When I move the pain is real sharp."

"Right," agreed Ann. "Sally told us that you probably had a few fractures."

"Sally? Sally Fontaine? The Naturalist who is also a nurse?"

"Yes, that Sally."

Douglas felt under the covers and found his bare chest sore to the touch. "Why didn't she bind me up?"

"We suggested that but she said that nowadays they don't bind the chest for fractured ribs because it impedes the lung action and can cause pneumonia or other complications."

"Oh."

"Lucky for you, your eye will be as good as new. Soon as the swelling goes down. Except for the ribs and bruised knuckles you should be much better by tomorrow."

A peculiar look began forming on Douglas's battered face.

"What's the matter?"

He blushed. "I have to go to the bathroom."

"Well, you can't just right now. The maintenance woman gave me a big tin can that you can use."

"No way."

"Look, Douglas, I'll step out in the hall if you are so darned shy. You do your thing in the can. Nielsson doesn't want anybody to know where you are just yet. Officially, yesterday and last night didn't happen. Vern and Henry are covering your tracks so there won't be charges pressed or an investigation."

Douglas started to protest but Ann stepped out into the hall and closed the door.

"Shit," he mumbled. The noise from the can was loud, tinny, disgusting, he thought. In order to urinate he stood up. The effort sent pangs of hot misery through his left side. More disturbing was the realization that he was completely naked. His tall, bruised body was clean, too.

Ann opened the door, catching him shaking off his penis. "Finished?" She was giggling again.

"Good timing," he mumbled.

"Here, give me the can and I'll empty it."

Clutching the blanket about him Wolf Man limped over to a chair. Soon the young woman returned. He could tell that she was enjoying every moment of his embarrassment. "Can I have my clothes now?"

Again that laugh, "They aren't here."

"Not here? Well, where are they?"

"Tina, Melanie's friend, took them home. She said she'd get them all washed and ironed and back to you first thing tomorrow when she comes to work. Besides, Nielsson doesn't want you to go anywhere."

He was getting angry. "What am I supposed to do in the meantime? Run around naked?"

Ann giggled. "Guess you can continue clutching that blanket, but I like you better without it." A look of devilment appeared on her face. "Or, I have a cute little apron with ruffles that you can wear."

"God damn it! Get me some clothes." Impassive, the woman remained silent. He added, "Who cleaned me up? Sally?"

"Nope." Ann was enjoying the situation. Douglas was glaring in anger. "Melanie, Tina, two of the other girls, and of course, me."

Douglas's face flamed. "Why in the hell didn't you drag me up and down the street without anything on? You perverts!"

"Come on, Wolf Man. Those girls risked their lives for you. They deserved a little reward, the pleasure of checking you out. They liked you, Douglas."

He didn't respond.

"Fay said you had cute buns and she didn't know how such a skinny man could have such a well-rounded butt."

"Oh, god! I suppose they saw the front of me too."

"Of course. So did I. We all agreed that you have very nice parts. Now, really, you should feel flattered."

He was cussing under his breath, loosing control. Things were happening to him. Even with the pain the idea of five or six women looking at his nakedness somehow thrilled him. Douglas moved to hide his growing erection deeper in the folds of the blanket.

Ann, suddenly serious, smile gone, walked barefoot to the window and pulled the slightly raised blind down. Turning, she dropped her robe revealing the whiteness of her exquisite body.

The pain of rising from the chair made him dizzy. "I think I am going to be raped."

"No. Lie down on the mattress. On your back. I'll get on top and do all the work. Tomorrow it will be your turn to do pushups." His resistance, never really there, fled. The blanket fell on top of her robe. "Ohh," she gasped as she saw him in his fullness. Carefully, slowly, the two positioned themselves on the narrow mattress.

Strange how peculiar thoughts enter one's head at surprising times. Douglas, for a second, thought that Glacier National Park certainly had a lot to offer.

*

Late October, 1984

"You've got to OK my move to another room." Virginia was, in her usual manner, almost yelling at Vern Nielsson.

He smiled, already knowing the reason. "Why do you want to do that, Ginna?"

"Why?" she yelled. "Why? God damn it! I can't get any sleep, that's why." Virginia was the only employee who could cuss without Nielsson protesting. He'd given up on her years ago. The irate maintenance woman had caught her breath again. "Every god damned time I think I can get a little shuteye those two wake up and go at it again. Damn! They keep me so hot I can't stand it. Talk about things that go bump in the night! Too bad the U. S. doesn't have an Olympic Fuck Team. Those two would get the Gold Medal."

Vern's patience ended. "That's enough, Virginia. Don't overstep your privileges here."

"What god damned privileges?"

"You know what I mean." Embarrassed Nielsson gazed helplessly at the ceiling of his office. "The ladies in the outer office can hear you."

"Hell, they don't—"

"Enough!" Vern's roar of anger stilled the thwarted woman. He was breathing hard with frustration. Some time passed before he could speak. "Now, just listen to me. OK?"

Frowning, not the least bit intimidated, Virginia plopped into a chair. "Maybe if my name was Ann instead of Virginia I could get some of that stuff."

He whispered, "Will you please shut up?" The humor of the situation began to frustrate him and Vern struggled to keep a smile from forming on his face.

"Good. Now we can talk rationally. Don't interrupt." He cleared his throat.

Puzzled, Virginia said, "It's OK Vern. Go ahead and spit."

Nielsson ignored the comment. Automatically his fingers reached for the magazines that weren't there. His powerful hands moved as if they were straightening the missing reading material on a table that also wasn't there. "Now Virginia," he looked the woman straight in the eyes. "You know why I let Douglas and Ann stay there. He needed care. I needed a place to hide him until Henry got the Blackfeet under control. What I didn't need was for the public to catch on to why Douglas is here."

"Why is he?"

"None of your business." He frowned at his error. "And I mean that.

"The other reason is that there isn't enough money to heat the whole dormitory. The way it turned out we only have heat, water and power going to two rooms and the lady's shower." Vern couldn't help himself. "And, I don't believe you mind sharing the facilities with Wolf Man, as you call him."

"Hell no I don't." Virginia grinned. "The other day I walked in and he—"

Both of Vern's hands went up in protest. "No. No. I don't want to hear about it." The two Indian women in the outer office did though and they frowned when Virginia's story was cut off.

"Yeah. OK. But, what about my sleep. I'm so damned—"

"Ginna you're enjoying the arrangement a lot more than you want to admit. Just let it be for a couple days more. Then Douglas will go out into the back country again."

"If it doesn't snow."

Vern scowled again. "Yes. This is a peculiar fall. More like the end of August."

He got back on track. "So, Ginna, cool it. Put cotton in your ears or better yet, enjoy the noises. You might learn something." He couldn't believe he had said that.

Virginia laughed. "Vern, you old son-of-a-bitch. You are a phony aren't you? That moral shit and all."

"Shush!" The embarrassed Ranger smiled. Leaning over his desk he whispered, "I wasn't in the mountain troops for nothing.

"Now, get out of here. Go empty a garbage can or something."

Virginia laughed. She'd never realized what good friends she and Vern were. "Wish I'd known you when—"

"Ginna, will you get out?" Vern clomped to his feet and threw open the door to his little office.

Caught listening, the secretaries jerked their heads back to their paperwork.

*

Still Late October, 1984

"I want a Back Country Permit!"

The demand was stern, almost threatening. Ann looked into a pair of pale green eyes. Instantly she didn't like the man.

She had unlocked the St. Mary Visitor Center and was packing a few brochures the regular staff had left for possible late-season visitors. Massive wooden shutters covered the towering windows, leaving only a smattering of skinny sunbeams filtering into the center of the vast dark room. Instantly Ann became nervous. She was trapped, alone, if the man meant her any harm.

Using her most authoritative voice she responded to his demands, "Well sir, this place is closed for the season."

The stranger frowned. "Surely you can get me a permit. There's no one in the back country now, is there?"

Strange question. Ann apprised the visitor who had moved inside, blocking her from the door. Oh, oh, she thought. Bad situation. "Sure I can, Mister." She slipped from behind the counter, crossed the room, grabbed a blank permit and record book from behind the Back Country Desk. The alarm system was disconnected. Ann was on her own.

"We can go outside and sit on that big rock in front of the VC." He glared. "In the sun," she added weakly. Ann felt much safer outside. She was a strong woman and could likely outrun the stranger. Or, deck him, she thought.

"My, what a beautiful day. You're lucky to be going on an overnight this time of year."

"How much do I owe you?"

"Nothing. No charge for Back Country, Sir. I'll just fill this out for you.

"Name?"

"What do you want to know for?"

"Regulations. For your safety. We can't issue a permit to someone unless we have a name."

"Moses." The name stunned her. The man was carrying a staff.

"Last name?" Ann realized she was making a mistake and began thinking how she could get out of issuing the permit.

"Jolly."

"What?"

"Moses Jolly. Anything wrong with it?"

"No. No, Sir. Address?"

Ignoring the question the stranger said, "Look, I want this for ten days."

That was her way out. "But, sir. We aren't permitted to issue anything beyond five days. It is a safety factor, especially this late in the season."

"Who do I see?"

"About what?"

"About a ten-day permit. I've got to have a ten-day permit!" Anger clouded his almost handsome features.

Ann scowled back. "Well, the only one who has that authority, who is around today, is Hannibal Simms. He's law enforcement and is over at the station. Go talk to him."

"You mean," the man's posture was threatening as he grasped the staff with both hands, "you're telling me that you won't give me the permit? That I have to go all the way over to the Ranger Station to talk to this Simms person?"

"Sir, you can get angry if you want to, but then you likely will get turned down for any back country overnighter."

"What if I just go, Lady? Then what? You can't stop me."

"I can't but the other officers can and will. You would get more than a citation." Ann wished the man would swear or do something normal, but he didn't.

"Very well. We shall see." Turning, the irate hiker hurried across the parking lot to the only car. His.

Ann sighed with relief. She was shaking uncontrollably. "What a way to end a season."

*

A Few Days Later

All of the very few remaining park employees were waiting for the good weather to break. Instead, day after beautiful day blessed October with Indian summer beauty that even the old-timers couldn't remember happening in past years.

Douglas and Ann were sitting on the porch of the 1913 Ranger Station, which stood up above the flat land near the southeastern end of Upper St. Mary Lake. "What are you thinking about, Wolf Man? Pretending you are Chance Beebee, the 1913 Ranger?"

"No. I think of him though. He's a local hero, a legend all right and he certainly was a man's man, but—"

"But he killed bears, lions and wolves. Right?"

"Right." Douglas expressed his thoughts. "He should have known better. Known what he was doing. John Muir did. Teddy Roosevelt knew the West was in danger, even though he hunted big game. Beebee should have known that he was killing something important. He lived in the wilderness and couldn't even understand what it was all about. Most men were that way but that's no excuse."

Douglas gazed northward, eyes taking in the beige short grass prairies awaiting the winter onslaught of elk and deer.

Across Upper St. Mary Lake, mirror still, the meadows between the water and the forested slopes of Single Shot Mountain wavered slightly in the unseasonably warm sunlight. Douglas imagined the world, there on the other side of the lake, as translucent, ethereal, spiritual. "Perhaps the word, 'other-dimensional' is better."

"Huh?" Ann stirred from her own daydream.

Around the corner of the cabin a gyrating swarm of tiny, black gnats appeared. The miniature insects fluttered irritably into the faces of the young couple. Both laughed.

"Oh well." He quit swatting and stood up. "I've got to get back anyway. Virginia's checking me out of the dorm first thing tomorrow, you know."

Ann reached for and grasped her companion's hand. Douglas was always surprised how strong and warm the woman was, even her grip.

"Time for all of us to go, Ann. Soon as it snows." Both automatically looked to the west, up the lake toward the still open Logan Pass. They saw only sunshine. No clouds.

Fingertips scarcely touching, the friends cut through the sparse forest, which led them to the service road just below Glacier District's parking lot. Two snowplows stood grotesquely on the otherwise empty blacktop surface. Most of the other vehicles had been moved back to the West Side or returned to the interagency motor pool. Somewhere, either across the lake or on the road to Many Glacier, Hannibal Simms patrolled the late autumn paradise so devoid of humans.

Ann took the lead and turned to walk down the little path from the office to the dorm. Meg Oftie opened the headquarters door. "Hey, you two! Been looking for you. Want to hike in to Belly River with Ken and me?" Ken was the seasonal patrol ranger for the northeast area of the park; also Meg's husband.

"Well, I don't know," Douglas began.

Ann cut him off. "When?"

"Tomorrow morning. Early. We really want you two to go with us. We'll stay overnight at the Ranger Station up there."

"What's the occasion?" Douglas was getting curious.

"Some guy didn't come out on time," grinned Meg. "We think he purposely disobeyed instructions and plans on staying out for five days over his allotted time."

"Oh, him. He's trouble. That's what," Ann explained.

"Yeah? Humm. Maybe that's why Ken's making me pack my trusty little pistol."

That did it. "Yeah! Ann and I will go with you." Douglas smiled. Lately he had become bored with conventional patrols.

Ann didn't like his facial expressions. He was hoping for some excitement.

"Ann?" Meg wasn't letting Douglas speak for her friend.

"Yeah. I guess. OK."

*

CHAPTER 10

The Last Full Day of Autumn Weather, 1984

Mobile homes, in a somewhat neat but irregular line, marked the northern end of the tiny hamlet of Babb. "Up there." Ken, the driver of the Bronco, motioned with a thrust of his left arm, thumb pointing west. "Up there's where the Babbits heard the Big Foot."

"Babbits?" laughed Meg. "Ken, you are really something." She loved her "really something" very much.

The driver accelerated the truck until they were going 70 on the straight road. "Yeah," he responded, proud of himself for daring to bring up such a subject. "Anyway, did you ever hear that story, Doug?"

"Henry told me all about it." Douglas didn't want to hear anything weird on this trip, the last of the season.

Ann, disappointed that Ken had been silenced, peered out the left, back seat window. "There's Chief Mountain. Douglas, sit back so I can see." She was peering across the seat from the right side.

Not really majestically, more mystically, Chief Mountain towered above it's surrounding mountains. The single, flat-topped spire rose into the perfect indigo sky. All four humans looked, catching glimpses of the Blackfeet's sacred mountain. Ken eased up on the gas-peddle. Chief Mountain, as it often did to observers, had caught the four adventurers in it's somber mood, a peculiar presence, which emanated from the spire to envelop the land around it.

Ann sighed. Meg looked wide-eyed as if the view was the first time she had seen it. Her husband broke the silence. "You folks know that little gentleman who runs the store at Carway, just across the border in Alberta?"

No one responded but Ken knew they were listening.

"Well, I like to go up there. When I come to the border stop the Canadians always ask, 'What are you entering Canada for?' My answer is always, 'Oh, I'm going to the station over there to get some gas and have a pot of tea.'" Ken slowed the vehicle, clicked on the left turn signals and wheeled the Bronco on to the Chief Mountain International Highway. He continued to speak. "You know, those are the only times I drink milk in my tea. Funny." He thought about that and forgot what he had been telling.

Several miles later Ann exclaimed, "Look. See that dirt trail? That's the road the Indians take to the mountain."

"Yeah," agreed Ken. "Also goes to Slide Lake. Good fishing, really good, although the trout aren't particularly large. There's a cabin on the shore if any of you want to go there. You can get the keys from me."

Ann squeezed Douglas's hand but he ignored her.

Their road steadily increased in altitude. The little party arrived at the Chief Mountain Overlook on the northeast side of the highway. Chief towered high into the azure western sky. Remembering, Ken continued the story he had begun miles back. "What I was going to say was that one time the Canadian gentleman who runs the gas station was pumping fuel into my vehicle. The guy at Carway."

"Uh huh." Wolf Man wanted to hear the rest.

"We were both gazing at Chief Mountain and I said something about how beautiful it was. The proprietor agreed saying, 'Yes. I always look at the mountain when I come outside. One day I looked over there and I saw—'"

Ken's voice choked. "He didn't finish the sentence. I looked over at him and he was crying."

No one spoke. Meg sniffled slightly. All sat staring at the holy mountain. "You know," added Ken, "they say that up there, somewhere, is a sacred burial ground, just like in the Robert Redford movie, Jeremiah Johnson. Feathers, strips of cloth, hair, all that stuff. If a White man gets caught in there the Blackfeet beat up on him."

"Good!" declared Ann. "I once told a campfire audience about how sacred Chief Mountain was and I suggested that they not hike in the area. Boy, did I get a reprimand."

"From whom?" Wolf Man wanted to know.

"Emerson. Sometimes he's a pain in the you-know-what."

"That figures," commented Meg. Emerson was Ann's seasonal supervisor.

The warm day, blue sky, hazy mountain slopes, and especially Chief Mountain caught the couples in a peculiar mood, a feeling that they were a part of an eternal existence, yet, at the same time, so very mortal. They were, just as the season they were enjoying, dying. Everything ended.

Just before they got to the "Closed for the Season, Chief Mountain Customs Station" on the Canadian border, Ken wheeled the Bronco onto the blacktopped extension of the highway, which was a parking lot for backpackers. Beneath the overhanging evergreens sat a large, brown vehicle.

"That belongs to the missing backpacker," explained Ann. "I remember it from the other day."

114

"A Lincoln? A Lincoln Continental up here in the woods?" Ken shook his head. "Must be rich."

"He talked like he was. The way he tried to boss me around about the Back Country Permit."

The land dropped away from the parking lot taking the Belly River Trail down-slope through a dense coniferous forest, winding along the contours of the mountain. There was no reason to hurry. They'd meet the tardy hiker on his way out.

Meg gave Douglas and Ann a knowing smile. They dropped back allowing Ken and his little wife some privacy.

There were Magpies, long tails spread in streaks of black and white, their cries echoing in the otherwise silent forest. Once, far away, a raven called. The sun glinted golden shafts through the branches, a few beams reaching the needle-mantled earth.

Ken and Meg were waiting for them where the trail broke out of the forest revealing a beautiful open valley with the Belly River flowing busily through it's center.

"Isn't this something?" beamed Ken, pleased to be showing off his assigned area. "You should see it in July and August. All flowers. Lupine virtually covers the slopes. God, I love this place."

Ken's enthusiasm was catching and the couples became more animated, quite talkative, relating past experiences; holding hands where the trail allowed them to walk side-by-side.

Douglas thought of Julie and how they had walked along the Red Eagle Trail. He dropped Ann's hand. Understanding, yet hurt, she dropped back to bring up the rear. Perhaps, she thought, when they would get to the cabin he'd forget, for a while. Happily for her she was right. Ken and Meg, quite a ways ahead of them, were talking excitedly about something. The patrolman and his wife had stopped just short of the Belly River Ranger Station.

"Look at that, Meg. Oh man, do we have a problem." Ken was standing away from the cabin, pack held on one arm, right hand frantically reaching inside the just opened flaps. He pulled out the stock of his shotgun, then the barrel. "Dang, we've got troubles here. Look at this mess." Wooden shutters, ripped from a window frame, lay strewn about, torn and bitten into pieces. The front door of the sleeping cabin had been wrenched from the entrance, so that it hung suspended by only the single top hinge. Judging from the damage, the bear had entered through the window. Why it had torn the door off its hinges was a mystery. "He probably didn't like the idea of not walking out of there," wryly commented Ken.

Emergency rations, always kept in back country cabins, had been destroyed by the beast's fury. Flour that had been in a tin can, plastic containers of dried fruit, canned meats and vegetables, all lay strewn about. Most of the cans had puncture marks in them thus creating partly dried messes of various juices.

"I hate this." Ken shook his head in frustration. "I love bears and when some dumb bruin does something like this I'm afraid those ass-holes who run our country will get fed up and destroy them. Thank God for the Endangered Species Act."

"What now?" Ann was nervous and a little scared, as were all four of the hikers.

Ken looked about the meadows and scattered trees. "I hope that son-of-a-bitch isn't watching us from out there somewhere."

"Thanks," muttered his wife.

"First we all get armed. I mean ready to shoot." As he should have, Ken had taken charge. In all they had the shotgun and two 45s. Ann's little pistol was virtually useless if the bear returned. "As of right now nobody goes anywhere alone. In fact, we all stick together. Even if someone has to take a shit."

"Ken!"

"I mean it, Meg. Remember these grizzlies can outrun a horse. We stick together."

"Too bad we don't have a high powered rifle," commented Ann, as she looked at her little 38-caliber revolver.

"Yeah. I didn't expect this," confessed Ken.

"Tell you what. We'll walk down to the trail intersection and look about for a while. Then we'll come back here, clean up this mess, and get a good night's sleep. Tomorrow we'll try to pick up the hiker's trail. First though, I'll call Nielsson on the radio and tell him what we've found here. Frankly, I'm not too happy about our situation, and I'm not trying to scare you."

Everyone was apprehensive. All four stood close together, scanning the areas where trees met meadows. The shadows seemed particularly dark, more so than they had been half an hour before. Douglas was checking his Magnum. "Let me see your revolver, Ann." The weapon looked so tiny in his hands. "If we see a bear don't shoot him. You might hit him in the balls and he'll only get madder."

No one laughed nor even smiled at Wolf Man's stupid joke.

"A little levity on my part," he mumbled.

Actually, Douglas was having a pretty good time. The danger of the situation had brought him alive, almost tingling with anticipation. If only the girls weren't along, he thought. He feared for their safety. Nielsson couldn't be reached at St. Mary but a radio transmitter up on one of the high peaks allowed Com Center, Communications Center on the West Side, to pick up on Ken's transmission.

The Back Country Ranger had moved away from the group for the radio conversation. He returned still frowning. Douglas began to get the impression that the frown was halfway phony and that Ken was having fun too, in a way.

"What did they say," asked Meg.

"Be careful. They'll think of something."

The three listeners moaned their disappointment.

"Oh, come on." Ken was a little angry at their reaction. "Give Headquarters some credit. We've got a misbehaving endangered species working here. As far as we know, the bear didn't do anything but break into our cabin."

He was right. Help would come the next day.

"Ken, Honey. I've got to pee." Meg whispered it.

"Here we go. Everyone to the outhouse. Three stand guard and we all take turns. Don't anybody listen, though."

His response brought nervous smiles from the women. The worse was over. On such a beautiful day how could anything be threatening?

Body functions appeased the foursome began cautiously walking toward the trail junction. Their progress was intentionally slow. Ann, who had excellent eyesight, walked in lead position, looking for sign of the bear's passing. Nothing.

"Maybe he didn't come this way," suggested Meg. She was referring to the bear.

"Could be", admitted Ken. "Could be he just didn't walk the trail but was hunting over there along the west bank of the stream."

"Maybe he didn't come this way at all. He might be in Canada by now," hypothesized Douglas. No one believed his theory. The bear was up ahead somewhere.

*

Ann and Douglas sat on the rock surface of a raised slope where they could see the surrounding countryside. Dawn Mist Falls tumbled weakly in the low-water season of an October without rain.

They had split up, contrary to Ken's original command. Not that anyone wanted to. The problem was that the lost hiker had to be found; hopefully be warned of the danger. Ken and Meg were moving upstream, checking out the Cosley Lake Campground. Douglas and Ann hiked the northern trail along the main stream of Belly River, looking for footprints, or paw prints. They found nothing. Not a trace of animal life. Not even the delicate hoof marks of mule deer. "What do you think, Wolf Man?" Ann loved calling him that.

"That guy's dead. I can feel it. Something bad has happened."

Hoping the bear hadn't killed the stranger Ann suggested, "Maybe he fell somewhere."

"Yeah. I just feel he is dead, though."

Ann looked at her companion's face. What she saw made her want to shiver. She shivered. He was enjoying the situation. She realized that her Wolf Man was where he belonged and she was an intruder, having no right to be there. Being a woman had nothing to do with it. Ann was untrained and virtually unarmed.

"I don't want to frighten you, Ann."

"You already have."

"Yeah. Guess so." He considered whether to continue his thought. "If worse comes to worse, I'll try to shoot the bastard. There's no guarantee with a mad grizzly, if that's really what we have here. So, in that case, you duck down into a crack or jump into the brush, or hide somewhere and don't move no matter what. No matter what, Ann. Stay put 'till Ken shows up."

Ann paled.

"Did that scare the shit out of you or what?" He was smiling.

"OK." Her agreement was almost inaudible.

*

"Three o'clock. Let's go."

Ann jumped at his voice. "Darn you, Wolf Man. Don't talk so loud."

Her companion laughed. The contrast was considerable, Ann angered and afraid while Douglas was enjoying himself.

The couple made their way back along the trail, slowly, cautiously, taking in every detail, still looking for signs of the lost hiker, or the bear. When they arrived at the trail junction, they found that Ken and Meg had not yet returned from checking out the Cosley Lake Campground. Ann's anxiety increased. She worried that their friends had run into trouble.

"Here they come," reported Douglas. He and Ann watched as the married couple moved rapidly along the north side of the stream that drained Cosley Lake.

"Hi, guys!" Ken appeared relieved to see them. "Time to get back to the cabin and clean it up so we can sleep there tonight. Got to put the shutters and the door back on."

Remembering their condition Douglas cynically asked, "What shutters?"

*

Dawn came late, as it does so far north in October. Milky mists bathed the valley, hiding whatever creatures might have been there.

Douglas, standing in the doorway he had just opened, shivered and breathed in the early morning chill, then let out twin spurts of moisture-laden air from his nostrils. The creamy jets slowed, widened, and evolved into brief clouds of minute water droplets. His exercise was not unlike the actions of the Great Bear. Tears came to his eyes. "Jeeze, the cold sure clears one's sinuses." When he spoke, a frightened, teeny blob of gray fur scurried across the floor seeking the sanctuary of the enclosed sink.

Ann arose clothed in heavy socks, tight-fitting long underwear and a flannel shirt. Wolf Man stood watching her movements, admiring the firm legs and perfect bottom.

"Nice, eh?" Ken smiled slightly.

"Yeah."

Somewhat embarrassed at the remarks he had initiated Ken added, "Congratulations."

"Just friends," explained Douglas. Turning he nearly bumped into Meg, who had moved toward the door.

Sensing what he had on his mind she greeted, "Morning, Glory. I see you are up and at it."

He wondered what she meant.

Breakfast for the couples consisted of hot tea, slices of pound cake, and canned apricots.

By the time they stepped outside, the fog had begun to dissipate. Swiftly, yet cautiously, they hiked upstream, retracing the previous day's route. Along the Belly River a water ouzel cried pleasantly in the morning cold. Moments later the tiny bird was seen hopping about in the shallows of the stream.

The morning was splendid. Yet, all four humans sensed something that they could have only described as a tenseness in the atmosphere. Near Gros Ventre Falls Ken said, "Look" and pointed to the west. High up, almost lost in the dazzling sunlight, cirrus clouds were appearing, coming over the Mt. Cleveland massif.

119

Distant rumblings, not identifiable at first, transformed into the rapid whop, whop, whop, whop of a helicopter. Sharp of eye, Meg saw it first, a tiny black dot scurrying down the valley from Glenns Lake. Something was hanging below the helicopter, suspended by a long cable.

"Bear trap" identified Ken. "They'll be taking it to the cabin, in case the critter comes back. Which it won't."

"Right" agreed Wolf Man.

"Anyway, we are supposed to stay here until they return. Won't take long." Ken had conversed with Com Center earlier that morning. "Thank goodness the radio works."

The couples sat on a knoll so they could observe the Cosley Lake trail through their binoculars. Each had a pair.

"Wish the chopper would hurry," declared Ken. "I don't like those clouds building up." Waiting was difficult. A whole hour passed.

"Shit." Douglas was expressing his anxiety.

"Here she comes." Meg had seen it first again.

"How do you do that? I have excellent eyes but I didn't see the chopper when you said that." Ann sounded envious.

"She practices by spotting men," grinned Ken.

His wife ignored him.

The incoming helicopter wasn't large at all, a privately owned tourist chopper contracted by the National Park Service for one trip only. Besides the pilot, two passengers could squeeze in uncomfortably, if the far right passenger stuck his leg outside of the cabin. Deftly the skilled pilot touched down in a small meadow. Earlier in the year a trail crew had removed all pieces of brush and other items that could be sucked up into the rotor blades thus creating a primitive heliport. Douglas laughed with happiness. He loved helicopters, especially if he got to ride in them over mountainous terrain.

Two park employees in Class B uniforms stepped out. Bending low, avoiding the spinning blades, they walked hurriedly toward the waiting couples. One, the taller man, Douglas recognized. "Hi Gene," he yelled loud enough so that he could be heard over the noise of the whomping rotors. They had been together the day the Great Bear had been caught in the snare trap. The man grinned and waved.

The other ranger, an older man, shook hands with Ken and then introduced himself to Douglas. "Wade Leonard."

As often happened, the new arrivals ignored the two women.

Leonard spoke. "You have a plan?"

"Yes." Ken was pleased that he had been asked by his superior. "We are going back up along Cosley Lake. Meg and I saw sign that our missing visitor might have camped there. Maybe he went on to Glenns Lake."

"We didn't see anything up there as we flew down just now," Leonard reported. "Better change plans here." He became silent, frowning in contemplation. "Damn. I hate it when I'm pressed for time. Too easy to make a fatal mistake for someone."

Douglas and Ken looked puzzled.

"Big storm's coming. A real son-of-a-bitch." Everyone looked to the west. The cirrus clouds were higher above the horizon, streaking for the sky's zenith. Gray, puffy clouds began appearing along the Continental Divide.

"See here you men," Leonard had decided, "the situation is serious. Likely the man is dead. He could have fallen or drowned, but from the condition of the cabin," Leonard peered at Ken, "according to your report, I'd guess he met a bear that didn't like him.

"The women will fly out. We can't take any chances. Have them stow their gear in the chopper and climb in. We don't have time to drop them off at St. Mary, so you guys can pick them up tomorrow, at West Glacier."

Ann agreed with the plan. It made sense, since neither she nor Meg were trained nor well armed. But, she thought, I wish Wade Leonard would look at us just once. Just recognize that we are here. He didn't.

"Get going you two. You don't have much time to get back before the blizzard hits."

No time for good-byes. The women ran to the helicopter, threw in their packs and climbed aboard. Seconds later the vehicle was again airborne and once more became a black dot scurrying up-valley, racing the oncoming weather front to the Continental Divide.

"Here!" Gene Hodgson thrust a Winchester shotgun into Douglas's hands.

"Thanks."

Hodgson, knowing the lay of the land almost as well as Ken led the group along the trail to Elizabeth Lake.

Once, stopping to take a breather, Wade Leonard spoke, "Time's running out. If we don't find him at Elizabeth Lake we'll have to return to St. Mary and get snow equipment."

Douglas instinctively looked toward the approaching storm front. The sunbathed mass of clouds seemed no nearer. The great stone wall was blocking the oncoming weather. Thinking about that, he realized that when the buildup finally slipped over the divide the storm would rush downhill in tremendous fury.

Upstream from Dawn Mist Falls the trail continued nearly due south, while the course of the Belly River curved westward, making a rather graceful arc. Further up trail the men once again encountered the river. Even in October there were muddy, swampy spots. Hodgson stopped at one such area. "We're on the right trail. Look boys."

In the mud, partially dried, was a single, rear paw track of a large grizzly. On top of the bear's spoor a booted human footprint had destroyed much of the animal's track. Coincidentally, or was it, two twigs had fallen in such a way that they had created a cross. "Look at that, will you." Ken nearly whispered the sentence. "He did that on purpose. Placed his foot smack dab in the middle of the bear print."

All four men felt the dawning realization that what they were about to experience would not be ordinary. None of them had ever seen where a human had so purposely placed his foot upon a large grizzly paw print. People, even the most insensitive ones, made a point not to step where a grizzly had left his spoor. Such human behavior was a result of respect and awe for the animal but it also reflected ancient and not-so-ancient spiritual feelings. Superstition, some would call it.

"Who is this missing person we are looking for?" Gene Hodgson queried, puzzled at the act that had been performed.

Perhaps premonition, maybe sensing what they would find, all four checked their weapons again. Not only did Douglas make sure the Winchester was loaded but he also opened his pack, extracted the Magnum 45 and strapped the powerful revolver's gun belt around his waist. Tying the holster so that it's narrow end held snug against his thigh Douglas grinned sheepishly. "I'm kinda' scared," he admitted.

Elizabeth Lake, long, of well-proportioned shape, was a compliment to whomever it had been named after. Douglas remembered sitting with Julie, high up on the Ptarmigan Wall, looking down on Elizabeth Lake. They had marveled at the gracefulness of the shoreline, the purest of blue water, and the surface that had been unblemished by not a single breeze.

The east shore gradually met a rising slope, which slowly at first, glided upward into the forest. In contrast, the west side, the one their trail followed, rose abruptly to culminate above the glacial cirques of Natoas Peak, 8,384 feet high.

Douglas's thinking of Julie and their day at the Wall was interrupted by the searchers' arrival at the lower, northern end of the lake.

"Now what?," asked Ken, still somewhat chagrined because his search plan had been rejected.

Wade Leonard looked about the valley, his mind aware of the rapidly weakening light. When he spoke he did so mostly to clear his own mind for the decision he would have to make. "We've got three campgrounds up here. The nearest one is," he pointed to the trail leading along the eastern slope, "just a few hundred yards from where we are. The next closest one is the upper Elizabeth Lake Campground. Number three, God help us, is way up there at Helen Lake. I sure hope we find our wayward camper before we have to go to Helen. In fact, I don't think we have time."

Ken was using his binoculars, systematically scanning the eastern mountainside.

"See anything, Ken?"

"I don't know, Doug. Take a look just where the trail disappears." All four men trained their binoculars on the location.

"Seems like that's a tan, light brown something-or-other just below the trail," reported Hodgson.

"Let's go men," ordered Leonard. "We'll check out Gene's 'something-or-other.'"

They all felt it. Something more than the oppression of silence before the storm. More than the weakening sunlight and the first streamers of cloud sifting down the eastern slopes of the divide. What awaited them, there in the brown grasses of late October? A killer bear? None wanted to admit that such a creature existed. A corpse? No one wanted to find the grisly remains of the camper. Under the circumstances none felt that they could deal with a mutilated corpse. Perhaps they would find something else, more pleasant. Civilization, only a few air miles away, seemed like another very distant world. Douglas shivered and looked nervously at Ken's frightened eyes. They were on their own.

Wade Leonard knelt beside a backpack. "Boys this is weird. Looks like our missing hiker slipped off his backpack and left it here on purpose. And, then went," he looked about for clues, "where?"

Wade untied the drawstring that held the large flap in place. "Let's see what we can find.

"A ground cloth." He pulled the blue, plastic sheet from the pack's interior. "Oh, oh. Look here." One edge of the plastic had been ripped by something sharp.

Wade pulled out the next item. It was the rain flap that went over an alpine tent. "My, my. And this is torn to pieces. See." He pointed with his right index finger. "Teeth marks. Claws did this over here."

Douglas felt the dried, clear substances surrounding the teeth puncture marks. "Look's and feels like saliva."

Other items, a hat, white towel slightly muddied, and sneakers were extracted from the pack. All contained large tooth puncture holes.

Ken spoke. "But, the pack isn't damaged at all."

"Right," agreed Wade before anyone could respond. "What do we have here?" The ranger looked at his men. "Wolf Man? How do you see it?"

Douglas stroked his chin in an old man's way. "Could be," he paused, "could be that the hiker had set up camp, gone out walking, maybe to Lake Helen. When he returned he discovered that a bear had torn his camp to pieces. Hurriedly, because these things weren't folded up, he just stuffed in the main salvageable items that his pack would hold and headed out, to get away."

Wade nodded. "Good thinking. Then what?"

"Well, we didn't find his tracks going back so he either went up this trail to Redgap Pass or Ptarmigan Tunnel. Or, taking the obvious course, because his car is back at Chief Mountain Customs, he headed north and is likely in this area somewhere. Probably dead. Maybe hurt. Could be he's just scared shitless and is hiding somewhere around here."

"Any other ideas?" Wade looked at the men. Ken and Gene shook their heads sideways.

"OK. Let's go to the campground."

*

The rangers cautiously approached the camping area, not knowing what awaited them. Campsite 2 contained the remains of an alpine tent. Shreds of blue and orange cluttered the earth. One particularly large piece hung, as if purposely draped, over a limb. Besides tent pegs they found a Coleman stove glistening weakly in the soft daylight, a twisted useless mass of metal. Another pair of sneakers, bits of clothing, punctured tins of fruit and dried food containers littered the ground.

"Looks like he came back from hiking and found the camp destroyed. Musta' piled what he thought was salvageable into the pack he was carrying." Wade spoke what all four rangers had concluded. "Just as you guessed, Douglas."

"Then what?" Hodgson's question was more like a demand.

"Somewhere he met that bear," Leonard replied.

Douglas and Ken searched the area and at the same time cleaned up the campsite. Besides a huge pile of bear dung they found nothing. Wade and Gene Hodgson returned from the lake.

"Find anything?" Ken did the asking.

Leonard shook his head negatively.

The fine sleet that had been falling turned into a heavier rain. No strong winds yet. Ponchos were donned for protection. "Whew! Some shit!," Wade grimaced. Fog began forming along the shoreline.

"Look boys," Wade was in command. "We're screwed. I'd guess this one will fuck up my record. Unsolved. Christ, we can't even find the kill spot or one god damned piece of clothes that he was wearing. For all we know he is still alive." Glaring at the fog he continued. "The chopper made it in safe, so the girls are OK." He had called in their location.

They began retracing their route. That was when the bones were spotted by Douglas. "Pure luck," they all realized.

*

Douglas squatted, knees far apart, buttocks close to the ground, not noticing that his muscles were beginning to ache. Tiny gray pellets, the beginning of another sleet squall pecked harmlessly at his uncovered head. Before him, partially obscured by mud and aquatic vegetation, long bones, human bones, protruded from the black ooze of the lakeshore. Fascinated with the remains of what was not-so-long-ago a human being, he studied the scene that lay before him.

Though somewhat indistinct because of the spongy soil and decayed matter the rangers had easily identified the giant pad with its scythe-like claw marks an inch and a half in front of the main impression. The print was the spoor of a very large grizzly bear.

Ken was snapping photos of the macabre scene from all angles.

"Take plenty of black and whites, too," ordered Wade Leonard.

"Got them. Doug, hand me the plastic bags. No sense of you getting muddy too." He began extracting the long bones. There weren't many of them. Two badly chewed radius bones emerged from the mucky lakeshore and were deposited in a black bag.

"Here." Ken handed the remains to Douglas. "Tie off the end."

Next came half of a fibula, from a lower leg. The remaining four bones included a complete femur and the right thighbone of the victim. All were covered with shredded remnants of human muscle and skin.

"That's it," declared Ken.

"Only four?" Wade sounded incredulous.

"Only four." Ken washed off his forearms and hands in Elizabeth Lake's pristine water. "God. I won't forget this for a while. Here." Ken handed the second bag of remains to Douglas. "Tie off the end."

Wade Leonard was fully in command. "At least we found a body, whoever it is. Probably the hiker. That saves our necks. No son-of-a-bitch can say we abandoned a park visitor to the elements. I also got ahold of Nielsson on the radio. We devised a plan. Isn't a good one but tough shit."

Leonard was rubbing his balls. He always did that, no matter where he was, if he became anxious about something. The men could tell what he was doing under the poncho and they smiled. He ignored them and went on rubbing. Some of the tenseness had left the little group.

"He continued swearing. "This isn't some little piss-assed snow shower. That oncoming wall of black is a full-blown blizzard. A big storm means that our killer bear is going to den up real soon. They always wait for a storm. That means that the den is near here and that big son-of-a-bitch is likely staggering around, full of red meat, waiting for the snow so no one can see him enter the den." Wade took a long drink from his plastic water bottle.

"Nielsson and I agree. Likely we won't find the bear until spring. Maybe never. Maybe whatever wild hair got up his ass will go away and he'll be a 'good' bear again. Who knows? Could be he is sick and will die soon."

The men were watching his face, not certain what their boss was trying to say.

"Hell! You boys know god damned well we always try to figure out bears as if they were humans. Which they aren't. Try to think like it would. Wild. Savage. A 'B E A R'. Not a sniveling Smokey the Bear. If you do that mentally then you'll realize we can't follow his thinking. Each of us will come up with a different answer to what the killer is up to." Wade paused and added softly, "Grizzly's are too damned smart for us."

Ken was getting anxious and Wade noticed his fidgeting. "Hold your horses, Ken. We'll get out of here soon."

Wade's Army background showed. "Listen up men. Vern Nielsson and I decided. Ken's truck is back at Chief Mountain Customs. If we don't get it out today he won't be able to dig the thing out until next April. So, we are heading back the way you folks came. Down Belly River." He grinned.

Douglas was beginning to appreciate what a tough character Wade Leonard was.

"What about us?" queried Hodgson, who had caught on that only Ken and Leonard were going to Chief Mountain Customs.

"Gene, old boy, that is the fun part," grinned Leonard. The stress of thinking gone, he had stopped scratching. "We don't really know for sure whose bones these are. Not really sure. Only ninety nine percent."

"So?" questioned Hodgson.

"So maybe that Bible reading asshole got away. The cold water could keep bones and flecks of meat looking fresh for a long time. We might just have some other poor bastard's bones.

"What if the dumb ass got away? Where would he go?"

"Back to Chief Mountain to get his car," volunteered Douglas.

"Not necessarily, Wolf Man. Maybe, just maybe he was smart enough to realize that the quickest way to safety would be Ptarmigan Tunnel."

"Or Red Gap Pass," chimed in Ken.

"Sure as shit hope not. The tunnel is the shortest route out of here. From there the trail's all downhill to Swiftcurrent and safety."

"Maybe he got confused and went to Helen Lake," argued Ken.

"If he did that then it's tough titty 'cause we don't have time to get to him. Besides," added Leonard, "we are pretty certain the hiker's dead. So, Gene, you and Wolf Man get your asses on up the trail. Check out the junction to Red Gap Pass but don't go that way even if you see signs of the missing hiker. The blizzard would get you. Go for Ptarmigan Tunnel."

Ken was still arguing. "Ptarmigan Tunnel's closed. I locked it myself."

"Yeah, but when they get there the doors will be open again. Ben Widley will be waiting for them."

"Widley?" Douglas groaned. "If he knows I'm coming up he'll lock the damned doors again."

Leonard remembered what he had heard about the argument over the leg hold trap. "Yeah. He might," teased Leonard. Frowning, "You've got to stop making enemies around here Jakowski."

Douglas, seldom called by his last name, knew it was prudent to drop the subject. It was his turn to give a command. "You guys have a long haul ahead of you so give me the bones. Gene and I'll divvy up the rest of the evidence."

No one argued. The task completed, without comment, the four men set out for safety.

Hodgson and Douglas's route was a grinding uphill climb, all the way to the tunnel. The rain, with an increase in trail elevation became sleet again. Both men feared the higher, flat rock trail would glaze with ice.

"Got your crampons?" wheezed Gene.

"Are you kidding? Do you?"

Hodgson shook his head "no", then continued uphill. Soon they reached the trail junction, the other route leading to Red Gap Pass. They peered through the sleet and fog and could see nothing beyond a hundred feet or so. "I suppose, if he is alive, he'd be dumb enough to go up there," Gene conjectured.

Douglas disagreed. "He wasn't dumb. Just crazy. There's a big difference. What's left of him is in my pack."

"Hey!" Gene shouted back at Douglas, "What if the bear came this way?"

The thought of meeting a grizzly on the narrow trail sobered them completely. Douglas called ahead, "The bear isn't stupid, either. Just us." Both men wished the remote possibility hadn't been mentioned. With the ponchos on, their weapons were not handy for rapid action.

Sleet began piling on the trail, rolling in the wind to the sides of the rock-slabbed route. Soon walking would become hazardous if not impossible. "Great plan," yelled Gene, referring to Leonard's orders. Higher still, where the trail became a narrow notch on the rock wall, sleet was gradually replaced by brittle, half-melted-then-frozen-again snow. More elevation was gained. Real snowflakes dominated the vague world in which the two men struggled. Both were relieved to see the snow.

Up, up, higher yet, the trail led them toward the tunnel. Snow had meant temporary safety from the danger of ice but they encountered powerful winds, blowing with hurricane force, whipping the packs about them, nearly throwing the men off balance. Douglas considered taking the loose poncho off but decided that the rubberized material provided protection, holding in some of the warmth his body was releasing.

Half a foot of snow piled up on their route. Halfway to their destination the depth became ten inches. Their situation was becoming grim again. Neither could see more than eight feet ahead. They had to concentrate on taking steps to prevent nausea and disorientation for there seemed to be no up or down in the white world about them.

Douglas could see only a vague black shape, snow splattered legs with booted feet rising and falling ahead of him. His nose ran profusely and the arctic chill of the powerful winds brought tears to his eyes. Yet, Wolf Man felt an exhilaration, all tension gone. Powerful leg muscles, protected by woolen trousers, flexed, relaxed, flexed, relaxed, carrying Douglas ever higher up the face of the cliff. He experienced joy in feeling the power of his body. Gene must have been experiencing the same sort of thrill for he quickened the pace slightly. His snow-blurred movements became easier and rhythmic.

Beyond Douglas's companion the trail appeared to be angling somewhat to the west. They must be near the tunnel entrance. Gene stopped suddenly causing Douglas to collide into his snow-covered body. Through the large white snowflakes, no longer assaulted by the main force of the storm, they recognized the heavy, black iron doors of the north entrance of Ptarmigan Tunnel, the sharp contrast of darkness seeming to block any further progress. The doors were closed.

Just outside the entrance, covered by several feet of snow, an odd shape huddled against a man-made stone wall. The two men looked at one-another questioningly. Sheltered from the winds they were able to hear a peculiar sound emanating from the snow-pile. Both grinned. The weird noise was someone snoring.

Hodgson brushed the snow away, revealing the just-awakened face of Ben Widley. He groaned. "Hi, boys. Decided I'd take a snooze while I waited. Brought my fart sack along so I wouldn't freeze." Widley crawled out and rolled up the down bag. "Had to shut the doors to keep the snow from drifting in."

The three men kicked the snow back from the tunnel entrance just enough to pull one of the doors open so they could squeeze through. Inside, the darkness enveloped them in a bone-chilling cold. Widley and Gene, in unison, slammed the door shut, causing an echoing, clanging noise. Secured, the lock was snapped shut. Ptarmigan Tunnel was once again closed and would remain so until the heat of next summer's sun melted the snow.

*

CHAPTER 11

October 31, 1984

"Not only were we glad to see Ben Widley, which I never thought I would be, but we walked out of the dark tunnel's south entrance and there were three horses waiting to take us down the mountain. Boy, did they look good to me."

Douglas added, "The ride down was beautiful. Surprisingly, there was little wind. Wet snow clung to the trees and covered everything in a mantle of white."

Vern Nielsson slapped his knee, experiencing in his mind the beauty of the Wilber Creek drainage. His wife, Evelyn sat next to Wolf Man, on the couch. Their two daughters sat on the floor, Cindy with her back against Vern's chair and Carolyn sprawled on the rug beside the coffee table. Nielsson cleared his throat. "Wish Henry was here. What did Martha say, Mother?"

"Henry is over at Duck Lake again. Something about some Alberta fishermen misbehaving."

Vern scowled. Absentmindedly he straightened the already perfectly positioned magazines on his reading table. "Guess we might as well get on with it. Cindy, will you take notes of what's said?" Not waiting for affirmation he looked at Douglas. "She can write in short hand, you know."

"Not much more to report, Vern. Just those human long bones. Hardly a scrap of tissue on them. And, no clothing. That's what got us the most. Not a thread anywhere in the area. I just don't see how a bear could do that.

Vern thought a moment. "That particular grizzly was upset about something. Just think of the condition the cabin was in. No overwhelming scent of food there, no bacon, no sweets. Yet, that bear not only tore the shutters off the window but he ripped the door open too. I've got a feeling he was just plain sick. Worms, maybe."

"Oh, Daddy!" protested Carolyn.

"Well, Honey, that's reality. That poor old bear might have a gut full of worms that is consuming most of the food he's eating. Not only did his stomach maybe hurt but he could have been starving to death."

Douglas didn't say that the search team had also thought about parasites.

Evelyn asked, "Did Wade collect any droppings to check?"

"In fact he did." Looking at Douglas, Vern asked, "You boys found some bear poop at the campground too, didn't you?"

"Daddy!" protested Carolyn again. She was teasing.

Vern smiled. He loved to have his women scold him.

Douglas, no longer shy in their presence, reached out and took three oatmeal cookies from the plate. The women exchanged glances of humor.

"You see, Douglas, I can write this death off as the result of human stupidity, not really a killer bear. Not the result of another human being involved. This killing was different than the others we are investigating."

"I agree, Vern. Especially with the Bible stuff."

"Yes. Well, tell us about that. Give us the details on the religious aspect of the case."

"OK," he agreed. He sat silent for a time, recalling the events as they had transpired.

"We were searching along the shoreline of Elizabeth Lake. Just a little ways from the waterline Gene Hodgson found the Bible." Reaching for a paper bag Douglas explained, "I brought it along. Thought you'd like to see it." He took the book out of the brown paper and unzipped a clear plastic freezer bag. "Here." He handed the black leather-bound Bible to his superior. The girls and Evelyn crowded around Vern so they could see the object.

"If you notice, the four fangs went into the Bible, nearly all the way through. The two upper canines penetrated the front. See," he pointed, "the top incisors also went through." Turning the Bible over, he continued. "The lower canines also penetrated. The bottom incisors merely scratched the cover. That wasn't a very powerful bite. Neither did the bear rip the pages. What we have here is a clean penetration and release. Not the act of a mad grizzly. I'd guess the man dropped the Bible at this point."

"Dropped?" inquired Cindy. "You mean the Bible was up off the ground?"

"That's exactly what I mean." He reached into the sack again. "We found this letter still folded neatly within the Bible. No teeth marks." Carefully he opened the white page of notepaper. "It reads:

October 28, 1984
Dear Mother,
I have found the Beast.
You will be glad to know that I am going to seek
him out and destroy the Anti-Christ once and for all.

131

Blessed be Jesus Christ.
Your loving son, Moses

"Doesn't make sense does it?" asked Douglas. "How did he get The Beast connected to the Anti-Christ?"

"Moses," repeated Evelyn. The victim's name had not been mentioned before the letter was read.

"Yes, Moses," responded Vern. "His name was Moses Jolly. From Dallas."

Douglas handed Vern the letter. "There's more."

"Oh? What else did you find?"

"Find is right. When I got home last night I went through the whole Bible looking for information. Didn't find a thing, not even his name. That is until, almost at the end, in the book of Revelations, there were certain verses neatly underlined with pencil. Can I read them to you?"

Nielsson waved Douglas on.

"OK. Let me get my notebook out." He reached once more into the brown bag. "Here it is. The first one." He found the page upon which he had copied the verses.

"The Book of Revelation, Chapter 11, vs. 7. Jolly underlined the following:

'When they have finished their testimony, the beast that comes up from the abyss will wage war against them and kill them.'"

Douglas's voice, purposely dramatic, chilled the room. When he finished the verse, he was met with silence. All were looking at him.

"Ahem," he wiped is lips with his right hand. "And the next one:
'Revelation, Chapter 13, 2nd verse.

'The beast I saw was like a leopard, but it had feet like a bear's, and its mouth was like the mouth of a lion.'"

Vern spoke. "I can visualize what happened. This man, Moses Jolly, was a religious fanatic of sorts. He came to Glacier because he had read Night of the Grizzly or the Saturday Evening Post story or something else as gruesome. So, Moses had decided that evil was here, in Glacier. Evil being the beast."

"Yeah," agreed Douglas. "Let me read this to you. The last one marked."

"Thank goodness," whispered Evelyn.

"'Revelation, Chapter 13, 18th verse.

"'Wisdom is needed here; one who understands can calculate the number of the beast, for it is a number that stands for a person. His number is six hundred and sixty six.'"

"Oh," moaned someone. The daughters had moved to the couch, one on each side of their Mother so they could touch her for comfort. Douglas, crowded, had slid to the floor.

"That's it, Vern."

"Yes. Well. Tell me what you think happened."

"Jolly had set himself up as the World's savior; the chosen one to rid the planet of Satan. OK?"

"I agree so far. Go on." Vern was proud of the young man.

"So, like you said, he came to Glacier and went into the back country looking for the Beast, sees a giant paw print, somewhere along the Belly River. Maybe another one at Helen or Elizabeth Lake. That was his big opportunity. Moses Jolly goes hunting for the Beast with the Bible as his only weapon.

"No luck. No Beast anywhere. But, when he gets back to his camp he finds it destroyed." Douglas paused, thought a moment and then continued.

"I'd guess that the condition of the camp upset him somewhat. It would me. Maybe he began to realize that he wasn't the Savior after all. Maybe he was really scared. I don't know." He paused again.

"And? What next, Wolf Man?"

Douglas smiled slightly for Vern had called him by his nickname.

"What happened next could be that Moses panicked. Stuffed all that useless stuff into his pack and lit out for safety.

"Just a guess, but I think he met the bear low in the trail to Redgap Pass. He turned and hurried down to the lake. The bear, likely only walking fast, was catching up. Instinctively Moses turned toward his old campsite. A mistake. He should have headed north. No matter. The grizzly was closing in.

"Now his only chance was God."

"He could have climbed a tree," suggested Carolyn.

"Well, yeah. Maybe. But, that guy really didn't know much about surviving out there."

"Then what?" Vern was enjoying watching his protégé think things out.

"Uh, well, then he placed his pack on the ground. Takes out the Bible and moves toward the grizzly. About that time he must have known he couldn't get away and he must have been terrified. He realized he wasn't facing the Beast but a live very wild animal that was going to kill him. The beast was a real, physical grizzly that was pissed off about something."

Douglas realized his verbal error. Everyone ignored the remark.

"You know, he could have been yelling. Praying loudly. Anything to bolster his spirits. The bear simply walks up, not running, and Jolly uses the only weapon he has, the Bible. He stuffs it in the beast's mouth.

"No miracle happens. God doesn't strike the grizzly dead. Big mistake. Woops. So, he runs."

"You can't outrun a bear." Carolyn stated what they all knew.

"That's right," agreed Douglas. "Wade Leonard thinks the victim ran into the lake and that's why we didn't find a kill spot. No blood."

"No bear can eat 180 pounds of meat and bones at one meal. But, figures Wade, in his fury the grizzly could have dismembered the body and dragged the arm and leg pieces up to shallow water for a feast."

"Now, I know that doesn't make sense. No clothes and all."

"Perhaps Mr. Jolly was naked." Cindy blushed as she spoke.

Vern beamed with satisfaction.

Douglas thought about that. "Yeah. You know it could be. He could have neatly piled his clothing somewhere and we just didn't find it. But, we're never going to know anymore. If we find anything in the way of evidence it won't be until when Vern?"

"Late June or early July, maybe."

"Yeah. Well." He had concluded his report.

Vern nibbled on a cookie. Crumbs fell on his massive chest.

"Daddy." Evelyn nodded toward her husband's shirt.

"Oh. Yes." Absentmindedly he brushed them off onto the rug. The simple unconscious act brought lightness back to the group. One of the daughters laughed softly.

Vern was thinking. "Douglas, the season is over. That old bear has likely denned up. If he does have a mass of internal parasites, he could die before spring. My guess is that we will never find him. I hope not." Most of what Vern said was repetitive.

"What I want you to do is drive down to Bozeman and have the lab people check the bones carefully. I'll handle the Bible, letter and other personal effects. Widley's men got Moses Jolley's vehicle out of the parking lot up at Chief Mountain, before the snows drifted it in. Barely made it. Hannibal's men will check the car over but we don't expect to find anything that will help our case.

"You remember Helen Grigsby?"

"Yes. She's the Assistant Personnel Officer that spoke to us during the Seasonal Training."

"That's right," Vern smiled. "She brought your payroll check over yesterday along with a letter for me from the Superintendent.

Douglas, I was ordered to send you home until after the holidays. From what I understand Fish and Wildlife want's you for a short-term project at Tule Lake, California. Something about Snow Geese. You'll report back here in April or May, depending on how much money I can get."

Douglas appeared pleased. Then his brows furrowed. "Can I have my trailer back next year?"

"Yes. I prefer that." Nielsson hesitated, glanced at the women and finally asked, "What about Ann?"

Wolf Man's face crimsoned. "We are good friends."

"Yes," agreed Nielsson. "So it seems."

The living room remained silent for some time.

"Will Ann be back next summer?" Douglas inquired.

"Very likely. If she wants to. I can recommend that she be re-hired but I don't have the direct jurisdiction over seasonal naturalist hiring."

"I appreciate you doing that. Thank you."

More silence.

"Well, Mrs. Nielsson thanks for the refreshments. Guess I'll see you folks next year then."

The Nielssons didn't like good-byes so they were not verbally exchanged. Carolyn escorted Douglas to the door just as she had done on his first evening in the park. "Good bye, Wolf Man." She kissed his cheek. "We love you."

Flustered, he stumbled out the door. Damn! he thought. She does that to me every time.

*

Deep within the primeval forest that bordered Medicine Grizzly Lake, the Great Bear stood, observing the large fluffy snowflakes drifting lazily downward. Lowering his massive head the giant licked a thin layer of accumulated snow from a fallen Spruce. The act was refreshing, somewhat clearing his sleepy head. Lazy, stupor-like, the fat creature wobbled slowly toward the rock outcropping with a split limestone cavern at its base. The Great Bear had chosen the site for his hibernation den.

Nearly to his destination he stopped and began snuffling in huge masses of the chilling air. Just as had happened in the springtime, when the grizzly exhaled, clouds of condensed moisture whirled about his head. Only this time, denning up time, the bear-made clouds were ignored.

No danger sounds found his ears. Only clean scents of forest and dampness met his olfactory nerves. The snow thickened. Not so far above, the winds were picking up in intensity. Instinct told the Great Bear that the approaching storm would be the one that would seal the land with a frozen white blanket that would last until spring. His senses and training told him that under cover of the storm his den was secure. He would not be seen entering the black slit opening to the little cave.

The bear's instinct was in error. The Great Bear was observed. Dark eyes watched from another rocky outcropping, downwind from the den. The eyes belonged to another creature, one that had observed the den selection two days previous. The creature had memorized the lay of the land. He knew what the area would look like under a winter accumulation of snow. Almost toothless, the leering figure carefully stalked toward Atlantic Creek, not far from the den. His gaunt frame, tall and graceful, swung along displaying great strength and endurance. The felt hat, speckled with snow, sported a lone jet-black raven's feather.

Hunkering down deeper into the folds of the blanket that covered his shoulders, Fang began softly chanting an ancient song of the Old Ones, those of the evil spirits.

*

CHAPTER 12

February 1985, Dayton, Ohio

On a Friday evening the Jakowskis' attended the Dayton Ballet at the old, decaying Victory Theater. Peeling walls, faded, worn stage curtains, and yes, even a few broken seats could not and did not detract from the elegance, the history, the memories that the great old structure contained.

They arrived early. Catherine loved to watch the crowd. Actively involved in supporting the ballet, she spoke of the old days.

"My sisters and friends used to come here on Saturday afternoons. Eat popcorn. Always sat up in the balcony." She turned as if to make sure the balcony was still there. "Sometimes we would come in the evening, sneaking in greasy hamburgers and fries. As long as we bought a coke and popcorn the management ignored us.

"Little kids, down in the front row, just behind the orchestra pit, would throw popcorn on to the stage so they could watch the rats scuttle out to feed."

"Suppose there are rats here now, Mother?"

"Lord, I hope not! No, not up here. Maybe down in the catacombs, where the old dressing rooms are located."

"Mother, do you remember a long time ago, a story you told us kids about this theater being haunted. You were kidding weren't you?"

"No. Not that time. Of course I don't know if the stories are true." Catherine paused, as if finished with the topic.

"Well? Are you going to tell me again, or aren't you?"

"Not much to it. The story goes that someone committed suicide by jumping off the balcony."

"That's not much of a fall."

"Look. I just tell them. I don't explain them."

Douglas laughed, realizing his mother was the source of the response he used so often. "So what's scary about that? A little fall."

"In the days when we came to see the Three Stooges and other B and C movies, really corn-ball stuff, attendance was way down. The story goes that sometimes during the week, when nobody was in the balcony, the projectionist, the man running the projector, would look out of one of those little rectangular windows and sometimes he would see a man standing off to the right, a few rows down, just standing there, looking in at him."

"I bet that scared him, didn't it?"

"No. As a matter of fact, no. The movie operator didn't feel threatened so he'd look back. A couple of times, I think, the operator went outside of his booth, into the balcony, but the figure had vanished."

Catherine had warmed to the topic.

"I remember a school group coming here to investigate poltergeists, ghosts, whatever. They were from Beavercreek or Vandalia or somewhere like that. A suburban group. No silliness like Ouji Boards or Tarot Cards.

"Their teacher taught psychology. Several adults were chaperoning the venture. They had rather sophisticated electronic sensory equipment. Don't ask me what that included."

"Ghost busters," exclaimed Douglas.

His mother stopped talking.

"Hey, don't leave me hanging. What happened?"

"Nothing much. The group camped out on the stage. Slept in sleeping bags. "During the night they heard peculiar noises such as footsteps echoing from the dressing rooms below."

She halted again.

"And?"

"The recorders were on all night. They played the tapes back. Although the investigators couldn't make out any words they had recorded human-like voices. Men and women. Mostly a man's voice."

Douglas pondered that. Again the supernatural stuff like the coyote on the Duck Lake Road. "What do you think about the stories, Mother?"

"Me? Think about them?" She frowned. "Well, I have a very deep faith in God, as you know. I also believe we modern products of evolution, we Western Civilization Citizens, worshipers of Freud, Darwin, physics, mathematics and so-forth, have discarded and refuse to consider very large segments of what reality includes."

"Like what?"

The house lights had dimmed. Catherine interrupted their conversation. "Now, watch, Dear. Over on the right aisle. Just before the program begins."

Recorded music emanated from behind stage. The first ballet segment of Dance Overture was about to begin. The audience became silent, attentive, waiting for the dance to commence.

Two female figures flustered down the right aisle, one a middle-aged woman, the companion in her late twenties.

"Douglas, watch what they do before they sit down."

The women's seats were located front row, just a little to the right of center. They reached their reserved Row A, Seats Seven and Eight. Stage light reflecting on them. They turned, faced the audience for a moment and then sat down.

Catherine laughed softly. "We are here, everyone. You may start the program now."

"Well I'll be damned," exclaimed Douglas all too loudly. Embarrassed, he unintentionally pulled on the aisle arm of his seat. It came off in his hands.

"That scenario, my dear Son, is played out at the beginning of every program they attend."

*

The five-part Dance Overture concluded. House lights brightened slightly to allow late arrivals to find their seats. The soft pleasant glow enabled Douglas to read.

"Look, Mother," he pointed to his program. "What is Schubertiade?"

"I'm not sure. Hazel called to tell me that Gregory Robinson was filling in on the male part. He's the Black dancer that did the Spanish thing."

"Yes. Powerful man." He loved teasing his mother. "He has nice buns, eh, Mother?"

Unashamed, Catherine responded. "Yes, I love to watch him move."

"Steptegean," explained Douglas.

"What?"

"Steptegean," he repeated. "Some groups of people, especially from Black Africa, have big butts. They store fatty tissue in their buns for sparse times, when there is a food shortage. It's a survival thing."

"You scientists! Ruin everything, even romance. Just shut up and watch." She was a little angry.

A moment later she spoke again, summing up her previous discussion. "Anyway, with Barbara Pontecorvo and Gregory Robinson dancing together, Schubertiade will be fantastic. They are such powerful dancers."

Her declaration was an understatement. The Old Victory Theater lights lowered to darkness. Curtains rolled noisily open revealing the two dancers statuesque, waiting for the music to begin.

Not gradually, but all at once the audience was captivated with the sensuous, muscular undulations, swift, expressive, rhythmic movements.

The dance was not coarse or offensive. Yet, undeniably the movements reflected lovemaking, basic passions, desires, even the act itself, without displaying obscenity. The dullest husband, the most frigid wife, knew, fantasized, and experienced the passions their eyes beheld.

Quickly, all too soon, the dance ended.

The audience, stunned, sat in silence. Somewhere in the balcony a lone man began applauding, thus breaking the spell. Pandemonium broke loose. In mass the theatergoers rose to their feet and cheered, whistled, and enthusiastically clapped their hands.

Douglas looked at his beautiful, still-young mother. She was wiping tiny beads of sweat from her upper lip. "My God!" she gasped.

How magnificent the experience had been. The audience would never forget Schubertiade.

Intermission

Regaining their composure, couples began moving to the aisles. Some hurried outside to smoke. Others, to cool off in the February chill. Women dared look into their companion's eyes with obvious desire. Some men, a few, their macho self images shattered, avoided their spouse's, girl friend's or mistress's looks of passion. They didn't like not being in control.

Here and there, secretly mostly, male couples held hands. A few women clasped their female lover's fingers in tender embrace. Schubertiade had made the night a time for love.

*

During the intermission, sitting nearly alone in their down-front seats, left side, Douglas and Catherine gazed at the viewing box, which was slightly above and in front of them. They couldn't help doing so for the suspended room was just a mere fifty feet away. Douglas's gaze drifted back to the orchestra pit. Just at that moment, his mother's hand grasped his wrist, closing tightly. He followed the direction her eyes were looking and found himself once again peering into the box seat area.

The tiny observation room was no longer empty. Obscured somewhat by deeper shadows a grayish, male figure stood looking down upon them. Somehow, the face was visible, clear in features. Chalky skin, hollow, black eyes, slightly ruffled hair, a trace of a smile (or was it a smirk?) on the thin lips. The specter glared down at them, not really malevolent but somehow threatening.

Mother and son both felt, they knew, the obscure figure was looking directly at Douglas. Almost imperceptibly the head nodded, as if in recognition and then, with the rest of the form, it slowly faded away.

*

"Every year I get a mid-January chill and I don't warm up until May," Douglas complained. "I've got three more months of misery ahead of me."

"Cheer up, Douglas. You'll be heading for Oregon in a few weeks." Mrs. Jakowski wheeled her car around the corner as she spoke. The red Porsche splashed up Brown Street spewing out scissortails of repugnant, gray mush.

The young man shook his head in displeasure. The ugliness, the filthy, monotonous slush was everywhere. Parked autos wore irregular coatings of various degrees of melted ice, snow and sickening smears of salt from the treated streets.

"This stuff will rust your car right out from under you," he grumbled.

"So? I'll get a new one."

Douglas gazed at the pavement parallel to the street. Sidewalks were no better, long ribbons of mushy gray melt-water, lighter stretches of re-frozen snow, and a few concrete rectangles of dry, bare pavement. It seemed the merchants were attempting to provide their customers with safe walking in front of, at least, some of the stores.

Down the hill from Dayton's south suburbs slid an electric trolley, sparks showering like minute fireworks each time the wheels rolling on the overhead wires hit a wet contact. Douglas's mother swerved her car in order to avoid the yellow vehicle's spray.

Splat! The Porsche's windshield sported a thick layer of muck.

"Good shot." She was laughing.

"Well, it's your car. Not mine."

She ignored her son. "Look there! That white vehicle is pulling out." She wheeled in to the just vacated parking space that was parallel to Brown Street. "Good timing, eh?"

Douglas was enjoying being a complainer so he ignored her good fortune. "Mother, why don't you back up a little bit so the front wheel will slip off the curb?"

"Who wants to be perfect?"

"Me."

"That is what a Mother gets for taking her good-looking son out on the town. Now look. Don't call me 'Mother.' I want them to think I've still got enough pizzazz to interest the young men."

"You do, Mother. You do."

Before she could open the driver's door Douglas had hurried around the car, through the wetness, to help her out. Beaming, because of the courtesy, she said, "Chauvinist."

"Yes, Mother. You love it."

Brown Street became a challenging barrier of ice and water. Holding his mother's arm, Douglas supported her so that her tiny feet wouldn't slip. He felt the ice water filling his left shoe and coldly penetrating the other.

Douglas really hated winter in the city. His jesting was not all a charade. Every Ohio city, every mid-western city, was to some degree like Dayton. Cincinnati was gray. Columbus's sidewalks and streets were a mess. Cleveland's pavements were also gray but frozen solid. All were disgustingly dirty.

Slicing along the darkened storefronts the chill, penetrating, damp winds sought out openings in coat collars, sleeves, and swept unmercifully up ladies dresses. Catherine pressed closer to her son's giant frame, seeking protection from the turbulence.

The Jakowskis reached the restaurant's doorway, encountering two couples exiting.

"We could have waited," protested one of the women.

"What? Wait an hour and a half? No steak's worth—-" His words blew southward, riding on a particularly strong gust of arctic chill.

The entryway, dimly lit and feeling colder than outside encouraged the young man and his mother to hurry into the restaurant proper.

"God, it's dark in here," Douglas grumbled.

"Now let me do the talking and stop complaining. Let's have some fun. I haven't been in here for half-a-year or more." Catherine was beaming with anticipation.

The elegantly dressed hostess smiled at the couple from out of the gloom. Recognizing the local celebrity, she greeted, "Good evening Mrs. Jakowski. Are you here for dinner?"

"Yes. We came for two of the best steaks in town."

The hostess was looking Douglas over as she spoke. "I'm sorry but there will be a ninety-minute wait. Why don't you go into the bar and have some drinks?" Her voice sounded more like a recorded command than a question.

"We don't drink," smiled Catherine. "Douglas and I will just have to wait right here, by the door."

"Oh. Very well. I'll put your name down on the waiting list." The hostess turned away.

"Mother, why did you say that? I need a drink."

"You don't need a drink, Dear. Trust me. We won't be waiting long. Besides, the way Madeline looked you up and down something must be wrong. Check your fly, son. You aren't that handsome."

Both laughed. They were mother and son, but just as important Douglas and Catherine were good friends.

Twice the entryway door opened as more customers entered. Each time Douglas shivered. Under his breath, he uttered his favorite word of frustration.

"Mrs. Jakowski." The hostess was calling to them. "I've found you a table." She was smiling as if she had performed a miracle. "Follow me please."

"See?" smiled Catherine.

"At least she didn't say, 'Walk this way.'"

"Enjoy it, Douglas. Enjoy it."

They were guided through the gloomy smoke-filled room to a small booth where they could watch the activities in the bar area.

"Thank you, Madeline." Catherine unobtrusively slipped the young woman a ten.

"This is great, Mom. I'm not used to dating a celebrity."

"Money talks, Honey. They love my money, not me. There isn't anything wrong with being civil and generous."

Douglas smelled a fragrant odor. Looking up his eyes took in the exciting vision of a beautiful waitress. "Are you ready to order, Mrs. Jakowski?"

"No. Of course not." Catherine smiled throwing Douglas an impish look. "We'll have a few drinks first. You order for us, Douglas."

He did and the waitress hurried toward the bar.

"You see, my giant son, the management doesn't approve of customers milling around the entryway. If they can't make money off of you at the bar they get rid of you by finding you a seat."

Noise from the bar; loud laughter, some of it shrieking, some booming, most slightly inebriated good humor; people yelling across tables so their companions could hear them; shadows, dark, some almost diaphanous, lights emitting feeble projections that became trapped in the bluish smog of a hundred cigarettes, penetrating but a short distance. Douglas couldn't see the color of his Old Fashion. A Martini would have been a better choice, not so sweet.

Mother and son fell silent, overwhelmed by noise and the closeness of several hundred well-dressed, perfumed bodies. Douglas should have felt claustrophobic but he didn't. The winter evening had been what he missed most when he was in the West, culture, man-created beauty, being a part of a thriving, successful society. The bars of Babb and St. Mary belonged to another world, faraway on an alien planet.

The second round of drinks arrived. In the sanctuary of the crowded restaurant he sipped some Vodka. The woman watched him, proud of her son's masculinity, as he put the Martini to his sensuous lips.

"Ahh. That's better. Not so sweet." He swizzled the two large olives; gently marinating them in the powerful Vodka. "Here, Mother, have an olive."

How beautiful her delicate fingers were. Had they been a little darker they could have been Julie's. Quickly he snapped the intrusion from his mind. Thoughts of her were becoming less and less frequent.

"I've been reliving the ballet," explained Catherine.

"Me too. Thanks, Mom, for taking me."

She gave him the soft smile he loved so well. "You're welcome."

The woman's features changed slightly. "Have you given any thought to the man we saw in the box?"

"Not yet. What do you make of it?" He shivered and took another swallow of the Vodka. "What did it mean, Mother?"

She didn't answer.

Douglas recalled that last summer a coyote on the Duck Lake Road had performed the same eye contact, the same look of impending danger.

They continued to lounge in their little booth, casually watching their neighboring diners. Somehow, they both were enjoying the shadowy, smoky atmosphere surrounding them. "You have been home for a week and haven't filled me in on what you and your Indian friend have discovered." Catherine had become serious again.

"Nothing. We have found no sign of the missing visitors. Not one bone. Not one piece of clothing."

Catherine frowned. "Could bears do that? Not leaving any evidence behind?"

"Absolutely not. Maybe once, like that crazy religious guy I told you about, but not five more times. Not even twice. Bears do not purposely hide clothing and equipment." Douglas grinned. "You know that, Mother."

"Of course I do. That leaves murder as the only solution."

"Right." Douglas's smile faded. "We don't have a single suspect. No one with a good motive."

"How about Henry Two Feathers?"

Douglas's features reflected his pleasure in discussing Henry. "The Deputy Sheriff? He's something else. A real gentleman. You'd love him, Mother. He and his wife, Martha, are fantastic. As for Henry, well, it's hard to explain but we have become very close. Almost father and son. We respect each other a great deal."

"Good. You need that kind of a relationship, even at your age." Catherine wished Steven, her husband was still alive. The thought wasn't new. Every day she missed him.

"So," she tried to get away from thinking of her loss, "Where does the investigation stand?"

"Just a few weak suspects. Mostly Henry's. All very iffy. I have a few too. The Swift Current Ranger is an..." He stopped.

"Ass Hole, dear. Don't be shy." Catherine was teasing.

"Yeah." he laughed then continued. "A big, skinny Blackfeet nicknamed Fang. I'm watching him best I can. Henry says it isn't Fang. Probably right. What would the motive be except plain meanness?"

Douglas thought about what he had just said.

"And?" Catherine urged him on.

"Oh, I thought a seasonal might be our man. Although he hates me, he did me a real big favor. Maybe the killer or killers are some of the others on the West side who don't like me and I don't know why. Doesn't make sense.

"Henry is watching a good half-dozen suspects, some White and some Indian, who live on the reservation. Nothing concrete. That's just about it."

Catherine caught his hidden meaning. "Just about?"

"Yeah." He waved away a cloud of smoke from a nearby booth.

"Go on."

"Oh, you don't want to hear about it."

She waited for him to continue.

"OK. The cattle mutilation I wrote you about. Remember?"

She nodded that she did.

"I sometimes wonder if...." He stopped.

"Yes? You wonder what?"

Douglas felt slightly embarrassed. "It's only that I know the mutilations are real. What really convinced me was when the tissue samples I sent to my friend disappeared. Right there in the university lab." Nervous, Douglas waved the waitress over and ordered another Martini.

"What you are talking about Dear, is UFOs."

"Aw, Jeeze. I hate that phrase. Call them something else will you?"

"Is that what you think, Douglas? Visitors, aliens, whatchamacallits; they are responsible for the missing people?"

"No!" he frowned. "I mean, yes. Maybe. Who knows? The whole thing is crazy. Except for my new friends and the beautiful park I wish I'd never become involved in the investigation. Now I'm stuck. I'm no cop. I told Nielsson that."

"What did he say?"

"The first time he listened. After that, he simply ignored me."

"Worse yet," he continued, "there are jealousies involved. People are out to discredit Vern. I'm sure some wish I'd just go away. I make them nervous. Henry says the Blackfeet really respect me." He paused grinning, "Except for those I've pissed off."

He looked up realizing he shouldn't have said that. "Sorry, Mom."

"That's OK, Dear. This time."

He wasn't certain whether she was scolding or not.

The steaks arrived. Although they could not see them in the gloom, the meat was delicious, incomparable in flavor. With his mouth full, he mumbled, "Well worth waiting for."

*

February, 1985

Far up the headwaters of the Missouri River, even beyond the vast snow and ice-bound high plains, where the North Fork of Cut Bank Creek reaches higher still in a southwestern sweep toward Morning Star Lake, there is a meeting of waters.

Beneath five or so feet of snow a stream, another tributary of the Cut Bank flowed gently in darkness, awaiting the thaws of spring when the trickle would become a roaring torrent.

The human, an ominous, gaunt-looking, lightless figure, bent under a heavy burden, crunched its web-footed way up-valley, following the landmarks created over the centuries by Atlantic Creek.

146

Heavy snow filled the exhilarating air with soft, downy flakes of exquisite design and variety. Hardly a sound was discerned, except for the wind up high, far up the slopes of Triple Divide and Mt. James peaks.

Sensing his location, Clarence Kipp, nicknamed Fang, spoke to himself. "Triple Divide. Let's see. The snow coming down, depending on where it falls, will, in springtime, melt and flow westward down Pacific Creek to the great ocean of the same name. Or," he continued, "maybe the snow will be on the north face of Triple Divide Peak. Then the water will descend to Hudson Bay Creek, then to St. Mary Lakes, the river of the same name, to Alberta, and eventually enter Hudson Bay. The only thing left is Atlantic Creek, which drains into the Missouri and the Mississippi. If that happens then the water will mix with the warm semi-tropical Gulf of Mexico."

Clarence, the black, snow-splotched being, smiled at his knowledge for he was very intelligent and well-read. He was self-taught, to a large extent. The walls of his well-insulated shack were lined with books. Not the classics. Not of science or math, but volumes of history, native lore, geography, even psychology. He had experienced his knowledge of natural history rather than obtain it from books.

Neglected by an alcoholic mother, father unknown, he had been rejected by all of society, even by the few he called friends.

The Indian adjusted the stiffening body inside the Hudson Bay blanket. Even he, Fang, was tiring from the exertion of snow shoeing up the valley with nearly two hundred pounds on his back.

"Chinga," he swore, using the only Spanish word in his vocabulary. Not far now. The lake should be up ahead. Just a short struggle remained. The tragic man's destination was not Medicine Grizzly Lake. He looked about for the landmark, a badly lightning-blasted top of a hemlock.

There it was. The tree. Shorter looking. Partially buried under the snow. Shattered top swaying in some unseen current, half a hundred feet above him.

The den lay hidden against the hillside, beneath the long, snow-blanketed limestone crack.

Comprehending what the Great Bear would do when it emerged from the long sleep, Fang tossed the bundle off his shoulders, careful to grasp the red and white blanket so that the cloth unrolled sending the naked, dark-skinned corpse deep into the snow. "Fucking Comanche," Fang hissed.

With an almost sadistic effort, the Indian rolled the dead man over so he was spread-eagled, legs upslope, arms out nearly straight at the sides. The task was difficult in the soft snow and he gasped for air, inhaling the oxygen-rich, snow-sprinkled gasses.

"Ha!" To Fang the scene was funny. The man's genitals were exposed, whitening fast. "Maybe," the wild man mumbled, "A raven will peck your pecker, you son-of-a-bitch!" Throwing back his head the man, believing that he was possessed by the evil ones, screamed his passion into the muffled sky.

Tightening the thongs on the snowshoes, he began chanting a medicine song, one not heard often by the Blackfeet, or anyone else. He sang of his guardian, the evil one; ancient verses praising the hairy giant he knew lived not so very far away.

In contempt for White Men and for the spirit of the slain Comanche, Clarence yelled, "Sasquatch!"

Within a deeper darkness, far down in the stone crack den, the Great Bear stirred. Somewhere far above, up above the snow, eerie notes of a flute weakly permeated the heavy atmosphere. The Medicine Grizzly grunted irritably, rolled his massive head upside down and placed a paw over the exposed right ear.

Unknown to the Great Bear, a springtime meal lay freezing in the snows above, awaiting its inevitable consummation.

*

CHAPTER 13

May, 1985

Back in his dilapidated trailer along the shores of Lower St. Mary Lake, still without running water, Douglas sat in his rodent-infested recliner chair and waited, his trusty Red Ryder BB Gun pumped and ready for a mouse to appear. The depression over what he had found at Tule Lake waned and he laughed to himself because he was holding his Dad's old toy gun, ready to wipe out the first moving rodent that showed it's beady eyes. "To hell with politicians, sportsmen and developers."

Thoughts of his father carried his thinking back to his home. The Jakowski house was unpretentious but very comfortable, reflecting the good taste of his mother and father. The latter was dead. Vietnam hadn't killed Steven. His father had fallen asleep while driving home from Cleveland. He had simply gone off the freeway at seventy-five miles an hour and died.

Home, was in a southern suburb of the sprawling Dayton, Ohio metropolitan area. The tiny community, Oakwood, surviving among it's giant neighbors only because of the wealth of the inhabitants, possessed a pleasant, yet somewhat unimaginative name. Many, including the Jakowskis, simply called their city "The Dome."

Outsiders called the village "The Dome" too, but not usually with affection. The simple fact was that the small community had everything it's citizens needed so there was no point in going elsewhere. Some, a few, never left their sanctuary. Although Douglas disliked urban living and the arrogance of the well to do, he did respect and at times enjoy many of the residents of "The Dome."

The few high school friends he kept in touch with had done well; most of them. There were a couple of lawyers, one doctor, and several young business executives. One or two had gone off to the Peace Corps, the military, and a very close friend, the Senior Class President, was successfully driving a taxi in New York City. That was what he wanted to do and Douglas was happy for him.

His acquaintances of his own generation often fulfilled more than the mundane, mothers' bridge club expectations. Rebellion was in their blood. One lovely young lady had spent her senior high school year in Tunis, as an adopted member of a prosperous Tunisian family. A former friend was serving time in a Peruvian prison, the charges being possession of drugs. Another female class member was working with Richard Leakey, in Kenya. Others, most of them who had the stamina, were still laboring to obtain PhD's in such diverse fields as Chemistry, Philosophy, and Foreign Relations. The majority had gotten their BA or BS. Others had served a stint in college, then quit or flunked out and returned to "The Dome" to take up positions in their father's business.

Douglas had gotten as far as a MA in Wildlife Management. He wanted a Ph.D. but had somehow gotten sidetracked.

"PING!" The BB, moving so slow that the mouse saw it coming, struck behind the rodent's left eye. The tiny creature died instantly. Douglas realized that his de-mousing program was doomed to failure. Chances of an injury that would result in lingering pain were too great. He'd have to get a cat. Perhaps he could borrow one for a week or so.

Yawning, feeling cramped in the smelly recliner, he stood up and opened the trailer's door.

Evening breezes gently rustled the newly emerging leaves of another summer season. From Lower St. Mary Lake came the raucous fussing of gulls. Nearby, in the greening willows, a sparrow sang his beautiful territorial song. He sat on the floor with his long legs outside, dangling so that his feet touched the remnants of his front, wooden step. The weight of winter's snows had crushed the crude structure into a jumble of wood fragments.

Unknown to the young man, a tiny, reddish-brown speck of life scrabbled its way around the corner of the doorframe and disappeared into the semi-darkness of the room. By the time he slipped under the covers the intruder had progressed to the edge of the bed. Body heat, the warmth of the man's blood, drew the tiny creature across the pillow where it found the safety of the human's red hair. Without hesitation, the minute creature disappeared into the tangled mass.

*

"You've got a call from California. Can you come over and take it?"

Douglas was showering in the dormitory. The woman's voice startled him. He looked up to see Edna White Cloud standing in the doorway. Her voice was barely audible over the noise from the splashing water. "What?"

"You've got a call from Fresno. It's that TV guy, Jess What's-His-Name. You know, the one that followed everyone around last summer taking videos of their hikes and talks."

"Yeah. Yeah." He turned his back to the woman. "I'll be right over."

Edna smiled, staring at his white bottom, waiting.

Irritated at her boldness, yet pleased and sexually stimulated, he gave up. He turned off the water and, with a towel fluffing his wet hair, faced the anticipating woman. The next time he looked she was gone.

"Damn!" Since the night of his ill-fated excursion to the St. Mary saloon, resulting in five women undressing and bathing him, it seemed every female in the valley was trying to get a look at his penis.

He dressed swiftly, still somewhat wet, and hurried over to the office. Edna was whispering to the other, older secretary. When they saw him entering they both giggled.

His face clouded in a flash of anger. "Which phone?"

"You can take the phone in Vern's office. He's gone for the week." Both women were looking at his crotch.

"Damn," he muttered in frustration. "Hello, Jess?"

"Hey Douglas. Good to hear your voice. How's tricks?"

"OK, I guess. I'm getting a little tired of this place, though."

The voice from California chuckled. "Well, I'm sending you some blowups taken from my video tapes of last summer. Should arrive in a few days. Still get your mail at the office?"

"Yeah, I do. But, what's this all about?"

"I'm not asking you any questions, Douglas. Just trying to help. Last summer I figured out that you were looking for something." Jess paused. "Or somebody maybe."

"You coming out again this year, Jess?"

"Nope," responded the California voice. "My position got phased out. Irrelevant, I guess. Who wants to improve interpretive activities?"

"Sorry about that. I liked your work. Since you won't be here, I'll tell you a bit of what I'm doing. Maybe I am looking for something. Let's say I am on a special assignment."

"Gotcha! OK. I won't say anymore over the phone except be sure to look close at the photos. I've got miles of videotape and maybe my observations don't add up to anything. But look anyway."

"Thanks, Jess. How's Patty?"

"Fine. Real fine. We're a great couple. Getting married come July. She's pregnant."

151

"Great." Douglas's enthusiasm was genuine. "Congratulations, Jess."

"Thanks. Say, be careful. If my hunch is right the person you are looking for is one mean S. O. B."

"Right. I will. Thanks again, Jess. What do I owe you?"

"Nothing. Take care of the park for me. It's a special place."

"I promise. No sweat." He hung up.

Douglas slouched in Vern's chair for some time, thinking about the call. In the outer office he heard the women speaking in hushed tones. The walls were thin plywood and the door a mere shell. He opened the door and walked out. Both women were busy shuffling papers. Neither looked up.

They had heard his half of the conversation. What had he said? Did they know his secret? Then he remembered his comment about being on a special assignment. He had blown his cover. Any comment to the women would only worsen the situation.

Douglas slammed the door when he left the office. Edna looked at her companion and held her index fingers about a foot apart, an exaggeration, and said, "Wow!"

Wolf Man heard the laughter as he headed back to the dormitory. Fucking women!

*

The early May summer weather had submitted to late winter by the end of May. Ferocious winds roared off the snowy peaks, screaming downhill to assail the valley residents. Slam! Another burst struck the little white church on the hill in Babb. Douglas sat halfway down the left side. With very few exceptions the worshipers were Native Americans, Blackfeet, Piegan, and perhaps a Cree. They said Mable Jenkins was Cree.

Wolf Man loved watching the youngsters. Their dark faces were beautiful, animated, full of life. Black hair. Dark brown eyes, faces still unmarked by the harshness of living, reflecting soft, bronze skin.

The Babb Catholic Church was a special place for Douglas. Magic. Little bursts of magic happened there. The congregation knew that too. He felt that he belonged there, in the eighth row, left, praying on the hard board kneeling benches. When there, in the Babb Church, he felt very close to God.

Outside the storm worsened. Wave-after-wave of cold air assailed the wooden structure. Windowpanes snapped. Beams, hidden in the ceiling and behind the walls cracked sharply from the onslaught. The whole church strained as if it was about to take off, go sailing downhill to smash to pieces in the meadow to the east.

Father Picard entered, escorted by two adult "Altar Boys." Some old Catholic traditions still held. The priest, an excellent actor, looked about at the faces staring up at him; then he seemed to appraise the safety of the ceiling. Having everyone's attention, Fr. Picard smiled.

"When they decided to build a Church here in Babb they selected this location, on top of our little hill. It does have a wonderful setting. The view is great. Of course those people knew they wouldn't have to sit in here during a wind storm." The congregation enjoyed the little joke.

Julie would have laughed. Julie. He hadn't thought of her for a couple of days. Wherever he looked, he saw a reminder of the beautiful young woman. The Lower St. Mary Lake's shoreline on which he lived had also been her home. She had worked at St. Mary. Julie had gone to this church, sat in the very same pew that he now occupied.

Worse than the memories of Julie, was the fact that Ann hadn't returned yet. Her season wouldn't begin until around the twentieth of June.

The service ended; he couldn't remember the sermon and only a vague recollection of taking the Host at communion.

"Body of Christ."

"Amen."

Douglas liked Communion better in the churches that distributed wine with the bread. The ceremony was more relevant. Funny thing to think about now.

People were leaving; casting furtive glances his way. The strange red-haired man looked very sad, very lonely. A very old lady, supported by her granddaughter, managed to ever so slightly touch his shoulder. The contact startled him. He looked into the ancient one's eyes and smiled.

He waited until they had all left before he arose and walked to the door. The chilly blasts were still assailing the fleeing churchgoers. Car and truck doors slammed. Motors roared to a start. Vehicles bumped and wiggled down the rough lane that led to Babb and Highway 89. Douglas sat in his wind-battered Toyota, somehow getting a peculiar satisfaction out of the fury of the storm. The violence reminded him of his beloved Great Plains. The grass would be high enough in Nebraska to be whipping rapidly in the relentless westerlies of spring.

Fr. Picard locked the empty church and got into his pickup truck. The little structure would remain empty until the next Saturday, unless someone died. He looked at the young man sitting in his yellow car. The priest waved. Douglas faked a smile and waved back.

Satisfied, his goal of being the last car off the hill achieved, he drove the tortuous short trail downhill to Babb. He checked to see if anything was coming on Highway 89, then swung out onto the highway. Across the road, leaning against the front of Thronson's store, stood a tall, lean figure. He swung his car off the road to look. Fang. The figure was Fang, leering as he had done the summer before. The near-toothless Indian almost ceremoniously raised his right, middle finger in an act of contempt, holding it so Douglas could see.

"Up yours too," Douglas mouthed so that the man could read his lips.

Fang, delighted with his obscenity, grinned open-mouthed, revealing the single ivory tooth.

He drove on toward the St. Mary River, crossed the bridge and headed south intending to go to his trailer. The temples on the sides of his head throbbed. He felt flushed, perhaps coming down with a cold or fever. He hoped it wasn't the flu. Yet, he was hungry and very lonely. On an impulse, he swung the car into the parking lot of the Lakeside Cafe. No other vehicle was there. He entered the restaurant.

"Hello, Douglas." Mary, the proprietor, was working the restaurant alone.

"Hi, Mary." He slumped onto a seat at the counter. "Got any huckleberry pie today?"

"Yes." The woman was eyeing him apprehensively.

"Coffee, too, I guess."

"You OK?"

"Yes. Well, not really. I don't feel too well. Coming down with something."

Mary frowned. "Maybe you should go to the clinic in Cardston."

"Yeah. Guess I will tomorrow. Thanks for the suggestion." He gulped down his glass of ice water.

"How about iced tea instead of coffee?"

"Good idea, Mary. Thanks." He forked a piece of pie and shoved it into his mouth. "Umm. Good pie, Mary."

She smiled at the compliment.

"Seen Henry around?" He missed his old friend.

"Nope. He and Martha went to Lethbridge for a few days."

"Oh. Too bad. I need to talk to him."

"You don't look so hot." Her eyes reflected her concern. "Look, you don't have to eat the pie. It's on the house. Go on home and go to bed."

"No. No, I'll be all right. And the pie's just what I need," he lied. His voice was without life, stripped of emotion. He finished the pie, gulped down the remaining cold liquid and asked for the bill.

Mary looked into his eyes. "Sometimes, like I think now for you, it is time to move on to some other place."

He gazed back, trying to catch the meaning.

"It is time that you go on with your life."

"Yes. You are right, Mary. After this summer. I have to finish my job here and then I'll leave."

"Good-bye, Douglas." Her words sounded final.

Confused, the pie churning in his stomach, he left the cafe. He arrived home just in time to throw up outside of the door to his trailer.

Except for the throbbing headache, the evening brought a lessening of nausea and pain. Perhaps, he thought, he didn't have the flu after all.

Twice during the night disturbing dreams wakened him. Each time a cold chill seemed to permeate the trailer. Each time he heard the scurrying of tiny rodent feet, a sound that he detested.

The first nightmare was the worst of the two. He and Henry Two Feathers, not his mother, were at the ballet. The apparition was standing in the box again, staring at him. In the dream the ghostly eyes emitted blood red, widening rays of light. He, whoever he was, laughed madly allowing trickles of blood to flow down the sides of the ghastly mouth. With extended index finger, the horrible creature pointed directly toward him. Henry seemed to fade away, fleeing the scene. Wolf Man was left alone with his hellish tormentor.

He jerked upright, coming fully awake with a spasm of muscles. Instantly, he became dizzy and fell back gasping, cold chills enveloping his body.

"Oh. Wow," he whispered to himself. Soon he was once again asleep.

Streaks of light were shooting above the moraine-lined eastern horizon when he awoke again.

The second dream had placed Douglas and Henry on the Duck Lake Road. The scenario had been simple, easy to comprehend. Henry stopped his truck for some reason and looked out the driver's window. Suddenly he became Henry and Henry, now the passenger, gaped in frightened disbelief. He opened the passenger's door, jumped out and fled up the hill toward the Billedeau Ranch. Confused, he turned, looking toward the northwest. There, standing without movement, the coyote stared into his eyes. To the young man's amazement he could see tears flowing down the animals muzzle. Coyote was crying.

Douglas slowly let go of the dream, rising up out of his sleep. His eyes were blurred. Reaching up to rub them he discovered that tears were flowing down his cheeks. "Oh, God," he gasped, not comprehending what was happening to him. Rising, he found the water bottle and gulped down mouthfuls of the stale but still refreshing liquid.

Maybe, if he opened the door he'd feel better. Cold, chilly bursts of the last of the storm worsened his weakened condition. Below the doorsill, lay the pool of last nights vomit, shining faintly, a greenish-blue shimmer of slightly digested Huckleberry pie.

He threw up the water and went back to bed.

He couldn't sleep. Neither could he think clearly. Morning waned into afternoon. He tried some more water and kept it down. Somehow he had to get to St. Mary or somewhere and get help.

"Hey, Wolf Man!"

Douglas struggled to his feet.

"Come on out. I know you're in there."

He opened the door to find a complete stranger, an Indian in his thirties, standing alongside a red pickup.

"Huh? What do you want?"

"Hannibal Simms sent me."

"What for? I don't know you." The incident wasn't making any sense.

"Says Two Feathers might be in trouble. Found his rig in the Cut Bank Campground."

"No. There must be some mistake. Henry's in Canada."

"No he ain't. Anyway, his truck ain't in Canada. She's parked at the C. G."

"The what?" Douglas couldn't think.

"In the C. G. That stands for campground. Boy, you ain't very bright."

Douglas struggled to comprehend what was being said. "Why did Simms pick you to come here?"

"Nobody else around. Sunday, you know. Simmsey's on road patrol so you need to get to Cut Bank." The visitor was getting nervous. "You'd better get your ass in gear. Simms wants you at Cut Bank. Henry might be in trouble."

"Uh, OK." He shut the door and stood wobbling, trying to think. He couldn't, much. "Henry's in trouble. Truck's at the campground. Simms wants me there. Doesn't make sense.

"OK. Get dressed. Better take warm clothes. My gun. Let's see. Yeah. Water. Both bottles of water and Bufferin. Jeeze, I'm sick."

He made the drive to the Hudson Bay Ranger Station without having to stop once. He was feeling a little better and guessed that he could handle things down at Cut Bank if there was no one else that could go. Just as the strange Indian had said, the station was closed. No one was there. Thinking a little clearer he entered the office and switched on the radio.

"Damn. I can't remember the call numbers." Severe ringing in his ears was wearing him down. He pressed the transmission button.

"Simms, this is Jakowski. Over."

No response. He tried several times more.

"Oh." He was too weak to think of cuss words. "I'd better go. Henry might really need me." For some reason he glanced at the office mail pigeonholes and saw he had an envelope. The package was a 9 X 12 brown envelope. Not really thinking clearly he jammed the thick piece of mail into his daypack. Surprised that he had the pack he asked himself, "Now, why did I bring that thing in here?"

He went to the restroom and splashed cold water on his face. Somehow he had to clear his head. The body chills were gone. Instead Douglas felt hot, sweaty. He gulped down two more Bufferin. "Better not overdose." The throbbing headache was worsening again.

How could a half an hour seem like a day? He puzzled over his question. The journey had been almost too much for the nearly delirious man. There had been a near-accident. A red sports car had honked angrily when Douglas had crossed the top of Divide Pass. Wolf Man had strayed over the centerline.

Later, on the way down, he was still talking to himself. "Oh. Must be careful. Got to help Henry. Why did Simms want me to do this? Huh?"

Route 89 turned in to one agonizing curve after another. "Got to be careful. Slow down. Woops. Nearly lost it." He talked his way down, off the mountain, navigating the tortuous route that wove along the headwaters of the South Fork of the Milk River. The road was the same one he had taken the year before, when he had first arrived at the park. He didn't recognize any of it. But he did see the dirt road angling off to the west, heading up toward the Cut Bank Camp Ground.

Unfortunately for Douglas a barbed wire gate straddled the access road. He was able to get the crude arrangement of wires and sticks open but then he didn't have the strength to close it again.

"Shit. What am I doing here?"

"Hey. I'm cussing. Must be getting better." He scratched at the inside of his left forearm. Then, he scratched at the right forearm.

"Hey. Look there. Tire tracks." He was speaking out loud so that he could concentrate better. Coasting the car in neutral he extracted the revolver from his pack. In so doing the manila envelope fell between the seats, landing on the back floor. He saw that the weapon was fully loaded.

"Fishing must be good here. Good fishing. I'll come back and go fishing." He scratched his arms.

No one was at the Cut Bank Ranger Station.

"Jesus" he exclaimed. "Isn't there anyone around anywhere today?" Then he thought. Wait a minute. I see only one set of tracks going in. Can't be Henry and Simms both. Which one?

He was beginning to sense that something was wrong with the Indian's story. He slowed down, cautiously peering into the forest.

The yellow Toyota labored over an open meadow that was situated north of the stream and above the campground. He could see the wooden outhouse, almost hidden by the new leaves on the willow trees. Just beyond sat a blue Chevy truck.

Who's is that? I've never seen that one before. Or have I? He slid the Toyota through a nearly melted snow bank, then stopped. He didn't see anyone or anything suspicious. He just sat still, watching, listening. He heard only the gushing of the swollen stream. Half an hour passed. Another ten minutes slipped away. He was tiring. Attempting to remain alert sapped his remaining energy.

"Holy shit. I've got the runs." He threw open the door and shakily stepped out. The fresh air helped a little. Strapping on the gun belt he dropped the 45 into the holster.

Last winter's snow lay in splotches; gray, squishy piles that were, he thought, somehow still more attractive than the dirty snow and ice of the city he called home. His footsteps alternated between splashing and sucking noises. Even in his semi-stupor he realized that the left boot had a leak.

The outhouse door was stuck. He felt his body fluids oozing out of his rectum. "Shit!" He pulled hard and the door grudgingly stuttered open. Pants and shorts were dropped just in time. Almost. Splow!

The diarrhea blasted out then settled into a long succession of noises, trickles and minor splashes.

"Oh god does that feel good. Ahh. Must be the flu after all."

He sat in the privy a long time, completely fatigued, gazing out through the open door, looking at the small trees of the forested valley.

"No. Not that. Son-of-a-bitch!" There was no toilet paper. "God-damned government. Can't spring for a simple, cheap, fucking roll of toilet paper." His anger drained him of additional energy. His vision blurred when he stood up. Waddling awkwardly, holding his pants, weighted with the heavy weapon, he lock stepped his way to the nearest snowdrift.

Douglas continued to verbalize his thoughts. "What a mess. My ass is covered with shit and my arms itch like poison ivy." The last remark brought Douglas to a halt. "Poison ivy? There isn't any poison ivy around here." Letting his pants slump onto the soggy earth he unbuttoned the left sleeve of his flannel shirt and slid the red checked cloth up to reveal the skin of his forearm.

"Oh, no." His voice whispered softly. "That's a rash." In disbelief, "Oh, no. I've got Rocky Mountain Spotted Fever. Good Lord, help me!" He felt fear course through his body replacing the chills.

"Oh, God. I've got to get help."

Pants down, horrified at realizing he had tick fever, he didn't hear the soft splashing steps behind him. Something struck him just to the right of the top of the spinal column and he collapsed face down into the wetness of the snowmelt. He was still awake, sort of. Senses told him he was hearing roars. Through numbness he experienced sharp something's ripping his shirt and trousers. Cold air chilled his exposed backsides. Vaguely he thought of the Great Bear.

No, he thought. Not a bear. No bites to the neck or thighs. But, those sounds? What was it? A human roaring?

His eyes blurred. Blood was flowing from his scalp, mixing with the ground water. His right eye saw pink just before he fainted.

How long? Seconds? Minutes? Not hours. The daylight had not progressed westward. How long had he been unconscious? He tried to move. He couldn't.

My God, I'm dying, he thought. The left nostril was submerged in a shallow pool. Snow floated inches away from his left eye, the clear one.

Funny, he thought. My left nostril is underwater but my left eye is clear.

Sort of pretty. The ice and snow. Bits of bark and dead leaves all mixed up with the whites and grays. He drifted off again.

Woah. Must have fainted. About time for an out-of-body experience, he thought. That would be different. Funny how my mind is clear. Must be dying and I know it. Am I saying this stuff out loud? He wasn't.

Strange. That poem I read once. What was the name? About a soldier who was shot or something. He wondered, Uh, what was that line?

"I heard a fly buzz..." something or other. Yeah. A fly landing on the guys face just before he died. Unload a pile of eggs. Maggots. The horror of the thought didn't penetrate Douglas' mind. He remembered the poem.

"I heard a fly buzz, before I died." Emily Dickenson, he recalled.

Oh, God. Desperate, breathing becoming rapid, making short-lived bubbles in the snowmelt.

No flies here. Too cold.

Too cold. Getting numb. Numb.

A few seconds later. Seems warmer. Maybe warmer. Wolf Man fell into a deep sleep.

*

Henry Two-Feathers found his badly wounded friend lying in the puddle nearly an hour after the assault had taken place. Douglas was barely alive.

*

CHAPTER 14

May 1985

"Out. Everybody out."

Startled, the two secretaries, a law enforcement seasonal, and Donnie, the Blackfeet maintenance man all jumped at Vern Nielsson's authoritative command.

"Go over to the cafe. Do something for an hour. Don't hang around outside." They all hurried to the door and clomped down the wooden stairs. Vern crudely printed, DO NOT DISTURB, on a sheet of copy machine paper and Scotch-taped the notice to the outside of the entrance door.

"Now," he looked at Henry Two Feathers, "go ahead and call Douglas. I'll be outside, far enough away that I can't hear your conversation. Use the phone in my office."

Henry, surprised at the help he was getting, thanked the District Ranger. Thinking for a moment he asked, "What's the prefix for Dayton, Ohio? I've only got the last seven digits."

"513." Vern had a knack for remembering numbers. Henry shut the office door and began dialing.

Catherine answered the phone.

"I'm sorry to bother you again, Mrs. Jakowski. This is Henry."

"Thank you for calling. Douglas wants to talk to you. I'll wake him."

"No, don't do that. I can call back."

"Please stay on the phone. Douglas needs to talk to you."

There was a long pause.

"Hi, Henry." Douglas's voice was weak, very low.

"I can hardly hear you. How are you doing?"

He was slow responding. "I'm better I guess. My back really hurts. The worse part is the fever. Even with the shots I'm having a hard time shaking it."

"You take it easy, friend."

Henry's word, "friend" pleased Douglas. "What have you found out? I've been home two days now. Guess that makes the attack a week old. Today's Monday, I think."

"Yes." Henry placed a sheet of paper on Vern's desk and wrote down the time and date. He intended to take detailed notes of their conversation. "Now, Douglas, tell me what you saw. I'll write everything down so go slow. You already told Vern that you didn't see the attacker. Was there anything else strange?"

"Only one set of tire tracks going in to the campground. Then, there was a blue truck."

"Yes, we know about the vehicle. The Cut Bank Ranger owns it. He drove in early in the morning and didn't come out until the day after you were attacked."

Douglas, voice getting weaker inquired, "What was he doing?"

"Usual patrol to the Snow Lake and Medicine Grizzly Lake campgrounds. He didn't know about your attack until he called in at five. His check-in time. There wasn't anything he could do that late in the day so he remained camping at Snow Lake. On the snow pack. I'm sure he was there because he complained about the mosquitoes being so bad up there."

Douglas gave a faint laugh. "Yes. I remember them from last year. Oh." Douglas paused again. Henry could hear talking in the background. "Look, Henry, I'm pretty weak. Could you talk to Mom? Tell her what you know. OK?"

Henry, somewhat emotional, answered, "Sure Douglas. You get well real soon, will you?"

"Yea. Thanks."

"Henry? This is Catherine."

They heard Douglas click off on the bedroom phone.

"How is he Mrs. Jakowski? He doesn't sound so good."

"Call me Catherine. He isn't feeling too well. Pretty weak from the fever. He's got pneumonia, you know. His back bothers him the most. No fractured spine. No broken shoulder blade. Thank goodness."

Henry blew out his breath in relief. He hadn't known how extensive the injuries had been.

"The pain comes from damaged back muscles, badly bruised. That's why we keep him sedated. The good news is there is no permanent damage. At least the doctors think there isn't."

Henry remained silent.

"What are the scratches on his back from?"

"I don't know, Mrs. Jakowski, but I can guess. I'd say someone tried to make it look like a bear attacked Douglas. Pretty sloppy job. Must have had a garden tool or something. You know, those three or four pronged things used to loosen up the soil."

"Oh. Thank goodness he had a lot of clothes on. The doctor says there will be just a couple of permanent scars on his back and one on the calf of the left leg." Catherine continued, "What about tracks? Douglas said there was some snow on the ground."

"Like I told you yesterday I came back from Lethbridge early. I was out of cigarettes and drove up to the Lakeside Cafe. The lady who runs the place told me that Douglas was ill so I decided to check up on him. Amos Larson, a road maintenance man, saw Douglas turn in at the Cut Bank road junction. That's the reason I found him a bit later."

"No tracks then?"

"I don't think so." Henry was embarrassed. "When I saw Douglas lying in the puddle I didn't take time to look around. He was half-drowned and nearly dead from hypothermia. By then the rain had started in again. Heavy. Later, when Donnie, a maintenance man, and I returned to the scene all we found was slush. Even my prints and the marks where I dragged Douglas to the truck were almost gone. Really a bad stroke of luck, that rain."

Catherine remained silent, thinking about what Henry had just said.

"Mrs. Jakowski? Are you still there?"

She startled out of her silence. "Yes. Oh, yes. I was just thinking. I'm taking notes."

"Me too."

"Henry, Douglas told me to tell you something very important. He said for you to go to his trailer and read his journals. There are two of them. One is personal. They are easy to find, behind the bed somewhere. He said that maybe there is something in them that will give you a clue, help you solve the puzzle."

"Are you sure he won't mind? Diaries are private thoughts, you know."

"I'm certain of it. Henry, you can't imagine how high a regard my son has for you. Go ahead. See what you can find." As an afterthought Catherine added, "When you are through with them Douglas wants you to send the journals along with his other personal stuff. He's afraid the government will get ahold of them."

"All right, Mrs. Jakowski. I'd better get on that before the Park Service lawmen beat me to it."

*

Reluctantly, the old man unpinned the sheriff's badge from his shirt pocket. Breaking and entering wasn't exactly legal. He would commit the act as a private citizen. Shielding his eyes from the brilliance of the match flame, Henry lit a cigarette. In spite of his precautions the flare-up weakened his night vision. He swore to himself, irritated with his habit.

Another thirty minutes passed. No one seemed to be moving about. Only three vehicles had passed on U. S. 93 during that time. No traffic on the radio, either. He'd leave that behind, locked in the truck's glove compartment. But, not his revolver. That would go with him. He wasn't really certain what he was about to encounter.

Chill winds found their way through the slightly rolled down window of the truck's cab. The not-yet completed darkness revealed white caps rolling on Lower St. Mary Lake. He shivered involuntarily. Late May can be damn chilly, he mused to himself.

Another half hour passed. The darkness became complete. Squinching his eyes shut, the lawman opened the driver's door and as he did the dome light came on. With eyes closed he stepped down onto the moisture-saturated path that would lead him to the trailer. Henry slammed the door. "What the hell!," he said aloud. He never did seem to be able to get in and out of a sheriff's vehicle quietly and at the same time not cause a light to come on.

As was his habit, his right thumb snapped open the leather thong that held his Smith and Wesson securely within it's holster. His left hand clutched a small wrecking bar.

No unusual sounds. Wind. Faint splashings from the lakeshore below. Aspen and birch leaves rattling on invisible branches.

Henry had been to the trailer several times so he had little difficulty feeling his way along the invisible path. He reached out and found the pole that supported the electric line. The moist wood felt familiar to his work-worn hands and somehow the insignificant contact gave the man reassurance that what he was about to do was necessary. Douglas's trailer gave off a faint glow, even in the deep shadows of the forest. Henry remembered that it was a dull, dirty cream color, badly rusted.

He found the door. As expected, a heavy lock prevented easy entry. Certain now that he was unobserved, Henry clicked on his flashlight. What he saw caused him to smile; the first smile since he had found his injured friend. Although the lock was expensive and sturdy, the hinge, which it prevented from swinging aside, had been screwed into the metal frame. Anyone with a screwdriver could easily gain entrance. Henry had one.

Once inside the trailer, the door lock secured from the inside, Henry switched on the lights. What he saw was very familiar to him. The inside was immaculate. Personal items were somewhat strewn about but other than that there was no dirt or disorder.

The little trailer had more room than one would expect. Besides the compact cooking area there was a table with twin built-in benches. What was probably considered a living room held a table, two wooden chairs, a recliner, and shelves of books, papers, records, tapes, and professional equipment. At the far end of the room the inhabitant had thrown a mattress on the floor and an unmade bed covered it. To the rear of the living room a door led to a very small bathroom.

The lawman knew exactly where to look for the information he was seeking. Behind a stack of college papers he found the two loose-leaf notebooks with the Montana State University logo printed across the fronts. They were the diaries of his young friend. He lifted the documents from their not-so-obvious hiding place and stared at them, almost in awe.

Turning, Henry opened the tiny refrigerator and took out a Bud Lite. A faint spray of moisture and gasses issued from the opening as he popped the top. Sighing he took a long draught of the cold liquid. The effort caused a shiver to roll rapidly down his spine.

Curious and feeling a little bit guilty, the lawman opened the thicker diary. Immediately he laughed heartily. On the cover page, in heavily scrawled script he read:

THE DIARY OF DOUGLAS JACKOWSKI
A Damn Fine Man!

White men never failed to make him laugh, if they had a sense of humor. Douglas was one of them that did. Not that he didn't really believe he was a good man, but he didn't go around boasting about it. That is, he hadn't, Henry corrected himself.

True to his professionalism, Douglas's first entry was a copy of the letter from Elwood Lenning, Glacier Park Superintendent. It was brief, non-informative, just a short letter of introduction that had made the initial contact to Douglas, the wolf researcher. The letter indicated that Douglas wasn't being asked to come to Glacier. He was being told.

Henry's eyes quickly scanned the following pages, sparsely containing evasive correspondence between Douglas and the Superintendent. Then he found the page describing the arrival of the wildlife expert.

Lighting another cigarette, Henry sat back in the easy chair, which took up nearly half of the living area, and read the few lines. He knew the story. Age may have doomed the Sheriff to aches and pains but his memory was excellent. He thought about that awhile. Probably inherited, Henry decided. Ancestors of this very land had no written language. No diary to fall back on. Only memory. All of the old legends were half-truths, but history never the less. He was a product of that old way. Yes, the stories were as vivid in his mind as when Douglas had related them to him. Eyes a bit watery, not completely from the acrid smoke, the old man sank deeper into the chair and recalled from the recesses of his mind the details of the day the Wolf Man came to Glacier.

*

The trailer door flew outward in a hinged arc, slamming violently against the rusty exterior front wall.

Amidst a thick cloud of acrid, grayish-tan smoke the lean body hurtled outward, away from the doorway. Landing with a soggy thud the man-figure supported itself on quivering hands and knees, head lowered, glasses askew.

Gasps, quivering inhalations for breath, competed in sound with retchings, terrible coughing, and raspings deep within the throat and lungs. Driblets of saliva yo-yoed down each side of the contorted mouth before thinning out and dripping to the ground. Tears flowed from water-blurred eyes.

The man in agony was Henry Two Feathers.

"God-damned cigarettes," he panted. "I've got to stop smoking that crap." Already the trailer was clearing of the cigarette smoke, the chill winds of yet another unseasonable cold spell rushing inside the warmer interior, cleansing the structure of tars, nicotine and all the other poisons Henry's system craved.

His plight was rather serious. Normal breathing came slowly. Each time he had one, the seizures seemed worse. Dampness penetrated his uniform trousered knees. Sweat, resulting from the exertion of his dilemma, chilled Henry's lank body. He began to shiver. "Damn!" Still weak, he plopped on his rear end, chilling his still well formed butt. "There goes my hemorrhoids," he said aloud. The chill would certainly result in discomfort.

His mind clearing, Henry began thinking about getting up off the cold ground. His right hand automatically reached toward his shirt pocket, then stopped.

"Shit!" He swore in good Douglas style. Grasping the nearly empty cigarette pack Henry angrily tore it from the pocket and hurled the cellophane-covered container into the weeds. Trembling still, moaning a bit, he awkwardly pushed his torso upward, got his right knee in place and successfully raised himself to a standing position. He was panting, somewhat stooped in posture. The clean air soothed his tormented throat and lungs. Mind clear, once again, the diary incidents flooded back like paintings, flashing portrayals of a young man's life, just a year before.

Time to go home, Henry thought. First he wanted to tidy up a bit; put the trailer back in order. Collect the beer cans. Two of them. Dispose of the remnants of a snack. Collect the cigarette butts.

Cigarette butts.

Henry looked about, finally locating the pack lying in the wet grass. One cigarette, there were just two left, was hanging partway out of the opening, collecting moisture. "Damn," expressed Henry, carefully sliding the semi-soggy smoke back into the protection of the container.

*

Henry couldn't make himself go home. Exhausted from concentrating and lack of sleep he drove the two miles to the Lakeside Café, where he consumed a large plate full of ham, eggs, and whole-wheat toast, the latter amply smeared with orange marmalade. Henry liked orange marmalade.

He raised his cup for a sip of coffee and the mind-thing clicked in. It happened that way. Always had. Henry did his best thinking in a trance-like state, all else blocked from his senses.

*

"He's been sitting like that for most of half an hour."

"How long's he been here?" She didn't get an answer.

The owner of the Lakeside Cafe had just returned for the noon rush and was questioning Lisa, one of her two waitresses. All three women were behind the counter, staring across the room to the table where Henry Two Feathers sat. A faint smile played on his lips. Otherwise the man was motionless, right elbow on the table, the upright forearm holding a half-full mug of cold coffee.

"Should I bother him?" queried the younger of the two waitresses. "I could offer him some hot coffee."

"No, don't bother him," the proprietor responded. "Henry's thinking. He's OK. I've seen him do this before."

"But," argued the other waitress, "his eyes are all bloodshot and it looks like he's got snot all over his shirt."

"Hush! Leave him alone. He's had another bout with cigarette smoke. I've seen that happen before, too." Sighing the owner added, "You two mind your own business. I'll ring up Martha and warn her that Henry needs some care." She slipped out the door to use the phone at the adjacent service station.

With cup still suspended by index finger and thumb, Henry was recalling incidents in Douglas's personal diary. He even remembered some of the dates.

Sometimes the second, personal diary, had skipped days. One time a whole week had been unrecorded. Notes had become incomplete sentences, sometimes lacking adjectives, verbs or even nouns.

The late entries in the second diary were a record of the breaking down of self-discipline. The previous year Douglas had become overwhelmed with the disappointments of love, responsibility, and the inability to come up with a single strong indication of who the killer might be. Too many backcountry hikes. Too many dead ends of suspects. Everyone seemed innocent. There was no one left. Not enough time to keep a diary; not to do a good job. Exhaustion had often prevented Douglas from writing entries. The spring hiking in the deep snows of the current year had worn him down again.

Most of what Henry had read from the early pages of the second, personal diary, reflected experiences of little consequence. Only a few incidents were worth his time to take mental note. The lawman had failed to write anything down. One entry might contain a clue. So thought the older man.

Henry placed the coffee mug down on the oilcloth-covered picnic table. Immediately his waitress was at his side with a new mug of hot coffee. He smiled, mostly with his eyes, and the woman, pleased at his recognition of her act, turned and walked back to the cooking area.

Yes, he remembered, the date was August 12th., 1984. The beginning of the Perseus meteorite shower. Entirely unrelated. The display of shooting stars happened every August. On the 12th something unusual and perhaps significant had happened to Douglas. That was the date of the war dance in the back of the pickup truck up at Logan Pass.

He extracted his worn notebook from his shirt pocket. It had replaced the once again thrown away pack of cigarettes. One of the earliest entries recorded the names of the misbehaving Blackfeet.

The leader had been Gordon Plenty Walks. The Blackfeet's reputation was tarnished by a long list of arrests and citations.

Henry decided to check up on the malcontent. "Maybe, just maybe Gordon is one of the killers I'm looking for."

*

The Next Day

"Come on, Hot Shot. You have a run to make. The sheriff called just minutes ago." Martha pulled the covers off of Henry's aching body.

"Yeah," he grumbled. "I bet it's right next to the office and he wants me to run all the way over to Browning."

"No. You're lucky. The call is just up the road a ways. A man called Badwater says he's lost a steer. Something strange, I guess."

"Anyone with the name of Badwater can't be lucky," grumbled Henry.

"Hurry up. I've got breakfast ready for you. Really, it's lunch. You've slept through the noon hour." Martha was worried about her aging husband. Four hours of sleep wasn't enough.

*

Grumbling to himself, Henry whipped the pickup off the road. He had arrived at the site of the current problem. Two local men were standing above the right ditch, watching him approach. One was the rancher, Joseph Badwater. He was easy to identify for he stood a mere five feet tall but weighed over two hundred pounds. The man was powerfully built. Not sloppy fat.

Comanche, thought Henry in genuine prejudice.

The rancher didn't speak. The other, a younger man, fidgeted nervously. "Hi, Henry!"

"Sheriff Two Feathers, to you, boy."

The youngster grinned at the name causing Henry to scowl at the insult. The rancher was also displeased and grumbled something to his companion. Few Native Americans laughed at their tribal names.

Turning his anger-filled eyes away from the boy, Henry inquired, "What do you have for me, Joseph?"

"Dead steer. Been mutilated." Joseph didn't see any point in wasting words. Careful, so as not to destroy any possible clues, Henry stepped down into the ditch. Methodically his eyes scrutinized

169

every visible inch of the dead steer. The creature's left ear and eyeball were missing. Pulling the head up, the lawman found that a considerable amount of blood had soaked into the dusty soil.

"Humm," was all that he said.

The young man couldn't stand the silence. "Well? What do you think? It's one of those spooky mutilations, isn't it?"

Henry stared at the young man as he slowly lit a cigarette. Nervous, the man shifted his gaze to a clump of sagebrush. The sheriff ignored the question and asked one of his own. "What are you doing out here, Charlie? I don't see your Chevy."

The younger man laughed. "Naw! Me and Gordon Plenty Walks found this cow. He dropped me off at Joseph's so I could call this in. Gordon had to get on home."

"I just bet he did," responded Henry. Then he corrected, "This is a steer, not a cow." Turning to the rancher the sheriff reported, "This isn't a regular mutilation, Joseph."

"What do you mean?" The squat stockman glared in hatred. "Sure as hell it is." His voice was low and steady.

"I don't know anything about what hell has to do with this steer but look at those cuts." Henry paused waiting for a response.

The youth blurted in. "What do you mean? Eye's gone. So's the left ear. What do you mean not a mutilation? It's one of those god-damned space ships done this," argued Charlie. "Them Aliens did this!" His voice was trembling.

"Yeah?" the sheriff retorted. "Well, if that's the case your aliens wore cowboy boots because there are four sets of tracks here. Yours, Browns, mine and Gordons."

"So what," argued Charlie. "It's a mutilation, isn't it?"

Henry ignored him. "Listen carefully, Joseph. This steer was hit by a vehicle. If I call for an autopsy the vet will find massive bruises, likely along the animals left side."

Charlie started to protest.

Holding up his right hand in a demand for silence, Henry countered, "Now, just you be still for a minute. I'm talking to Joseph. This is his animal.

"As I was saying, someone hit this steer. Look at the gravel on the road and in the steer's hide. Whoever did it slid the steer into the ditch, cut it up a bit to make it look like a good old mutilation. But, it isn't. The cuts are simple, no distortion of tissue, considerable bleeding. Besides, the magpies are waiting for us to leave so they can continue the feast."

"What do you mean, 'feast'?" Charlie was fidgeting again.

"Hell, man! There's fresh bird shit on the cow's neck. The magpies have been pecking out the eyeball; having a real good time. Ask Joseph. He knows. Carrion birds don't touch a mutilated animal. Right, Joseph?"

The stocky rancher looked away.

"Right." Henry answered his own question. "Don't make me go to the trouble to explain what all I see in the gravel; the attempts to smooth out the skid marks and all that stuff.

"Now Joseph, if you want to prosecute Gordon and Charlie let me know. You'll win. I can assure you that. You'll win a settlement."

Again there was no response, only a look of black anger. The rancher's plan had failed causing his temper to soar to the breaking point. Charlie giggled nervously, then moved back, away from Henry. Joseph's muscular body was tense, considering jumping the lawman.

The crisis ended when Henry flipped the leather strap off the top of his revolver holster. At the same time, his hand closed around the stock. "Don't try it, Joseph. I'll drop you and Charlie before you get halfway to me."

Henry walked back to the truck. Reaching inside he lifted the radio speaker to his mouth. "Browning Dispatch, this is Two Feathers on Duck Lake Road."

The dispatcher affirmed that he was receiving.

"I'm here with Joseph Badwater and Charlie Win. Joseph lost a steer to a hit-and-run. There are no missing cattle. He has decided not to prosecute so I'm going back home. Signing off." Communicating over the radio was not one of Henry's strong points. Without taking his eyes off the two men he got into the truck.

Joseph couldn't let it go. He had to make a threat. "One of these days someone will get you, Henry."

"Yeah? Like someone did to that kid down near Heart Butte?"

"Huh?" The stupid sound came from Charlie's open mouth.

"Sure. Tell this boy about it, Joseph. He doesn't know."

No reply.

"All right. I'll tell him. He'd better realize what kind of people he's dealing with."

Henry directed his words to Charlie but his eyes never left the rancher. "Somebody killed a seventeen year old boy. Cut his heart out and nailed it to a tree where the youngster's father found it. Nice trick, eh? Tribal politics."

Joseph growled. "You're goin' too far."

"Oh? Well, you made the threat. I'm just saying what I think." Henry smiled and added. "You with the killers on that one, Joseph?"

The rancher almost lost control. He would have died if he had.

Smiling, Henry concluded, "Well boys, have a nice day."

*

Henry's pickup swung around a slight curve in the dirt road. There, sitting, just over the fence, a coyote watched as Henry braked to a stop. The animal stared at the lawman, eyes intent, obviously interested in Henry. It looked at the lawman and then, turning it's head, seemed to look back down the Duck Lake road to the little settlement of houses.

Chilled, Henry, feeling the coyote's eye contact, thought that he was being given a message. The animal would look at Henry and then turn and look at the houses.

"My god. What am I dealing with here?"

He knew what the coyote was telling him. "See Millie." At the moment he comprehended the message, the coyote turned and loped away, back up the hill toward the Billideau Ranch.

"I must be imagining all of this." Henry knew he wasn't. "If I go home and tell Martha this she'll say, "Listen to coyote, Hot Shot. Go see Millie."

*

That is exactly what she said.

CHAPTER 15

June 1985

Millie's house snuggled on the leeward side of a hill, which continued downward to meet the choppy waters of Duck Lake. Henry stopped his truck so that he could take in the view. If he went ahead, as he knew he would, Henry Two Feathers's life would change, the few years he had left following a far different course than what he had experienced up to the present early June day in 1985. Not comprehending what that thought meant frightened him.

He sat there recalling what he knew about Millie. He knew a great deal. Millie, Martha and Henry were friends.

Millie Starbuck was a White woman, somewhere between fifty and sixty years of age. Widowed in 1977, the result of a hunting accident, the lonely woman had chosen to develop her very unusual extrasensory powers. She had been born with a Prophet's Veil, a thin membrane beginning at the eyebrows and covering the lower portion of her face. That had been in Midway, Kentucky. The doctor, carefully snipping the unusual tissue from the infant's face had told her mother to keep the membranes. They were very important. He had cut the tissue in half, rolled the pieces up and inserted them in two glass vials. "Don't loose these. They are very valuable." Within a short time, someone broke into their home and only the membrane pieces were taken.

After her husband's death Millie told fortunes for a while. That bothered her. She could see bad as well as good in a person's future. At first, she stopped working with friends and later quit altogether. Not only was Millie able to see an individual's future, but she was said to be able to contact the spiritual realms. Those that didn't know Millie very well, laughed at her and thought she was a little bit crazy. Most of the Blackfeet and Millie's neighbors and friends knew that Millie Starbuck was blessed. She had been touched by God.

Henry smoked his cigarette down until the fire nearly scorched his knuckles. "Damn," he muttered softly. "I might as well get this old carcass on down the road."

The shingled roof of Millie's house was the color of the gray, dried ruts that the locals called a road. Wild roses sprawled just inside the ditch, having escaped from the woman's flower garden. Roses sprawled everywhere up over the fence that had once been white, across the irregular borders of the lawn, and even threatened to intrude upon the failed vegetable garden Millie had attempted to create.

Many seasons of winter snows had taken their toll of the fence and what was once a rose trellis. Beyond the house, several outbuildings lay smashed from the same weight of whiteness that descended upon the habitation each November and stayed until April.

"Ah, well. This is for you, Douglas," the man stated. Carefully crushing the butt in the truck's overloaded ashtray, Henry geared the vehicle into low and crept toward the home of his old friend.

"Hi, Henry. Come on in. The dog won't bite."

There was that promise again. Henry knew better. "Tie that mutt up or I'm heading for home."

Laughing heartily, Millie dragged the half German Shepherd, half something else to a dilapidated shed and forced the door shut. "Now your butt's safe, Henry."

Agonizingly slow, the old man unfolded himself from the pickup's front seat and stood up. "Your main street here," he waved toward the chuck holes, "ruined my kidneys."

"Aw, come on. Get in the house and I'll brew you up some herbal tea."

"No thanks." It was his turn to laugh. "The last time you did that for me I had gas for two or three days."

"See. Herbal tea's good for you. Cleans your gizzard so you'll feel better."

The two friends entered the little cottage. A transformation seemed to occur, more like a metamorphosis, coarseness left behind, replaced by the soft somewhat quaint warmth of a special friendship. Although daylight was nearly ended, the windows magically glowed cheerily with brightness. Lace curtains, delicate, starched, smelling of Montana dust, diaphanous panels gently hanging down over the full length of the windows, accentuated the last direct rays of the sun. Each sheet was pulled to the side and held by a short loop of the same material.

Henry took in the softness of the windows, thinking of a time long ago when he had visited another White woman's home, in Great Falls. It too had been enchanting. There had been huge ferns on Grecian pedestals standing about that room.

Millie had pushed ahead of the man and was busy in the far corner of the room that also passed for a kitchen. Water noisily gurgled into a teakettle. A cupboard door softly clumped shut. China cups rang on china saucers. Strange how a White woman's home differed from an Indian house. Most Indian homes were sparsely furnished, very utilitarian, uncluttered.

"I seen you sitting up the road there, Henry. I'm glad you decided to come on in."

Smiling, he turned and sought out the easy chair he knew was not Millie's favorite, not her throne. Henry's emaciated frame sank deep into the fabric finding relief from the stress of supporting the large, bony torso.

"I baked you a strawberry pie. I was looking for you a couple of hours ago. The pie's cold now. With June days so long, I should have known you'd show up about now."

"Eight o'clock, Millie," informed Henry.

"I suppose so." The house held no clock, no timepiece at all.

"Howie sure performed wonders with the lights you had him recess in the window frames," Henry admired. "Looks like noontime just beyond the curtains."

"Most of that's sunlight, still. But, they're on. I only turn them on when friends come to visit. When a bulb burns out I've got to get Howie over here again to change the blessed thing. I can't afford much of that."

They sat in silence for a while. Henry, absentminded, poked a crystal dangling from an unlit floor lamp. Light rays emanated out from the long, many-faceted crystal, shooting out flashes of reds, greens, and almost every other color of the light spectrum. Crystals hung or sat on bookcases, from curtain rods, all of the lamps, everywhere one looked. Otherwise the room was soft, subdued, warmly carpeted, strange, beautiful. Above all, the atmosphere was feminine.

Henry's eyes settled upon his hostess. Unblinking, Millie returned his gaze. The cold and heat of many years had somewhat creased the woman's face, but Millie's peculiar, soft beauty still remained. She knew that some men found her desirable. One of her few pleasures came from knowing that her sensuality still aroused the males she dealt with.

Millie had tricks too. Knowing that Henry was coming, Millie had removed her bra. Now, as they talked, she laughed inwardly as each movement, carefully orchestrated, resulted in her still-rounded breasts bouncing slightly and quivering noticeably beneath her cotton blouse. The game pleased her. A woman should be proud of such power. A woman should be generous, in a discrete, tasteful manner. Millie was feminine yet she was master, rather than mistress, of what transpired in her house. No male dominated her, not for the last thirty-four years. She had learned how to govern.

The teakettle sang loudly. Henry's eyes admired her jeans-covered bottom as she moved artfully to the stove.

*

Settled, each with a cup and saucer balanced on their knees, the two friends were ready to talk. Stained plates and forks were all that was left of the strawberry pie wedges.

"That's coffee, Henry. Instant."

"Yes. Smells good. Thank you. I wanted to finish my pie first."

She explained, "I knew you were coming. Late this afternoon I got vibes that Henry Two Feathers was in trouble and was on his way for help. What I don't know is what the trouble is all about."

Henry, as unemotional as possible, told of Douglas's experience in the Cut Bank Campground. Then, he told her of the first and recent coyote incidents, up on the road, just a mile or so away from where they sat.

Millie's smile faded and a frown of concern creased her features.

The lawman, once he got started, couldn't stop. Millie listened to his story about Douglas. All of it. When he finished, two hours later, the woman simply said, "Well."

"Look. I'm worn out. I've spent hours and hours of recalling things, events, sentences, images of last year and early this year. Frankly, Millie, I'm all memorized out. The old ways don't come easy to me. I'm too much a product of the White Man's culture. Simply, I'm finished. Somebody else has to help me now. I just can't do it."

Millie sat, unmoving.

"Look." He was slightly irritated because she had not responded with advise. "Do you mind if I step outside and have a cigarette? My nerves are sorta' on edge."

"Go ahead."

The night air felt good. Chilling but refreshing. Off to the west the horizon still glowed from the vanished sun. Henry turned, looked up, and found the faint crescent of a new moon, drifting low on the darkening horizon.

One of Millie's neighbor's dogs barked. Another mongrel responded from further away, down by Duck Lake. Her own dog, still in the shed, remained silent. A bat, attracted by the mosquitoes that Henry's warmth had accumulated, darted a few feet from the man's face. The cigarette glowed with each inhalation, the addictive need diminishing steadily. He dropped the smoldering butt on the walk and crushed it with a booted foot.

"If you can find it, pick up the cigarette and bring it in, Henry," ordered Millie. She had opened the front door.

"Oh." Irritated, he peeled the remains off the concrete. "Shit," he wheezed.

"If it's out, throw that thing in the waste can under the sink."

He wet the butt under the faucet.

Millie was sitting in her recliner, as if she had never left it. Eyes partly closed. Something had taken place during Henry's absence. "Henry, I can't help you. Coyote sent you to me for help and the only help I can give is to refer you to someone else. I'm not Native American and only an Indian can provide you with the kind of aid you are seeking. I think that wise old Coyote knew what I would tell you."

"Who?" Henry knew he wouldn't like her answer.

"Sweet Grass Woman."

"No!" Henry jerked in his chair. The man's exclamation of protest reverberated throughout the little house. Somewhere in the shadows two crystals pinged together, as if startled. Calmer now, "No, Millie. I can't. I won't go to Sweet Grass Woman. That old lady is different. You know what they say about her."

Millie nodded in the affirmative, letting her friend rid himself of his frustrations.

"No, I won't do that," he repeated. "I will work this thing out as I've always done before. There's a killer out there, somewhere. I'll get him. I will. I'm really good, Millie. You know that, don't you?"

Henry was nearly pleading but his friend remained impassive, unmoving.

"I said I can't and I can't. I promised." Henry licked the beads of perspiration from his lips.

"Promised? What do you mean, promised?"

"Hell, Millie. This is all crap! I don't believe in ghosts or witches, or the little people or any of that stuff. Spirits? Bull crap!"

"I don't like that last word."

Henry ignored her. He was breathing hard. Fumbling he unconsciously searched his shirt pocket and extracted a cigarette from the open pack. Matches. Where were his matches? A flame leaped up before his eyes. Behind the flame Henry saw Millie's face, beautiful in the light, yet almost inhuman. He became frightened. His hands trembled.

"Here, Henry. Let me help you." She held the match to his cigarette.

Long inhalations. Lungs filling and constricting with hot gases. Exhalations. Bluish gusts of smoke rushing out, spreading anxiously into what had been virgin territory, for tobacco smoke.

His hands were still shaking. The woman remained impassive, watching the smoke with half-closed eyes.

For an instant, observing her beauty, seeing her nipples just behind the soft cloth of the blouse, desire flooded his senses. He made an almost imperceptible movement. Millie, knowing his thoughts, slightly shook her head sideways. Eyes silently communicating, "No, Henry. No."

"Jesus!"

The woman crossed herself. "Not in here, Henry. Not the Lord's name in vain." She meant it. Firm, strong words of admonishment.

He looked at the cigarette, waved the smoke away, got up and threw the half-used object out into the blackness of the night. Neither spoke for some time.

"You know, Millie," he was back sitting in the chair again, "I used to think there was only good in the world. For most of my life I indulged in the fantasy that God, who or whatever God is, could not have made, created evil. I had it all figured out. Evil wasn't evil. It was man's weaknesses. Evil was nothing more than our lacking goodness and common sense. That's a good philosophy, isn't it?"

The woman didn't respond.

"So, if evil exists, in me for example, it really isn't what it seems to be. All I have to do is do good to negate my failings. And, the best part of my philosophy was that through good works man could destroy any semblance of evil. God understands. God helps us overcome ourselves in times of inconsiderateness or downright meanness.

"That's what I believed, Millie. Almost all of my life.

"And then I had a dream. Two really. Both nearly the same with some variations." He became silent, withdrawn.

The woman whispered gently, "Tell me."

Time seemed to stop. They remained unmoving. Eyes of the man smoky, recalling the past. Hers alert, seeking his horror.

"Well." They both jumped when the first word left his lips. "Both times I was asleep, on my back. I don't usually sleep that way. I snore when I sleep on my back. The noise bothers Martha.

"Anyway, in my dreams, if they were dreams, they were both so vivid, I was lying outstretched in bed, kinda' like a corpse is placed in it's coffin, when with lightning speed, something from the foot of the bed grasped me. This sounds stupid." He paused, trying to decide if he should continue.

"Go on, old friend." She reached forward and put a hand on his knee, a brief touch of compassion.

"Dark tentacles entwined about my body, pinning my legs, my hips, wriggling horribly upward, then about my chest. Squeezing my lungs. Crushing my heart. In one dream the thing had multiple heads, you know, like in that Greek tragedy."

"Medusa?" she guessed.

"Yeah. Maybe. I don't know. But, the second time, the worst, a single stalk terminated in a swollen, round eyeball, moving up my frame, staring into my eyes; coming closer and closer to my face." Henry's voice became raspy. He cleared his throat. Millie handed him a tissue. "Thanks. Both times I knew what I was encountering. A demon. Evil. Both times something, God, chance, whatever; saved me. My arms became free. The last time, the one I remember best, my anger at being attacked by the evil thing overwhelmed me and with great strength I grabbed the head, the big bulge in which the eye was seated, where it joined the long, supple stalk, and I squeezed my hands around it.

"The evil thrashed about, angry, intent upon it's objective, to kill me or worse. But I was stronger. You see, my anger, based on good, was stronger than the demon's evil. I knew I was winning and I silently shouted corny things like, 'Be gone with you.' 'God is with me!' 'You'll not get my soul!'

"Like I said, corny sounding words I'd never say out loud. Maybe I learned them in church or Sunday school.

"My left hand, still grasping the base of the smooth head stalk, a lot like a seed pod, squeezed harder and made a sort of a fist at the same time. With my right hand, fingers working, I poked and shoved and poked and poked, stuffing the evil into my fist until the head, the eye, was gone."

He wiped the perspiration from his forehead and face. Millie didn't move.

"The worst was yet to come. I awoke, flat on my back. Arms on my chest, I think. I'm not sure. My breathing was almost non-existent. My heartbeat seemed very weak. I was so cold! The whole area about me was cold. That was reality. The awareness hit me that something was really happening. Something bad. Maybe I had a dream but the truth was that something evil was nearby.

"I began praying. Rapidly. To myself. And I felt tremendous strength. The cold retreated and warmth returned.

"Tired, I stopped praying to rest a bit. The cold crept back, moving up my legs, my spine, enveloping me again, only that time there was no visible evil. Only the cold.

"Well, Millie, I prayed again. The cold went away. Each time I stopped the cold returned but it became weaker and weaker and finally whatever it was never came back."

The old man's eyes sought out those of the woman, his friend. "You see, Millie, there is evil. I have seen it and felt it."

Quiet words but strong with conviction, "Evil does exist and I am afraid. I am afraid to get involved in the old ways of my people."

He wasn't quite finished and Millie knew it. She waited for him to continue.

"You see," he flexed his shoulders and neck, trying to relax, "when I was a young man, Barking Fox in Flowers, my grandmother, told me one day, 'Henry, stay away from the old ways. The old ways are strong. Some good is there but also bad. Henry Two Feathers, you must not let anyone talk you into learning about the old ways, about the medicine that can come of it. The old ways are powerful and you are not strong enough to deal with them. They would destroy you. Go to church. You are a good Methodist. Love God. Do not seek what is past, what must die with your generation."

He was finished. The story had been told. He appealingly looked at Millie.

"Sweet Grass Woman, Henry. You must go to Sweet Grass Woman."

"Oh, lady! How can you say that? You sit there after hearing me explain why I can't and you calmly say, 'Sweet Grass Woman.' No arguments. No logical reasoning. I'm just supposed to go get myself messed up in the occult with all that damned mysticism and heaven knows what else!" He was getting angry.

Millie smiled, her body partially hidden by the softness of the recliner. She smiled from the shadows of the chair, the dimly lit room that was her life. She smiled and remained unmoving.

Slowly at first, almost unperceptively, a light of sorts, a radiation, encircled her frame. The aura, rose pink in hue, wavered, strengthened until the woman's body glowed brightly, obscuring her physical form. Then, gradually the light intensity weakened, retreated, disappeared. From the recesses of the room crystals tinkled musically, cheerfully.

Millie, still smiling, spoke. "Color pink is love. Go home, Henry. I gave you a sign. Go home to your Martha and sleep with her. When the time comes, you will know what to do. These things are real. You are blessed, my dear friend. Accept what is truth. Your grandmother was wrong. You are strong. You will prevail in what you must do."

*

Henry, shaken by the experience, drove carefully along the primitive road. He spoke but once.
"Damn women. They sure are weird."
Henry went home to his sleeping Martha.

*

CHAPTER 16

Far up the long, broad sweep of the high plains grasslands, above the gentle, yet sometimes rugged slopes of the Missouri River Valley, the land rolls on and on in vast, sweeping undulations.

In the old days, a century and more ago, the earth actually waved, bending to the great winds; a Sea of Grass, Conrad Richter wrote, almost unbroken from Mexico to the upper reaches of what is now known as Alberta and Saskatchewan.

Between the Milk and Cut Bank rivers on the west and the Sage and Milk on the east, for the Milk River arcs in a long graceful northern curve, there are places even today where the grass in early summer grows brilliant green. Later in the warm season the short grass becomes slightly golden, lighter and lovelier than wheat, dried under the sometimes-scorching summer sun.

One such area, bisected by a few "improved" gravel roads, perhaps the most enchanting of all, is called the Sweet Grass Hills.

Henry sat in his pickup, savoring a cigarette, exhaling the light blue smoke while absorbing the beauty of the land that rose before him. I wish Douglas were here, he thought.

They, the young man and the time-worn deputy, had occasionally talked of the Great Plains. Henry, for the most part, had listened. He had understood of what his young friend spoke.

Douglas had described how one could sit on a rise in Nebraska, or North Dakota, or Kansas, almost anywhere on the plains and watch the day end. Usually the sun set, a ball of red fire extinguished by the western horizon. For a while, a whiteness clung to the earth's rim until it, too, disappeared.

In the east, opposite the setting sun in the west, was where the most impressive phenomenon took place. Far, far away a low, thin line of darkness began to materialize on the eastern horizon. As the observer watched, what appeared to be a horizontal cloud grew thick, advancing nearer. At first, there was nothing really spectacular about the approaching shadow of night. Then, depending upon the observer's sensitivity and imagination, the black wall rose as if it were advancing to envelope the hills, the grass, the observer. And, the approaching night was doing just that.

Douglas had told Henry how sometimes he trembled in fear as the great darkness, now not really black but rather bluish black, rushed westward consuming all that lay before the observer. Fields, grain elevators, trees, houses and barns, all would disappear into the advancing gloom. His eyes would flash with the thrill of recollection and his voice sometimes trembled. He had told Henry about experiencing day's end several times, but he'd never really got to the description of when the advancing night engulfed him. Perhaps he couldn't find words adequate enough to properly explain the sensation that overcame him each time the blue-black night reached him, out there, often alone, on the Great Plains.

Carefully, although June was not the fire season, Henry stubbed the half-inch butt in the ashtray, eyes watery, not from tobacco smoke.

Douglas had become his friend, the son he and Martha never had. On that June morning in 1985, Henry struggled with the realization that he might never see the young man again. He sighed deeply.

The pickup moved back on the graveled surface and slowly headed north, toward the rising hills.

What was it that Douglas had said? ...something about the difference between men and women. That, with few exceptions, women could not comprehend why some men had to experience the wild places. The spirits of men like himself would languish and expire without the closeness to the good earth. Women could rationalize why such men didn't really need the "out-of-doors" as they often called it.

Douglas had said he thought the nature thing, be it mountain climbing, sailing the seas, hunting, fishing, or simply just being there, was beyond not only women's but most men's comprehension. Without the nature experience, such men as himself and Vern and Henry would simply wither and die spiritually.

Henry wondered if his young friend had been correct. He doubted that he had. Millie knew. His wife, Martha seemed to understand, too. She never complained about his fly-fishing or why he loved law enforcement with all of the frustrations and danger that went with it. She knew the job put him outdoors most of the time. And what of her own way of absorbing the things around her? He had caught her watching Chief Mountain many times. Often, while he fished, his wife would lie in the grass or go exploring, finding, in her own way, the very comprehension that Douglas thought women lacked.

Now, on that June afternoon, he drove ever closer to meet another woman; a person who would alter his life forever, an individual knowledgeable in the old ways, the part of reality that he feared.

"Ah, well." He shook himself free of his sadness and concentrated on the land about him. The hills were splendid. Balsamroot wagged hairy leaves and yellow-flowered heads in the slight zephyrs of an unusually calm day, a temporary calmness. Here and there Indian paintbrush boldly rose amid the greenery, upper leaves, sometimes a brilliant scarlet, or yellow, or orange, nearly obscuring the true flowerets of pale yellow luster. Sweet grass, for which the hills were named, grew everywhere, the new stems already rising tall, seeking the early summer's sun.

Once again, he pulled his truck off the road. He couldn't rid himself of Douglas's words.

"You know Henry, "if you put a Bushman from Africa or an Aborigine from Australia in jail they will die. I don't see why our own society can't accept the same human trait in our people, yours and mine. We are trapped in what is called Western Civilization. In a way, it is prison, too."

His friend's frustrations had been difficult to understand. Henry had almost always done what he wanted, within reason. But, he realized that he was living where he wanted to be. Most of the people he called friends were not displeased with their environment. Well, there were becoming to damned many tourists. And the Canadians! He simply couldn't comprehend living deep in the White Man's world. Why, he'd pack up and leave.

Douglas's words about environmentally concerned Theodore Roosevelt, Meriwether Lewis, Sigurd Olson and Barry Lopez, had no meaning whatsoever. Henry didn't have any idea who Olson and Lopez were.

Better forget Douglas's thoughts for now. I'm confused as it is.

He guided his pickup on to a dirt trail that passed for a lane. The truck rattled over a cattle guard. No cattle had been seen for some time. Bit by bit the road gained altitude, until he found himself on a small hilltop, surrounded with almost unbroken grasslands. A small house squatted in a lovely little valley. Its unpainted clapboards glistened dully in the June sunlight. There were two outbuildings, a freshly painted shed and an outhouse. He guessed that a vehicle of some sort was lurking in the shed.

He drove the last quarter mile in low gear, thinking of putting the truck in four-wheel drive. The pickup slipped down the eroded ranch lane. Henry's experienced driving prevented it from high centering or falling into one or two very deep potholes. The vehicle came to rest on a flat bench of land.

No one was in sight. Two non-pedigreed hound dogs lay basking in the sun. Neither was curious or ambitious enough to rise up to see what had arrived.

Henry picked up his holstered revolver from the rider's seat and placed it in the glove compartment. Not having the weapon available caused him to feel a small flutter of anxiety. He got out of the truck.

Although the month was June, each footstep resulted in gray dust wafting upward in tiny irregular spirals. No grass grew on the ranch yard. No flowers blossomed along the sides of the small house. In the rear, a large vegetable garden seemed to be thriving. "Must have a well," Henry guessed. It was obvious the residents did not waste the precious water.

From the back door of the house a clothesline stretched outward, supported by occasional four-foot high stakes. At the far end, the rope terminated with a knot tied in a loop to a hook that was screwed into the doorframe of the outhouse.

A woman was standing in the doorway of the house. She was heavy. Dumpy was the word. Her hair was pulled back and tied in a bun. Her dress was faded, worn from years of service. Aware that he had met the woman somewhere in the recent past, he politely removed his hat. "Hello, Tina."

The woman looked at the approaching stranger for a moment, then swung the screen door open. "Come in."

He habitually stooped as he passed through the door.

The woman waved at a wooden chair. "Sit down."

The little one-room house was immaculate. Bare pine boards, the floor, glistened with cleanliness. He felt certain that the woman had scrubbed them that morning. Nine dusty scuffmarks recorded where his boots had touched the floor. "Sorry," he apologized. The woman's eyes accepted his words. She sat down on the remaining chair.

Beneath the southern window, one of two such openings, a bare, severely scrubbed table stood alone. Behind the silent woman a large bed occupied a corner of the room. There was nothing else. No lamps or vases, no reading material, no utensils. Henry looked at the Spartan cupboard doors behind which the bare essentials were stored.

The two Blackfeet watched each other in an unstaring, respectful manner. Wondering if his trip was for nothing, he opened his mouth to inquire of Sweet Grass Woman. Before he could utter a sound, the woman spoke.

"She is emptying her bowels."

"Oh." Clear enough, he thought. They waited in silence.

Wood scraped on wood.

"You can look out the door if you want to."

He nodded his thanks.

The little outhouse door was open. Emerging from the shadowed interior was an ancient figure, severely stooped, maintaining her equilibrium with the help of a very crude home made cane. The old woman was wearing a faded, cotton dress. Yellowish, worn moccasins protected her feet. The woman's hair, pure white, hung about her face, tumbling down her shoulders, combed and cared for yet still seeming disheveled. He wondered how she could see through the strands covering her face. Expending considerable effort the bent figure got the outhouse door shut. Her feeble right hand reached out and found the rope. Grasping the lifeline, Sweet Grass Woman began her long journey back to the house.

"She's blind," Henry blurted out.

"Yes."

"Should I go help her?"

"No. You watch. When she comes close, you sit down and wait."

Soft plumping sounds, feet placed down firmly, cane poking into the dust, marked the woman's progress. Her companion opened the door and virtually lifted the old one over the threshold. Old one spoke; soft, unemotional words that he couldn't quite hear. The woman interpreted for him, a smile for the first time appearing on her face. "She say's that the little house smells pretty bad. She tells me I should throw lime into the hole and cover up the shit."

The old woman was still mumbling. The other woman laughed.

"She says she thinks a spider bit her on the butt." Enjoying the attention she was getting, Sweet Grass Woman chuckled as she patted her emaciated rump.

The companion woman helped the old one onto the bed, propping her up with several brightly decorated pillows. Henry smiled. The flowers stitched into the fabric were poinsettias ringed with laurel. Merry Christmas, he thought.

"Move your chair over here." The younger woman motioned to a position alongside the bed. Henry moved his chair, careful not to scuff the floor, and sat down.

The blind woman began to speak, in a dialect he couldn't understand.

"She says you are to take your jacket off. Too much of a smell of stale tobacco. Here," she reached out, "I'll hang it just outside the door. That way, anyone coming will know our old woman is busy and will not interrupt us."

He was beginning to like the younger woman.

So sudden that it startled him, "So! You are Henry Two Feathers."

"Yes, Mother."

"Ha! Mother. That's nice. You call me Mother and I'll call you Henry."

"Fine. That is good."

"I've heard of you, Henry. I know about your work. Most of our people say you are a good man."

"And the rest?" he joked.

"They don't like you and a few say you are a no good son-of-a-bitch."

"Shame!" The other woman scolded her old friend. "You behave now." Turning to Henry she explained, "The older this one gets the worse her words are." The Old One waved the woman away. Tina moved her chair to the doorway, sat down, and silently watched.

For a time, there was only silence. Henry took the opportunity to study the Old One's features. Her skin was very dark, heavily wrinkled. Beneath the loose strands of hair two milky, sightless eyes stared out, unable to penetrate the thick cataracts that had grown over the lenses. Cheekbones, sharp beneath a skinny face, seemed to be holding the blind orbs in place. A just-as-craggy chin completed her features. She had no teeth.

Sensing what was going on she spoke, "I never was very pretty."

"Why," protested Henry, "I think you are very nice looking now."

"Humph!"

"When I was young, my mother told me that you were old," he informed her.

The toothless gray head and her companion both laughed.

"Now you must be near one hundred years of age."

The women laughed again.

"Henry Two Feathers, you are not so good in your counting. I remember the year of the great starvation."

"My God, Mother, that was the winter of 1883-84. You can't remember that far back."

Chuckling, the blind woman replied, "Oh, Henry," suddenly becoming very serious, "Oh, but I wish I didn't. The great starvation. The slow death."

She turned her head as if peering out of her right eye. Sweet Grass Woman continued. "That old Almost-a-Dog. He was a Piegan. Almost-a-Dog made a liar out of the government agency. They told us that 247 of our people had perished because the government didn't send us the cattle to replace the buffalo. They said 247 had perished. You know what that man did? Every time he was told of someone dying he marked his stick. Make a notch in this old willow stick that he carried with him. 555. We lost 555 of our people.

"Remember? Sure I do. We lost so much. So many. I'm old, Henry. Real old. And I'm not telling you how old. Just real old."

Her features changed, as if throwing off a bad memory, which is what she did. Looking up at nothing visible to her, Sweet Grass Woman asked, "Why did you come way out here, Henry Two Feathers? What do you want?"

Her questions surprised Henry. He had assumed that somehow she would know the answers without his telling her. Her eyes, reflecting moisture covering the whiteness of her affliction, appeared calm, waiting for a response.

"You expected me to know, didn't you?" Turning her face toward where her companion sat, "They all think I know everything." There was nothing emaciating about her laughter. "I'm Old-Woman-Know-It-All." She laughed again.

Tina, reading his thoughts, explained, "Grandmother likes to laugh. Everyone is so solemn around her she has to create her own humor."

The old woman sighed. "That's right. Like you, Henry."

"Now, Henry, I know about the boy you call Douglas. Several people have spoken of him. Why don't you tell me all about the boy with the funny White Man's name. He is why you came. You are after the one who hurt his back, aren't you?"

"Yes, Mother. I'm looking for a murderer, but not as a law officer. I'm hunting for this man because Douglas is my friend."

"Good. Henry, it is good that you do this. Before you tell me the story, my friend here will perform a little ceremony. Not long. The cigarette smoke lingers and as it is stale it will bother us in our business." Turning toward where she knew Tina was sitting the old woman ordered, "Get me a small twist of sweet grass."

Fascinated, Henry watched as Tina removed the small bundle of still green grass, placed it in an earthen bowl and lit it. Light, fragrant wisps of smoke rose, dancing around the old one's face. She inhaled deeply and with her skinny right hand she waved the dancing fingers toward Henry. "Breathe deeply, Henry. This is our incense, our medicine, our perfume, our great purifier. We used this powerful smoke at the Sundance ceremonies, when I was young. They still use it, I am told."

"Yes, the sweet grass is used in those ceremonies and in the sweat lodges," Tina interjected. "That is why the house smells so fresh. We burn the grass and the insects stay away."

"So that evil will not come," added the ancient one. "Now, be silent. Let us pray in our own ways for what we are about to do is a great thing. We must have the help that our ancestors called upon. Pray."

The old woman sat upon the bed, hands clasped, eyes closed, head erect, not bowed in submission.

Henry thought he should try to think a prayer. Our Father who art... The word "art" threw him. Sounded more like a man's name. He fidgeted a little, wondering if his visit was a mistake.

The Old One spoke, "You are not a religious man, Henry." Before he could respond she added, "That is OK. Your grandmother's instructions to avoid the old ways have clouded your mind. I feel that you will be very religious by the time your problem has been solved. Do you feel this, Tina?"

"Yes."

"Good. When you leave, you will take with you a bundle of sweet grass, to protect you and to help you pray.

"Now. The day will be warm. Tina has made lemonade. You see, we knew you were coming. In a little while, we will have lunch. You start now. When it is time to eat, Tina will silence you."

Henry began, the long story rolling out, every detail. The old woman sat unmoving, her white head cocked, listening carefully to what her visitor was saying.

*

"You stop. Rest your voice. Go outside and smoke. When you come back in we will eat."

*

Henry re-entered the little house to discover that Sweet Grass Woman was already eating.

Tina explained. "She likes peanut butter and jelly sandwiches. The old woman couldn't wait."

"I gum them," grinned the Old One. Crumbs stuck to the fragile skin of her shining lips.

"That's OK," Henry responded.

"It better be," she smiled. "I like Skippy Creamy, but you know, Tina has an awful time finding it for me. This jar," motioning toward where the container should have been, "my Great-Great-Grandson got it for me in Missoula. He's such a nice boy."

"The sandwiches look good," Henry lied. Then he tasted one and found them acceptable. They ate in silence, except for the Old One smacking her lips as she struggled to masticate the sticky sandwiches she was consuming.

"Oh!" Her exclamation startled him. "I've got to go again. The lemonade, you know."

Tina helped her to her feet and held on until the old woman got her legs going. She shook Tina's hands off her arm. "Stop that. Get the door for me. Where's my walking stick?" Slowly, what must have been painfully, Sweet Grass Woman, bent nearly double with arthritis, felt her way along the cotton rope to the outhouse.

Henry watched. A sadness rushed upon him. "I don't know what to say, Tina. She is so frail but her power is nearly overwhelming. Even I can feel it and I don't believe in this stuff. I didn't," he corrected himself.

"Yes." Tina had decided that Henry was acceptable.

They stood just outside the doorway, Tina and Henry, watching the ancient one sliding her long bony fingers jerkily along the clothesline, a stubborn refusal to accept help.

The daily wind had arrived, sweeping the grasses in columns of waving blades, row upon row, down the hillsides, converging it seemed, not upon the house but rather to consume the lonely little figure of Sweet Grass Woman. The dull skirt whipped about the Old One's legs, revealing yellowed moccasins and wrapped leggings binding the once rounded calves of legs that men had found beautiful. Not now. Ruptured veins hid beneath the bindings. Twelve decades of running, playing, jumping, child bearing and carrying heavy burdens had broken the lifelines beneath the skin, creating bulges, spider ruptures, and of late, a month or so, sores which defied any salve or lotion applied to cure the lesions. Soon, at last, she would die, go on to where her husbands, all three good men, well, two of them were, would greet her once again.

Sweet Grass Woman reached the door of the privy. Like the White Man's outhouses, hers had a half-moon cut into the door, carved all the way through the sturdy panel, thus admitting a feeble light. Opening the door with its stiff spring was the most difficult task, especially with the high wind.

One day she would fall. That would end her independence, as she enjoyed it. A broken thigh, mind drifting away, her soul trapped in a dysfunctional wreck of a human body. She would die here, in the Sweet Grass Hills. Not in Browning, with it's noises and filth. Not in that "Indian" hospital but here where the wind was alive and the sun poured it's great energy earthward, where at night the stars showed with such intensity that humans looked in awe and cried because of the heavenly splendor.

Above all, in her world of darkness, Sweet Grass Woman remembered the stars on a winter's night. They seemed so very close to the Earth. And, she thought, perhaps, just perhaps one of them would come down to her as one had done so very long ago, the starvation winter, and had somehow saved her life. Inside the outhouse, excrement dribbling from her wrinkled butt, Sweet Grass Woman thought of that peculiar experience which had started her on her course as a medicine woman; a Shaman.

In the privy, the air was cool, the stink trapped beneath the seat. The little breezes were soft, fresh with Tina's new layer of lime. The wind tore at the structure, as it did almost every day, but to no avail. She was safe in the dark world within her own personal darkness.

Sweet Grass Woman slept.

*

"What's she doing in there?" Henry's question was one of concern.

"Oh, she falls asleep sometimes," Tina matter-of-factly responded.

"Is she all right?"

"Sure. I'll get her out. Watch."

Tina reached out from the doorway, grabbed the rope and gave a mighty tug. The board holding the other end of the rope pulled out slightly from the outhouse frame and then slammed back in place.

Bang!

"There. That will wake her."

"Hope she has a good heart."

"She does," Tina assured him.

Up on the western slope, where heat waves shimmered and danced erratically, a whirlwind developed. The miniature funnel was invisible at first. Gradually picking up chaff, blades of still-green this-years-grass, bugs, all swirling around and upward, the phenomenon growing in intensity, the funnel, now visible, wove back and forth moving erratically downhill, reaching the barren yard just as the old woman struggled out of the toilet.

Too late to escape the unseen danger Sweet Grass Woman grasped the clothesline and leaned on her walking stick. Dust, an airborne mass of desiccated soil, struck her solidly. She seemed to falter, almost falling over, skirts sailing up over her shoulders. Then the whirlwind passed on, moving alongside the house and beyond.

Relentlessly the wind whipped at the white mass of hair, sweeping it across vacant eyes, merging the strands with the unplucked also-gray brows. A few hairs found the woman's gasping mouth and entered quickly, caressing what once had been sensuous lips and tongue.

Henry, watching the slow approach of Sweet Grass Woman, took in the prominent cheekbones, sometimes exposed ears with dangling lobes, and the sharp aquiline nose. He thrilled at the raw beauty he found there, in the old woman's face.

She reached the door. Henry started to open the screen. She heard his movement. "I can do it."

He drew back from the curtness of her tone.

Then, "Whew! The wind really whistles through your pants today."

All three laughed. They took up their old positions in the room.

"Now." Sweet Grass Woman was sitting on the edge of the bed. "You had just finished telling me about Julie. Go on, Henry."

As the lawman talked, Tina wiped the woman's dusty face and hands. Next, she combed the long hair into a semblance of order.

Henry continued his story. He concluded the account around three.

Sweet Grass Woman sat quiet for some time, eyes open, vacant eyes seeming to see. "So, old Coyote talked to you and Douglas. To you, two different times, a year apart."

"Well, not really. He didn't talk—"

She waved him into silence. "Yes he did. Not in words you could hear, but you understood him, didn't you?" She didn't wait for a reply. "Douglas knew that he was in danger. You went to see Millie. Now you have come to me for help. Don't reject Coyote's messages. Don't offend our old friend's help." The ancient face took on a scowl.

"I'm sorry that I offended you," protested Henry. "I have no experience with such......"

The old woman waved him into silence again

"Your problem, Henry Two Feathers, is that your grandmother had stubborn ways."

That was the second time she had mentioned his mother's mother. Confused, he asked, "What do you know about my grandmother?"

"I know her very well. I said, 'know' because I do not accept an end to the spirit at physical death. Neither do I refuse to speak of the deceased as our people do. That is one of the rights I possess as a medicine woman."

"A Shaman," Henry declared.

"Yes. If you wish. A Shaman."

"I suppose you believe that we wander about as ghosts or go to some unpleasant world."

"No. Those thoughts are wrong. You see, Henry, I am a medicine woman but more a Shaman, as the White people say. I am respected for what I know, the wisdom I have been given."

"By the Old Ones."

"May be. You could call them that. Yes. I studied the old ways. The old powers your grandmother told you to avoid, to fear."

He was surprised. "How do you know this truth?"

"She told me that she would not let you get caught up in the old ways of our fathers. You would be a modern man. A White Man. Your grandmother even refused to use her native name, Barking Fox in Flowers. Always she was Lydia. Never Barking Fox in Flowers."

"It's shorter." He shouldn't have said that.

"Quiet!" For a few moments she mumbled to herself. "Lydia means nothing. An empty name for a woman who turned her back on her people. 'Lydia', is an anathema."

Henry raised his eyebrows in surprise.

Tina explained. "Sometimes I read this old woman words from the dictionary. She likes 'anathema' because of the way the word sounds."

"Quiet!"

Silence. Somehow the atmosphere in the house was different. Tina appeared to have faded deeper into the wooden chair upon which she sat. Sweet Grass Woman's poise became almost regal. She held her head high, the face seeming to seek the ceiling.

"Now. No more nonsense, Henry Two Feathers. It is time to stay serious. Come here. Let me feel your face. I want to know what you look like. Humm. Fine nose for an old man. You don't drink."

"No, Mother."

"Good." Her fingers moved lightly over his features. "Good. Slackness of cheek muscles. Nice eyebrows. Cared for. Shows self-respect. Much hair for one your age. Is it gray?"

"A little. At the temples. Some strands here and there. Not much facial hair." She leaned forward sniffing his hands, behind his ears and even lifted his left arm to inhale his sweat.

He was embarrassed.

"Good, old man Henry. You stink of White Man's things but you are pure Indian. If you weren't, my dogs would have bitten you."

He doubted if they would have gotten up no matter what sort of creature he was.

"I had to be sure. You are a pure blood. Rare these days." Gently the hands shoved him away from the bed. Sweet Grass Woman was still sitting up, legs dangling from the side of the bed.

"Listen, Henry Two Feathers. Your grandmother was wrong. That time she was wrong."

"About what?"

"Listen. Be silent. I will tell you."

Sweet Grass Woman rubbed her aching knees. "Tina, help me in to bed. No. I'll leave my walking clothes on, like this morning. Just put my legs and feet on that old blanket. Then, when I have to pee again I will be dressed."

"Yes, old friend." Tina propped her old woman up in bed.

"Thank you.

"She was wrong, Henry, for you are not weak. Your spirit is very strong. You must not fear the bad ones that are part of the old ways. You are strong."

"I don't understand," he protested.

"You must learn the old ways. The evil you seek is more than just man. If you are to stop the murders then you must get help from our spirits. The good ones."

Henry felt trapped. "Well, I'm not sure—"

"Henry Two Feathers." She emphasized his name. "If you want to stop the killing you have no choice. If you love Douglas as your son, as I think you do, you can no longer decide or pick and choose what you want to do. Do what I say. Henry, you must do what I tell you."

"Well, OK."

"Not good enough. Say it."

"I promise that I will try to follow your teachings."

"Not 'try'."

Henry protested. "Mother, what if I can't?"

Sweet Grass Woman's voice trembled with emotion. "The Gros Ventre, who lived here before us, saw your ancestors coming across the plains so very long ago. Their moccasins were blackened with ashes from a plains fire. You are of noble blood. Your ancestors are great ones in the spirit world. They demand that you obey me. You will not fail them. Henry, look at me. I feel them here in this room. Now. You are one of them. Blackfeet!

"You will do what I say. Agree."

"I agree." His words were weak. Strong doubts rushed into his head. Was the old one senile?

"Now, Tina, we need some more lemonade."

A pained look came upon his face. He hesitantly said, "Mother, I've got to follow the rope."

"Good. For a while I thought your kidneys were not working. Go Henry. When you come back inside you will tell me anything else that I should know. Then we begin."

Henry got up, hoping that he could make it to the john.

The Old One added, "And don't pee just outside the door. Go to the outhouse. You men think you are something special with that thing you have."

*

Silence pervaded within the tiny prairie home. Tina had swept away the dusty footprints all three had created, mostly because of trips to the little house with the half-moon door. Stirring ever so slightly, the old woman broke the silence. "We have agreed. You, Henry Two Feathers and myself, Sweet Grass Woman. Let the spirits of our beloved ancient ones listen.

"Now is the time for the preparation for your vision quest. You are the oldest person I know of to seek a vision. But, you must. There is no other course to follow. Where would you like to go?"

"I don't have the slightest idea," he confessed.

"Yes you do, Henry Two Feathers. Now think."

He remained silent, not knowing what to say but realizing that what he wished he could do, he could have done in his youth.

Sweet Grass Woman spoke again. "In the old days, the medicine man would tell the boy or sometimes a girl where to travel for their personal journey to the spirit world. It was always three days journey here or three days journey there. In some tribes, the time was four days. I read about the coastal people of the Pacific, before I lost my eyesight. They, some of them, took four-day journeys.

"In the old days Blackfeet would walk to the sacred rock of the plains. Nowadays it sits, unbecoming, outside the museum in Browning. Others would go to Pitamakan Falls; Trick Falls as the Whites so disrespectfully call it. But, today we have the automobile and the truck, so the number of days fasting must be done some other way. Now, think, Henry. I know what is on your mind. If you were a young brave where would you want to go for a vision quest. Say it, Henry. You must permit yourself to ask for the journey."

He was sweating. "Well, I guess," mouth sticking with dryness he struggled to speak the words, "Chief Mountain; but in all due respect, Mother, I'm too damned old for that kind of a climb."

"Then, Henry Two Feathers, that is where you will go; must go." Tina nodded her agreement. He knew better than to protest. Henry also knew his legs were about worn out. Emphysema was working at his lungs, causing shortness of breath and sometimes dizziness.

"From now on we don't call our sacred mountain, Chief Mountain. That is a White Man's arrogant name," she explained. "Long, long ago, even before the horse came to our land, our sacred mountain was called Nina'istuko. That is what you will always call the home of our God. Nina'istuko. Say the sacred name, Henry."

"Nina'istuko."

"Good. You speak the sacred name as a Blackfeet, a Piegan, should." The old woman moved her head about, as if trying to see him. "Some say Nina'istuko is the home of the Thunder Bird. I don't put much belief in a god like Thunder Bird. My voices tell me the name is for children and the unimaginative mind of the White Man. Others, like me, this old crone, say the sacred mountain is the dwelling place of the Wind Spirit! I think maybe that is true. The Wind Spirit is true. He is outside today, tormenting any blind old woman with failing kidneys that he can meet on the trail to the half-moon house." She laughed. Her voice seemed remarkably youthful, rich, and vibrant.

"There is more, up there. We mortals... I learned that fine word from the dictionary... really can not recommend."

"Comprehend," corrected Tina. "Why don't you keep your words simple, old mother?"

"Yes. I will. What I mean to say is that man tries to describe God. Mostly, they make God appear as a man with oversized muscles. That is not true. Some others see him as a forest creature, a ghost, the Sun. Not so."

"How do you know, Mother?" he inquired. "Do you know what God looks like?"

"No! Man doesn't know what He looks like or what He is. We must just do our best to please Him as we live here on Earth."

Henry grew more curious. "Did you figure that out, Mother?"

"No. They told me. The others told me to accept God and not try to see Him in my mind."

"What others?"

The old woman was getting frustrated. Her fingers twisted the gray strands of her hair. Tina spoke. "Of this, Henry, my old woman cannot explain without getting upset." Turning to the ancient one she added," Now, Sweet Grass Woman, tell Henry what he must do."

"You will climb Nina'istuko. Up there the Great One will reveal how you can discover who harmed your friend, Douglas.

"Now go. I am very tired."

Henry left the two women in their little house. There was no more to learn. He, a Blackfeet, would be told who the killer was.

CHAPTER 17

Two and a half months before Henry visited Sweet Grass Woman, the Great Bear peered out of his den. A late winter avalanche had stripped away much of the protective snow that had covered his sanctuary's entrance. Cold, blustery winds had wakened him prematurely, penetrating even his thick fur and thinning layers of fat. Fortunately a heavy snow, over a yard deep, once again sealed his den shut, thus ending the bear's discomfort.

When the Great Bear, who enjoyed sleeping above all else, peered out again, April was a mere two days away. The winter avalanche had not only temporarily exposed the den to the winter elements, but it had covered the nearby dead human body with tons of snow, trees and other debris. Gradually the rocks, logs and brush, heated somewhat by the warmer weather of early Spring, melted the adjacent snow, creating fissures, caves, all sorts of openings, penetrating far down into the slide.

Sniffing deeply, the Great Bear smelled the ever-so-faint odor of the dead man that Clarence Kipp had deposited. Another smell, a dead mountain sheep, killed by the avalanche, guided the bear away from the human to a more easily accessible feast of carrion. The murdered man's body was forgotten.

Deep, soppy snow choked Atlantic Creek. Further downstream, beyond the Cut Bank campground, the bear found succulent young shoots of grasses, sedges, flowers, and best of all young cow parsnips. He languished in the low country for a long time.

One day the district ranger returned, riding his smelly horse. The time had come for the Great Bear to move on. During the following weeks he fed along the North Fork of the Cut Bank, digging for bulbs, rodents, anything edible. Once he came upon a lion kill, the deer only partially consumed. The carcass became the bear's property, much to the chagrin of the still-hungry mountain lion.

More people arrived in the valley. Two of them. The bear moved upstream to frozen Morning Star Lake. No food there. He went on to the even higher Katoya Lake, slept a few hours and then climbed to the pass.

On the June night following Henry's visit to Sweet Grass Woman, the Great Bear, now the Medicine Grizzly, topped out at a location the man-creatures call Pitamakan Pass. Pitamakan was Piegan, meaning Running Eagle, referring to the famous woman war chief of the Blackfeet Nation.

198

The Great Bear didn't know that, of course. Neither did he realize that he stood astride the Continental Divide or that he was looking down into the blackness of the Nyack Valley. The beast did enjoy crunching along in the snow of a bitterly cold, still night under a magnificent, full moon. He turned his enormous head to stare, perhaps in wonder, at the brilliant white circle that illuminated the rocky cliffs, snowfields, and the upper cliff walls of the deep depression beneath him. Beyond the Nyack, glaciers and massive snowfields clothed in last winters snow, gleamed, shimmered and sparkled as if the whole range of mountains was alive with moonbeams. The beast's amazing memory functioned again. The Great Bear knew that the Nyack valley was filled with bears, grizzlies. Some, perhaps, were in estrus, ready to mate. Hesitating only to plan a route of descent, the Great Bear plopped down on his ample rump and cautiously began sliding down the dangerous western snow slopes of Mt. Morgan.

*

"Are you sure you have everything you need?" Martha was driving the pickup.

"Yes. What do I need? I'm not supposed to drag along all of my possessions." Henry was somewhat irritated. Nervous. He always got that way when he was about to leave Martha behind.

She bit her lip, tears blurring her vision. She understood her husband; what he was about to do. He had no real choice if he was to remain a man. "You'll do just fine, Henry."

He noticed that she wasn't calling him Hot Shot.

"Thanks for the words, Martha. I appreciate your support," then added weakly, "and prayers."

Her head turned toward him in surprise, their eyes fixed momentarily upon one-another. Henry never spoke of praying. "Don't worry." She was changing the subject. "I'll look after the cattle and horses."

"You always do."

The pickup labored up the International Highway, the road that went to Chief Mountain Customs. She eased up on the accelerator, wanting to prolong their togetherness. Henry knew what she was doing and remained silent, feeling a tightness growing in his chest.

She asked, "Which road are you taking?"

"The second one. It's a little steeper, I think, but shorter," he explained.

"There's the first one. Up there." She pointed.

"Yes."

The truck moved on.

"Now listen, Martha, I have to leave my revolver with you. So, I don't want no low-life to see me get out here."

"OK."

"You just keep going. Don't stop except to let me out." She nodded her head, "yes." She knew her voice would break if she spoke.

"There, Martha. There's the road."

She slowed down, swung the truck around and stopped. Desperately she whispered, "Henry."

The old man reached out and clasped his wife's right hand. "I'll be all right, Martha. Honest."

"Yes."

He could barely hear her word.

The truck was idling at the gate.

They kissed.

"I love you, Martha."

"Yes."

"Now, get out of here! Don't forget to pick me up in three days."

She couldn't answer. The truck gained speed, became increasingly smaller until a rise in the road hid it from sight.

Oh, god, he thought.

*

Women make men cowards, Henry rationalized. He was standing just inside the protection of the first trees up slope from the road, scattered alder and fir. His gaze went back to Montana State Route 17, called the International Highway because the United States section ended at the Canadian border crossing. Anxiety over leaving Martha, so vulnerable at her age, fifty-seven, laid heavily upon the unarmed lawman. I suppose things would be worse if we had children, he thought.

Henry reached for the cigarettes that would have normally been in his left shirt pocket. They weren't. "Drat!" he hissed, realizing that trying to not swear was almost as bad as not smoking. "My only two vices."

His thoughts went back to when Sweet Grass Woman had ordered him to leave the cigarettes behind and to smoke no more. Obeying the medicine woman, he had tossed the half empty pack on the table as he walked out, followed by Tina. "I wouldn't be surprised if she didn't smoke them herself," he had protested.

"She will." Tina smiled at his perception. "The old lady smokes in the outhouse."

Grinning he had asked, "Are you sure?"

"You bet," Tina had replied. "We caught her once. She had tried to light up and got too close to the toilet paper. We nearly lost her. Some of her hair burned."

Standing in the seclusion of the trees he thought, Well, I hope she enjoys them for I sure could use a smoke. His hands were shaking badly. When he turned to advance up the trail his mind left Martha and his life behind him. The transition from the domestic man's environment to one who is on an adventure was complete, intense, without remorse.

Between the treetops puffy clouds, slightly darkened at the base, hinted of rain. Otherwise the day was fine, cool, slight breeze teasing the spring flowers, rustling the leaves a little bit. He was very much aware of the beauty of the world he was moving in. Somewhere, low in the trees ahead, a warbler peeped unobtrusively.

One set of truck tires since the last rain, Henry reported to himself as he read the imprints in the primitive road. Someone else was ahead of him, further up the mountain. Maybe, he thought, the tracks belong to Billy Smith. He hoped so.

The Slide Lake trail was steeper than he thought it would be. Breathing became an effort. His legs began to feel weak, inadequate for the task ahead. The first mile of walking in and out of ruts, dodging rocks and puddles caused his feet to hurt. Cowboy boots were not for walking. They were the only kind of footwear he owned.

Another slow mile grudgingly fell behind the seeker. Then, a third. Henry was beat.

"Hey, Lawman." The voice startled Henry. "Back this way."

The greeter was leaning against a wreck of a Dodge pickup. Henry stood, weaving a bit, catching his breath. When he was able, he spoke. "Well, Sam Hunting Bow."

"Don't call me that shit, man. I go by Sam Kennedy. Come on, Old Man, we got to walk up along this creek a ways. Think you can make it, Old Man?"

Henry tried to ignore the punk.

People had made several trips from the pickup. The trail of flattened grasses was easy to follow. Their destination was a table of relatively level earth, vegetation partially removed. Alongside the quick-flowing stream a small, nearly smokeless fire burned hotly. A few yards from the fire stood a peculiar looking roundish structure consisting of scorched, carbon-blackened hides and matting loosely attached to a willow frame.

Henry looked at the sweat lodge. "That's it?"

"That's it," grinned the disheveled-looking Sam. "You've got a real treat ahead of you."

"I wouldn't be surprised. Where's Billy?" asked Henry.

"Upstream there. Some place. Probably saying his prayers. "Or," Sam added, "taking a shit." The man's tone was contemptuous. Henry sat down in the grass to wait. Sam opened a Coors and chugged it down. "Ahh." He exhaled and threw the empty can onto the ground.

Henry looked away, trying to ignore his crude companion. He was thirsty and already very hungry. Time passed slowly.

"Hey, man!" Sam Kennedy's voice was loud and coarse.

"My name's Henry."

"Yeah. Yeah. I know." The man was leering at Henry. "I forgot to tell you." Sam belched loudly, then continued, "Billy says for you to take your clothes off and put this on." He threw Henry a skin loincloth.

"I'll wait 'till he gets back."

"Don't give me no shit, Lawman. He said do it as soon as you get here."

Henry was trying to control his anger. If the situation didn't improve soon, he vowed he'd go home.

Sam watched Henry undress and out of meanness grinned when he saw his genitals. Very angry, embarrassed, Henry moved away from his tormentor and sat down on a small rocky outcropping. The hardness hurt his butt. Attempting to ignore the beer guzzling Sam, Henry sat, eyes downcast. Bare feet met his gaze. He hadn't looked at them in daylight since he was a kid. They were so ugly. Big and skinny, the bones seemed to be enlarged, lying just beneath the pallid skin. The middle nails of his left foot were black, ready to come off. Henry had dropped a pipe wrench on them.

"Stupid thing to do," he muttered. "Maybe I should try to meditate." Henry had never meditated before so his attempt failed. A few early season flies found his nakedness. Then the mosquitoes came. He was miserable.

Billy Smith found Henry futilely waving his arms at the insects. "Hi, Henry. How you doing?"

"I'd be better if he wasn't here." Henry motioned toward Sam.

One glance was enough for the holy man. "Pick up those cans and put them in that empty sack."

Sam grumbled but obeyed. Henry was surprised. Sam seemed to be afraid.

"Now, get out of here."

"Huh?"

"You heard me. Get out of here. You're drunk. You are desecrating this mountain."

"I'm doing what?"

"You heard me. Get out."

"Ok. Ok. Man—" Sam grumbled down the grassy trail.

Henry was pleased at Billy's power to control the drunk. The medicine man wasn't very large, just five and a half feet tall. Well built though.

"I'm sorry, Henry," apologized Billy. "Sam was the only one I could get to put up the sweat lodge. I've got a hernia and can't lift much."

"No harm done," Henry lied.

"No. He's disrupted my mood." Billy seemed genuinely sad. "Let's meditate awhile. Clearing our minds of bad things, like Sam, will get us back on track. Here." He tossed Henry a stick of Cutters repellent. "Smear that on so the mosquitoes won't eat you." They both smiled. Henry was beginning to like his teacher.

"When we begin the ceremony the bugs will not bother you."

Henry hoped so.

*

CHAPTER 18

Evening, accompanied by a chill wind, descended upon the slopes of the holy mountain. The two men, initiate and Shaman, were eating lightly of dried buffalo and peculiar balls of dough which they toasted over a small fire that Billy had started from embers of the larger, special blaze.

"We will eat only a little bit, Henry. Here," handing him a mug of water, "drink this to wash the food down."

Henry must have looked surprised.

Billy added, "Usually the initiate fasts completely. However, you are much older than most so you need your strength. Go ahead. Drink."

The cold water, refreshing because the large canteen had been immersed in the stream, chilled him, yet tasted sweet and clean.

Billy's instructions on how to meditate had worked. Deep breaths had relaxed them both. Eyes closed, hands loosely clasped in his lap, allowed thoughts to come rushing into Henry's head. Martha, Douglas, the fence that needed mending, the unpaid medical bill, all in their own way worrisome, flowed through Henry's mind and although not resolved they had been met and fell from his concern.

Once Henry had become so relaxed he almost fell over sideways.

With the worries faced and discarded the sub-conscious mind took over and Henry remained in a trance-like condition for some time.

"Feel better?" Billy was smiling. Henry's chin had been imbedded deep in his chest, making normal breathing all but impossible.

Henry looked about, somewhat surprised. "Yes. I think so. I thought I was falling once."

"Good," declared Billy. "That means you were completely relaxed. Probably for the first time in your adult years."

"What about sleep?"

"That's different. The relaxation you just experienced is a far deeper form of rest."

Billy was watching Henry closely. "Head ache?"

"Yes. A little," admitted Henry.

I shouldn't have wakened you so abruptly," confessed Billy. "Tell you what, Henry, we will shut our eyes and I'll talk to you a bit. When you open your eyes again, the discomfort will be gone."

*

"Say, how did you do that?" Henry was impressed.

"Oh, I used a little hypnosis, that's all."

"Really? I've never been hypnotized before." Henry thought the experience was fun.

"Yes, you have," corrected Billy. "You use hypnosis on yourself very often. You just don't realize what it is."

Henry's face reflected doubt.

"Ever catch yourself daydreaming? Or thinking about nothing?"

"Yes. I guess so."

"That's it." Billy grinned.

Henry was uneasy about broaching the subject. "Say, I have a little problem with calling you 'Billy'. I don't mean that isn't a nice name but don't you have another one? One you use when you do this stuff?" Henry swung his right arm about encompassing the whole camp with his gesture. "A name that gives you more respect?"

Billy teased him. "Like 'Sir', or 'General', or 'Doctor'?"

"You know what I mean. For the ceremony."

Billy had been asked that question many times. "I don't like my Indian name, Throws Stones at Horses. The Blackfeet words for that are even worse. How about Poia?"

"Sounds good to me," responded Henry. He knew that the name was that of a legendary Blackfeet hero, a medicine man in the old days.

Billy smiled. "I like it. Not really my name, but, what the heck."

Henry noted that the cuss word 'hell' wasn't spoken.

Poia spoke again. "Darkness will be slow coming, since this is June. Not 'till ten, maybe later. So, let's start."

"OK."

"One more time, Henry. Drink this bowl of water. There is a little salt in it which will help you."

He slowly swallowed the slightly saline liquid.

"Now," instructed Poia, go urinate, over there in the trees. Have you had a bowel movement?"

"Yes. The herbal tea Sweet Grass Woman sent me cleaned me out real good."

"Good. When you come back we will start."

*

The two men had moved up close to the sacred fire, positioning themselves on a dirty, well-worn blanket.

205

"You just sit quiet, Henry."

"OK," came the deep voiced response.

Billy, now Poia, inhaled deeply five times. Each time he faced a different direction, the last one being up. He began to chant, a soft, nearly inaudible song that Henry couldn't comprehend. The prayers or whatever Poia sang were long, consuming a good quarter of an hour. The singing ceased. Henry felt surprisingly calm.

Poia, who had stood during the breathing and singing sat down again, facing Henry. "Henry, the sweat lodge ceremony is done in many ways by many people. The way we will perform the rituals will be the Lakota, the Sioux way. They call the sweat lodge Inipi. Say the name, Henry."

"Inipi." The sounds of the name came easily to Henry's lips. He thought they sounded familiar.

"Good," encouraged Poia. "Inipi." He became silent in contemplation.

"In the old days the Sioux were our enemy. Even today we Piegans, Blackfeet, hate them. And some Lakota despise us. Such feelings are foolish for we are all God's children. We are all from the same creation. Earth Mother spawned us out upon the surface of the Earth to learn how to become more like the Great One."

Henry thought about his dislike for the Pawnee and made a mental note to try to remove his prejudice. The same with the Comanche.

Poia hesitated again, while he planned his words. "The Sioux, when the White Man came, were something special. Of all the nations, the Sioux were the most mystical, the closest to understanding what this is that we all experience.

"I think the horse did that to them. The Lakota became spirits on horseback, riding far out on the great expanses of grasslands, arms widespread, sometimes staring at the sun, while the horse galloped beneath them, freely running where it wished, guided by the spirits. Horse and man became one, two beings entwined in their wildness, in their prayers, in their souls. If you or I, Henry, stared at the sun as they did we would go blind. Not the Sioux. At least not the holy ones. They were, I believe, spirits closer to God than any other people have ever been."

Henry thought about Poia's words. "Isn't some of that just stories? I always thought the Sioux were delusional. A little nuts."

Poia smiled again. "Very likely some of the stories are made up. Modern and so not true. But not all. Have you ever heard of Sitting Bull and how he broke a great drought?"

"I vaguely remember," confessed Henry. "Tell me about it."

"Those were the days of the terrible famines of the last half of the 1800s. As bad as our winter of death. The government failed to deliver the cattle allotment to the Sioux and they were suffering terribly. The buffalo were gone. Because of the heat and dryness the plains were naked. Just emptiness. Except for the deep-rooted plants like our sacred sweet grass, most plants were dead.

"One day, frustrated and very angry, Sitting Bull went to the government agent to tell him that the Sioux were dying. They must have food.

"According to what I was told the Agent flew into a bad temper. He shouted at Sitting Bull. Swore bad words at him. He tried to humiliate the great chief. Finally, out of breath and words, the Agent said in an angry voice, 'If you, Sitting Bull, are so great why don't you make it rain?'

"The great Sioux chief, the friend of Buffalo Bill Cody, stood up as tall as his stocky body would allow and replied, 'I will make it rain,' or something like that. Sitting Bull walked proudly outside of the agency house and plopped himself down in the middle of the dusty yard. He was facing west. The great medicine man began chanting his prayers. He prayed all day, facing always to the west. People coming and going on horseback raised dust clouds that settled over Sitting Bull until he looked like the earth itself. His voice, although his throat was very dry and dusty, never faltered. The White men laughed.

"Those who were there said that by late afternoon very small, dark clouds appeared over the far western horizon. They continued to grow for the remainder of the day, getting closer. The storm grew in power and intensity." Poia watched Henry's face and saw that the older man was listening intently.

"That night, as you have been told, the rains returned and the earth began to renew itself, bathed in the water from the Great One. Green things began to appear upon the earth once again."

The story ended, the example of Sioux spiritual power made, Poia arose, walked to the sweat lodge, reached inside and extracted a short, stout stick. Returning, he made his point. "Since the Lakota possess great spiritual power our sweat lodge ceremony will be based, much of it, on the Sioux tradition.

"Because the White Man is beginning to imitate our sacred ceremonies and because they and some of our brothers are charging Whites to experience a ceremony, you will not reveal what happens inside the sacred sweat lodge. This is a command."

"I accept the wishes of Poia, my teacher and spiritual guide," agreed Henry.

"Good!

"Sometimes those misguided fools use marijuana in the Sweat Lodge ceremony. That pleases some, but the wrong destroys any spiritual value the participants might have received, even from a paid-for-ceremony."

Poia looked at the stick, more like a small pole, which he held in his hands. "This," he explained after he was once again seated, "is the Beaver Stick, very important to the Blackfeet, Piegans, whichever you choose to call us."

"I prefer Blackfeet," Henry declared.

"Good. So do I.

"We use the Beaver Stick, sometimes, because of the legend of Manyan. I personally find that the Beaver Stick has great protective powers."

"I remember that name from my childhood. Grandfather told us that Manyan meant 'new robe.'"

"Your Grandfather was right, Henry. The Beaver Stick story tells us of a young man who is helped by a beaver family. When it became springtime, and he was to leave them to return home, Beaver Chief, the one who had made the lodge that Manyan was living in, offered the young man anything he wanted. He could take anything he desired home with him. Instead of riches, the Blackfeet youth chose the Beaver Stick. You see the young man knew that the Beaver Stick was the most powerful of Beaver Chief's medicine. The stick, this stick that I hold, protects the possessor from water dangers. The Beaver Stick will enable the medicine man or woman to cure people of illnesses."

Henry looked skeptical.

"When the water is poured on the holy rocks inside the sweat lodge Beaver Stick will protect you. Keep you safe from rock explosions, from scaldings, and will sometimes cure you if you have a sickness. You will carry this holy thing to the top of Nina'istuko. Never will you use it as a staff or tool of any kind," Poia added, "unless you know that you are to use it. Beaver Stick will let you know."

"Seems pretty heavy for me to lug to the top of the mountain and back," observed Henry.

"We do not know the size of the first Beaver Stick. I think it must have been small for Manyan wore it around his neck. Perhaps this size is not correct."

Henry studied the three-foot, barkless pole. Incisor imprints from a beaver's chewing, indicated how the pole had been stripped of bark.

"You will not take much with you, Henry; this wooden object, a sacred bundle and some dried sweet grass to use in your ceremony. That is all."

Henry sat listening, his face expressionless.

"What I now tell you is very important, Henry. Do not forget what I am about to say.

"A long time ago, in a cave far south, near a place the White Men call Indian Head, not so many miles from the Rio Grande River, a very holy man told me of an elder, an even more powerful wise man named Swift Eagle. I don't remember the Apache word for his name. Swift Eagle is remembered among the Apache for the wise words he would say. They were as if from the Creator himself. One thing he said must be remembered by you, Henry. Swift Eagle declared that, in his words, 'If you really need something, be prepared. Then it will come to you.'

"Repeat the words, Henry, so that I will know you are armed with this old one's wisdom."

Henry cleared his throat. "If I really need something, I should be prepared. Then, it will come to me."

"Good." Poia was pleased with how Henry had personalized the saying. Without hesitation Poia continued, telling Henry about the sacred sweat lodge. "Let me tell you that the poles are of willow saplings, cut not far from your ranch. I cut them myself, in a special way. Where they had grown, as in the old days, I placed tobacco. Do you know why?"

"Probably to thank the willow spirits for their gift of poles," guessed Henry. The concept was not unfamiliar to him.

"You are right." Poia was pleased with Henry's response. "Doing so, giving the tobacco, also helped keep me well while I built this lodge and while we perform the sacred ceremonies which will soon begin.

"Willow has a very special relationship with water, growing so close to the streams as it does. Water is much needed by us. Man. Water will be what you desire most when you are on the mountain. Here at the lodge, water will cleanse us as we pray.

"While willow represents the plants of our world, other things are also represented in the sweat lodge, the Inipi. You will find animals, birds of the sky, stones, the air, water and fire, all inside. For you see, the Inipi is a small world, a microcosm of all that God created. Each of those I mentioned have special powers that will help you when we are inside."

Henry volunteered something he knew. "My Grandmother, who raised me, used to do something with willow bark, when I had a headache."

Poia smiled. "That's right. The bark contains the same medicine we now use by taking aspirin."

The medicine man, having lost his chain of thought, held his chin in his left hand. "Let's see. I guess I've covered the poles enough. Oh. The poles are set so that basically the round sweat lodge has four sides exactly parallel to the four main directions. North, south, east and west." He smiled, "I used a compass to make sure I was right." That completed the pole explanation.

"Now for the covering of the Inipi."

Henry was beginning to wonder if they'd ever get around to the actual ceremony.

Poia continued his discourse on the sweat lodge. "In the old days the Inipi was covered with animal skins, usually all buffalo. Sometimes others were used, like what we have here. This Inipi's covering consists of pieces of canvass and old, worn out blankets. My friends and I tell participants that the worn blankets represent human life, they having experienced many of the passions and emotions of man. Personally, I think that is an excuse so we don't have to use new blankets. New ones could become very expensive."

Henry, once again busy swatting mosquitoes, missed the humor of Poia's narration.

"Our Inipi has two animal skins. Sweet Grass Woman said this should be."

"Oh?" Henry was once again listening.

"Yes," smiled Poia. He smiled often. "The smaller one, the skin you see on the south side, there, to the right of the door is a coyote skin. I got it from a road kill. Coyote was known, in the old days, as a trickster. Our people regarded him as a deceiver, always getting people into trouble. Some consider Coyote that way today. I don't. Many of our people think there is nothing to the old stories, that Coyote is no more a minor god than you or I."

"Well," Henry confessed, "I agree with them."

Poia appeared distressed. "But, Henry, look what he did for you and the boy. He warned you both and even told you what to do to get you on the road to finding the answers you so badly need. You don't really think you imagined those incidents with Coyote, do you?"

He didn't answer.

"In your case, Henry, Coyote understood the seriousness of what was happening to so many people. You know. The missing ones."

Henry's mouth opened in surprise. "You know about them? The people that we don't know what happened to them?"

"Sure. I know. Sweet Grass Woman knows. Our tribal leaders know about the missing Whites and Indians."

"But why—," Henry began.

"We, some of us, have tried to solve the mystery. There are no clues. Our prayers have not resulted in our getting answers. Then, thanks to Coyote, you came to us for help. We needed you. You must realize that the prayers of many powerful leaders and our shamen are going out to the Great One, so that you will be successful.

"Henry, we would have helped you even if Douglas whatever-his-name-is, would have been the only victim. He isn't. We don't know what to do." Poia frowned again. "We fear that the new mystery, the disappearing people, will end just like the cattle mutilations of the 1960s. No solution." He looked appealingly at Henry. "They are still happening, you know. After all of these years we still do not know what is mutilating our livestock."

"I know." The possible connection between the missing people and the mutilated cattle frightened Henry. He had never thought that the answer to one could be the answer to the other type of death; if the people were indeed dead.

"Maybe," speculated Henry, "There is no connection at all."

"I hope not," whispered Poia. Both men sat in silence, their minds troubled by the unsolved mysteries.

The mosquitoes began searching for shelter from the falling temperature. Henry barely noticed that they had left.

Poia roused out of his contemplation. "The other animal skin you cannot see from here. He is our cousin, the grizzly bear. As you must know, the bear is a very powerful animal, the only creature that our warriors were afraid of. Bear symbolizes both life and death. When the bear, which I prefer to call 'Our Brother', is in his winter sleep he is very close to the spirit world. He dreams. Bear must know many wise things. Joseph Cannon, the Iroquois from New York who lives in Browning, told me that their old people say that bear can bring people back to life. For you, Henry, we will pray that our powerful brother will bring you rejuvenation."

I can sure use some of that, thought Henry.

"Once the lodge is covered with skins, canvass, robes or whatever, it becomes an Inipi, a truly living being."

Henry looked at the unmoving, very ugly, rounded sweat lodge.

Poia said, "The Nez Perce, from Coleville, say the Inipi is the body of our Great Spirit Chief. When you go inside you will sense that this may be true because you will know that you are in the body of something alive and authoritative. Something alive and strong will be dwelling in the darkness of the skin with so much power. Do not forget to pray for your health and good life as well as for the answers you seek. You cannot overwhelm the Inipi with your needs. He, more than a Catholic Priest, has heard it all before." Poia's tongue was thickening. He wasn't used to talking so much.

"One last item. Did you notice the pipe just outside the entry flap?"

Henry could still see the object in the fading light.

"The pipe is the Calumet, the pipe-stone. We believe the pipestone came from the blood of very ancient animals. Calumet represents the stones from the Earth that were the ancient ones."

Henry looked puzzled.

"Think about that some other time. I know what I'm trying to say but have a hard time with it," apologized Poia.

"On the pipe, over there, the one we will use, you will find the figure of the bear carved in it. This one was used because Sweet Grass Woman feels that the bear plays an important role in your problem. We had to get this from our cousins, the Bloods, in Alberta and it cost us some horses to just borrow it for tonight. The pipe is special, too, for there are twelve eagle feathers hanging from it. The feathers are representatives of Eagle, who is messenger of Wakan-Tanka, the Great Spirit.

"Wood, once again. The pipe's stem, as you would expect, is made of wood, representing trees and plants that give life. Each time the door of the sweat lodge is opened, the pipe will be smoked by us, inside the Inipi. When the pipe is not in use, I will place it just outside the lodge door flap, on the small, elevated altar."

Henry thought Poia had completed his instructions. He was wrong.

"I personally selected these round stones which are heating in our sacred fire. They are from Idaho, where the Earth sometimes opens up letting out her lava, the lifeblood of Earth Mother. These were selected because of their size and shape, like a man's head."

Poia explained the reasoning behind the stone selection. "Igneous rocks, volcanic, do not explode like limestone, stones from river beds, some granite and stones containing quartz. Granite is igneous, too, but some types cannot be safely used. Men have died because of shrapnel from such stones. My rocks of the melted earth will hold the heat for a long time. Neither will they disintegrate or crumble, when the cold water finds their surface.

"One should never drop or throw the stones of the Inipi. If I should accidentally drop a stone, I must place it back into the fire and chose another one. Perhaps, such a fallen stone doesn't wish to be a part of a particular ceremony. These stones, the heated ones, are brought into the lodge and from then on are referred to as Our Elders. The Lakota, under whom I studied, called the ceremonial stones Tunka or Tunka-shila, which means, Grandfather. They are called Tunka because earth stones are living things and have souls.

"Rocks were here before the Blackfeet and even before the Ancient Ones, who were gone before modern man arrived. My Lakota teachers told me that all life began with the rising of a great stone from the waters of creation. When stones are heated and glowing in the dark, we in the Inipi return with them to the first dawn of creation."

Henry, fascinated, thought of the first emergence of land from the great seas that once covered the Earth and wondered how the Lakota had known.

Poia sighed. "Truly, my friend, I am finished. You must promise me once again not to reveal the sacred ceremony, the sacred words, or the sacred songs to anyone."

Solemnly Henry declared, "I do so promise."

"Good! Now, Henry, do you have any diseases or weaknesses which may cause you to find harm in the sweat lodge?"

"My heart is good."

"Fine. Any problems?"

Reluctantly Henry said, "I have hemorrhoids."

"No matter, my friend." Poia thought, then asked, "How about asthma? Any lung problems?"

"I do," Henry corrected himself, "did smoke a lot. The doctor told me I had the beginnings of emphysema."

"That is important for me to know. I must watch you closely. I might have to shorten the sweat lodge ceremony." Poia looked concerned.

"Now is the time, Henry Two Feathers. Follow me inside and we will begin."

*

CHAPTER 19

Cold, penetrating, agonizing, intense iciness assaulted the near-naked man's body. Henry grasped the worn military blanket, trying to somehow coax the abrasive material closer to his goose-pimply skin. Dawn would come soon, he hoped. Henry's wristwatch was tucked away somewhere in Billy Smith's belongings.

He looked toward the northern sky, trying to see the Big Dipper or perhaps the North Star through an opening in the forest's umbrella of limbs and needles. Coniferous branches confused his view, presenting him with mere patches of open sky. All he knew was that the right side of his trail road, the one leading to Slide Lake, also met a faint hint of a path which, if he were lucky enough to find it, would lead him to the summit of Nina'istuko.

Standing there, in the middle of the trail road, he thought back to the sweat lodge ceremony. The conclusion of the activity had presented him with a dilemma. Fully prepared for the vision quest, he had found himself in a hostile, bone-chilling damp environment, the temperature having dropped into the upper forties.

"You can do what you want," Billy had declared, "I'm getting some shuteye." Thus expressing his disinterest in Henry's future, the medicine man had unrolled a sleeping bag and spread it alongside the dying embers of the sacred fire.

Above, a half-moon had glimmered weakly. Henry, already shivering, had decided to head up the trail road to the cut off leading toward the summit. He now stood somewhere near to the beginning of the trail he sought. The fickle moon had slipped behind Ninaki's summit. Or was it Papoose summit? Or Nanaki-Papoose's summit? No, he thought, That can't be right. The peak he could barely observe was further away, due west. Gable Mountain. That was it.

No matter. The geographical mind exercise solved nothing.

His moccasined feet were wet. Deerskin absorbs water so that it can become slippery and slimy in order to torment old men who attempt stupid things.

"Shit!" There. The word was out. Henry had tried. Really tried. He had gone through the rituals, passed out from the heat twice, nearly unable to continue, but he had done it. He had completed the four exercises of the sweat lodge ceremony. Thinking back he was sure the temperature inside the Inipi had been high enough to have the blackheads come shooting up right out of his back. Almost. But, this damned cold. He tried kicking his abused feet together. The exercise had worked in the past, had brought warmth to his feet many times. Not this morning. He kept hitting his ankle bones. Boots would have worked. But these moccasins....

The old man was agonizingly tired, very cold and extremely hungry. He mistakenly decided that he had never been so hungry. What to do? Not enough light to find the faint trail. Too tired to expend energy just to get warm. He'd walk. Things couldn't get worse. Wrong again.

The vision-seeker, struck out cross country, as the ranger's say. Dense foliage forced him ever to his left, when he wanted to travel north. Just go uphill, Henry told himself. Keep going uphill. Gasping for breath. Tripping, scrambling, falling to his knees, the man, no longer certain why he was there, floundered upward. At least he was becoming warmer. Now my damned, no, darned, he corrected himself, glasses are steaming up. Funny, he thought, how the left, down slope lens stays clear but the right one fogs over. A little bit silly, but curious, Henry reversed directions, adding on unnecessary distance, just to see if the right lens would clear. Instead, the left lens took on a gauzy layer of moisture. "Shit!" Henry wished he had a handkerchief. He didn't dare wipe his glasses on the sacred bundle. No matter anyway, I can't see a damned thing.

Not realizing he had sworn again Henry wondered what he was carrying in the awkward bundle that hurt his shoulders. The canvass was heavy, strapped to him like a pack. Thankfully, the old man realized that the burden was keeping his back warm. He stopped, took off his glasses and waved them in the moisture-saturated air. Dawn had arrived, or would come soon. Weak light began revealing the outlines of trees, rocks, and the general lay of the land. He forced himself to move on, pushing himself to struggle through the vegetation of a partially-open hillside.

He stopped. For a moment, a tiny infinitesimal second, the underbrush had ceased grasping at his bare legs. The vision-seeker retraced his steps. Slowly. One step. No. Another and yet another. There. Henry peered about him. The trail, he thought. This is the trail. Out loud he boasted, "I'm on the god-damned trail! Thank you, God, whoever you are." Henry's hand went to the Beaver Stick hanging at his left side. The wood felt soaking wet. Water. Henry thought that perhaps the Beaver Stick did have some magical power.

Good fortune, if that was what Henry was indebted to, seemed short-lived. Certain that the trail would lead him safely to the summit of the holy mountain, the old man plunged through the forest and instantly lost the route.

Brighter daylight saved him. Henry had memorized a topographic map of the area. His course had to continue northwestward, up the gentler slope of Chief Mountain's south flank. The steeper climb would come later.

The wet moccasins, good for gripping the earth with his toes, did not offer the protection Henry so desperately needed. Every step found a sharp rock, a tree branch or tiny pebble waiting to penetrate deep into the soles of his throbbing feet. He fell, hard. The awkward, bulky pack crashed down upon his neck sending glasses flying into an already high spring growth of plants. Brushing the hair back from his sweaty brow, he wished he had a hat for protection. His right hand came away, the palm covered with blood.

Panting, gasping, the old man stood up, readjusted the burden, and put on his retrieved glasses. The wound was on the butt of his hand, sliced on a sharp protrusion of limestone. Several steps revealed that the left knee had sustained an injury too, a twisted ligament. Not too bad. Half a mile further and he stumbled and hit the ground once again. Lying still he struggled to regain his composure. "Shoot!" he yelled at the thinning forest.

The sound of his voice, although not loud, resulted in responses from a pair of magpies. Flashes of white shot in straight flight between the stunted trees. "Whop, whop, whop," beautiful wings, feathers blue-black and intense cream, rising and falling in swift rhythms of flight. Henry watched the two birds flying so effortlessly into a deeper copse of trees. "Humm," he puzzled, thinking out loud, "Magpies are usually in open places, like the plains." The observer didn't realize that the creatures were moving from one small, open meadow to another. Once again he fell. His left foot, somewhat out of control due to overexertion, had slipped under a dead branch concealed in the duff of the forest floor. The fall was not serious. He managed to keep his glasses and pack where they belonged.

Time to rest again. There was a rock adjacent to the branch that had tripped him. A good place to sit. He could see very little. Trees grew very close together, blocking enough sunlight from the forest floor so that other plants could not grow under the canopy of needle-covered limbs. There was nothing to hear but his own breathing, and the pulsing beat of his heart. More of an anxious throbbing. For all he could sense he might be the only human on earth. "Earth Mother," he corrected himself.

Cold crept in, attacking sweaty back, shoulders, arms. His legs shivered uncontrollably as well as throbbed and ached, sending slivers of pain coursing up and down the skinny appendages of his tormented body. Something had to give. He was shaking spasmodically, his body nearing dangerous hypothermia. Arising he moved on, thus warming himself from the exertion. Each step was a minor victory. Before he realized what he had accomplished the forest opened for the last time and before him stretched the steeper slopes of Chief Mountain, Nina'istuko, rising above to his right.

"God, that's steep," Henry exclaimed, immediately realizing he had cussed again. Sun's rays, slanting in from the horizon of the plains, bathed his body in an infinitesimal radiance of heat.

He stopped. The man stood panting, looking at the strengthening daylight, not really comprehending what a pathetic figure he struck in his ugly breechcloth garment with the flaps hanging down to his knees. His head hung forward, back arched under the weight of the obscene-looking pack he was carrying.

"Look, God." He started to talk but the ridiculous sound of a winded man babbling to himself on a mountain slope made him revert to silently forming his words.

"I'm an old man", his voice reported to God. "I hurt and I'm tired. I went through the sweat lodge ceremony. Now here I am struggling along, really pooped.

"Poop really isn't a very nice word to say to God, I suppose.

"God, I gave up cigarettes and I'm doing this vision quest thing because Sweet Grass Woman and seems like everyone else thinks I should. That's OK. But, I won't make it unless I can relieve some of the pressure and frustrations by swearing. I just can't watch my language and do all this damned walking. I hurt to much."

He really got into his project of explaining his problems to God.

"You know, I respect you. When I cuss I don't mean to offend you. When I say, god damn something, the g in god is a small g. I don't mean you. I just need to cuss and let off steam because right now I'm all tensed up and I need to relax so I can make this climb to the top. I've got to let go.

"So, God, large G, hold your ears or look the other way or whatever you do to ignore us humans 'cause I've got to let loose."

He stood still, regaining his breath. Then, "Bull Shit!."

The drawn-out words swept along the rugged Chief Mountain slopes, weaving through the startled trees, rising up to craggy cliffs and soaring out into the wild blue yonder.

He thought, I've been around Douglas too much.

Far away an echo responded weakly, "Bull Shit." Henry had always cussed. No lightning struck him down. There were no clouds for it to form in. The earth didn't tremble. Nothing happened except he had made a deal with God. In order to carry out his quest the old man would swear a bit. Let off steam. Since the agreement was one-sided, God not really in on the deal, Henry remained a bit uneasy.

On a topographic map the distance up Chief Mountain appeared to be a short, but rugged walk. The only route to the top without involving rock-climbing, was the rather gradual south-western side. Henry moved painfully from rock to rock, stopping often, sitting for longer and longer periods of rest. Not only were his legs trembling but they sometimes buckled sending him down upon his knees, those scraped and bloody knobs, survivors of countless sudden contacts with the mountain's unrelenting surface. Henry had learned how to ease the knee-rock contacts by absorbing much of the blows with outstretched hands. They, too, became raw and bleeding. Compounding Henry's agony, the lungs, badly abused by a lifetime of smoking, were unable to function fully. The emphysema that was beginning to shorten his life, resulted in coughing, gagging, rasping seizures, further draining the old man's strength.

Early in the climb he remembered a lesson from his youth. Don't look up. Constantly looking at the route ahead would only cause discouragement. Watching the trail ahead, when one was climbing, only slowed down time, compounding the agony of the journey. Gradually the slope eased. Henry, noticing only that the climb was becoming less strenuous, had never-the-less deteriorated to crawling on his hands and knees; those bloody knees. He remembered a book he had read long ago, ANNAPURNA, a narrative of climbing the great mountain of the Himalayas. The book's author, Maurice Herzog, had written of a time he and a companion were so exhausted they could only crawl. Then they couldn't move and lay, unable to be heard, watching their friends in camp a scant few hundred feet away.

"I don't have a god damned camp to go to," grumbled Henry.

He stopped crawling. Not much of a slope. He pushed his glasses back up on his nose and looked ahead. What he saw was the summit. He was there.

Victorious, the old man struggled to his feet, reeled about in the thinner air, and nearly took a serious fall. "The summit, 9080 fucking feet. My god! Small g," he added. He collapsed upon a flat, rocky surface and rested for a long, long time.

*

Had he been asleep? Henry jolted upright, hoping he hadn't slept. Resting was permissible. Sleeping on a vision quest was not. Again he rationalized that somehow age should be a considering factor. Still, rules were rules. His pain-wracked body responded slowly to his movements. Empty stomach gnawed relentlessly like an open sore. The world spun about, gradually calming down to a slight feeling of dizziness.

The vision-seeker beheld the irregular, somewhat flat surface of Nina'istuko. Loose rocks lay scattered everywhere, resting on the still-solid crown of the eroding mountain.

Never had Henry experienced such wild beauty. Northward and perhaps a hundred miles to the east, the Great Plains shimmered, reflecting the emerald coat of early summer. The Sweet Grass Hills seemed nearby, only a few miles distant. He turned his gaze toward the awesome jumble of mountains within Glacier National Park. The Belly River valley nestled beneath the gigantic ramparts of Sentinel and Bear mountains. Cosley Lake lay, like a dark, turquoise jewel squashed between massive limestone castles. Upon the mountains' flanks last winter's snow shone so brilliantly in the morning light that he had to turn away.

Something began happening to Henry. From that point of time when he gazed off into the distances, the seeker sensed an alteration of his reality. His life-long paradigms, his belief system, the model for his existence, began crumbling, gradually being replaced by a new sense of being, of what human existence, the whole physical world's being, really was all about. The changes were slow, incomprehensible at first, never fully understood.

"Time to open the pack," he decided. No swearing. The coarse words were not necessary. Tensions were fleeing, retreating from the overwhelming peacefulness that Nina'istuko offered.

Henry's heart jumped. A miracle. He thought his troubled eyes had been cured, the near-sightedness and astigmatism gone. With near-trembling hands Henry removed his glasses. The world about him blurred, became less distinct. Nothing had changed. Disappointed, the old man also felt shame. He had done nothing to expect a favor from the spirit world, from God.

He unbuckled the straps and flipped the canvass pack open. On top, wrapped in clear plastic, were a few personal items.

Well, I'll be, he thought. Why, there's my comb.

Careful that the plastic would not escape his grasp and blow down the mountain, Henry placed the items upon a flat rock. Comb, a toothbrush and a small tube of Crest. Billy Smith had a lot of the

White Man's culture in him. He discovered another tube, containing First Aid Cream. Band aids. Even an Ace bandage. The latter would give support to his damaged ligament.

The small package had a tag with a large #1 written on it. "I guess I'm supposed to get cleaned up."

Descending downhill a short distance Henry began making himself more presentable. Thus far he hadn't touched the plastic bottle of water so he washed himself off a bit, put a little moisture on his hair and combed down the disheveled mass.

"What's this?" There were two more items left in the bag, a red bandanna and a bottle of sun-screen. "Good idea," Henry said out loud. His skin, unused to direct sunlight, would burn in the high altitude. He took care to rubb the scented, pink liquid over all of the body parts he could reach. Only the center of his back remained unprotected. He then rolled the bandanna and tied it around his head, creating a sweatband.

"Now I do look like an Indian, sort of."

The toiletry completed, Henry returned to the pack. The long flaps on his loincloth bothered him, getting in his way and chapping the inner thighs. Henry shed the garment and applied more lotion to the newly exposed parts of his body.

Inside the pack there were three more packages. One, he guessed by the shape, contained a ceremonial pipe. The label read, "#3," so he set it aside.

Instead he chose package #2, lifting it from the pack. The burlap bag's contents were heavy. He looked at the object for a time, trying to guess what it contained. With almost reverent care, he unwrapped the item.

Pale white, a buffalo skull emerged. Henry knew what the bones were for.

Billy had told him of the warrior that legend said had carried just such a skull to the top of Nina'istuko. He had placed the object upon the stone summit and had used the head-bone as a pillow while he prayed. Billy, then calling himself Poia, told Henry that years later Whites had removed the shattered bones of the original buffalo skull.

Looking about, Henry selected a proper location for his meditations. The buffalo skull was placed so that it faced eastward, toward the Great Plains, the home of the vanished great herds.

He didn't feel anything or even sense it's spirit, but Henry, by most standards raised as a White Man, knew the heavy object contained great power. He stood looking at the bleached skull for some time. Strange, the buffalo skull story came back to him in more detail than he had ever been told.

Years ago a member of the mountain tribes, usually enemies of the Blackfeet, came to Nina'istuko to seek a vision. The brave warrior was a Salish or perhaps Kootenai. Henry couldn't recall for certain. Once upon the holy mountain, the stranger was safe from his adversaries, the dwellers of the plains.

Unlike Henry, the man had been young and very strong, so he had ascended the great rocky peak with little effort. Because of his physical prowess, the warrior had carried a great skull of a bull buffalo all the way to the summit. The head-bones became the sacred pillow upon which the vision quester placed his head while awaiting the personal spirit of nature that eventually came to him.

At the end of the 19th Century, Henry remembered specifically that the year had been 1892, another young man, a White Man who was to become one of President Franklin D. Roosevelt's most valued cabinet members, Henry L. Stimson, climbed Chief Mountain. Another member of the Stimson climbing party, their Indian guide, Billy Fox, later told the Blackfeet that Stimson had found the remnants of the skull. Rumors were that later White climbers removed the shattered bones, taking them as souvenirs, soon to be discarded in their trash.

Henry became overwhelmed with emotion. He, Henry Two Feathers, had renewed the medicine, had returned the great spiritual power of the buffalo herds to Nina'istuko, home, some believed, of Thunder Bird, home of the mighty Wind Spirit. If nothing else came of his quest, that accomplishment would be reward enough. Perhaps, because of extreme exhaustion or maybe due to hunger and the physical pain he had shut out of his mind, Henry wept.

Solemnly, beginning his prayers, Henry placed the discarded loincloth flaps upon a slightly elevated rock slab, which would also accommodate his long body. Naked, suddenly proud of his human form, Henry seated the buffalo skull so that vacant eye sockets faced the point where the summer sun would first appear over the eastern horizon.

Cognizance, the sudden awareness of what the new day would bring stunned him. The morning would find the sun rising over the northern-most point of the star's annual journey across the heavens. The next dawn would be the beginning of the White Man's summer. Summer Solstice. The most sacred of days for Native Americans and peoples throughout the Northern Hemisphere. Coincidence? Henry thought not. He no longer believed in coincidences. Besides, Sweet Grass Woman had planned it all.

Within the elongated package Henry not only found a pipe but it was a Calumet, a red stone pipe minus the twelve eagle feathers. A very old tin, once holding Prince Albert Pipe Tobacco, was filled with the sacred leaves that made up the ceremonial tobacco. Henry also found a silvery cylinder containing kitchen matches.

He read the enclosed instructions, making special effort to memorize the pipe ceremony so he would always remember. Lighting the pipe Henry faced to the east, inhaled, then blew the light smoke, the color of fawn's hair, toward the sun that was still climbing toward the zenith.

Billy, Poia, had instructed Henry to make his own prayers. This he did.

Oh God
God of all life
God of rocks, clouds and water
Giver of life
Taker of life
Hear me as I pray
See me as I fast
Accept my spirit in its humbleness
Help me to find answers, the reason for my quest
Protect those for whom I pray
Oh, God
God of all life
God of rocks, clouds and water
Giver of life
Taker of life
Hear me as I pray

Again and again he softly spoke the words of his supplication. Each time the words flowed softly from his lips, anxieties fled. He had feared insincerity. What if the Creator sensed that he doubted what he spoke? What if a party of Whites came scrambling up the mountain to catch him naked? Then what?

He turned to the south and repeated the ceremony.

Then to the west.

Each time his fears diminished and he cared less about people finding him as he was. The vision seeker would ignore them.

He prayed to the north and then toward the immense blue indigo ocean above him.

This should not end with the sky, he thought. Inhaling deeply Henry blew the pale smoke upon the surface of the rocky summit, upon the buffalo skull, upon the tiny blue cluster of forget-me-nots hiding from the winds. "Earth Mother," Henry proclaimed. The old man knew that what he had added to the prayers was as it should be.

Ceremony concluded, Henry Two Feathers tapped the ashes from the pipe, then carefully wrapped the venerable object in the padded cloth from which he had taken it.

He waited, not knowing what to expect. Nothing happened. No spirit took shape. No mighty wind blew. Everything was the same, everything except Henry.

Within the Calumet pipe's wrappings he had found freshly cut sweet grass. There had been no instructions but the old man knew how to use it. Respectfully, he took the grasses, a few at a time, bent them, crushed the stems between his hands, and rubbed the ruptured fibers upon his body, the freed juices cooling his skin. The smell, as the name indicated, was sweet, refreshing to the nostrils, purifying. The natural scent mingled pleasantly with the faint odor of sunscreen.

He stretched out upon the rock slab, using the weathered buffalo skull for his pillow. The unyielding object caused the occipital bone on the back of his head to throb. Somehow he would have to endure the pain.

Bright sunlight, for the Earth's star was directly above Nina'istuko, bore into his closed eyes. Even with eyelids closed the brilliant pink, the color resulting from his eyes' blood vessels, was barely tolerable for even a short time. Round, black spots and curlicues of something like hairs or dust particles, floated, rushed, stuck and paraded across his pinkish vision.

Henry slipped the bandanna over his eyes. The adjustment carried sunscreen to the moist corners of his corneas, resulting in stinging sensations. Conditions worsened as a few flies found the prone man's nose, ears and genitals. This isn't working, he thought. Beads of sweat, forming in the hollows of his arms, tickled as they ran down the sides of his chest.

He inhaled deeply several times, holding each breath for a moment, then slowly, completely forcing the oxygen deficient gasses from his lungs. He shook his wrists and twisted his ankles in an attempt to relax. Time seemed to stand still. Confidence faltered again. It seemed he was getting nowhere. He'd never get a sign from any spirit. Nothing!

The mountaintop stillness of noon dragged into mid-afternoon. Out of the west a slight breeze explored among the irregularities of the summit. The air movement brought comfort to the frustrated man. An hour later the comfort had become a chill wind and he found himself wishing the heat would return.

One lone cloud, unseen by his sheltered eyes, rose above the massif of the distant Mt. Cleveland. Another gray accumulation appeared. The clouds sailed alone for a time then were joined by a parade of white, puffy clouds with dirty, gray bases. Once the sun disappeared behind a vaporous mass. Henry, not doing well with his meditation and prayers, immediately felt the drop in temperature. He peeped out from under the bandanna. The sun re-emerged.

Evening found the sky splotched with cumulus, all sailing gracefully eastward, to their evaporation over the hotter plains. He sat up. The time had come to open the last package, the roundish, bulky one.

*

CHAPTER 20

Piegan legend, not well substantiated by historical fact, tells of a time, early in the 19th Century. The Piegan, Blackfeet as they are now called, were famous for their long journeys of personal exploration. Sometimes the young men would travel a thousand miles or more, one way, just to be doing something, seeking adventure and learning about the world.

One year great fortune came upon the powerful nation. The returning buffalo migration brought with it an all-white yearling calf. To possess a white buffalo robe was the greatest gift that the spirits could give. Prosperity, expansion of hunting territory, many healthy male babies, all sorts of advantages were enjoyed by the tribe that possessed such a holy robe. According to the legend the Blackfeet killed the calf. Lavish ceremonies were given to give thanks to the great buffalo spirit for allowing the white robe to come into the possession of the Blackfeet. The word of such a gift had flown across the plains making Blackfeet enemies envious and wishing they had fallen upon such good fortune.

Then, one summer, enemy warriors, Henry thought they had been Comanche, stole the white robe and fled all the way to what is now New Mexico. A war party of Blackfeet went in pursuit. The thieves were finally attacked and the white robe was re-captured. Deep in hostile country, the successful warriors hid the sacred robe in a cave, because they thought their chances of escaping were slight. They did elude their pursuers and returned to their homeland.

A few years later the survivors of the journey, along with a few younger men, decided to return to the south and bring the white buffalo robe back to their people. They traveled on foot, at night, and lay hidden during the day. In this way they were not detected by other warriors. Such traveling took a very long time but their tactics enabled the little group to safely pass through the territory of the Crow, Cheyenne and many other powerful tribes. The men finally stole some horses, retrieved the white buffalo robe from the cave and safely carried the garment home to their waiting people.

Flash backs of the tale reminded Henry that the warriors claimed to have gone all the way to Santa Fe. Often the story included the fact that they had met Kit Carson and had become his friends. He believed that at least that part was true. Those particular details of the legend were quite specific.

On the 20th of June, 1985, as dusk advanced from the east, Henry gazed down at the opened third bundle. Before him, neatly folded, lay the ancient, badly worn, now much smaller, white buffalo robe. Stunned, he sucked in air between clenched teeth. His heart seemed to stop, too. The old man reeled dizzily, blood draining from his head. What an honor. The sacred white buffalo robe. He was looking at the legendary robe atop Nina'istuko. What stronger medicine could Henry Two Feathers possess? There was none.

Fearful of touching the robe, he succumbed to necessity and held the heavy covering in his arms. Tiny white hairs drifted off into the evening winds, perhaps an offering to the other spirits.

He positioned himself cross-legged, facing east, toward the rushing darkness of night. Not surprised, Henry experienced the same sensations Douglas had reported about the advancing blue-blackness, the frightening apprehension that the observer would be engulfed in the blackness of death. Soon only the top of Nina'istuko remained illuminated. All else below hid in the shadows of the new night.

The old man turned, repositioned the robe and watched the waning sunlight, streaked with shadows of mountains to the west, weaken more, and finally succumb to the night spirit.

Clouds were still patchy. Here and there larger accumulations blotted out the still faint lights of stars and the planet Venus. More knowing of it rather than seeing, he experienced a small rain storm cross the Belly River country and rise up the west slopes of Nina'istuko, thus cooling the land and depositing a heavy shower of rain. Carefully, respectfully, he folded the robe and returned it to the inside of the pack. His tattered army blanket followed. With all items safely tucked away he re-positioned himself in an upright, cross-legged position, facing the rapidly advancing shower.

The rain attacked Chief Mountain with gradually increasing intensity. Large droplets assailed the man's face, shoulders, and legs. His whole body became a mass of streaming rivulets rushing down the chilling skin, then flowing along the rock shelf that was his altar. At first the old man welcomed the rain. Nearly a whole day had passed without a taste of water except for the tooth brushing. He opened his mouth, tilted back his head and stuck out the parched tongue. Cold rain found the opening, caressed cracked lips and inner mouth. Water splashed and coursed over his face, into his big ears, down the wrinkled body, stealing warmth as it went, replacing body heat with chilly wetness.

He began his prayers. He slowed the breathing process, lowered his body's metabolism. The seeker, in spite of the cold, fell into a deep trance. Even thinking ceased. He sat there upon the wet stone, impervious to the frigid rain that assailed his naked body. No shivering occurred. The man, his soul, had retreated beyond physical response, deep into the inner recesses of his mind, where he waited for nature's assault to subside.

Lightning, distant and far above, streaked the clouds, reflected downward disclosing the peculiar motionless man figure. The image glistened black, a deeper shadow in a world of near-total darkness. Thunder, beautiful and spiritual, boomed and rolled in the clouds above. He did not respond to the noise either, but remained unmoving, unresponsive to the natural world about him.

The rain, ever so slowly, slackened to fleeting bursts of moisture, then stopped completely. The cold wind blew the water from the rocky shelf, from the cracks in the buffalo skull, and dried the human who sat so very still. Slow, he stirred, rising out of his self-induced trance, amazed that he had accomplished such a feat. Eyes opened. He looked unseeing into the blackness of the night. Out on the plains the lightning still danced above the earth.

Fingers moved. Toes wiggled. Then an arm changed position. Legs, aching from the long held cross-legged position, began moving in a spasmodic fashion. Breathing became natural again. Blood flowed faster to the chilled surfaces of the body. Shivering, intense shivering wracked the human form.

Satisfied that he had allowed enough time to be fully awake, he opened the pack. He stood, combed the water out of his hair, placed the blanket upon the rocky shelf, sat down and wrapped legs and feet in the cover. From the pack he retrieved the white buffalo robe, safe, dry, not desecrated or harmed by any careless act. Taking great care and in a respectful manner he positioned the sacred garment over his back and shoulders, clutching together the edges, thus protecting the chest. One fragment, remnants of a leg, was placed over his head.

In such a manner he attained warmth once more, the great pleasure of comfort driving away the misery that the rain shower had tried to impose upon him. The clouds, the tail end of the storm, slid eastward. The heavens became splendid in magnificent starlight so intense that he was able to see objects, rocks, the world that was the top of Nina'estuko. Henry didn't think much. Neither did he pray. Only his eyes moved, seeking something he knew not what. The mysterious warmth continued to radiate from the mystical robe that was his protection.

One time, just before the first signs of dawn, a meteorite streaked across the heavens, a brilliant blue-green flash shooting earthward, angling along the curvature of the planet. Nervous, he looked about him, seeing only dark shadows. He hoped he would not encounter the Star People. His anxiety puzzled him for he really didn't believe in their existence; or did he? Sweet Grass Woman did. Millie had talked about the strange beings from somewhere else. He had heard others, too. Jack Ball. Elaine White Ribbon swore they were real. Maybe he did believe in them after all. Perhaps they were the very spirits he was trying to contact, up there on the holy mountain.

Nothing materialized. His anxious moment passed. His body had experienced too much heat. Too much cold. Miles of painful walking. No food for a day and a half. Only raindrops for moisture. No sleep for two days. He lapsed into a near coma and remained in that condition for the remainder of the night and through the dawn of the beginning of the summer solstice.

*

The Alpha Male lapped refreshment from the stream that flowed just beneath Miche Wabun Falls. The wolf was unaware of the name so he could not puzzle over the significance of such a title.

In the world of civilized man discussions, even heated arguments resulted from the peculiar name. The problem was, and is to this day, that Blackfeet, Cree and Chippewa languages each contain the name, or words very similar. Some say Miche Wabun means "The Great White Rabbit." Others, offended by the idea that such a lovely falls could be named after a hare, swear that the words refer to "The Great Spirit," which, they argue, is certainly not a rabbit by any stretch of the imagination. Elders of the Cree Nation profess that the meaning of Miche Wabun is "Great Day Coming," or "Great Dawn." Perhaps, because of what transpired there on that Summer Solstice of 1985, the original meaning was indeed "Great Dawn."

Alpha Male, leader of the wolf pack that had recently been frequenting the Crypt Lake area of the Canadian section of the Waterton-Glacier International Peace Park, peered cautiously about, saw no danger and drank again, the agile tongue deftly carrying the clear liquid to it's eager throat. The lead wolf's intent had been to scout further up the stream, the North Fork of the Belly River. The area usually abounded in ungulates, especially deer. Marmots, ground squirrels, voles, and a myriad of other tasty morsels also lived in the narrow valley and along the adjacent mountainsides.

Between the movements of taking in water and the raising of the head for another cautious look around, something happened to the wolf. Yellowish-brown eyes took on a puzzled expression. Something incalculable, enigmatic to the beast's comprehension had occurred. His plan to hunt along the shores of Wabun Lake faded from the wolf's memory. Confused, not really knowing why, the beautiful animal headed northward, running to meet his pack, the black female and their five juveniles.

At the same time the Alpha Male changed his course, another wolf pack, one that was also exploring south of the Canadian border, loped along the snow covered trail between the Hole-In-The-Wall and Brown Pass. Just as the Alpha Male near Wabun Lake did, the other pack leader stopped, his sudden action causing his female to collide with his rump. Snarling, the confused male leader snapped at his companion, baring the long incisors protruding from his open jaws. In submission the female fell to the ground, turned over, and offered her throat to her dominant mate's fangs. He ignored her. The male's eyes seemed transfixed, questioning.

Moments later the three adults and two juveniles were heading toward the Bowman Creek drainage which would provide them with easy access to the high, wild valleys of the Livingston Range and beyond.

*

The mid-morning sun heated the mountaintop with solar energy rich in ultra-violet radiation. The flora, plants, grew behind rocks, in crevasses, anywhere there was partial shade and protection from the strong winds of such an environment. Sometimes the plants grew beneath or behind past living vegetation, the skeletons of the plant world. Others, a few, displayed reddish leaves and stems, the peculiarity enabling the genetically adjusted flowers and grasses to endure the deadly high altitude radiation.

Chief Mountain's fauna, the animals, did likewise, burrowing wherever there was soil, spinning their webs in shadows, lying close to the cool underside of rock protrusions. Some, such as ants and flies seemed impervious to the sun's energy, merely moving faster when the temperature rose.

Larger creatures, some protected by fur of reddish brown, gray, and even orange, bathed in the sunlight, soaking up the heat they so loved, the warmth that they so seldom had to enjoy.

Nina'istuko was the home of a family of Hoary Marmots, a mountain variety of groundhog. Half a dozen rock rabbits, picas, or coneys, depending upon which name White people preferred, scurried about already gathering grasses for the next winter's hard times. One coney, sounding his warning call of "Geek!", scurried past the old man, almost brushing the human toe which protruded from the blanket. The little animal's slight streak of buff, a movement across Henry's peripheral vision, roused him from his open-eyed stupor. He raised one hand to his forehead and realized that he was really sunburned. Fear of a bad burn brought the sleep-drugged mind back to awareness. Fumbling in the pack, he found the sunscreen and liberally applied the creamy mess to his forehead, face, ears, neck, arms, legs, every portion of his body that he could reach. He kept rubbing the lotion on until he had used the container's entire contents. No matter. The next day would bring his defeat, death, or most likely both. Re-rolling the bandanna he tied it on his forehead, as he had done before. He wasn't sure that he had any moisture left in his body to produce sweat.

With great difficulty he stood up, took a few weak steps, wavered and quickly sat down again. Vertigo dominated his mind. The world, Nina'istuko, wobbled, shimmered, and spun before his eyes. I must be loosing my mind, he thought. The temptation to drink from the canteen dominated his thoughts for a while. For just a moment his thoughts were turned to food, but the dizziness had eased his desire to eat.

The burnt forehead began to sting. He arched his eyebrows, thus wrinkling his forehead. Yes. His face hurt. Fascinated, he continued to wrinkle the skin, almost enjoying the pricks of discomfort and the burning sensations that remained.

Well, where is my sign? he asked himself. No eagle hovered, not even in far distant skies. No mountain sheep or goat suddenly appeared to graze on the summits sparse vegetation. Why didn't a mountain lion appear? A lynx? Really, a pack rat or a snowshoe hare would be a welcome sight, if it were his sign. The coney, having disappeared among the rocks, he observed nothing larger than ants, flies and the sweat bees who had found his altar, now smelling of his perspiration.

He forced his mind back to the sweat lodge ceremony. Somehow, he had to get his mind functioning again. Let's see. North stands for the red stone. North's messenger is the bald eagle who gifts the seeker with reproductive powers, good health and self-control. Well, too late for that reproductive stuff. I hope. Smiling because of the memory, his voice, cracked and raspy, he said to the morning sun, "Well, not much success there." Not having a child was the bitterest of pills for Henry and Martha to swallow. He looked down at his uncircumcised, shriveled penis wondering if the thing would ever rise again. Likely the last few days had killed it.

Thinking was exhausting but he continued.

East. Yes, the sunrise of Summer Solstice. I saw the dawn, I think. Henry looked about, confused. Yellow stone is the symbol, the golden eagle the messenger who dispenses wisdom, understanding, and gratefulness.

"Why," he said out loud, "I don't think I have any of those either." He peered toward the east. No eagle soared. No huge wings flapped in the light blue sky.

He thought some more. What's next? South. South is the easiest one to remember. White stone. The great white crane gives the seeker rebirth, life renewal. White crane gives man his destiny. He thought about "south" for a while, considering the life renewal concept as a hopeful possibility. The only direction left was west. He couldn't figure out why the black eagle was west's messenger. From west the seeker acquired renewal, just like south. He remembered that it was from the west that the rainstorm had come. West provided man with purifying water, thunder and the nitrogen-rich lightning, nature's great fertilizer.

Hey, he thought, west has given me the water and the thunder I heard. Maybe west is my special direction. His idea didn't make sense. Oh well. He again slipped away from the physical world, moving into a shadow world of vagueness, of muted thoughts, unfamiliar realities, if they were that. The man didn't sleep. Henry had simply ceased to function mentally and physically.

*

Young legs, muscles firm, carried the small party of Ranger Naturalists out of the forest onto the scrubby, still partly snow covered, rocky western side of the Chief. Except for water bottles and sack lunches carried in daypacks, the five adventurers had little else but their clothing.

Someone had told them that upon the forested slopes of Chief Mountain there were Indian holy places, cemeteries and sites like seen in the movie, "Jeremiah Johnson". Every now-and-then White people would stumble upon the sacred places of prayer. Feathers, rawhide thongs, willow prayer circles, bits of cloth, all sorts of paraphernalia hung from tree limbs or lay about the holy ground. The young rangers had also been informed that if Whites were caught nosing around those locations the Blackfeet would run them off, sometimes severely beating the intruders.

Due to the danger involved the rangers had opted to sleep overnight at the Slide Lake ranger cabin. In the morning, the morning of the first day of summer, the little group of two men and three women hiked to Gable Pass. From there they struggled along the east slope of Ninaki Papoose, thus approaching Chief Mountain without traveling out of national park territory.

Diane Morrisey, one of the five hikers, thought about the Indian lore she had read before arriving at Glacier. New to the St. Mary station, the young geology student was not yet accepted by the Native Americans on the staff. Neither did she fit in with the more boisterous, sometimes promiscuous veterans of last season. Like the night before in the cabin.

The training season had just begun, just a few days old. The veterans would begin work when they returned from the hike to Chief Mountain. Diane had a week and a half more of training to endure before she would be allowed to deal with the public on a full-time basis. Perhaps their knowing one-another from the previous year was the reason her companions had so easily paired off and slept together.

The ranger cabin had been small. Sounds of love making at first disturbed her. She had buried her head in her pillow, embarrassed, even in the darkness. Her hiding place hadn't worked. Her body heat forced her to uncover her head and shoulders. Surprised, the young woman found that the amorous sounds excited her. The humor of her situation had caused her to smile, her reaction hidden, thank goodness, by the blackness of the cabin's interior. Each time someone reached an orgasm she giggled softly. The noises were so silly, so animalistic at times. The listener wondered if she would ever get to sleep.

The rains that had descended unmercifully upon Henry Two Feathers also fell upon the cabin drowning out all other sounds, even those of mice scurrying about, investigating the intruders' packs. Diane's feverish body had eventually cooled and sleep had come to her.

"Hey, Diane! What's your hurry?" David, one of the rangers was calling to her.

Patiently, waiting for the others to catch up, the small woman brushed the crystalline snow from her gaiters. Her companions were right. No need to hurry on such a lovely day. The others were resting on an area of dry limestone, where the sun had eliminated last winter's snow.

Still thinking of Indian lore, Diane recalled her second day on the job. For some reason part of the program that had been scheduled for the second week had been moved up. All the naturalists from the west side as well as the Hudson Bay District group, had gathered outside the St. Mary Visitor's Center. Diane remembered a dark haired beauty that shyly hid behind one of the building's buttresses. Two other Blackfeet women had also been present, all three members of the Glacier Natural History Association staff.

The purpose of the meeting was to hear Tommy Many Swans speak. He was a revered chief of the Browning Blackfeet, a sort of P. R. man. Tommy had concluded his talk by speaking about Chief Mountain, how sacred the place was, how White people sometimes desecrated the dwelling place of the Indian gods and spirits.

Diane's supervisor had smiled cleverly and said, "I've been told the Blackfeet still practice the Sun Dance Ceremony. Is that right?" Everyone present knew the ceremony was prohibited by Federal law.

Tommy became uneasy. Hesitantly, not wishing to be rude, he admitted that the Sun Dance was still practiced.

The supervisor, relishing his cleverness, pulled on his neatly trimmed beard. "Where and when will this year's dance take place?"

Tommy Many Swans seemed embarrassed and perhaps angry. Instead of answering, the speaker turned his back on the audience.

Diane had felt ashamed.

That afternoon the same supervisor had instructed the naturalist staff that they were not to discourage visitors from climbing Chief Mountain. "After all," he explained, "most of it lies within park boundaries."

Those incidents, Tommy's lecture and the supervisor's White arrogance, had resulted in the five naturalists' expedition to Chief Mountain, to experience for themselves such a special religious shrine.

The two couples had passed Diane as she reminisced. She picked up her steady stride and easily caught up with them. The walking was strenuous, bodies consuming oxygen as quickly as lungs could bring it in. No surplus for needless conversation. She looked at her wrist watch. 2:07. They were behind schedule. Greg, the strongest of the climbers, was up ahead, steadily approaching the summit. Diane forced herself to catch up. The others were scattered below, slowly progressing upward, each selecting his or her own route.

She caught up with Greg right on the edge of the mountaintop. "Look, Diane," her companion gasped between breaths. "Do you see what I see? Here, take my glasses."

Diane put the binoculars to her eyes and made slight adjustments. A dark lump, partially covered by a light, yellowish substance, was sitting on the top-most rocky shelf of Chief Mountain.

"What is that?" she asked.

"I don't know. Looks like a man." The peculiar covering slipped off the human form. "It's an Indian," whispered Greg.

"Let me see again," she demanded. Greg had taken back his glasses.

"Why, it is. He's a man." Diane didn't realize her statement was peculiar. "Look again, Greg. That's an old man. You can see the gray in his hair."

"My god, Diane. He must be on some sort of vision quest." Greg frowned. "Best we don't disturb him." Concerned, he thought a moment. "Let's go back and tell the others so they don't bother him."

"They'll want to stand on the summit. Why don't you steer them over there?" She pointed to another rocky high spot. "I think that rock is just as high as the place where the Indian is sitting."

"Yeah. Ok. Come on."

"No. I'm going to make sure he is all right."

"No," protested Greg. "Don't interfere. Let him alone."

"I will. I've got to make certain he is alive, that he's OK."

"You be careful. Let him alone, Diane."

She ignored her companion. "Just keep the others quiet." Cautiously the young naturalist stepped toward where Henry sat. So that she wouldn't startle the man, she angled away from his position, then moved closer beneath where he sat, where he could see her.

The man's features were impassive, large nose unmoving, eyes closed, lips slightly opened. She drew nearer until she realized the old man was naked. Curious, she stared. Still not satisfied that the inert figure was alive the naturalist continued to look finally perceiving a slight movement of stomach and chest. He was breathing. Her eyes moved upward, straight into the open orbs of the old man. He was looking at her. Strange. She wasn't afraid. She smiled slightly, nodded her head and backed away. The Indian's eyes closed again.

*

Evening arrived. Henry Two Feathers still had not received a sign, a personal communication from any member of the spirit world. Unless....That White woman. Had she really been there, just below the rock slab, Henry's altar? He thought he had hallucinated. There had been no perceptible sound. He had simply opened his eyes and there she was, staring at him. He recalled how their eyes had met, his and the girl's. Short cut hair. Brunette. Eyes so close he could see they were hazel colored with flecks of ebony blackness. Then he had shut his eyes. When he once again opened them the girl, the apparition, was gone. Certainly, he thought, not a spirit that could help an old man who was seeking a murderer.

His condition was weakening. Another night could kill him. Best to watch the approaching night sweeping across the plains, obliterating everything, just as Douglas had said.

He tried to stand, but legs too long in one position were numb. Muscles refused to respond to the brain's commands. He pulled himself forward, off the slight rise of the stone shelf, his altar. If he could move forward just a few feet he would be able to watch the shadow of night sweep up the sheer flanks of Nina'istuko.

Below, highway 17 had disappeared into the darkness of night. The blue-black flood of lightlessness swept up the slopes of Sandy Ridge. Sherburne Peak, to the south, seemed to be swallowed up in a matter of seconds.

He was frightened. What if the approaching night was death itself? Maybe even the end of the world. Exhaustion, dizziness, claimed his mind. Panic-stricken the old man crawled back to his altar of stone. Grasping the white buffalo robe, he wrapped the garment tightly about his trembling torso. He would look to the west. Concentrate on the light, the weakening sunlight, he told himself.

Silhouetted against the white streak of the western horizon, the last rays of summer solstice, a figure sat staring, unmoving, the thing obviously watching the peculiar antics of the man-creature, Henry.

The wolf had never observed a human performing in such a manner, crawling around on all fours, dragging its legs, somehow turning itself into a pale white blob. Alpha Male sat on his haunches, tongue lolling out to the side, eyes taking in the funny spectacle.

Chills coursing through his battered frame, he watched in near disbelief. A wolf. The wolf spirit was there, with him, Henry, atop the sacred mountain. His chills were not from the cold of evening. The buffalo robe still preserved his body heat. The blanket once again was insulating Henry from the cooling rock slab.

What should I do, Henry asked himself. He had never seen a spirit before. He couldn't think. Neither could he pray. One couldn't cry out, Hi, Wolf. The thought seemed disrespectful and stupid. No mental message came to him, no thought transferal from beast to man.

Bored, the man-creature hadn't done anything for quite some time, Alpha Male stood up, turned quickly and hurried down the mountain to find his waiting pack. The animal didn't wonder what had compelled him to climb way up a mountain that held nothing of interest except a strange acting human.

Seeing the wolf seemed to give Henry energy. He stood up, straightened out the blanket so it would provide not only protection from the cold limestone but could once again be used as a wrapping for his bare legs.

The night was beautiful. High in the darkness of night the Big Dipper, Ursa Major, shone familiarly, two of the constellation stars pointing directly at the North Star. The suns of Cassiopeia flickered strangely like colorful candles in a far-distant cathedral of emptiness. He didn't know the names of constellations nor even planets. He did recognize the North Star and Venus, sometimes. Turning his gaze slightly he found the crescent of the moon sneaking unobtrusively across the night sky to it's hiding place below the western horizon.

A light clicked on. Henry, coming alert, watched the peculiar wobble and bobble of the rather dull illumination move toward the north. Suddenly the light was gone. "Russian satellite." He knew what that light had been. He had seen them many times, moving in their polar orbit, sailing from south to north.

Unlike the previous night there was no breeze and not a cloud appeared. Starlight, the composite of millions of tiny dots of light, once again illuminated the mountaintop. The buffalo skull glowed dimly, beckoning for him to place his tired head upon the unyielding pillow.

Henry wondered about the wolf. The animal had seemed real. There had been no message such as, "See Millie." When he saw the wolf he somehow knew that his long vigil was completed. A person didn't normally observe a wolf, just sitting there, especially not on top of a mountain such as Nina'istuko. The sign, the totem, however vague, was Wolf. Not many spirits had greater power, strength, superior wisdom, than Wolf. Henry knew that soon he would be guided to the one who had attacked Douglas.

Finally he could sleep. How long has it been, he wondered. Forty-eight hours? No. Much longer than that. And, he could eat. There was nothing for him, though. Water. He could quench his great thirst.

Hands trembling, the old man extracted the canteen from the pack and unscrewed the cap. The skull. Henry poured a token of water over the top of the buffalo skull. "Thank you, brother", he prayed.

His gulps were slow. A mouthful, then wait. A few minutes later he swallowed again, the cold water, in spite of it's staleness, felt wonderful. He dribbled a few drops upon the filthy, sweat-salt encrusted lenses of his glasses. Gently he rubbed them with a bit of plastic, poured water over them again and then set them aside to dry in the cold night air.

Sleep. He needed sleep. Relocating himself, he took his initial position, body outstretched, facing upward, head resting on the hard surface of the skull. He closed his eyes.

*

Later, before midnight he guessed, his eyes blinked open. A light, a strobe light perhaps, flashed on for a fraction of a second. When it came on again the light was a considerable distance from its original position.

Flash! The light had reversed course and was in the northern sky. Another flash. That time east of the previous one. He thought of sitting up to watch, for what he was observing was peculiar indeed. Instead, his eyes closed and he slept.

*

Once again he awoke. The moon had drifted to just above the horizon. Flash! That light again. Then another light. Flash! Flash! More than one. Two or three. Perhaps five or six. Lights were flashing everywhere. Henry beheld the unexplainable performance and decided he'd better get up. Again, he fell asleep.

*

The moon had set, drifted behind the great mountains to the west. One flash. That was all. Then, a brilliant meteorite, glorified in intense blues and greens, just as the one the night before, only much larger, sailed across the heavens leaving a slight cerulean trail behind it.

"What was that?" Henry wondered.

The exhausted man slept well past dawn.

*

CHAPTER 21

What a glorious day, he thought.

'Glorious' was not a word that he ordinarily used, not part of Henry Two Feather's usual vocabulary. He was beginning his journey down from the summit of the holy mountain.

That girl. He recalled the young, pleasant face of yesterday's visitor, up on Chief Mountain. Before him was a rock cairn, rocks piled up one upon another. From the top of the pile, anchored with a piece of stone, a red bandanna fluttered in the early morning breeze. He found a note, scratched on a piece of brown paper bag. "Look under the rocks." Carefully he removed the top layer of stones finding, in a hollow area, a plastic Ziploc bag. Inside there were two peanut butter-jelly sandwiches, half a dozen shortcake cookies and a badly bruised apple.

Rarely had he tasted such delicious morsels. Ingesting the food gave him the strength needed to safely make the journey back to State Route 17. Perhaps all of his energy hadn't come from the food. Henry's body felt amazingly strong, the downhill distance short, progress far swifter than that agonizing climb of two days before. More good fortune. Without even trying, he located the trail he had so easily lost on the way up; soon he arrived at the site where the sweat lodge had been.

He found his belongings, all of his clothes, just as Billy had promised, hanging from a limb out of reach of bears and rodents. How splendid he felt, once again wearing a shirt, trousers, and boots. The cotton socks were pure luxury, so warm and soft on his bruised feet. Inside his back trouser pocket he found an ironed, white handkerchief with which he could clean his glasses. That Martha, he had thought. She thinks of everything. In truth, he had put the handkerchief in the pocket himself. He just didn't remember.

He crouched alongside the little stream and washed the lenses of his glasses. Once clean and dried they were much more serviceable. He could see without trying to ignore spots and dried perspiration. As an afterthought he washed the dust and filth from the sacred beaver stick.

Sensing danger, the lawman stood up and faced the direction from which the sounds came. Someone, an intruder, was walking along the same path he had just traveled.

"Well, Sam Hunting Bow," Henry greeted.

"I told you that my name is Sam Kennedy. My names Kennedy, you old fart."

Henry smiled. "Why aren't you home looking after your wife and kids? You neglect them, you know."

The intruder's face scowled with rage. "That's none of your fucking business, you dumb shit."

Henry continued smiling.

"You're gonna' get yours, Ass Hole. I come back just for you, Lawman."

"Came," taunted Henry.

"Huh?"

"You said, 'I come back.' You should have said, 'I came back.'" He enjoyed correcting stupid people. His tormentor quivered with rage. "You wouldn't hit an old man with glasses on, would you, Sammy?"

"Just watch!" Sam had lunged forward, the power in his stocky legs propelling him across the little clearing.

Henry stepped aside. Sam saw the beaver stick, glistening with water from the stream, arc slightly just before it slammed into his neck. The attacker went down.

Repositioning the pack upon his shoulders he spoke to the fallen foe. "Have a nice day, Sammy." Sam didn't hear.

He found the intruders car parked further down the Slide Lake trail road and stopped long enough to unscrew the valve stems from all four tires. Throwing the bits of metal into the brush had given him great satisfaction. "Have a nice day, Sammy," he repeated.

*

Chuckling at the recalled incidents, Henry took off the pack and carefully placed it on the earth so that the Calumet pipe was safe from damage. The white buffalo robe protected the pipe from accidental bumps.

How wonderful to be alive. Golden sunlight glistened between pale, quivering aspen leaves. Insects fluttered and zipped about from flower to flower in some incomprehensible flight plan. Down there, beside the highway, the environment was so gentle on that June day, so very different from the summit, just a few thousand feet above where he waited.

Henry detected the pickup scooting up Route 17. She was exceeding the speed limit again and for once Henry didn't mind. He hurried down to the road, slipped under the barbed wire gate as deftly as a youngster. He opened the just-stopped pickup door.

"Hi, Hot Shot!" Martha was beaming with happiness.

"Hi. How's my girl?" Henry climbed in and embraced his wife. She looked at him in amazement.

"What happened up there?"

"What do you mean?" he responded.

"Here I was expecting to get Babb Rescue to take you to the hospital and you are behaving like a kid with the hots."

"Never mind," he chuckled. "Just get me home so I can shower, shave, and fill up on your fry bread and honey."

"You've got it, Hot Shot."

Martha took Henry home.

*

"Now what?" Martha, her patience gone, couldn't resist asking. Three days had passed since Henry's dramatic return home. The first day consisted of his eating everything she put in front of him, plus sleeping. The only unusual act he had performed was to write a letter to Sweet Grass Woman. Martha had taken it to the Park Cafe where one of the medicine woman's descendents picked it up.

Henry acted as if he didn't hear her query.

Her man was driving her crazy. He actually repaired her old clothes washer. The job was tacky, crude by anyone's standard, but it worked. Henry had cut a piece off of the side of a tin can, cut two slits in the base and inserted the metal onto the rim of the tub. Now, instead of water spraying out onto the floor of the utility room the metal deflected the spurt and the water fell back into the basin. He was very proud of himself.

"Are you all right?," she asked.

Finally realizing that Martha was speaking to him he responded, "Sure. Never felt better." He walked out to the barn and puttered about all that afternoon.

On the evening of the third day since his ordeal, Henry, humming some indistinct tune, smiled happily at his wife.

"Henry, don't take me wrong," began Martha.

"Why, I'm not taking you anywhere, Sweetheart. Just relax."

Martha wouldn't be ignored. "Now that is what I mean, Henry. You act funny. You don't smoke anymore. Thank the Lord for that small blessing. You don't swear either. Why Henry, you don't even give the Republicans hell for their insensitivity toward Native Americans."

She looked him in the eyes. "Henry, are you sick or something?"

"Yep. That's it. Love sick. Let's go to bed and mess around."

Martha pushed him away. "You old fool. Get away." Although pleased with his advances she frowned again. "You aren't well. I know it. I haven't heard a 'damn' or a 'hell' or anything stronger since you got down off that mountain.

"What happened up there? On Chief Mountain?"

"Nina'istuko," corrected Henry.

"I know the Indian name," Martha declared.

He smiled at his Blackfeet woman. "What happened up there? I can't tell you, Martha. You know that. If I could, you'd be the first to know." He was enjoying not being able to tell her everything.

"Well, I don't miss the cigarette smoke and your hacking cough but I really liked my old Henry better than you."

"You'll get used to me."

They heard a car door slam. Footsteps, hard heel strikes made by boots, pounded on the sidewalk just outside of their back door. Martha opened the door before the somewhat startled young man could knock. "Hi. Looking for Henry?"

A young Blackfeet, hair in a pony tail hanging down below the man's waist, nodded that he was.

Henry appeared at the door, then stepped past his wife. "Hello. Won't you come inside?"

"No. I've got to get back. I work in Cut Bank, at the super market. My boss, he let me off to deliver this message to you". Not certain that Henry understood what he was saying the man added, "It's from my old grandmother."

"Yes," acknowledged Henry, "I recognize you from someplace. You are one of the old woman's descendants."

"Yes. Here," he handed a white business envelope to Henry. "I've got to go now."

"Thank you very much."

The man headed back to his idling automobile and Henry stepped back into the kitchen.

Martha, not usually so inquisitive, asked, "What does it say?"

He read the short letter to himself. "I can't read all of it to you. You know, the totem thing. What my totem is has to be kept a secret."

Martha looked disappointed.

"But," he added, "She doesn't give me much help. The last half of the note reads, 'You know what you have to do. Let your heart guide you. I can't help you anymore. Trust the OLD WAYS.' She capitalized Old Ways," Henry explained.

Martha was still frowning. "Not much help. You are all alone again, Henry."

"Not really. The part I can't read to you tells me that my totem is very strong. That the old spirits, the powerful ones, are with me. The good ones are."

"And the evil ones?" Martha asked.

Henry shrugged.

"Well, I hope she is right, that old lady."

"She is, Martha. She is."

*

The St. Mary Visitors Center was busy with tourists. Outside, the east parking lot held several RVs including a gigantic motorized home. People, visitors, were scurrying from vehicles to the center and then, after a few minutes inside, they would hurry back to their cars and campers.

The winds, as they often did in June, blew down-valley, rushing along the mountain slopes, kicking up white caps on Upper St. Mary Lake, then sweeping over the flat prairie, gaining velocity before they assailed the vulnerable park visitors.

Henry sat in his truck, watching. Usually, in the past, he would have been smoking. Not anymore. The change was beyond his comprehension. He had kept his word to not smoke when he left Sweet Grass Woman's house. For some reason or other the desire had left him at that moment. No withdrawal. No nervous physical reaction. That didn't happen when a heavy smoker quit, but it had happened to him.

He got out of the pickup, left hand holding on to his Stetson, which was trying to sail away.

Clank. Clank. Clank. Tireless, loud, in fast cadence, the flagpole snaps that held the American flag collided with the metal pole. Henry hurried past the offensive noise, seeking the comparative quiet of the busy center's lobby. He held the door open for a little boy who was vainly attempting to get inside.

He saw who he was looking for. The dark haired girl he had seen on top of Chief Mountain stood behind the Information Desk sorting brochures. He walked up to the desk.

"Thanks for the food, young lady."

The girl looked up questioningly. She didn't recognize Henry with his clothes on.

"You know," he smiled, "the peanut butter and jelly sandwiches."

"Oh!" She put a hand to her open mouth. Her eyes were wide in surprise. "Oh, you are the Wolf Man."

It was Henry's turn to be surprised. "Wolf Man? How do you know about what happened up there?"

The young woman stood silent for a moment. "When we finally finished placing the food inside the rock cairn and stuffing the hole shut with rocks we turned around and there, just a short distance away, we saw a pack of wolves. There were seven of them, just sitting there watching us."

"Did they scare you? Being so close?"

"Why no, I don't think we ever thought of being afraid. Funny. We should have been afraid, I guess. They were so beautiful."

She explained, "I called you Wolf Man because when we had hiked down a ways we turned to get one more look at them. The one wolf had moved. He was heading for the mountain top."

Henry realized that the animal must have sat there watching him for several hours.

She asked, "Did he hurt you?"

"No. No. Wolves don't hurt people."

The girl responded, "That's what I've been told. We didn't know whether to climb back up to where you were or just let whatever was going on up there take it's course."

"Thank you," said Henry. "You made the right decision." He liked the girl very much. "What is your name, young lady?"

"Diane Morrisey."

"Here, Diane, this is your bandanna. Martha, my wife, washed and ironed it for you."

He changed the subject. "The office told me that Vern Nielsson is over here somewhere. Is that right?"

"Yes. Mr. Nielsson is talking to the new naturalists and sales people. All but me. He shouldn't be long. He doesn't seem to be the type who enjoys making speeches."

"Thanks, young lady." He started to walk away.

"See you, Mr. Wolf Man."

Again the new title startled him. Thoughts of Douglas rushed in to flood his spirit with sadness. He missed his young friend very much.

*

244

Vern Nielsson fled the auditorium in a near panic. So many people looking at him. So many highly educated people with a better grasp of the English language than he had. Back in the auditorium his voice had echoed, vibrating off the concrete beams and wooden paneling. Fresh air. He needed to get outside where a person could breathe clean air.

The District Ranger was the first one to the refreshment table. In fact, the polite applause was still sounding, perhaps seventy pairs of hands plopping together, reflecting Vern's kind words of appreciation that they would be working for him, indirectly. The harassed man grabbed a handful of his wife's oatmeal cookies from the table without breaking stride.

Henry moved swiftly to intercept the ranger.

"Come on outside, Henry. I've got to get some fresh air."

The two friends stopped to drink at the outdoor water fountain. Vern, still looking distraught, handed Henry a cookie. "Let's walk over to the bridge where we won't be bothered."

A sidewalk, between the east and west parking lots, guided the two men toward the river and the path leading to the St. Mary campground. Sunlight, the intense, glaring sparkling brilliance accompanying a windy June day, paled the Russian olive bushes, displayed the bent grass stems and made the wildflowers appear like streaks, moving strokes of vivid color from an artist's brush.

The trail led them between thickets of willows. The air was wild with hissings, the snapping of green willow branches, and the gurgling of the St. Mary River. A third of the way out onto the wooden bridge the two men stopped.

"We can talk here," Vern explained. "If anyone comes along they won't be able to hear what we are discussing. Besides, the wind will blow our words away." Both men leaned on the high railing, peering downstream, away from the brightness of the sun.

"Hear anything about Douglas?" Henry's question came abruptly, barely concealing his emotion.

"No, Evelyn called Mrs. Jakowski two nights ago. No change. Well, that isn't quite true. Seems he's making some progress. Henry, we might as well face the fact that Douglas won't be returning for some time. The doctors say his complete recovery will take nearly two years. The injured shoulder muscles are the problem. The good news is that the prognosis is that he will be just as good as new. Probably no back pains or anything. Quite amazing. Like a miracle has happened.

The Indian returned Vern's gaze without comment. His face was impassive, calm, not showing the intense relief the man was experiencing.

"You heard what I said, didn't you Henry? The wind makes it hard to hear."

"I heard you," the lawman responded.

Unable to read his friend's emotions or thoughts Vern changed the subject. "What about your job? Is the sheriff cooperating?"

"Yes. He's really a nice person. I've got a few more days of leave time. Then, if necessary, I'll likely take some sick leave. But, I don't want to."

Vern's mind was filled with questions but he remained silent, uninquisitive, respecting Henry's privacy.

The two men began searching the banks, the swift-moving channel, and the tiny pond, hoping to find a sign of beaver at work. Unsuccessful, they turned and walked to the upriver side of the bridge, into the glaring sunlight. A few bank swallows darted past, strays from the swarming mass of bug eaters that nested and fed near the Going to-the-Sun Road bridge, a stone structure just a mere eighth of a mile upstream.

Finally Vern spoke. "They, the young kids, are calling you 'Wolf Man', Henry."

"Yes," he smiled, "I just found that out."

"Do you want me to stop that?" Vern tried to see his friend's facial expression. "Some call Douglas that, only for different reasons."

"No." Henry's countenance remained transfixed, impervious to any emotions resulting from memories of Douglas. "No, let them be. They have a good reason to call me that."

"I know." Vern had been told about the wolf incident.

The friends stood silent once more.

Vern broke the mood. "I got a phone call from Jess whatever-his-name-is, that AV guy we had working around here last summer."

"Oh? That California person that followed everyone around with a video camera?"

Both men laughed.

"That's the one," responded Vern. "Last name Champion. Now there's a California name for you. Champion. Seems he had called Douglas just before the incident. He told me he had sent Jakowski a large manila envelope of pictures. Blowups of frames from his video camera.

"Anyway, I asked Jess why the pictures were important and he wouldn't respond. You know, those California folks are always afraid of a lawsuit."

"Did he say what they were of?"

"Wouldn't say, but he told me to find them because 'They might help you solve your mystery.'"

"All this came out after I told him Douglas was badly injured. That he had been struck from behind."

"So, what did you do about it?"

"I went to the trailer. They weren't there."

"No," agreed Henry.

"Say, how many times have you unscrewed that hasp on the door?" Both men smiled.

"You don't want me to break a good lock do you?" he chuckled.

Vern continued. "I got on the phone to the West Side and do you know where they are?" Vern didn't wait for a response. "Law enforcement found the envelope behind the front seat of Douglas's Toyota. Laying sort of between the seats."

"So, what are they of?"

Vern looked to see if anyone was within hearing distance. Several campers from the St. Mary campground were standing on the bridge. "Look Henry, you'd better get over there and take a look. Andy Daniels said he'd let you see the photos but he can't let us have them."

"That's really big of him," Henry responded. Vern shrugged his shoulders. Neither man was fond of the West Side lawman.

Henry explained, "I want to see the photos before I say anything else. Let's meet tomorrow, around five. Is here OK?"

Vern got an idea. "OK, but why don't you come over for dinner? Evelyn and the girls miss you."

"Sounds great. But, let's meet here first. Unless the photographs change my mind I'll have a proposal for you and the family had better not get involved." He hesitated a moment then asked, "What does District say about Douglas's real assignment? I don't suppose they are very happy."

Vern made a noise of disgust. "Personnel, and especially Strickland, down in Denver, wanted to dump me. No retirement. Nothing."

"Sounds like they saw a way to save some tax payers' dollars."

Vern held up his hand to silence his friend. "I'm really lucky. The Regional Director flew down here and we talked over at my place, one whole evening. That lady is something else." Vern nervously

247

cleared his throat. "Not only did she come here rather than calling me to Denver, to the slaughterhouse, she understood, Henry. She really understood what I was trying to do.

"But, no matter what my motives, I bent the rules. Hiring Douglas under false pretenses. I didn't tell her my friend in Fish and Wildlife knew what I was up to. No need to give him grief. I already cost him a good man, Douglas."

Henry looked concerned. "So, she did dump you."

"No. No. We made a verbal deal. That's all. Next summer I can retire. I agreed to do just that. I've got a lot of leave time coming so I'll be out of here come the first of the year. She agrees to take the heat until then, if there is any."

"And the case?" asked Henry.

"Well, Law Enforcement is running the investigation concerning what happened to Douglas. As far as everyone except you and I are concerned no one else has been harmed."

Henry thought about the missing men.

"No one else, eh?"

"No one else, Henry. No one missing on government property. No mystery, except where a couple of men got to that left their cars abandoned. Nothing to do with Glacier except they apparently came through here.

"Well I'll be darned," exclaimed Henry.

Vern looked sharply at his friend. He had said "darned," and back at the VC Vern thought he had heard Henry say, "Gee whiz."

"You OK, Henry?"

"Sure." Henry wondered why Nielsson had asked. "Let's go. I'll meet you here tomorrow at five. If I can't make it in time I'll call. OK?"

"OK. Then we can walk home and have some of Evelyn's cooking. What would you like?"

Henry didn't hesitate. "Pot roast, home made noodles, and mashed potatoes."

"Consider it done."

The two men walked back to the visitor's center.

*

The Next Evening

Henry stood, back leaning against the wooden railing of the St. Mary River bridge, watching Vern hurrying along the trail, appearing smaller between the otherwise impenetrable willows that choked the swampy south shore.

"Sorry I'm late," the ranger apologized. "Every time I talk with West Side maintenance I get stuck listening to a dozen complaints which have nothing to do with us over here."

Henry nodded in sympathy. "We're sure lucky to have the crew we have at St. Mary."

Nielsson caught his breath, for he had been almost running. Henry waited calmly. The ranger took deep breaths, his massive chest rising and falling, reminding Henry of a blacksmith's bellows. "That's better. I can talk now. What did you find out, Henry? Did you see the photos?"

"Yes."

"Yes what? Do you know anything new?"

"Vern, I can end this bad situation for you."

"What's the catch, Henry? What are you talking about?"

"The catch is that I'm going to ask you to stick your neck out one more time."

"Wait a minute, Henry. I told you yesterday that I almost got sacked. I've got my family to think about. My retirement, you know."

"Yes, I realize that. The fact is I can end the killings once and for all."

"You know I want that. My God, Henry, you know how I feel. But don't ask—"

"Let me explain." The lawman checked to be certain that no one was coming along the trail. "Something happened up on Chief Mountain. To me."

"Yeah, I told you I know about the wolf."

"More than that. I don't even understand everything. Seems I keep seeing more, visualizing incidents from the past. They all aren't from your world, Vern. Mine neither. Not the world I knew before I climbed Nina'istuko."

Nielsson was silent, waiting for his friend to proceed.

"Sometimes I see visions. I have dreams. Part of what I experience is like flashbacks. Other times. Some long ago. Maybe I imagine things." He paused trying to find the right words.

"I see spirits, Vern."

Nielsson looked incredulous. "Yes. Sure you do."

"Well, I can't help it. Ever since I came down from Nina'istuko I seem to have visitations."

Nielsson was becoming angry. His best friend was getting weird on him. Vern didn't like nor accept weird beliefs.

249

"I'll give you an example, Henry suggested."

The ranger started moving away, thinking of going back to his office. "Is that what you had me come here for, Henry? Mumbo-jumbo? Next thing you'll be telling me there really is a Sasquatch."

Henry ignored the caustic remark. "Just listen, Vern. If you want to end the killings, just hear me out. OK?"

Nielsson didn't answer but his backward movement had ceased.

"My supernatural experiences are simple to explain. The hallucination, I suppose you would call it, began as soon as I got home. I took a long, hot shower and felt pretty good. Not really tired anymore. Not sleepy, that's for sure. So, I walk over to the sink to comb my hair and I look into the mirror to check how my sunburned forehead is doing. For a moment I saw myself, not a pleasant thing, you'll agree. Suddenly, I wasn't me."

Vern's scowl deepened. "What do you mean you weren't you?"

"Just that. I was looking at someone else. One of the Old Ones. He had long black hair. Braided. His face was not normal. Something strange about it. I can't think of the right words."

Nielsson remained silent.

"At first I was afraid but my fear gradually changed to acceptance and now respect."

"Now?"

"Yes. Every time I look into a mirror I see him."

"I'm sure a psychiatrist has a label for such delusions."

"Yes. I've thought the same thing. Only, each time I seem to grow in understanding. Like the Old One is teaching me things."

"Messages? You get messages?" Nielsson was skeptical again.

"No, not really. But, each time I seem to learn a little bit more. Things that I can't possibly know from the past."

"Like who killed the missing people. The ones we think are missing," Vern suggested.

"Right. Oh, they are dead all right. No question about it anymore."

Nielsson, still disbelieving, asked, "Can you take me to their remains?"

"I suppose so. But, I won't. Why raise a mess? We need to terminate the problem with as little publicity as possible."

"I'm for that, Henry. It's just that I can't accept this stuff you're dishing out on me."

Turning his gaze from the river Henry looked the ranger straight in the eyes. "I can stop the killings. I can see that justice is done. No messy details left to explain." Henry paused for effect. "If you cooperate with me no one will know what happens or most important, that anyone was murdered in the first place."

Nielsson blinked. What Henry said was too good to be true. "There must be a catch somewhere. What is it?"

Henry smiled. "I don't like holding out on you, Vern, but there's a Judas goat in the flock."

"An employee? Is that what you are saying?"

"How about, 'someone you know?' Forget my first attempt to be subtle."

"Do you mean...."

"Don't ask me anymore."

Vern realized that Henry had just told him that someone on his staff was involved. "Hell fire and damnation, Henry. We've got to prosecute whoever it is. That's our way; the modern way."

Henry simply smiled.

The friends stood looking upstream, along the smooth surfaced ponds that lay south of the river's rushing current.

"Look there, over by that log," whispered Vern. "Kind of early in the evening but that beaver is floating fresh cut branches back there to his lodge." The animal's appearance seemed to have erased any thoughts of the killings from their minds. The beaver, a female, but the two men didn't know that, gracefully carried a willow branch between her jaws. The leaves at the small end of the branch dragged behind in the still water making rippling v's, which wriggled outward toward both banks of the dammed pool.

Vern broke the stillness. "What do you want me to do?" His voice was soft, yielding to his friend's wishes.

"Close Cut Bank."

"Then what?"

Henry chuckled. "That's it, Vern. Invent a bear incident. Something. Close up the place."

"What do I do about the Bear Management people? What about my ranger, down there?"

"Those are problems you will have to deal with. I'll do the rest."

"I don't know, Henry. There aren't many places in the Park Service where a suggestion like yours would even be considered. I realize that by the way you are acting and what you have just said that this is an Indian problem. I know you are being guided by Sweet Grass Woman." Vern turned and looked at Henry. "I met her once, Henry. About two years ago. Amazing woman. If she wasn't involved I'd flat out say 'No.'"

"You don't have any choice. I'm your only chance of stopping the killings without creating massive problems for you and the park. What would happen if you didn't help me would result in the end of your career and Douglas's and lots of other fine career people. That woman from Denver would get the ax. You know that, don't you?"

Henry looked Nielsson in the eye, "There have been seven killings now."

Nielsson swallowed hard. "I thought as much."

Vern had some questions. "When, Henry? Where? How do you plan on pulling this thing off?"

"Two days from now. Keep that place empty. Close all the trails including the ones along Triple Divide and Pitamakan."

"Those are it? That's easy. There aren't any other trails going into that area. Besides, both routes are still snowed in."

"Good." "Make sure no hot shot snow hiker sneaks in."

"Consider it done. Day after tomorrow, eh? For how long?"

"Oh," grinned Henry, "just two days."

"And that's it?"

"That is it. No questions asked. Ever."

"OK", sighed Vern. "I sure got myself into a ball buster this time."

Henry smiled because of Vern's off-color remark. The two men shook hands.

"Henry, I'll sure miss 'retiring' from the service."

"Why, you old rascal you, I'll see to it that you slip out of this mess like cat shit off a hot tin roof."

*

CHAPTER 22

Sighing, the rumble emanating from deep within his chest, the Great Bear stirred slightly beneath the weight of the female's head and left foreleg.

Sunshine, brilliant summer's life-giving rays, caused the male to pant heavily. Pesky flies had found his face, creeping into the moist corners of his eyes, walking ticklingly across the bear's muzzle. Irritated he rolled away from his mate, an almost black female he had been copulating with for several days.

Before her, the Great Bear had mated with a larger, lighter colored grizzly. He had remained with that one for five days. Never before had he found so many willing females. This June was the first time his natural promiscuity had been sated. The Nyack Valley was a sexually hungry grizzly male's paradise.

Interest declining, the mighty Bruin was thinking about moving on. Perhaps he could find a third willing female with a high estrogen level. The previous evening he had detected a provocative odor drifting up slope. The scent was faint but he could locate the female it belonged to, if he searched.

He sat up, looking about for no reason in particular. His restlessness caused his female to moan softly, her sleep having been interrupted.

The grizzly pair was far up the east slope of the valley, above the heavier forested slopes, lying in meadowland splotched with trees, rocks, and shrubs. Hiding in the shadows, snow-banks, dirty with bits and pieces of dead vegetation, continued their slow meltdown in the warm, early summer's heat.

Once again, the huge one's mind was not his own. Another force, spirit, took control. Confused, but not resisting, the male grizzly, once again the Medicine Grizzly, left the female and walked up the west slopes of Razoredge Mountain.

Abandoned, the female merely sighed and slept again. Likely another male would amble along.

*

Paws throwing up splatters of refrozen snow, the Crypt Lake wolf pack scampered across the icy Triple Divide summit. Long tails sailing behind, the wild dogs thrilled to the downhill slopes just beneath the Continental Divide.

The previous night they had taken a precarious route, through the land frequented by the human animals. Their run had taken them along the eastern fringe of the St. Mary Campground, fording the river at the exact location where a frustrated juvenile grizzly had killed and partially consumed two young, foolish, concession employees. The year had been 1980, the only year that the campground had been closed.

In 1985, when the wolves passed by the camping area, a lone camper's dog barked nervously. From the moraine above St. Mary Village, two more experienced hounds roared with anger at the wolves' intrusion. No matter. The pack scampered across the Going-to-the-Sun Road and raced through the great expanse of meadowland to the south. A coyote, hunting for hares or some other morsel, had observed the wolves approaching. Crouching low into the grasses she trembled with fear as the much larger members of the dog family cavorted along on a faint deer trail. That was how Alpha Male had led his family safely through man's land.

For all of the exhilaration resulting from the high slopes awakening to the new day's sun, the Crypt Lake pack was tiring. The journey had been long, over twenty miles, all traversed during the darkness of a no-moon night. One of the yearling pups was lagging behind, but the leader, the Alpha Male, didn't slow his pace until he found seclusion in the forests above Atlantic Creek.

One-by-one the pack flopped, exhausted, upon the needle-covered forest floor. His female, tongue lolling out of the side of her mouth, head lowered in submission, walked over to her mate and nuzzled Alpha Male's nose and mouth. Her love for him was intense, far greater than what she felt for their offspring.

Soon, bodies touching, the couple slept.

*

The other wolf pack, the one that had been exploring near Hole-in-the-Wall when the spirits called, were still traveling toward Medicine Grizzly Lake. Their route up Razoredge Mountain paralleled the Great Bear's trail. Soon they would drop down off the precarious slopes that would take them to the southeastern edge of the lake. Upon finding shelter, they too would fall to the earth and sleep, basking in the sun's rays.

Medicine Grizzly, the Great Bear, was already nearby.

*

Clarence Kipp parked his battered Ford truck underneath an alder thicket, just behind the Blackfeet campground, which was on the south side of Cut Bank Creek. He sat waiting, making certain that no one had observed his arrival. He had plenty of time. Eight or nine miles separated the lone figure from his destination, Medicine Grizzly Lake.

Henry Two Feather's message had said for Clarence to meet him two hours before dusk. "Easy doing," the man said to his truck. He could run the distance in two hours. "No sweat."

Before he had turned into the campground he had checked the road to Cut Bank Campground. A sign, a bright orange sign with bold, black letters, indicated the area was closed due to grizzly bear activity. Not likely, the man had thought. Yet, the Medicine Grizzly could be back. Sitting inside the truck, he cautiously swung the cylinder of his revolver open. Yep. Full load. Six cartridges sat in the chambers. He got out of the truck shutting the door so softly a nearby squirrel didn't hear the slight metallic click. His hand slipped back to his right hip and came to rest on the wooden handle of a long knife. Its sheath was leather covered with soft, fringed buckskin.

Clarence pulled his ebony-colored hat down, so that the generous brim shielded his eyes from the bright sun. To himself he said, Black hat. Bad guy. The man enjoyed his self-image. The thick lips on his skinny face spread wide in a hideous smile. Only one tooth showed, like a stalactite hanging down from the roof of his mouth.

Careful not to leave a trail, Fang disappeared into the forest he knew so well.

*

Those delicious Cow Parsnips! In the old days the Blackfeet and early White intruders used to slit the young stalks into quarters, lengthwise. Then the tender stems would be boiled until they were soft and palatable. Bears loved the fleshy plants too, before they became hard and impossible to digest. A large black bear was chewing away on the spring crop, chomping, slobbering, gulping, making what humans would call sickening noises.

Henry heard the bear's mastication. The animal's location was where the trail to Medicine Grizzly Lake split from the route to Morning Star Lake. He was pleased that the blackie was there. His presence meant no grizzly was in the neighborhood. The two species were not compatible. He stooped at a muddy spot, to study the bruin's tracks. The paw prints were huge, larger than most grizzly spoors. No mistake about it, the sign was that of a black bear. Claws were short, close to the end of the toes. The man was impressed with the animal's size.

*

The Great Bear, the Medicine Grizzly, had taken the long way back to the valley where he had slept through the winter months. Just as he had left, the giant had chosen to flounder through the drifts of Cut Bank Pass along the Continental Divide, to Pitamakan Pass and the lake below.

By the time he reached Morning Star Lake, he began to catch whiffs of the black male, who was still feeding some distance down-valley. The Great Bear growled menacingly, head weaving back and forth in an irritated manner, raised hackles emphasizing the hump, the enormous muscle positioned above his shoulders. He was becoming angry at the black bear's intrusion, all thoughts of copulating mere shadowed memories. Someone, a black bear, was in his valley, eating his cow parsnips, digging up his lilly bulbs.

Emitting another low, mumbling growl the Great Bear hurried on down the trail.

Fortunately for the black male, he heard and smelled the Medicine Grizzly coming. Without hesitation the intruder fled up the north slope of the Cut Bank Valley.

Both wolf packs, now resting on adjacent sunny slopes a few hundred feet above the valley floor, watched with mild curiosity as the black bear galloped uphill, traveling a path that ran between the two packs. None moved. They were where they were supposed to be. That they knew. The Alpha males lay patiently, waiting for whatever it was that controlled them to let them know what they were to do next. Of course, they didn't comprehend why they waited.

*

Henry Two Feathers arrived at Medicine Grizzly Lake about the time the sun was directly overhead. Nearly effortlessly he found the human remains, the rodent-chewed bones of the dead Comanche that Fang had carried to the lake. With meticulous scrutiny, he gathered the grisly parts and one-by-one dropped them into the holes of the still melting avalanche debris.

Task completed, Henry lit the Calumet. Smoking and praying in Blackfeet, the warrior helped the Comanche soul, if it still lingered nearby, to cross over, to enter the world of transformed spirits. While he performed the ceremonies coming to him from the Old Ones, he marveled at what he was doing. Such strange behavior for a modern man.

He received no recognition from the Comanche soul, no spirit rising out of the mass of broken trees and shattered rocks. His responsibility completed, Henry Two Feathers returned to the lake. There was much to do before his first visitor was scheduled to arrive.

*

Fang, Clarence Kipp, saw Henry sitting motionless before a yet-to-be-lit wood fire. The young Blackfeet stood watching the lawman, trying to determine what the old man was up to. Henry didn't move, his legs crossed, upper arms at his sides. Fang decided that the man's hands were folded. His head was erect so likely he wasn't sleeping. Silent, Fang observed the older man for some time.

"Well, aren't you coming in to talk?" asked Henry, his back still to the surprised Fang.

Silence.

"Come and sit down so we can talk our problems out."

Fang didn't respond.

"Shall I call you Sa'iyi, for I think the name fits, Crazy Wolf?"

Still no answer. Henry realized that the quickest way to get Fang to respond was to insult him. "Since I hear nothing from the warrior who lurks behind my back I guess I will have to call him Kishenehn, No Good."

"You don't have to interpret the words to me Old Man," declared Fang. Angry, the tall warrior walked out of the forest to confront his tormentor. "It is you who should be called Kishenehn, Old Man. Law Man." Fang spoke the words with an insulting slur.

Henry let the affront pass. He waited until Fang stood before him, the powerful, slim body quaking with anger.

"I got your fuckin' note. What do you want?"

Smiling, with the wave of an arm Henry directed his adversary to sit down. A small willow mat lay where Fang was to locate his behind.

The young man sat upon the woven pallet. Both were silent for a time, Henry deep in what appeared to be contemplation, Fang calming somewhat. Finally, Henry spoke. "Let us smoke from this sacred Calumet." He knew the young man facing him in such anger would not dare to decline the invitation. To do so might offend any spirit residing in the dried-blood colored pipe.

Henry puffed smoke to the four directions and up. Then he blew smoke toward the ground that separated them.

Surprised at Henry's last movements, Fang took the Calumet from the old man's outstretched arms. Serious, eyes intent with concentration, the younger Blackfeet performed the ceremony meticulously. He hesitated, almost handed back the pipe but then solemnly blew smoke upon Earth Mother.

Henry smiled his approval. The Calumet was laid aside. The two men were silent again.

A woods wren flitted about, low in the foliage, it's impressive voice scolding incessantly. The younger man grinned. "Little wren is angry because you are here, Old Man."

"No, you know that is not true. Our little brother enjoys scolding. The noise of his sounds makes him feel brave." Henry paused, then declared, "You don't need to make noise because you know you are brave. Isn't that true?"

"I'm sure not scared of an old man like you."

Silence again.

"You call me Old Man. You know what the Blackfeet word for Old Man is, don't you?"

"Napi," whispered Fang, feeling that he somehow had been tricked. "The trickster. What tricks are you playing here, Old Man?"

"Only good ones. Actually, no tricks at all. I can't risk offending the sacred medicine that I possess." He waited for Fang to question what the medicine was. When he didn't, Henry spoke again.

"I don't like the nick-name your so-called friends and everyone else call you, Fang."

"I don't like it either, man. They don't say it to my face, like you do. If they do, I punch them out."

Henry noted that the 'old' had been dropped. "Neither do I like calling you Sa'iyi, Crazy Wolf. The name is not complimentary. I called you Kishenehn, No Good, only to get you to come sit with me."

The young man was interested in the way the conversation was going but he remained silent.

"Clarence Kipp is a White Man's name. Why do you use it? Your father's name was Elk Tongue, Ponoka'w Uzini."

"Yeah," laughed Clarence, "named after the man who traveled all the way to Mexico and received the dreaming pipe from the people of the south lands. Peyote or maybe marijuana, huh?"

"I doubt that. Your father was named after a very great man," declared Henry.

"That son-of-a-bitch! He'd get drunk. Beat my mother. Fuck my sisters. Do things to me. If he were alive, I'd see that his days were numbered. I'd kill him!"

The man was almost out of control. Henry sat impassive, waiting.

"Ah!" Clarence waved his hands in frustration. "Don't know why I told you that shit! It is not your business."

"You are right. I'll not speak of him again. Before I show you my medicine, let's talk about you. Not about your family."

Suspicious, the young man watched Henry, trying to figure out what he was up to.

"Sweet Grass Woman told me you read many books. Good literature."

The medicine woman's name caused Clarence to forget his anger. "What about Sweet Grass Woman? Why does she talk about me to you, Lawman?"

"Because you are related. Blood relatives. Your mother is descended from her. If your mother had lived longer she might have told you that."

"You're putting me on."

Henry grimaced. "That's a White Man's phrase. I don't like it. Speak as a Blackfeet."

Clarence opened his mouth to swear but decided to remain silent.

"Your last name, Kipp. That's not your father or mother's family name. Where did you get it?"

Clarence laughed, thinking his answer would be funny. "From the saloon, where I hang out, sometimes."

"Seems you have a problem with names, eh, Clarence?"

"So what if I do? Who cares?"

"Me. Sweet Grass Woman, your old grandmother. Probably your sisters. Maybe lots of people care. I don't like your choices of names. I think I shall ask the Ancient Ones to allow me to give you a new name, a good name. A Blackfeet name that you will be proud of."

Clarence looked interested.

"I can name you Loneman, Nitaina. That's Blackfeet. But, I like Nit-awahka better. The name of Lone Walker. He was a great man. You are a lone man, Clarence. You walk alone, a Nit-awahka, he who walks alone."

"What are you getting at, Old Man?" Clarence had forgotten about the Blackfeet word, for Old Man. 'Napi'.

"Nothing. Only that if I were you, I would rather be called Lone Walker than Fang or Kipp. What do you think?"

The man didn't respond. He thought, and rightly so, that Kipp was an honorable name.

"OK. At least for now, today, I will call you Lone Walker and you will call me Henry. OK?"

"Yeah. Yeah. all right." Clarence was visibly pleased.

"Now, getting back to your reading."

"Listen, Henry, what I read is none of your business."

"I know that, but we have a couple of hours to kill before the others arrive and we might as well talk about something you are interested in."

Clarence wondered who the 'others' were.

"Who is your favorite author?"

"Why are you asking me these questions? What do you know about books?"

Henry smiled. "Good question. I went to Montana State University for two years."

"What did you do, flunk out?" Clarence thought he was being funny.

"Yes, as a matter-of-fact I did. But not before I had some darned good literature courses under my belt."

"'Under my belt', is a White Man's phrase." Clarence laughed at his own cleverness.

"Who is your favorite author?"

"There you go again." Realizing where he had picked up the phrase he shook his head. "Oh, man! I sound like that creep, Reagan." Clarence shook his head in dismay.

"Who is your favorite author?"

"You don't give up, do you? It's Hemingway. He's old stuff but I like what he writes."

"Hemingway, eh? Why him?"

"Why, that guy had balls. He was a real man. Took no crap off anybody. That's the way I am."

Henry agreed. "Yes, I'm sure you are." Then he added, "Hemingway lied."

"He what? No, you've got to be joking. Trying to make me mad. Make me Sa'iyi; crazy."

"Nope. You're wrong, Lone Walker. He really did lie."

"Come on. When? How do you know?"

Henry was warming to the conversation. "Did you ever read Hemingway's account of the Americans entering Paris? Liberating it from the Nazis?"

"Naw! Never read it."

"Well, good old Ernest wrote about a great celebration among his companions. You know, wine and all that stuff."

"So?"

"It never happened. Researchers and historians interviewed the other men named in the story. There was no great celebration where Hemingway was, outside of Paris. Besides, he killed himself. Blew his brains apart with a shotgun."

"Sure. I know that. So what? He had the balls to do it, that man."

"I agree but I don't approve of his suicide, though."

"Look," Clarence was becoming exasperated again, "I'm tired of this stuff. So what if what you say is true? What's the point?"

Henry smiled. "I like Hemingway, too, Clarence Kipp, Lone Walker, Nit-awahka. But he had faults and he made mistakes. Just like you. Just like me."

Clarence frowned. "I think you are making one big mistake right now."

"I don't think so," argued Henry. "You see, Lone Walker, Hemingway doesn't have any chance to correct his mistakes. You and I do. Let's just wrap all this talk up by realizing that there are always other choices, alternatives, be they favorite authors, getting out of a bad mood, or choosing a course of action."

Henry reached for the pack he had carried to the top of Chief Mountain. He flipped the already unfastened cover back and reached inside. "Now we will look at the medicine we have with us." Slowly, carefully Henry Two Feathers lifted the worn white buffalo robe high above his head. The unfolded skin, hanging down in front of his face prevented Henry from seeing Lone Walker's expression, but he did hear the young man gasp. "You know what this is don't you?" he asked as he lowered the robe.

Lone Walker nodded in the affirmative.

"Good. You must believe in the white robe's powers. That is important."

"Yes."

"You must also stop the worshipping of the evil Old Ones."

"But," argued Lone Walker, "my totem is the Sasquatch."

"See. You are wrong again. On two counts. Number one: The Sasquatch are not evil. They are just a small population of peculiar, intelligent, upright-walking animals that have telepathic abilities. Do you understand that?"

Lone Walker didn't respond.

"Good." Henry acted like the young man had agreed. "They are not your totem. That is the second point on which you are wrong. You have no totem."

"Yes I do," protested Lone Walker.

"No you don't. You have been lied to. Deceived. How it was done I don't know. Perhaps you don't either. You haven't ever gone on a vision quest. I checked with every shaman I know. You have no protective spirit."

"How do you know all of what you say?" Lone Walker was loosing his temper again.

Henry pointed at the robe. "I know. Believe me."

"Well, just maybe I ain't good enough. Maybe I am evil."

Henry countered. "What is that 'ain't' stuff? You don't speak that way except to impress your old buddies. Right?"

"I guess so."

"Lone Walker, don't you realize that this conversation shouldn't take place? Here we are, two Native Americans, out here, risking our lives, and we talk of literature and ethics as if we were two intellectuals. How can this be?"

Lone Walker shrugged his shoulders.

"Why, man, we are two intelligent human beings. That is why our words come out as they do." Henry had grabbed the offensive. "As far as I can tell, you haven't killed anyone, have you?" Henry didn't wait for an answer. "You did get conned into hauling all those bodies around and disposing of them. That is a White man's crime which would get you twenty years in prison."

"So? I got paid," grumbled Lone Walker. "You are going to turn me in, aren't you?"

"Wrong again. This is a tribal thing and it has to do with the old ways." As an afterthought he asked, "What have you done besides acting mean?"

"Well I almost killed a guy once or twice."

"That's not news," responded Henry. "What else?"

"I sort of worship the Old Ones, the evil Old Ones."

"That will stop if you want it to. We have the medicine here that will help you change that habit."

Again, there was no response.

Henry said, "We have a couple of hours. Likely more. Take your mat and go back to that large fir and sit down. Try to pray to the good ones for once. Meditate. You can chant if you want to but as soon as it gets dark and I light this fire, shut up. Don't move. Don't even take a leak. If our medicine is as strong as I think it is, we, you and I, will come out of this in fine shape." Henry hesitated, not certain if he should take the next step, as his dream spirits had directed. "Nit-awahka."

The young man stopped and waited for what Henry was about to say.

"Nit-awahka. Come here. Give me your knife."

Lone Walker retraced his steps. "I have a revolver, too. I won't give it up. All this is too new to me. You ask too much. Things are happening too fast. I am still Fang."

"You will not use the revolver. The weapon is as useless as a dead stick. This I have been told."

"Yeah? I haven't, so I'll keep it with me. I came here known as Fang, Kishenehn, the no-good-warrior of the Blackfeet."

Henry waited for the young man to continue.

"Now, I am suddenly Lone Walker, a most honored title. Yet, I have done nothing but talk to you. Why do you confuse me like this, Henry? Let me be."

"Give me your knife," Henry repeated.

Hesitantly, the knife was handed over. "Good." The old man placed the deadly looking blade inside the pack.

"You have passed the test of trust that I was told to give to you. Nit-awahka, you are worthy of the next steps. Sit, there, across from me. No, over there where we will not be so close.

"Good. Your ancient grandmother, Sweet Grass Woman sends her blood child a gift, a thing having great power."

Henry rummaged around inside the pack, pulled out a different knife and tossed it to Lone Walker. The force of the throw, the blade sailing toward the startled Blackfeet, created a dangerous weapon. Lone Walker's reflexes were excellent. He grasped the knife's handle, just behind the blade, as it came just inches from his exposed chest. For an instant anger flashed in the recipient's dark eyes.

"A long time ago this knife was given to our people in just this manner. The weapon can only be passed on in like fashion. Look." Henry opened his shirt revealing a stab wound in his chest. "It's not deep. I am not as fast as you but my reflexes are still very good."

Lone Walker knew of the knife.

Henry explained, "According to our history, the legends, Bear Mother presented this knife to a Piegan warrior the same way I gave it to you. She also gave him a song to go with it. I will try to sing it. Don't worry, the verse is short. Learn it now." He sang awkwardly in their native tongue, "A knife is just like dirt thrown against me." He repeated the difficult chant several times. "Now you sing."

"Lone Walker, without hesitation, sang in the high voice of the northern plains people. Over and over he chanted, "A knife is just like dirt thrown against me."

Simplistic, the true meaning promised strength and protection from the knife owner's enemies.

"Look at the handle, Lone Walker. Tell me what the handle is made of."

"Bone. I know this story. The knife's handle is made from the jawbone of a grizzly. The knife has great medicine because I caught it in the proper way."

"You are right. What else, Lone Walker? What else did the mother bear give to our ancestor?"

"She told him how to paint for battle. How to make the marks of power."

"Yes," agreed Henry. "Now, let us prepare for battle. Put the sacred knife into your sheath and we will prepare for war."

Where is all of this stuff coming from? Henry inquired of himself. I open my mouth and it just flows out as if I have always known of such things. Can this be happening? Perhaps I am dreaming.

In wonder, because they suddenly knew how the facial paints were to be administered, the two Blackfeet warriors rubbed the thick red ocher upon their faces. When the jelly jar was empty, Henry replaced it in a zip-lock bag. Martha wanted her jar back. First Henry, then Lone Walker ran their fingers down the other's face, scratching away the already drying paint. The results were hideous. Long, narrow streaks of skin showed between the otherwise solid layer of dark red.

Henry, his glasses once more perched on his nose, read the notes he had entered in a National Park notebook. "We have prepared for battle. The red ocher and stripes will protect us from our enemies." He looked at his companion. "Repeat my words, Nit-awahka. Just as I spoke them."

"We have prepared for battle. The red ocher and stripes will protect us from our enemies."

"Lone Walker, you can go sit down beneath the large fir tree."

Now, his companion spoke. "They call you Wolf Man."

Henry smiled. "Yes."

"Why do they do this? Is it because of the White Man they sometimes call Wolf Man?"

"No. I cannot tell you. Perhaps later you will know without my telling you."

Lone Walker retreated into the forest and sat down.

Henry, frightened at what was to come, prayed, "Earth Mother protect me from the evil ones."

He received no answer.

"They are all one, our gods," Henry told himself. He began, "Our Father who art in

Heaven......."

*

CHAPTER 23

"Ssssshhhh." Up high, above the forested slopes, a cold breeze was blowing. "Ssssshhhh," it said, a continual slightly wavering rushing of chill Pacific winds, eastward moving, hurrying overhead to touch the Great Plains with a summer chill. There are times when the icy force tumbles down slope, but not often.

Once, a more powerful invasion of cold bitterness shook the fir boughs, severely rippled the surface of Medicine Grizzly Lake, and forced the glacier lilies to bow their lovely heads in even deeper submission. Startled, a red shafted flicker that had been feeding on the insects hiding in a dead snag screamed out his shrill alarm and fled on red-flashing wings to more sheltered feeding grounds below.

Henry, sitting beside the lake, shivered and wondered why White Men chose to camp in such inhospitable places. His prepared, unlit campfire was situated on the lakeshore, just inside a National Park Service designated campsite. A moment before he had been swatting mosquitoes. Now he was trembling with cold. "Might as well play the part," he murmured, placing a large raven's feather in his hat band.

Across the lake, up the slopes to the divide, the sky was paling, turning to a faint yellow-olive sheen. From the old bear den, out of rocky cracks, flowing from musty, fallen trunks, oozing up from the black mucky soil itself, all from Mother Earth, a spiritual presence slowly asserted itself, filling the little valley with whisperings not quite audible, of images not really discernible. Awed, Henry sat spellbound, slipping into a trance-like state of mind.

Lone Walker must have felt them, the Old Ones, too. He began softly singing words Henry did not comprehend, the man's voice, falsetto in pitch, climbing and falling not unlike an enchanted flute.

Henry's coldness left him. He closed his eyes and sought the Great Ones, his heritage. They passed before him, those at first unrecognizable ancestors; some handsome, others frightening, savage. One, a woman, rode her spotted pony upon the plains. She was stocky, plain in features, more manly than woman. The horse, eyes wild, pulling against the twisted-hair reins, stopped and pranced soundlessly before his vision. The warrior, the war chief, the male maiden, looked down upon Henry Two Feathers.

He whispered in astonishment, "Pitamakan!," The image was Running Eagle, Pitawma'hkan, wildest of the wild, bravest of the warriors of long gone days, great War Chief of the Piegans. When he spoke the apparition smiled broadly, hair unruly, tresses blowing across her prominent brow. All that, Henry saw with eyes closed tightly. They, the Old Ones, paraded before him, dancing, walking, riding, each revealing their soul's identity in their own fashion.

He, Henry Two Feathers, thought the vision was ended. Nothing remained but the flowing grasses, the great expanses of emptiness he knew so well. Far away, a tiny figure appeared on a knoll where the grass grew short. He couldn't see what it was at first. Then, he realized the kicking thrashing movements were those of a baby, a human baby clothed in white doeskin. The baby moved. Now it was crawling. The baby must have grown, Henry thought. As the being moved downhill, it stood erect and waddled awkwardly. Then, older still, the clothing changed to tan, simple of design, a little girl hopped and skipped through the grass, down the slope into a hidden depression. When she appeared once again, the skipping had ceased. Henry beheld a beautiful maiden, lithe in form, supple as a willow. Love, desire rushed to his breast and he trembled with the thrill of seeing her. The woman.

Still strong of limb, creases beginning to appear on her still distant face, moving through the grasses of time, form bending some, aging, older, older still. White streaks in the raven-winged hair. Grayer. Whiter. Snow white. The transformation of spirit was crossing the flat prairie upon which Henry seemed to be sitting, coming ever closer.

Slower now. Severely bent. A limp in her walk. She leaned upon a crude, familiar looking stick, clothing drab, worn, of many patches. She was before him. Raising her feeble head, she gazed directly into Henry's face. He shook with fright. The old woman's eyes were milky. She was blind. Sweet Grass Woman! Henry thought he had shouted her name.

Abrupt, within one blink of his eye, the spirit changed form again, to the lovely maiden. Rushing, sweeping, as if upon a strong summers breeze, her ghost enveloped Henry in warmth, love, acceptance, such as he had never-before experienced.

"Unh! Unh! Uh!" Henry jumped awake, thrilling to what he had seen. Turning, he looked toward Lone Walker. His chanting had ceased. A lone evening sunbeam, angling nearly horizontally through the tree branches, was bathing the young man in quivering illumination. Lone Walker sat still, moisture flowing down the scratched furrows of his painted countenance. He was crying.

*

The great Sun Father fell behind the high, naked limestone buttresses that towered skyward just west of Medicine Grizzly Lake. What little color the sunset possessed went unseen by the two Blackfeet warriors.

Henry stood up, stretched, then shuffled stiffly back toward the fir tree where Lone Walker still sat. "You OK?"

"Yeah, I guess so," replied the younger man.

"Good. Me too. You'd better take a leak now, if you're going to. Go back up there," Henry motioned, "on the other side of that clump of bushes. We don't want them to smell your urine and know you are here."

"OK." Lone Walker stood up. "What am I supposed to do when they come, whoever they are?"

"Darned if I know." Henry was certain his companion knew who were coming. He added, "You scared?"

"Yes. Plenty scared," confessed Lone Walker.

"Me too. Wish I had a smoke. Or a stiff shot. Even a few cuss words would help."

Lone Walker was puzzled. "Why don't you let loose?"

"Somehow I can't," confessed Henry. "I haven't been my old self lately."

The two men spoke softly, delaying their separation. Finally, Henry made the break. "Gotta' go." Turning he walked slowly back to where he had been sitting.

Earlier, in full daylight, he had gathered moss and twigs, all hanging dry far above the moisture ladened forest floor. Henry struck a kitchen match on a dry rock and inserted the tiny flame into the 'birds nest' of dry material. A crimson flame shot up, growing swiftly, becoming a roaring campfire. Shadows recoiled from the fire light, hiding behind trees, stumps, shrubs, boulders and fallen trunks. Large sparks shot upward as a result of the incineration of bits of dried sap and dead insect bodies.

For a moment the man became anxious, unable to find what he had hoped to extract from the pack. Visibly relieved, the old man took out a plastic bag in which something was carefully matted with facial tissues. "Thanks, Martha," Henry said to his not present wife. He held two peculiar, somewhat rounded pieces of red cellophane, mounted in cardboard frames. Henry slipped each frame onto his glasses, the red material covering the lenses. He secured them firmly with minute ribbons. When he put his glasses over his ears and nose, Henry wore a pair of lightproof glasses. No flash of light or campfire flame could diminish his night vision. Small delicate sidepieces protected his peripheral vision from light intrusions.

The two men waited. Evening became the intense blackness of night. Above, the stars twinkled their deceptive reds and blues and whites, pulsating, each one having a special visual characteristic.

Henry became chilled, his back feeling the heatlessness of high altitude nighttime temperatures. Up above, on the divide, the winds had calmed, as if resting, awaiting the next dawn's emergence. He placed another piece of wood on his fire. The burning branches made a white man's fire, large, too hot for comfort. He hoped the wood supply would last.

Again he counted, checking his mental time schedule. Four p.m. Add one is five. Then three hours for travel. Perhaps two hours for preparation and planning. His guests should have arrived an hour ago. Maybe, he thought, they will wait until I give up and leave. Catch me along the trail. Henry vowed that he would wait. The unheard voices, the Old Ones as Lone Walker called them, told him to be where he was. Henry would stay put. The enemy had to come to him.

*

They came up from the Cut Bank campground, walking single-file, the last man riding a horse. Their progress was unhurried, almost silent. They knew they had Henry Two Feathers cut off from escape. Their quick investigation, a few phone calls, revealed that nothing unusual was happening at the St. Mary Ranger Station nor at the Sheriff's office. The Indian police were not even close to the park. Henry was theirs for the taking. The old man couldn't climb out of the glacier-carved valley. He had set his own trap.

The dark-shadowed man in the lead, somewhat ahead of his companions, was short, slender, like a coiled spring ready to release his physical power. The man wore thin, soft-soled moccasins so that he could feel any twigs that might otherwise snap underfoot. He was a killer. Trained in the Special Forces of the military, the Blackfeet was an expert in annihilations, the taking of human life.

Next in line, after the killing machine, strode another Native American, not Blackfeet but Miami. He was new to the group, having, at the last minute, been recruited simply because he possessed a gnawing hatred for Henry Two Feathers. Just the thought of killing the lawman brought joy to the unstable man's spirit. No real, deep-set grievance. Simply, he hated the deputy sheriff because Henry had issued him a speeding ticket.

The last man on foot and the one on horseback, bringing up the rear, were White Men. One was very tall, powerful of frame. The other, the rider, wore the backcountry uniform of the National Park Service.

Hours before the giant one had received a sealed envelope. Inside he had found a message:

Medicine Grizzly Lake, tonight.
If you don't show I'll give my information to
the FBI.

Henry Two Feathers

Panic. What to do? If he ran, they would catch him for sure. So, he had driven over Marias Pass to East Glacier to tell his companions-in-crime.

The giant and the East Glacier man, the one on horseback, drove to Kiowa, up the twisting jeep trail, through the barren hills, to where the other one, the ex-Special Forces killer lived. They needed him to put Henry Two Feathers down. Fortunately, they thought at the time, the Miami, the one who hated Henry, was also staying in the dilapidated trailer. Neither man thought the newcomer was a threat. Later, if it became necessary, he could be dispensed with in the usual manner. Or, better still, if everything fell apart, as it might, the Miami could become the scapegoat. A dead one.

Henry had set no trap. That fact seemed apparent. Although vague, the lawman's message indicated that he knew that the recipient of the note was responsible for the suspected murders. Or, perhaps Henry was referring to something else. Shooting in the dark, so to speak. Maybe the lawman wanted in on whatever he thought they were doing. Perhaps he wasn't what he appeared. Maybe he too, would relish the fun of slowly torturing a human being, of slicing the bound victim until their knives drained away his life's blood.

What had begun as an idea one night in 1983, that had brought the two White Men so much perverted joy, had grown into a habit. Careful selection. The victim had to be alone, away from friends and family. Better that he be a drifter. Two of the past victims had owned automobiles. The vehicles had presented a problem that had been successfully resolved. The others owned little or nothing. Such down-and-outers made much safer candidates for the sharp knives.

Now Henry Two Feathers had to be silenced, and maybe their two companions as well, but both men were afraid of the trained killer. Things were snowballing; getting out of control. Perhaps Henry should be the last to go. Better to wait awhile or maybe never take another victim.

Unfortunately for them, Fang had disappeared. They couldn't find the tall, skinny Indian who did their dirty work, the disposing of the bodies. Two hours wasted in Browning, looking for him. They had even risked driving to St. Mary, thinking they would find his pickup at one of the bars. Fang would be needed again, after they were finished with Henry.

That stupid Fang, thought the one on horseback. For one who seemed so intelligent, Fang had easily fallen for their mumbo-jumbo crap about the evil forces. All that nonsense about the Old Ones and the stupid Sasquatch fable. The man just didn't make sense, always talking about spirits directing his life, causing him to be mean, to perform acts of aggression. Burning black candles. Praying to his ancestors. Cult shit, thought Duane, the ranger. Fang's belief system had made him a perfect patsy, doing all of the dirty work for the two tormentors. He was good though, thought the Cut Bank ranger. No one ever found a body that Fang had disposed of. At least not until right now. Perhaps, if last winter's avalanche above the lake hadn't happened, all of this problem with Henry wouldn't be taking place.

Anyway, thought the ranger, Fang's usefulness may have come to an end. Some way or another they would have to kill the skinny Blackfeet with the lone incisor, after he had removed Henry's body from what was to be his death site. Too bad there wasn't enough time for fun-and-games with the knives. The man thought on, his common sense, always a little lacking, a thing of the past.

The ex-Special Forces killer, others called him Chief, was enjoying himself. Self-confidence was the name-of-the-game and he had it. Silent, swift of movement, the trained assassin stealthily glided along the trail. He thrilled with anticipation. Two years had passed since he had killed the Marxist mayor on the Mediterranean island of Pantelleria. The garrote had been the weapon. Decapitation the cause of death. Chief missed the thrill of taking life. Tonight would be different. Nice and simple. Henry Two Feathers, armed with a gun, would be dispatched by the killer's knife. Nice and easy. Blade penetrating upward, straight under the ribs to the heart. Twist it. That's what he relished, the turning of the blade inside a man. Then he'd leave. He didn't trust his companions. Head for Oklahoma before his dumb-assed White companions got caught. He'd blend in well with the Native American population of the southern plains state. His partners in crime would soon meet their end. He could almost smell it. Best to get away tonight, after the fun.

The Miami, the shadow following Chief, had met the killer in a saloon near Whitefish. They had immediately become friends, but not because they had much in common. They both liked boozing. Jonathan, the Miami, hailed from West Virginia, one of the disappearing Native Americans who frequented the hill country. He'd never gotten along with the Shawnee who also lived nearby. He could never accept the fact that he wasn't a full blood. So, at age sixteen, Jonathan had lit out for South Dakota and the Rosebud Reservation. The Sioux didn't like him either. They had enough problems with their own youngsters. The young drifter moved on to the Rocky Boy Reservation. Two years later he moved to Browning. On a lonely Friday night, just outside of town, Henry Two Feathers had pulled him over and given Jonathan a ticket. Too bad, Henry-Ass-Hole, Jonathan thought. I'll get a piece of you tonight.

When the group arrived at the switch-off to the lake, the seasonal back country ranger became badly frightened. He had delighted in tormenting the helpless victims but Henry Two Feathers was somewhere up ahead, waiting for them. Something could go wrong. The horse, smelling the fear emanating from its rider, neighed anxiously.

*

Lone Walker heard the men coming up the trail. The wind had died. Only the very faint splashings of the nearby stream broke the cold stillness of darkness, except for the crackling of Henry's fire. Strange, thought Lone Walker, that Henry trusts me so completely. What assurance did the deputy have that the tall, powerful Blackfeet wouldn't kill him? The warrior reached for his revolver. The feel of the handle was reassuring. Then, of course, Lone Walker carried the knife, the one with the jawbone of a grizzly for a handle. He listened. The muffled clop, clop, clop of a horse's hooves, barely audible, stopped. They must have seen the fire, Lone Walker thought.

*

Ears straining, Henry searched the shadows about his campfire with hidden eyes. Even with night vision the lawman was unable to discern objects much beyond the circle of firelight.

He heard them then, coming boldly along the trail. They would be able to see the campfire by now. A horse blew out its breath. It must be tethered down the trail apiece, he guessed. Unless someone stayed with it. Henry hoped not.

Dark figures, moving warily, single file, coming toward the fire, somewhat bunched together. Henry realized he could take all three if he used his revolver. Then the crisis would be over. If he killed them then, he would never know why. Never find out what had motivated them to become murderers.

The shadowy figures stopped. Henry heard a slight murmur. Probably arguing who is going to be first. He waited in silence.

The three men were puzzled. The lawman's eyes seemed peculiar looking, not appearing normal in the firelight.

The big man came first.

"Come on in, you fellows. Come in out of the cold. There are some logs for you to sit on. There," Henry pointed, "across from me."

The Miami started to move around the fire.

"No," Henry calmly stated. "You sit with the others."

Something in the voice made the Indian stop. He studied Henry carefully and decided that the lawman might have a weapon under the white robe that was spread across his lap. The Miami was right.

"Well, Jim, I was expecting you about an hour ago. Just about gave up." Henry smiled pleasantly.

Jim Ballard glowered back.

"And you, Duane. You are supposed to be a lawman of sorts, a backcountry ranger, eh? I didn't expect you to be in on this. I heard your horse just now. Come to think of it, I suppose you are the one who did Douglas Jakowski in. Am I right?"

The ranger was silent.

"That's right," declared Ballard. "Too bad you lost your buddy, eh, Henry?"

"But I didn't, Jim. You see Douglas isn't dead like you thought. We just kept that little detail secret. My friend is on the road to a full recovery. Does that bother you?"

Duane looked panic stricken.

Chuckling, Henry chided, "You lose, ranger. He'll finger you and off you'll go for life."

"Bullshit!" yelled Ballard. "Plain bullshit!" He was getting edgy. Where was Chief? Why hadn't he killed Two Feathers by now?

Smiling made the killers nervous. He smiled again. "How about you, Miami boy? Are you going to be a lifer too?"

"What's it to you, Ass Hole?" The boys voice trembled slightly.

Henry ignored the insult. "Know what this is, Jonathan?" He stroked the white cover across his lap.

No response.

"This is the white buffalo robe of the Blackfeet. That's what this is."

All three were impressed. The Miami fidgeted and acted as if he was about to flee. Ballard and Duane got the idea at the same time and grinned at each other. The ranger whispered, "The robe must be worth big bucks."

Henry chuckled. "Big bucks? The sacred robe isn't yours to sell."

"We'll take it from you, dumb ass."

"Oh? Ballard, is that right?" That smile again.

"All right. That's enough. How did you find out about me? How did you know?"

"A video camera did it. The year before you were hired. Not much of a clue. Just a few frames of a hearing in the St. Mary dorm. In the lounge area. The room was full of rangers and several clergy members who were trying to find out what happened to their missing friend."

"So?" Ballard was confused.

"So?" Henry echoed. "Why Jim, you were in the back of the room smiling. I was there that day. No one thought anything was funny. There was nothing to laugh at. A priest was making an impassioned plea for help and you thought it funny."

"One smile? That's it?" Ballard wasn't convinced.

"Three smiles, Jim. You smiled three different times. Now that is darned peculiar. You certainly didn't have stomach gas."

Ballard and the backcountry ranger exchanged worried looks. Where was that Chief?

*

Chief inched slowly forward, approaching Henry. No reason to hurry. If Henry heard him, then there would be shooting and Chief wouldn't get to use his knife; wouldn't be able to enjoy the feel of the steel blade grinding into Henry Two Feather's spinal column. Chief had decided to strike there rather than thrusting into the heart. He thrived on variety.

Easy. Each step was important. Concentrate. Move slowly. Be a shadow, a shrub, nothing out of place. Chief was part of the black night. Another step, found a sharp point on a fallen limb. Halt the decline of the foot. Raise the moccasin carefully off the stressed branch. Move it to the right. Ah. No obstruction; nothing to go snap in the night. Chief was still out of the firelight, back in the darkness a good fifty feet. There, ahead, was Henry, his hat with the raven's feather silhouetted in the flickering light. Stupid old fart, thought Chief. Easy one. He raised the left foot to move closer, the thrill of the anticipated execution strengthening, surging through his body.

"Schissss." Jawbone of a grizzly handle, blade razor sharp, the sacred knife sliced neatly through the soft tissue of Chief's throat, beneath the Adam's apple, while Lone Walker's hand closed firmly over the killer's mouth. Not much struggle. Quick realization, then fading senses. Chief's spirit fled the straining body, to be met by the others, the Old Ones of the Blackfeet.

Lone Walker grinned. Coup, he thought. Now I am a true warrior, a Piegan warrior. He lowered the slight figure to the waiting earth and returned to his willow mat beneath the large fir.

Henry barely heard the gurgling sound, the pulsing away of Chief's lifeblood. His adversaries apparently hadn't heard anything. They were on the far side of the crackling fire. Henry hoped that the dead man wasn't Lone Walker.

"The real mystery, to me," revealed Henry, "is why? Why did you kill seven men and con Clarence in to disposing of the bodies?"

"Eight," corrected Ballard, his confidence returning somewhat, thinking he might shoot Henry if Chief didn't hurry.

"Yeah," chimed in Duane, the backcountry ranger, thinking their situation might not be as bad as he had thought. "Fang only disposed of four of them for us. That dumb son-of-a-bitch and his spirits. Shit!"

Henry ignored Duane. "Why, Ballard?" Henry repeated.

"For fun." Both killers laughed.

Henry hadn't expected such a macabre solution to his question, to the mystery.

"That's right," declared Jim. "Just for the fun of it."

Henry still couldn't accept the answer. "Just for fun? No cult activities? No selling of body parts? Not even revenge?"

Ballard looked anxiously into the blackness behind Henry.

"He isn't coming, Jim."

"Who? Who isn't coming?"

"Whoever you had sneaking up on me. I'd guess he is heading for the happy hunting ground about now."

Anger consumed their previously growing calmness.

"Who's out there?" demanded the ranger.

Henry remained silent, his hand on the hidden revolver's trigger.

"OK, you old fart. Your time is up," declared Ballard.

Bass notes, long, faint at first, rumbling from the darkness, rising in pitch, drawn out, accelerating higher and higher into the wild call of the wolf.

The Miami yelled, "That's no wolf. Who's doing that shit?" He jumped to his feet.

Henry sat quiet.

"Get him," ordered Duane, meaning Henry.

Up on the north slope of the valley Lone Walker's wolf call was heard. The two packs, now merged as one, responded. First the Alpha males called. The lead females howled. All twelve wolves cried their primal message of the hunt.

"Those are real," Henry simply stated.

"Jesus!" exclaimed Duane. His horse, tethered down trail, screamed in panic, lunged and thrashed. Breaking free, she galloped wildly down the hill, heading for the little ranger station adjacent to the campground.

"Your horse, damn it," shouted Ballard. "Get it. Don't let the son-of-a-bitch get away." Duane stood frozen. "Go after it, Jonathan!"

The Indian didn't move either. The wolves were getting closer, baying now, rushing toward the firelight.

Ballard, still in control, ordered, "Easy boys. Wolves never attack humans. Don't let a little noise scare you."

Quiet, controlled, Henry spoke. "Those aren't ordinary wolves. You'd better stay put."

"Oh, God!" yelled Duane. "Kill him, Jonathan. For Christ's sake kill the bastard!"

The Miami didn't move.

The wolves were closing in, just a few hundred yards away. Alpha Male of the Crypt Lake pack smelled the fresh blood first. Not comprehending its spiritual transformation into something other than a wolf, the powerful animal roared a signal and turned toward the dead Indian's corpse.

Lone Walker, realizing they were almost upon him, leaped into the limbs of the fir tree he had been sitting under. Both packs found the corpse simultaneously. Incisors slashed and ripped through the dead man's clothing, tearing the body open, ripping out chunks of flesh, entrails, organs. Pack dominance was forgotten, each beast on his own, tearing for food, hot, steaming flesh. Blood splattered all over the earth, upon the tree trunks, turning the wild ones an unseen red, a lightless crimsonness. Two whole days and three nights without food, then the hot blood of Chief was more than the wolves could tolerate. Greedily, growling, snarling, the snapping of teeth pulling off mouths full of human muscle, they consumed most of the Indian's body within minutes. Just as quickly they stopped. Sated, they smacked their gore-covered lips, calming somewhat, allowing the spirit forces to regain control.

What was that over there? Fire. Still figures resembling men animals. Curious, the calmed packs circled the fire on three sides. On the remaining perimeter of the firelight the cold lakeshore hid within the darkness, reflecting only starlight and occasional bursts of snapping fire.

The four men, Henry and the three opposing him, sat silent, afraid to move, watching the pacing wolves, their eyes catching the glowing embers, reflecting red. For all the watching men knew, the animals were the souls of devils, awaiting their chance to drag the humans to hell.

Ballard cocked his revolver.

"Don't shoot," whispered Henry. "They might rush us." The ruse worked. Jim eased the hammer forward.

What made the situation almost unbearable was the fact that there was barely a sound. The wolves, seated around the fire glow perimeter, watched silently. The three men huddled together, fear making them impotent. Henry sat alone, outwardly impassive.

Duane began sniffing first. "What the hell?"

Then, Ballard detected the foul stench.

Jonathan, seeing them stare at him, slid away, along the log, careful to raise his bottom.

"You shit your pants!" Duane, nearly out of control, jumped up and screamed at the Miami youth. "You shit your fucking pants! Christ! Get away from me, you bastard."

Jonathan, his face contorted in fear, embarrassment and humiliation also leaped up, their sudden movements and Duane's yelling caused the wolves to come alert, standing, waiting for the strange beings' next move.

The firelight revealed a shiny stain of wetness from the man's groin half-way down each leg.

Duane reacted again. "Ugh! Get away from me, you chicken-shit son-of-a-bitch."

The Miami's temper flared. He thought of jumping Duane, but the ranger held a revolver.

Henry laughed softly, his chuckling easily heard by Jonathan.

Henry. The deputy. He'd get him. The old man seemed helpless enough, sitting there huddled under that white buffalo robe.

Ballard began laughing too. Duane chimed in. The noise rose to fill the forest with echoes of near-mad hilarity.

Jonathan, proud of his Miami heritage, screamed, "Shut up! You hear me? Shut up!"

The men quieted, but then as the fouled man stepped toward the fire a black glob of feces slipped down his pant leg and plopped on his boot. Horrified, the youth shuffled to extract the offal. In doing so his boot squashed the turd. "Ah! Ah! Oh, shit!" he raged.

The others roared with renewed laughter. He looked so funny, scraping his boot on a glowing ember. "I'll get you!," he screamed, and since Henry was the unarmed one, he stepped toward the old man, knife clutched in his right hand. Jonathan's forward momentum hurled him toward Henry, who was about to fire the hidden revolver.

"Smack!" Out of the blackness sailed a blade of steel upon which a grizzly bear bone handle rode, striking the hapless Jonathan square in the forehead, the blade penetrating up to the haft. Mad with pain and terror the boy grasped the handle with both hands and pulled helplessly, trying to extract the steel that was killing him.

Both White Men were up shooting in the direction the knife had appeared from. They shot their weapons, reloaded and fired again until the chambers were once again empty.

The noise was deafening. Frightened, the wolves scattered back into the forest.

Henry didn't understand why he hadn't taken Ballard and Duane down with his revolver. The white buffalo robe still covered the man's legs, as if sheltering him from the cold. Henry thought that the holy robe was protecting him.

"OK." Ballard was regaining his self-control. "You all right, Duane?" The seasonal ranger nodded that he was. For some reason his voice wasn't working. Ballard continued. "We sit tight. Till dawn. Then we get the hell out of here." Looking at Henry he added in a loud voice, "If anything else happens Henry breathes his last breath. You hear that?" he yelled to whomever was still alive in the darkness.

"Build up the fire, Henry."

Henry Two Feathers complied with Ballard's demand.

He was worried about Lone Walker. Since the shooting, there had been no sound from the fir tree area. Neither did Henry understand why Ballard was letting him live. Maybe he considered Henry to be some sort of a hostage, an insurance policy for getting out.

Far away, back in the forest, the falsetto chanting of Lone Walker sifted through the trees and descended upon the campfire. The voice was weak, trembling, ghostly. Henry felt prickles of shivers coursing along his skin and knew that Ballard and Duane felt the same, only more so. At least Henry knew who the singer was. The night was not yet past half over. The singing, rising and falling in pitch and power went on and on and on, fraying the shattered nerves of the killers.

Then, sudden, complete quiet!

Duane and Ballard looked at one-another, more frightened now that the singing had ended.

"Take those damned things off your glasses," commanded Ballard.

Henry didn't respond.

"Did you hear me? Take them off, whatever they are."

"No, Jim. I won't."

Ballard began moving toward Henry but stopped and sat down again. They sat in silence.

*

Early in the morning Henry said, "We're about out of firewood." The flames were diminishing rapidly.

"Get some more then," declared Ballard.

"Are you sure you want me to gather dead wood? I might slip away." Henry didn't want to relinquish his position, leave the safety of the white buffalo robe.

Ballard thought awhile. "OK. Duane, you cover me. I'll break off some dead branches from those trees." The forest consisted of old but not large fir trees, each possessing many dead lower branches. Ballard's snapping them off created minor explosive sounds. "Maybe the noise will keep the wolves away."

Henry realized how the wolves had protected him by frightening the killers. If they hadn't been there this Wolf Man would have likely died. What am I waiting for, he thought? Why don't I shoot them? He had no idea how the situation would be resolved. All he knew was that he was waiting. He must be patient.

"You fella's should be used to this." Henry nodded his head toward the dead Miami youth. "Maybe you want to skin him to keep in practice."

"Shut up," warned Duane. "How do you know we won't slice away on you?" The ranger was thinking of doing just that.

"You won't because he is out there, somewhere," Henry responded. "He might be close. You have to keep watch."

What the deputy said was true. The men were more fearful of the knife thrower than of the wolves. Both sat, stupidly facing the firelight, peering into the darkness with weakened night vision.

*

Henry's adversaries hadn't noticed yet. Light, faint streaks of light, were invading the starry canopy. Almost imperceptibly the distant suns were dimming and blinking out. Henry wiggled his toes and ankles, flexing the leg muscles. Whatever was to happen would happen soon. He knew, as he had always known, the revolver was not to be used.

Morning prayers were silently offered, not only in the Indian way but also in the Christian manner. The old familiar words made Henry feel better. The new way, calling the Earth Mother and the Old Ones comforted Henry, too. Acknowledgment of not being alone gave the warrior confidence and spiritual strength. Repeating what he had realized the previous evening about the two ways of worship, Henry said aloud, "They are the same."

"What?" His soft-spoken words startled the dozing Ballard. Looking around the killer realized that dawn was approaching. The fire had died to feeble embers.

Ballard shoved Duane. "Come on. Wake up. Time to get rid of Henry and head out of here."

The old man removed his glasses and took off the night vision lenses. He threw them into the ashes, where they melted before erupting into flames.

"Well, well, well," grinned Ballard. "There he is, Mister America. I want to watch your eyes when we kill you."

Henry spoke. "Jim, I can't figure you out. You killed those folks just for fun? For thrills?"

"You've got it, Henry. That's the best way. No motive. If it hadn't been for that California man and his video camera we'd have gone on having fun until we got bored with it."

"But, you weren't even working in Glacier when you killed most of them."

"Yeah. I wasn't hired because I wasn't a vet. That really pissed me off. I lived in East Glacier that summer. Real easy for us to get together and dream up some fun."

"And so you and Ranger Rick here went on a killing spree." Henry caught a slight movement behind the men, in the forest gloom. He hoped Lone Walker wouldn't try anything foolish. Yet, time was running out.

"You didn't kill the hiker up at Elizabeth Lake, did you? Last October."

"No," admitted Ballard, "We didn't know about him until after his bones were found."

The movement wasn't Lone Runner. Henry tried to remain calm. He spoke a little too loud.

"Why the religious man, the priest or brother or whatever he was?"

Ballard looked puzzled. "What are you doing, Henry? Stalling?"

"No, but I do want to know why you hated Douglas Jakowski so much."

"That wolf man? That son-of-a-bitch!," exploded Ballard. "He humiliated me in front of all those trainees." The man panted with emotion. "I'd have killed him for sure. Not like Duane here. Leaving him for dead.

"Enough of this. Stand up, old man. Take what's coming to you." Ballard leveled his revolver barrel, aiming it at Henry's chest.

Still seated, stalling for seconds, knowing what was about to happen, Henry said, "Jim. I think you'd better reconsider."

"Ha! Stand up Ass Hole. I want to watch you flop."

Henry could see the man's index finger slip inside the trigger guard. With an involuntary eye movement, he looked behind his intended killer. Ballard caught the look and wheeled about expecting to confront the chanter, the one who had thrown the knife.

Too late. The Great Bear, the Medicine Grizzly, cleared the thirty feet in an instant, colliding with Ballard with a force that broke the man's left shoulder. Jim saw the massive teeth in the huge maw. The bear's muzzle was the last thing he saw before razor claws slashed away his face.

Duane screamed and ran for the lake, diving in, trying to swim in the shallow, mucky water. The bear was upon him, biting, slashing, tearing until the lake turned reddish in the faint dawn light. The grizzly's head plunged under the frothy water and emerged with jaws filled with unrecognizable body parts and shreds of clothing.

From its throat came the roar of the Medicine Grizzly, just as the Blackfeet had heard him so very long ago.

Ballard, faceless, was up on his knees, one arm dragging. Spellbound, Henry sat transfixed, watching as his enemy desperately attempted to escape. Life draining away, Ballard slithered in his own blood, senseless, unknowing, crawling toward the lake. For Henry, Ballard's journey took an eternity.

Covered with mud, Duane's entrails slipping off his back, the Medicine Grizzly met Ballard at the lake's edge. Huge jaws opened, engulfed and closed on the dying man's head. Bones crunched and snapped. Jim Ballard was no more.

For the first time, the Medicine Grizzly noticed Henry. Rumbling low in the chest he stepped toward the sitting man-creature. Henry didn't move. He couldn't.

The bear sniffed, peering at Henry across the still-hot embers of the fire. It didn't wonder why he had attacked the humans. The incomprehensible blood lust sated, the massive grizzly turned away and plodded wheezingly back up the trail toward Divide Pass and the Nyack Valley beyond. The majestic creature was again the Great Bear only, no more the Medicine Grizzly. Until the next time.

*

"Lone Walker!" Henry called out, not expecting a response.

"Yeah." The man's voice, faint, came from above. Henry watched as his new friend climbed down the ladder-like steps of the fir tree.

"What were you doing up there?"

"Man," panted Lone Walker, "I've climbed this thing at least five times. My arms and legs are all scratched up. No skin left, I think." He dropped the last six feet to the ground. "I don't think I can do that under normal conditions."

"I was worried about you, my friend. I thought you'd caught a bullet until you began that singing. Then, I thought you were dying."

"Yeah." Lone Walker was still breathing hard. "How'd you like that? Pretty good, eh?"

"Really effective," grinned Henry. "Kept them guessing."

"Man! Did you see the size of that bear?" Lone Walker was obviously impressed.

Henry held up his right hand, covered with splatters of Jim Ballard's blood.

"Yeah." Lone Walker got the message. "I guess you saw him."

Henry nodded, "Yes." He was feeling his age.

Lone Walker, as usual unpredictable, asked, "I can stand a hot cup of tea. How about you?"

"What?"

"Tea. I've got some tea bags and a little pan. We can take turns sipping out of it."

"Sure," agreed Henry. "I feel pretty shaky. Go over there to get the water, not here." He was looking at Duane's floating remains.

"Yeah," agreed Lone Walker. "Way over there."

*

"Typical June morning," announced Henry. What had begun as a sunny day was rapidly deteriorating. He slurped one more swallow of tea and handed the tiny pan back to Lone Walker.

"Say, Henry, can I have my knife back?"

"Sure, here."

Lone Walker slid the weapon back into its sheath. You were right. My gun wouldn't work."

"Oh?" Henry raised his eyebrows in interest.

"Nope. Somehow I couldn't make myself use it." The younger man thought about that. "Do you suppose we, you and I, were under the control of the Old Ones?"

"Don't know. I've sure been thinking about that off and on during the past twelve hours." Henry changed the subject. "I hate to ask, but I'm nosy. When you killed that man that was sneaking up on me, whoever he was, did you take his scalp?"

Lone Walker looked shocked. "Why no, Henry. That's a White Man's invention. I'm Nit-awahka, Blackfeet warrior." He stood up proudly. "Not some half-breed fanatic."

Henry was pleased. "Yes, you are that. Sweet Grass Woman was right when she told me to trust you. I almost didn't. You've been such an ass all your adult life."

"Yeah. You're right, Henry."

"By the way, Nit-awahka, you can take the jaw bone knife back to your old grandmother, if you can pry it out of that Indian's forehead."

Lone Walker was pleased. Placing his foot on Jonathan's face the warrior pried the knife loose from the split skull. While he cleaned the knife in the lake, Henry carefully folded the white buffalo robe and placed it around the Calumet.

"Look at us," declared Henry. "If we were White guys we'd be rushing around taking pictures, filling out forms, taping off this whole area."

"Yeah. Instead we relax, drink tea and enjoy the new day," agreed Lone Walker. "Say, Henry, was that really Natu'yi-ap-ohkyaiyo, the Medicine Grizzly?"

"I'm not sure, son. I'm not sure of anything right now. I suppose it was."

Lone Walker asked another question. "Were they really here last night? I thought I felt them and saw strange things."

Henry shook his head. "I just don't know. No. I'm not being truthful. They were here, Lone Walker. The Old Ones. And the sacred robe's medicine protected us. We just can't prove those facts are true. I think that is the way the Spirit People work. One never knows for sure."

The old man looked about him. "We really have a mess to clean up."

"No sweat," declared Lone Walker. "Scatter the hot coals all around the fire circle here. Cover up the blood. The spots will scorch away. When the rains come this afternoon the signs of what happened here will wash away."

"We still have the bodies," protested Henry.

"Say, I said no sweat. Remember, I'm an expert at body disposal," grinned Lone Walker. "I know a deep crack in a rock wall right near here. Just drop 'em in. Kaplunk. No one will find them, ever."

Henry was attempting to think. "And Duane's remains, out there in the lake?"

"I'll take care of it. See that fallen fir with the top in the lake? Bingo! Not much left of the jerk, but I'll sink him good, under there. Next year the fish will be bigger." He laughed.

"Doesn't anything bother you?"

"Yeah. I'm sensitive. I don't take ridicule well." The young man had become very serious.

"Yes. I understand."

"By the way, Henry, I'll catch the horse, too. Tonight, after I get some shuteye, I'll ride her over to the St. Mary stable, unsaddle him, just like Duane would do. Can you pick me up about four tomorrow morning?"

"Sure. Just be careful. I'll meet you at the 1913 Ranger Station. Then we can drive Ballard's car back to the West Side, or better yet, dump it off in Browning, where he lives in the winter time."

Lone Walker smiled at their cleverness.

"Lots of loose ends," warned Henry. "Two Federal employees turn up missing."

"Yeah."

"I'll handle the problems as they come. Don't worry; you are safe enough. This is an Indian problem and we are taking care of it. Right?"

Instead of agreeing Lone Walker hesitated and then asked, "Henry, could you loan me a twenty? My truck's about out of gas."

Henry took a bill from his pocket. "What now, Lone Walker? You've got a new image to live up to."

"Yeah," he agreed. "I've been checking out the Babb church for a couple of years. I might join. What do you think?"

"Sure, why not. Just don't confess any of this stuff."

Lone Walker added, "I think I'll get my teeth fixed. I really like my lone ivory but a good set of false teeth would help. The set I have now don't fit so I only wear them for eating."

"Good idea, son."

*

Richard D. Seifried

AFTERWARD

Douglas was mentally fussing, tired of reading and weary of the slow, steady progress of moving toward full recovery.

Lying around had produced some decision-making. The process was slow, but Douglas finally confessed to himself that his love for Julie had waned. The affair had been just that. Nothing more. He found himself thinking more often about the blonde woman he had made love to the previous year. Perhaps, he thought, he might write her a letter, or even go see her, if he ever got out of the stupid bed.

One day, a college friend, Bill Gwartney, stopped in to cheer up the injured man. He didn't. Gwartney had said, "You're lucky to be alive. So what if you take a year or so to get back in harness?"

Douglas had exploded. "Bull shit! I belong out there," waving an arm vaguely toward the West, "not here in bed with fake-smiling females spoiling me. Times-a-wasting. I've got big plans for my future, a Ph.D. to get, research. I'm sick of fun books!" He threw the paperback he was reading across the room.

Not knowing how to deal with his friend, Gwartney left.

An hour later, the convalescing patient was in even worse temper. "Where's Mother?" he demanded of the live-in nurse. "She's been gone for over three hours. I can't believe she would do this to me." He received only frowns of displeasure for his childish behavior.

Catherine reappeared late in the afternoon. Douglas was relieved. Immediately his mood swung. He was on a high. Motioning for his mother to come closer Douglas whispered, "Mom, I don't think the nurse likes me. Why don't you let her go?"

Catherine ignored his question. "Someone is here to see you."

"Someone? Henry?"

She laughed. "Henry says, 'Hi.' No, not Henry. Someone else."

"Come on, Mom. Cut the teasing. Who is it?"

Catherine walked to the open bedroom door and beckoned to the waiting someone.

A girl, blond hair tumbling to her shoulders, stepped inside. "Hi, Wolf Man." Douglas stared in amazement.

"I've come to nurse you back to health. That is, if you'll let me."

"Ann." Douglas whispered.

She kissed him solidly on the lips. His arms reached up, trying to envelop her body.

"Boy, am I glad to see you. I need someone to help me redecorate this room. All this white confuses me. I keep waking up and thinking I've died and gone to heaven."

"If you want me to stay, I'll help."

Catherine stepped outside the room and softly closed the bedroom door. She hummed as she walked down the hallway, the first time she had been happy since before Douglas's injury.

*

Martha was thinking. Her man was certainly something else. Ever since he came back from wherever he had gone, that old husband of hers seemed even more rejuvenated than when he came off of the mountain. Where does he get all that energy? Happy all the time. Quit his job. Retired early. Goes fishing most every day.

And young! Young ideas. Martha's cheeks crimsoned as she thought about him.

They were in bed. Gone to bed early again, her Hot Shot husband and she.

Martha lay there perspiring, left thigh propped over Henry's hips, part of Henry's favorite position. He called it "side saddle." The old boy had been going at it for nearly an hour.

Where does he get this energy? Where does Henry get all this pizzazz? Martha loved it, their lovemaking. Ten years of "not much" had suddenly erupted into "hot stuff." Henry called it a reward. For whom, she wondered? Martha's mind wandered off and she fantasized that Henry was really Clint Eastwood. The idea worked again. For her. Exhausted, she lay still, allowing her lover to continue his fun. Her mind wondered about people their age, still getting it on.

Religious, she thought of the Biblical characters, the old men who begat for decades past their normal time. Then there was St. Elizabeth. John the Baptist's mother. The Book of St. Luke, New Testament. Martha forgot about Henry's copulation. She recalled Chapter 1, 13th verse. John's father had been an old man, a priest named Zacharias. His wife, Elizabeth, was barren, just like Martha. "No children possible," Dr. Schmidt had declared. The difference was that St. Elizabeth became pregnant at an old age.

"Oh my god (small g)," Martha gasped, thus interrupting Henry's concentration.

"Huh? What's wrong?" Henry's face came up from the sheets. "Am I hurting you?"

"No. Not that." Martha took the plunge. "Henry, don't you think we should use a condom? You know, just in case."

THE END

ABOUT THE AUTHOR

Richard Seifried began his literary career at age twelve. He has successfully published two books, *NATIVE ENCOUNTERS* and *THE ADMINISTRATIVE HISTORY OF THE FLATHEAD INDIAN RESERVATION TO 1890*. He has also been published in many popular magazines.

During much of his adult life he has studied, taught and lived amid the wilderness areas of our Far West. Six seasons were spent in Glacier National Park, where he worked as a ranger.

He is a university-trained naturalist, anthropologist and writer. The author is also a member of Western Writers of America and the Ozark Writers Conference. He currently resides in Eureka Springs, Arkansas.

Printed in the United States
4703